The HEART BEATS IN SECRET

KATIE MUNNIK is a Canadian writer living in Cardiff. Her collection of short fiction, *The Pieces We Keep*, was published by Wild Goose Publications and her prose, poetry, and creative non-fiction have appeared in several magazines and anthologies, including *The Cardiff Review*. She is a graduate of the Humber School for Writers in Toronto, Canada. *The Heart Beats in Secret* is her first novel.

Praise for *The Heart Beats in Secret*:

'Textured and beautiful. Katie Munnik has a voice full of quiet passion and poetry'   Kate Hamer

'Munnik unfurls her story in quiet, reflective prose, but there is much to enjoy along the way'   *Town and Country*

'[A] powerful, multi-generational novel . . . full of secrets, stories and discoveries'   *Prima*

'Beautifully written and moving'   *Woman's Own*

'*The Heart Beats in Secret* is a spacious and yet densely woven work . . . beautifully written'   *The Cardiff Review*

Also by Katie Munnik

The Pieces We Keep: Stories for the Seasons

The Heart Beats in Secret

A Novel

KATIE MUNNIK

THE BOROUGH PRESS

The Borough Press
An imprint of HarperCollins*Publishers* Ltd
1 London Bridge Street
London SE1 9GF

www.harpercollins.co.uk

This paperback edition 2020
1

First published by HarperCollins*Publishers* 2019

A catalogue record for this book is available from the British Library

Excerpt from 'The Trail Of The Lonesome Pine' Words and Music by
Harry Carroll and Ballard MacDonald © 1927 Shapiro Bernstein & Co Inc
Shapiro Bernstein & Co Limited, New York, NY 10022-5718, USA
Reproduced by permission of Faber Music Ltd All Rights Reserved.

Excerpt from *Basho*, translated by Lucien Stryk, Penguin 1985

Excerpt from *A Doctor Discusses Pregnancy*, William G. Birch, Budlong Press 1963

Excerpt from *Everybody's Pudding Book*, by Georgiana Hill, Richard Bentley 1862

ISBN: 978-0-00-833699-8

Set in Adobe Garamond by Palimpsest Book
Production Limited, Falkirk, Stirlingshire

Printed and bound in the UK by CPI Group (UK) Ltd, Croydon CR0 4YY

MIX
Paper from
responsible sources
FSC™ C007454

For Mike, of course.

What are heavy? Sea-sand and sorrow:
What are brief? To-day and to-morrow:
What are frail? Spring blossoms and youth:
What are deep? The ocean and truth.

Christina Georgina Rossetti

For Columba Livia,
to be delivered after I am dead

Well, my dear, the house is yours. Regardless of what your mother might expect, I think it only makes sense. She wouldn't really want it anyway. All the way out here on the other side of the world, isn't it? Perhaps she might like to sell it and use the money, though I'm not sure that's necessary. She seems comfortable where she is. And she's never been one to look for windfalls or godsends. But maybe you could use a few, so I'm leaving it to you.

It's a good old house. Friendly in its way. I've been happy here. Don't worry, I wouldn't be offended if you sell it, and I won't haunt you. I promise. But before you decide anything, do come and see the old place. You haven't been out here since you were a child, and it may feel different to you now. So come and stay for a while. Long enough to get a handful of warm days — we do get them here, you know, the kind when you open the windows in the morning and leave them open all day, forgetting about them until the curtains blow in just before sunset, when the wind shifts. I have never figured out why it does that. I always meant to ask someone, but never got around to it. Does it happen elsewhere? Or is it only here in this house? Maybe you

1

know, my dear Pidge. Does anyone call you that any more? I must say, when I was drawing up the official paperwork, I had to be so careful with the spelling of your real name. Your mother was right – it has a lovely ring to it. But I was right, too, wasn't I? It is a strange name to saddle any child with. Yet you, my dear, wear it well. Felicity said that the other mothers wanted to use old-fashioned names, like the ones their grandmothers wore – Jean, Rosa, Edith. Or natural-sounding names like Oak and Ivy, which are only apt out there in the woods. But she wanted something distinctive for you. Oh, your grandfather laughed! It is a beautiful name, even a little fancy in the best way, though pigeons are just as common as the rest of us. But perhaps no one knows Latin these days so that doesn't matter. I hope you haven't found it a burden. We all burden our children, I suppose. One way or another.

I hope this house won't be a burden for you. It's only a house. Or a bit of money, if you want it that way instead. You would need to clear things out first, so that's another reason to visit. There may be a few things here you would like to keep. Books or photos, or sentimental odds and ends. It is all fairly old, but it has been useful. Useful or lovely.

When you come, you can take the car out, too. I've left that to you as well, though there's a man in the village who would be happy to buy it. Just ask at the hotel and Muriel will point you in the right direction. She'll also have a set of house keys for you, if there's any trouble getting them from the lawyer. You'll know her when you see her. I thought it best to provide local solutions so you don't need to go into the city unless you'd like to. There's more than enough to see around here. Drive out along the coast. Go see some ruins. Or the old doo'cots. There's a man named Izaak who lives near here. A few years ago, he put together a calendar with drawings of all the local doo'cots. Beehives and lecterns and all that. He's clever at shading and really captures the way light touches old stone. There should be a copy of it somewhere around the house. Maybe in the bookcase. I can't quite remember.

Anyway, be well, my dear. Be happy. Live where you like, but when you're here, do take some flowers to the kirkyard and think of me a little. And if you stay until they are ripe, be sure to eat all the brambles you can find.

With all my love,
Gran

PART ONE

1

PIDGE: 2006

LONDON AND BREAKFAST AT THE AIRPORT. JUST COFFEE and a scone – a crumbled thing that tasted of margarine, and the coffee was too hot so I drank it down quickly. It was only fuel. Mateo had arranged the rental car for me. He likes to do that sort of thing. Said that if he couldn't be there, he could at least help with the details. So he bought me a guidebook about local history. He planned out my route and bookmarked the maps. And he'd arranged the car. I could pick it up at the airport, then drive north to Edinburgh. I could have flown, but it was cheaper to drive. Mateo said I was crazy – these Canadians and their long distances – but really, I wanted the space. And the effort. I didn't want to be delivered to my grandmother's empty house like a package. I wanted to make a journey of it. So I'd drive straight through, listen to the radio, watch the weather. Then a hotel room for the night and a bus in the morning to Aberlady. Mateo had written all the details on a bit of paper that I slipped into my passport, and he also sent it all by email so I'd have everything in one place, if worse came to worse.

'Worst,' I said.

'What?'

'Nothing. But you mean if I lose the paper.'

'Well, yes.'

'I'll be fine, love.'

'Of course. I just want you to be looked after.'

'Thank you.'

After a pause, he asked me if I knew why.

'Why?'

'Yes. Why she left you the house. Why not your mother?'

We were sitting together upstairs in the gallery, side by side like an old couple, looking down into the garden courtyard. I'd hoped that we could have lunch – our last day at work together before I flew – but he had a meeting booked, so we just managed a quick chat in the middle of the morning. Bright sunlight fell in through the windows overhead, and the pale stone walls hushed the space like snow in a clearing. Everything was glass and granite, which suits Ottawa well. Like ice, snow and bedrock.

'Maybe she thought I'd like it,' I said. 'I might. Like it, I mean. You might like it, too. It's a good house.'

At one end of the courtyard, volunteers were setting out materials for a children's craft session – lots of coloured paper set on bright foam mats.

'You mean to vacation there? I am not sure about that.'

'There's a beach.'

'Not a real beach. Too cold for that, no?'

'Maybe, but it's lovely. With sand and everything. I used to swim there when I was a child.'

'Under a frozen sun.' He smiled and took my hand in his. He had beautiful Spanish hands, soft and perfect. Gentle. I tried to smile, too.

When I first knew Mateo, we used to meet here often. I'd pick up the phone when the shop was quiet and I could slip away and he'd leave his office or the archive to grab a moment together. We'd just sit. Maybe hold hands. I think neither of us could quite believe our luck. You don't stumble on love like this, do you? Just open your eyes one day at work and there it is. That doesn't happen. Except it does.

'I suppose I might sell it,' I said. 'A bit more money for the condo. Maybe we could afford a little more that way.'

'Yes, maybe. But there is another question. Did she give it to you or leave it to you?'

'What's the difference? She just wrote that the house was mine.'

'Money is the difference. Inheritance tax. But I am sorry to be talking about money when you are grieving. None of this matters. I only wondered. And wondered about your mother, as well.'

The volunteers were laughing now, their voices brittle at this distance, their hair shining in the falling light. Mateo sat with me for as long as he could, still holding my fingers in his beautiful hands. After he left, I took my usual route back through the European rooms to visit the Klimt. I like her. Her face doesn't change. In the shop, I sell a lot of postcards; so many people want to take her home. I want to ask them why. I wonder who they see in her eyes.

I pulled off the highway at a service station, a place where everything looked plastic and you could buy pre-wrapped muffins and coffee in cups to take away, or choose to sit at small tables and eat plates of fried eggs, ham and chips. I bought a boxed sandwich, a coffee and a chocolate bar I didn't want and ate in the car.

Over the border into Scotland, the highway narrowed, the landscape rising on either side, and the traffic thinning away. I expected rain. Or sheep. Or both. Everything was green – so much greener than home – and the April sun was warm through the windshield. Then before Edinburgh, I saw a sign for Birthwood. The sudden scent of home: cedar, wild garlic, pennyroyal and pine. I glanced away and back again, but there it was. I hadn't misread. Birthwood. She never told me it was an old name. A real name. It felt odd seeing it on an official sign. I wanted to stop and take a photo or turn off the highway to see – but to what end? Nostalgia. Suspicion. Romance. I kept going, driving north-east.

No more service stations now, just small villages with bakeries and convenience stores, low white houses with heavy black lintels, old stone walls. A few trees and, beyond them, fields that stretched out to the greening hills, then cloud-hills clustered up, grey against a grey sky. I turned the car radio on and off again. Birthwood must be a small place. There had been no sign of it on the map.

A crossroads, then, or the name of a farm. Insignificant but for the fact that Felicity had never told me about it.

This stretch of highway ran along an old Roman road. That had been on the map. Ancient history in ten miles to an inch.

When I was a child, the woods at home were timeless. Bas taught me people had passed among the trees for centuries, following the seasons and animals, coming and going and coming again. Others arrived from further away – traders, priests and settlers. For a while, they tried to stay, then moved on and built cities elsewhere. The forest returned and thickened, but Bas could still find their traces. He showed me wheel ruts and weathered split-rail fences that divided up the now-indifferent bush, crumbled houses and broken barns kneeling like fallen dinosaurs or other long-forgotten beasts stumbling towards extinction. The built history of people didn't last long. A couple of centuries at most. The trees themselves might almost remember.

Out here on the highway and beneath these bare hills, time felt different. Stretched and snapped. The Ninth Legion marched away at the end of my mother's childhood. Tacitus scribbled notes in my grandmother's living room. In the space between the Roman roads and the plastic sandwiches, you could lose your balance.

I could see why my mother left.

But that's not fair. It would be different if you were born here. This is one of the places where my mother was born. Not quite here, but down this road, anyway.

She used to count out her births for me. The first happened so early she couldn't remember it and she'd say that to make me laugh. Then she'd tell me about her mother's labour, her grandmother's flat, about her father who was a soldier and couldn't be there.

The second was a beautiful picture – light after rain, pavements shining and the clatter of pigeons lifting from the rooftops to wheel over the city, out towards the sea. She was young and everything was starting. She told me this story after thunderstorms or when I couldn't sleep. She stroked my hair, then whispered French rhymes in my ear.

There was a third story, too, but she wasn't good at telling it. She'd polish it and change it after arguments or when she was worried. I sat on our cabin's doorstep and watched the wind ripple the surface of the lake as she wondered aloud about the things we get to keep, the things we release and the way we might, if we're lucky, get to choose.

2

FELICITY: 1967

I LIED MY WAY INTO AN INTERVIEW. THAT'S WHERE IT started. I hadn't meant to, but what with the rain, my wet shoes and Dr Ballater that February, it happened. I wouldn't have planned it. I didn't have the nerve.

When I worked for Dr Ballater, I was docile. Polite. He came into my high school looking for a sensible girl to help with the surgery's desk work. Just for a few weeks before Christmas, he said. Miss Jones suggested I would be suitable and summoned me to meet the doctor in her office. He stood quite close to the door so when I stepped into the room, I saw him immediately. I don't think he meant to startle me; he just wanted to see how I might react. So, I didn't. Or rather, I politely said hello, shook his hand and sat down in the chair Miss Jones offered. Dr Ballater spoke in a soft voice, describing the work and the practice, meeting my gaze directly as he did so. I folded my hands in my lap and nodded.

13

Before the war, he may have been handsome, but now it was hard to tell. He had what can only be described as a splodge of a face. I suppose that's not kind, but I'm not sure how else to describe it. A puckered welt ran from above his left eyebrow, across his misshapen nose, and down to his chin. The skin around the wound looked raw and mottled. He didn't make me nervous – there were plenty of injured men around when I was growing up. Still I kept noticing how his skin pulled as he spoke and how each expression dragged on long after his words. It was difficult to act naturally. He seemed a kind and tired man.

I thought he was my father's age, and maybe he was. He said that when the war started he had only recently qualified. Like so many young men, he'd been persuaded by the call to arms.

'I assumed I would be given ambulance duty,' he said. 'Like the writers in the Great War. Instead, they planted me in a field hospital as a surgeon. That didn't last long. A bomb fell on us and they sent me home.'

He told me that on my first day. I guess he wanted to get it out in the open. After that, he never spoke about the war, nor did he speak about his return home, so I needed to fashion that part of the story myself. A long convalescence in a grand manor house somewhere in the west of Edinburgh. Daffodils on the lawn. Starched sheets and painkillers. I imagined a nurse with gentle hands. Soft eyes meeting his. And tragedy, too. There must have been tragedy because I knew he lived alone. That part of the story needed work. Maybe she was married; maybe she had died. Influenza perhaps, but that didn't strike me as wonderfully romantic. Maybe she'd been caught in an air raid. London then,

I supposed, but maybe Edinburgh. Mum had told me about the planes over Marchmont on the night I was born. Maybe Dr Ballater's sweetheart was killed that night. How strange to imagine.

This was how I passed afternoons at the surgery, keeping an eye on the mantel clock, and half dreaming out of the window. At quarter past four, Dr Ballater liked a pot of tea brought through to his desk. At first, that was my least favourite part of the day. The kitchen always smelled like bleach, and the bamboo tray felt too light to be sturdy. I balanced my way along the short hallway from the kitchen, and Dr Ballater opened the door just as I arrived. I hated knowing that he stood waiting for me, listening to my steps. That face behind the door. It was better when he walked back towards his desk and cleared a space for the tray. He opened a drawer and removed an elaborately embroidered tea cosy. The lost love must have made it for him, of that I was sure. He set it on the teapot with such precision and told me he was happy to have me. My typing was good, and the patients thought I was friendly.

He started asking me to join him in the afternoons. 'Just a wee blether and a cup of tea, wouldn't that be nice?'

He told me about his childhood in the countryside, not far from Biggar, about the hills there and the clear sky at night. He asked me how I liked school, about my parents and how they were feeling. Once he asked me what my plans might be for after school and I waffled nervously. I really hadn't thought that far, not in detail at least. I imagined a flat somewhere. Maybe over in Glasgow, though Edinburgh might be more practical. I would be chipping in with other girls, of course. Cooking small meals over a hotplate, sharing adventures. The previous Christmas, I'd worked the January sales in

Patrick Thomson's, and one of the other temporary girls talked on about her bedsit, which sounded exciting. I could imagine that. But just what I'd be doing there, I hadn't a clue. That wasn't an answer to Dr Ballater's question. So, I said I was looking into university and might read geology. It didn't sound unreasonable as I said it.

He suggested that nursing might be a better fit.

'It's a good life and there are always those that need helping.'

In the end, that's what I did. Signed up for the new degree programme at Edinburgh University and found a flat-share which was cold and nowhere near as romantic as I'd hoped. We all worked hard and stayed over in the hospital when we could, to keep warm. Sometimes, we went for coffee or to the films, and on Saturday evenings we were welcome to join the boys at the student union for the weekly dance.

The spring I graduated, one of the medical students invited me to the May Ball and I cut my hair like Sylvie Vartan, bobbed and fringed. I barely knew him and we danced until they turned the lights on. Was that polite? I suppose it was. Then he walked me home to my student digs in Marchmont, a long beautiful saunter along Coronation Walk. The cherry blossom was thick overhead and underfoot – blossom soup, blossom salad – and the night was so clear and almost bewitching, but he was certainly polite and I wished he wasn't. I climbed the stairs alone and felt a little guilty for my loneliness as I fell asleep. In the morning, I caught a train home to East Lothian to see my parents, the sea and the sky dirt-pearl grey.

There was a job waiting for me with Dr Ballater. That worked out rather well. My parents were happy to have me home again, and we all knew that it wouldn't be a permanent arrangement, but in the meantime, I could save up for a car. I banked my money in an empty margarine tub on the shelf next to my alarm clock.

For the next five years, I worked for Dr Ballater. Each year, I weighed and measured all the schoolchildren, and inspected their scalps. I bought that car and established a rota of housebound widows who might benefit from a visiting nurse. In the autumn, I helped with the kirk jumble sale. In the spring, it was the Easter tea. Mum couldn't be bothered with all the village business, as she called it. She was far happier pruning the trees in her orchard or foraging about in the hedgerows. Sometimes, she would have the minister's wife round for a cup of tea or Muriel would come up from Drem, but mostly, she and Dad lived quietly and left the social affairs to me. I found I liked it when the village ladies dropped by the surgery with invitations and requests for assistance. It kept me busy and helpful. Cheerful, as befits.

Then it was February 1967 and I noticed snowdrops beside the surgery door. Maybe they grew there every spring but I only noticed them that February afternoon when the front windows were open and Dr Ballater was whistling, a thin, windy whistle, lilting and sweet.

I opened the door softly, hung my coat on the hook in the hallway and checked my hair in the mirror. Combing it back into place with my fingers, I wondered if it might be time for a trim.

Dr Ballater was still whistling when I entered his room and noticed the tea tray was already placed on his desk. He asked me to marry him.

Abrupt as that.

I said nothing, and he apologized, the meat of his face flushing red.

'I should let you come in the door properly. I should let you settle.' He turned away from me, adjusting the mugs on the tray. 'Can I pour you a cup of tea?'

'Yes. Thank you, Dr Ballater.' The words felt brittle in my mouth.

'George. Please,' he said, and his hands shook a little as he filled a mug, or maybe it was just that the pot had been overfilled. 'There. Milk? Sugar?'

'Yes. Please.'

A splash and then two spoonfuls, heaped, and he placed the mug in front of me, awkwardly passing me the spoon, too, in case I wished to stir my tea. I did and then crossed my ankles.

'So, will you?'

'I . . . I don't know. I didn't . . .'

'No, no. I've rushed things, I'm sure. You didn't expect this. I can see that now. But I do . . . I should think you will need to marry someone. You are not the kind of girl who wouldn't. I should be glad if you would have me. I can always find another nurse.'

The wind caught the curtain, blowing it out into the room with a curve like a bell, and I thought of those snowdrops outside. They must have been there every year. They must.

'Here, this is for you, Felicity,' he said, my name sounding too soft as he held out his hand stiffly, giving me a twenty-pound note. 'Take it. You might like to go buy yourself a dress from Edinburgh, or something of that ilk over the weekend, and think, think about it. We will speak next week.'

The steps out of Waverley station were always windy, and I hadn't worn my working shoes. My good shoes – low heels, patent leather toes and a clever covered buckle – made an unfamiliar click as I climbed the steps. I'd worn my trench coat, too, which might be protection against any rain, but wasn't really warm enough at all. The weather was bright and brisk with thin grey clouds wisped high over the castle as I walked towards Woolworths. This was silly, I thought. I didn't need a dress. I didn't want a dress. Maybe I should head to the top floor for a coffee in the tartan-carpeted restaurant. Instead, I browsed the book selection. Twenty pounds would buy me a very solid armload of stories. But that wasn't what Dr Ballater had in mind.

So, instead I found a white pillbox hat made of thick felt, which matched my trench coat and looked stylish. I also bought a leather bag with a good shoulder strap and two stout handles. The kind of thing you might take for a weekend away somewhere. Paris. Bruges. Would Dr Ballater take me to Paris? Would we sit together on a terrace drinking coffee, or a glass of wine, even? If I said yes, I would find out, I supposed. That was the trick of it. I had to give him an answer and things were going to change whatever it might be. The shop girl wanted to wrap my hat and place it in a smart box, but I told her that I would like to wear it. She paused, then said, *Of course.* I told her I could carry my bag, too, just as it was.

I stepped out of the shop into a different day, the sky slate grey and a sharp wind. My mother would say that I really did need a pair of gloves, but the new leather handles felt good in my bare hand, and a brave face conceals all shivers. Which was something else she might say. I turned the collar up on my coat and adjusted my purse under my arm. If you didn't know, you might just think that I had arrived in town from parts far flung and sophisticated rather than dumpy old East Lothian forty minutes away. Yet if that was true, and if I were really that person, why on earth would I come here? What would I want to see? Old stones and old folk standing in the rain.

That morning, I'd told my parents about Dr Ballater's suggestion.

'Oh,' said my mother.

'And how are you going to respond?' Dad asked.

'I don't know.'

'No,' said Mum. 'It looks like you don't.'

'Do you like him? You do, don't you?' Dad asked. 'I knew his family during the war. Good people. He might be as good a chance at happiness as any.'

'I'm not sure,' said Mum. 'He is older, isn't he?'

'Felicity has always been an old soul.'

'Yes,' she said, and it didn't sound like encouragement. They didn't say anything else, just sat together at the kitchen table, over half-cups of tea and the crossword puzzle like every other morning for the last hundred years. I kissed them both and said I'd be home again in the evening in time for tea.

I crossed Princes Street towards the gardens, pushed along by a swift, rushing wind and my mind filled with the words of the old hymn – *so wild and strong, high clouds that sail in heaven along* – so filled, so full I could almost sing. But best not to. Spring wind or no, Edinburgh might not approve. I kept my peace and walked sedately into the garden. Past the gate, down and down the steps in my pinching shoes, no angel blocked the way, no flaming sword to bar my path, but a gardener walked towards me holding a giant arrow under his arms. He smiled and nodded at me and, looking the other way, I saw another gardener on the slope beside the steps, surrounded by dozens of small potted plants. I wondered if I imagined them, summoned them somehow. Only once I was sitting down did it occur to me that they must have been working on the floral clock. That would have been interesting to watch. Still, it felt so good to sit down and slip my shoes off for a moment.

You are not the kind of girl who wouldn't.

What the hell did that mean? What kind of girl was I?

Predictable. Suggestible. Polite.

The castle looked down from its rock foundation like Edinburgh's broken tooth against a threatening sky. I took off my hat and folded it in half, opened it again and set it on my skirt. A sensible skirt my mother had made me in hunter-green tweed with flecks of purple. The kind of material that might be fashioned into an interesting tea cosy.

Then the rain started in earnest. Princes Street was crammed with cars, so I headed east. The North British Hotel has a lovely lobby, and I figured I could loiter there until it dried up a little. Stepping inside, I was surprised to see so many other women standing about. Mostly my age or younger, although also here and there, older women checking their watches and watching the crowd. A woman stepped forward, holding a clipboard. She wore her dark hair in a neat chignon, a serviceable broach pinned to her lapel.

'Your interview number, please. Do you have it to hand?'

'No, I—'

'Did you not receive one by post? With your interview invitation?'

'No. I didn't.'

'Oh dear. Another one. There have been so many slip-ups and confusions today. Some days run smoothly, and others . . . well, if you give me your name and details, I will add you to the list. Don't spend a moment on worry, dear. It will come right in the end. Teaching or nursing? Teaching?'

'No. Nursing.'

'Ah, my apologies. I'm usually right with my guesses. Clever of you to catch me out. And better luck for you. Not so much of a crowd for nursing here today. Your name?'

'Felicity. Felicity Hambleton.'

'Perhaps doubly lucky, then. By name and by nature. It will be your turn soon.'

'Thank you.'

She smiled and turned to speak to the next girl come in from the rain, a redhead in NHS spectacles clutching a soggy brown envelope to her chest.

So, nursing interviews. I'd never call it answered prayer, but maybe a way forward. I looked more carefully around the room and saw a sandwich board propped up near the reception desk.

Agnew Employment Agency:
Canadian Recruitment

Teachers:
Protestant School Board
of Greater Montreal, Quebec

Nurses and Midwives:
Various – Montreal, Quebec,
the Northern Territories

Near the doors to the hotel ballroom, folding chairs were arranged in a row, and girls sat waiting, shuffling along each time a name was called. Teachers or nurses: so that was the game. For some, it was easy to guess. I looked for wristwatches, writers' calluses, inky fingers. I could imagine chalk dust brushed out of tweed skirts that morning, shoes polished before bed last night. My own shoes looked the worse for wear, water spots marking the patent leather toes, but you pay a price for glamour in Scotland. And, as the lady said, I might just score a few points for being distinctive. I sat down, opened my handbag and applied more lipstick.

Let's see. Canada. The frozen north. What did I know about Canada? Cold and snow. Ice hockey. Indians. French. Oh dear. I hadn't thought of that. Any job in Quebec would require French, wouldn't it? Proper working French, which was likely a notch or two more advanced than *mes lunettes sont sur la table*. I tried to remember the other posters that hung on the French room wall at school. *Les légumes verts. Les saisons. Chaud. Froid.*

When my name was called, I was thinking about imperfect conjugations. What the hell – let it happen, whatever it would be. It was sure to be better than a walk in the rain. I picked up my new bag, smiled at the girl sitting next to me and stepped into the ballroom.

The interview was brief, the interviewer a thin, pale man in heavy glasses, sitting at one of the many small tables in the room, each with another interviewer just like him. He held a red Parker Duofold with a gold nib, but most of the notes were taken by the woman beside him. She sat very straight in her chair, her papers set at an angle on the tabletop, and she was writing with her left hand. She paused at the end of my name.

'*Avec un y*,' I said, quickly. 'Not *ie*.' The woman smiled. I crossed my ankles and straightened the hem of my skirt over my knees. The interviewer apologized for misplacing my details. There had been problems with the administration. Might I be able to send a fresh copy early next week?

'Of course, of course. *Pas de problème.*'

He asked about my experience and my training, nodding as I mentioned the University of Edinburgh.

'That is one of the reasons why we are here. The best programme in Europe, it is. We're lucky to be able to scoop up girls like you.'

'Are there no appropriate Canadian nurses?'

'Yes, yes, of course. Still, the Edinburgh degree programme is cutting edge, and there's a greater chance of real bilingualism here than, say, in Edmonton. Your French is good, I assume?'

'*Bien sûr.*'

'The proximity to France, no doubt. And the Auld Alliance, too, I should think. Now then, Church of Scotland?'

'Yes. Does that matter?'

'No, it isn't crucial. For the teachers, yes, with board regulations, but in the hospital, it can still help. Montreal is a city of Presbyterian expats, at least on the anglophone side.'

'Quite.'

'So, not the north? No grand polar adventure for you? Is it Montreal you want?'

'Yes. Yes, I suppose it is.'

His assistant spoke out in a clear, crisp voice.

'You will do nicely.'

'Thank you,' I said, but she kept her face set and slid an envelope across the table towards me.

'Here is a packet of information from the agency. In it, you will find a copy of the contract, details about immigration, and about Montreal as an international city. And, naturally, about the agency's involvement with your career. There are forms to finalize as well. You will find it all quite self-explanatory. If you have any questions, there are telephone numbers for our representatives in London.' She wrote a note next to my name, glanced at her watch, and looked past me towards the doors. All settled.

'Thank you,' I said again. The interviewer stood to shake my hand.

'You're welcome. Enjoy Canada.'

Outside, the rain had stopped, and the afternoon was brash with daylight. I stepped away from the shadow of the hotel and onto the still-wet pavement. Pigeons, hundreds of pigeons clattered up before me, a broad arc of flight over the gardens and, above the castle, the sky was slashed open into gold, bright gold. All those wings and gold, too. My breath felt sharp and new, and, away to the west, the pavements shone.

No one, it seems, is born just once.

3

PIDGE: 2006

MY MUM TOLD STORIES WHENEVER WE TRAVELLED. We'd be hitchhiking out from the camp in the cab of some truck, headed to Ottawa, or Montreal, and I'd sit up on Felicity's blue-jeaned knees, her long hair tickling my face as I leaned back into her skinny chest and all the way she'd make the driver laugh with her tall tales and stories, her toothy laughing smile. Sandy Gibb the Glass Man, astronauts at Expo and swimming pregnant in a moonlit lake. She could make a story of anything. Maybe I should have told her about this trip. I told the gallery that I needed time away to sort through my grandmother's things. They filed that under 'personal reasons' and then reasonably told me to take as much time as I needed. I told Mateo that I would need to organize the details of her estate, and he said that he understood. I told myself I'd be cleaning the bungalow. Before I left Ottawa, I'd imagined lots of cleaning. All those large windows and the wooden floors, too. Linoleum tiles in the kitchen. Then the bath to scour, old pots to scrub, and Persian carpets to shake out in the sunshine. It seemed like therapeutic work. Cleansing. Solitary.

Mateo said once that it was my aloneness that first caught him. I wondered if he meant loneliness, if he was mistranslating, but he said no, he meant aloneness. He said it was intriguing.

Maybe it was living at the camp with Felicity. There was lots of time then to be alone. In the night when she was at the birthing house. Or in the afternoon, when she opened her books and settled down to work at the small table in our cabin and she liked to have the space to herself, so she sent me outside. In the summer, there were always lots of children to play with, but as soon as the nights got too cold for tents, the field would empty and I'd be alone again.

When I was a little older, around nine or ten, Felicity started to take me with her to births, particularly when there were small children. She had me tell them stories and invent games to keep them entertained and distracted. Rika thought it best for children to keep away from a birth, but she never made rules, only suggestions. I'd heard Rika talking about this with Felicity one afternoon, and because they were talking about children, I listened.

'What about when a mum wants them there?' Felicity asked. 'Should we come up with some pretence to get them outside anyway?'

'No. Always only tell the truth. She needs to go so far into herself to open for the baby, and lies aren't going to help that.'

'And neither are kids in the room?'

Rika laughed. 'You got it, babe. It can be hard to open for one baby when you are listening to another one prattle.'

I lay above them on the top bunk with my *National Geographic*. They probably forgot I was there, but it didn't matter. They never kept anything from me. I'd heard everything, all the complications and contradictions. I learned how things can be difficult when babies come and how sometimes they don't. How it's possible to hope for two things at once. Release. Safety. Or time and space. I looked up from my magazine and let my eyes trace the lines on the river maps pinned to the wall. Blue ink meant water, and in this neck of the woods, the names were beautiful. The Ottawa, the Picanoc, the Gatineau, La Pêche.

'If she really wants them close, then make space by all means. But often she only thinks she wants them so that she can keep an eye on them. So, we give the kids a safe, cared-for space away from her, and likely she'll choose to be quiet and alone.' Rika was always teaching like this and Felicity wanted to learn. She'd come to the camp pregnant, and after I was born, she decided to stay and help out.

I tried to explain all this – the work, the help, the study, and Rika – to Mateo in our early days, but he was more interested in my stories of long days spent alone in the woods, of climbing trees and swimming naked and summer nights and winter afternoons spent in snowshoes out on the ice. I told him how I lay down flat on my back on the snowy lake and imagined the cold depth of the water hidden beneath me, the hollow sky above me. I told him that lying there alone, I felt contained like a coin in my own pocket and perfectly happy.

On my own, the travel felt long. I arrived in Edinburgh late in the evening and found the hotel, just as Mateo had suggested. In the morning, the streets were wet, and through the window in the hotel's breakfast room, I watched tourists with umbrellas, golf bags and suitcases pass by on their way to the trains. Pigeons huddled on the damp rooftops, and I drank strong tea, thinking about the house.

It sits away from the village and you can see the sea from the house, but not the sands. For the sands, you need to cross a footbridge and walk out past the flat lands, the marshlands and scrub trees. You pass through places where the way is lined by barbed-wire fencing, keeping the sheep in and the dogs out, and then places where the path is only a trace through open landscape. It is a bit of a walk to get to the beach, but a good walk.

Closer to the house, the shore is thick with black silt washed down from farmland nearby. A small stream cuts through the mud, a snaking path for the running tide. The bay is wide, open like a bowl, but the sea here is narrow, a silver band between East Lothian and Fife leading into the North Sea. When the tide fills the bay, it comes in quick and strange, leaving a wide sandbar dry across the mouth. That's where the geese gather at night and where the shipwrecks sit. Felicity never let me walk out that far. She said they were just rusty submarines left over from the war and not particularly interesting.

The house was a place we visited in winter because in the winter Felicity got homesick. Gran kept the back bedroom ready for us, just in case. She knew that Felicity found the white winters at the camp hard. The days were quiet and short, the trees were bare, the path deep with snow and she had to tuck my trousers into the tops of my knitted socks to keep me warm.

When it got too quiet, too cold, and too bright, she pulled down the army surplus backpacks from the rafters and filled them with sweaters, skirts, books and warm scarves. We'd leave behind the textbooks, their precise illustrations, and the river maps. Then Felicity would bundle me into my thick winter coat, rub my face with Vaseline to keep the wind away, and we hitchhiked off to the city to find the airport bus. We never had enough pennies to commit to an annual flight, but whenever we needed to, we managed to fly. Felicity said that this was yet one more advantage of staying away from the public schools: flight was always possible. She also said that there were ample books at the camp to fill anyone's brain usefully, and that if there was anything extra that I wanted to know, I could always ask Bas.

I could ask Bas anything and he gave me answers like small prizes slipped into my waiting hands. He was the one who told me pine needles keep you healthy like oranges do. He showed me how to hold hens' eggs up to a candle to see the chick growing inside, and taught me that adult loons leave the lake a whole month before their children every autumn. The next generation migrates alone, relying on instinct, and he said instinct was a feeling and feelings matter. In return, I told him all the things I knew. That some grown-ups kept their eyes open at the table when we said the blessing. That all my mother's hair was fair and curly – under her arms, too, and even under her skirt – while mine was dark and flat. That some spider-webs could outlast thunderstorms. That pennies smell like blood and blood smells like fish and that you couldn't smell bruises at all.

I suspect my gran had something to do with the *enough pennies* when it came to airplanes. We never had much. We didn't need much, really. Life in the woods wasn't about pennies, and mainly the camp was self-sufficient anyway. We grew plenty of food in the fields across the lake and sold what we wouldn't eat at the road-end all through the summer. Pies, tarts and deep baskets of strawberries and raspberries from the gardens, and wild blueberries from the rocky places along the lakeshore. What we couldn't eat or sell, we saved. Bas made berry schnapps and wine coolers, and throughout the summer and into the fall, the canning kettle boiled on the woodstove and the air in the farmhouse kitchen was thick with sugar, vinegar and cloves. Felicity said she came by canning honestly, and told me about Gran's preserves: rosehips, apple chutney, gorse wine and bramble jam. Saving things up must be in her blood and she crinkled her forehead a little fiercely when she said it, though no one would ever say she wasn't authentic. A good camp word, *authentic*. Rika used it like a compliment, as though some folk weren't and might only be acting. Did adults do that? I wasn't sure. When I asked Bas, he shrugged and pulled the dressing-up box from the cupboard, asking who I was going to be that afternoon. I acted out every story my mother told me. A pirate tree-nymph. A mountaineering beaver. Or my favourite role of all: the Blessed Virgin herself. Bas always made time for stories, layering me with blankets, helping me to belt a pillow to my middle that I might stagger my way towards Bethlehem. He played every innkeeper with arms open wide, and with a straight face and a shining eye, found a footstool for my swollen virgin ankles and wondered if I might like a mug of tea.

'I don't know,' I said. 'Did they have tea then?'

'I'm not sure. Maybe that comes later. It'll be the wise men who leave some with you, but I don't think you've met them yet, have you?'

'Are you foolish, Bas? Or wise?'

'Probably foolish, your holiness. Most probably.'

'I think you're wise. You know how to make bread. That's wise, isn't it?'

'Wise enough for this world. Would you like some jam, too, m'lady?' He spread it thick and I ate it stickily with fingers and lips jelly red.

Bas always knew what to offer, how much to ask, when to be silent or serious or good. He was good at keeping a story going. Much later, I realized the gentleness that took, and the strength.

Stories are fragile things, eggshell thin and porous.

After breakfast, I picked up a few groceries in a small convenience store near the hotel. Enough to live on for a little while, I thought, and there would be shops to explore in Aberlady once I'd settled in.

Then I turned in the car at the rental agency and found the bus. It shuddered out of the city, through suburbs, past rows of stucco houses with gravel yards or small lawns and the occasional incongruous palm tree. Most of the people on the bus were old, chatting with their neighbours, holding shopping bags. A pile of free newspapers at the front of the bus sat untouched, and I thought about leaving my seat to collect one but looked out the window instead.

The road passed on through small towns and smaller towns until at last the way opened up and I could see the colour of the fields and the line of the coast. The clouds had lifted, or maybe the wind had blown them back out to sea. It was a windy landscape, with small, crooked trees and hawthorn hedges along the roadside, and white birds hovered high above the waves, holding the wind in their wings. Then a wooded stretch, denser now, and in between the trees, old cement blocks sat heavily – anti-tank defences left over from the war. I remembered Felicity telling me about them, and about the railings set in the churchyard's stone wall. They had been sawn off when the country needed more metal for airplanes, leaving iron coins set into the stone. She showed me how to press my thumb in each one – one a penny two a penny – and how to climb up the *loupin-on stanes*, that long-abandoned set of steps that Victorian ladies used to climb up to their high horses.

Just past the church, the bus stopped and I collected my bags. I hadn't packed much because I wanted space to bring things home again. I wasn't sure what, but maybe Gran had left something specific for me to find. Heirlooms or papers or photographs. I'd search the house as if for clues and maybe find why Gran had left it to me. Felicity had trained me to look for stories, hadn't she?

I crossed the street to the hotel – a big whitewashed building with picnic tables and plant pots out front, trellises against the wall, and ivy. The door was open and no one sat at the desk in the front hall. I wasn't sure about ringing the bell. It looked as if it would make a great deal of noise. I stood there for a moment, examining the map laid out on the wooden counter, the coastline curved like the back of a fish, or like a belly facing the sea. Then, an old woman came through a door behind me and cleared her throat.

'Hello,' she said. 'Are you looking for a meal?'

'No. Well . . . I'm really here to collect keys,' I said. 'For my grandmother's house. Jane Hambleton. I was sent a letter that mentioned there would be a set of keys here. With Muriel?' I opened up my shoulder bag and pulled out the letter for the woman to read, but she just looked into my face with a soft smile.

'Yes, of course,' she said. 'That's me. And you are Jane's little Pidge. Felicity's, I mean. You and I met when you were small. You won't remember me, but your mother brought you here. And you look just like her. Except for the hair, maybe. The colour suits you.' She coughed a little laugh and asked about my mother. 'Is she keeping well? She's here with you too, then?'

'No, it's just me. She's back in Quebec. She's well. Happy.'

'Ah, yes. Settled there, I suppose. Such a shame that she couldn't make it home in time for her mum's funeral, but I suppose it was unexpected, wasn't it? And so quick. But such a shame. And just before your own arrival. She was so looking forward to seeing you. She told me so many times that you were coming and that you might pop in here first, and that's when she left the keys here. I think she was worried you might arrive when she was out for a walk or even down in the garden and that she wouldn't hear you. But I'm sure all that's in the letter, isn't it? Ah well, things come out as they will, won't they? Are you planning to stay long?'

'I don't quite know. There's the house . . .'

'Yes, I suppose it will need sorting through. All Jane's lovely things. And Stanley's books and papers, too. I don't think she let go of much after his death.'

'She left it to me. The house, I mean.'

'Oh, that's wonderful. It's a good house, a cracking garden. So, you think you might stay?'

'I live in Ottawa. My partner is there, and my work.'

'Of course, of course. Yes, you'll just be wanting to see it and sort, won't you? Well, while you're here, do pop in again. The kitchen does a lovely bit of lunch, if you ever need a meal. Cooking for one can be awkward, can't it?' Muriel reached over and straightened a messy pile of golf brochures beside the bell on the desk. 'But you need the keys and you must be tired. Just arrived, and all that way, too. Ah yes, here they are.'

She found a small brown envelope under the counter and slid it across the map towards me. It looked as if there might be anything inside. A wedding ring. Ashes. Dragons' teeth. I slipped it away into my pocket. 'Thank you.'

'Would a cup of tea help? You must be absolutely shattered. You've only just arrived, haven't you? You have the aeroplane look about you.'

'I'm just off the bus. I stayed in Edinburgh last night.'

'Well, you come along through here and I'll see about some tea. Unless you'd prefer a coffee?'

'No, tea's fine. Thanks.'

I followed her through the door at the end of the hallway, past a bar and a lounge with sofas and chairs and then into a larger room with tables set for lunch. White napkins and slate coasters.

'Sit anywhere you like. Do you fancy something to eat?'

'No. I'm not sure. I can't quite fathom what time of day it is.'

'Travel will do that. You sit down now. You'll feel better with the tea in you. Sugar, too. It does wonders. And I'll bring you a scone as well. You look like some bulking up might do you good.'

'Thank you. That sounds wonderful.'

I chose a small table by the window. My fingers picked at the flap on the back of the envelope and then ripped the paper and shook out the contents into my hand. A heavy mortice key fell into my palm and sat there like a finger bone. No wonder Felicity thought in fairy tales, if this was the key to her childhood home.

My mother's third birth came in bits and pieces. There were always sliced apples and something about the grass growing outside the cabin. She tried out new versions on me, changing the weather or time of day, approaching everything from a different angle. I liked it best when she began it in the afternoon. The morning story often featured rain and sometimes books left on the lawn. Once, she told me a fox ran across the grass with a vole in its mouth, and a crow shouted down from the trees, startling the fox so she dropped her prize as Felicity sat with me on the porch, watching. I didn't like that telling at all. But the afternoon story went like this: we were together on the porch, Felicity on a stump stool and me sleeping swaddled in a blanket that Rika had knit, lying in a cradle Bas had carved. The rain was over, and the weather would be dry now, so she sat slicing the apples into rings, then threading them onto garden twine to dry in the wind. I could see her hands doing all this; she did it every autumn. Out on the lake, a loon surfaced and called, and I woke gently, my eyes bright as water. I didn't cry or make a fuss and all afternoon, the loon sat there on the lake, calling and calling, and Felicity sliced all the apples and not one was wasted. Later, she'd hook the twine over a peg high up on our cabin wall, where the apple rings would grow dark and leathery. Felicity liked saving things to use later, saving up the seasons. I don't know why this story counted as a birth, but she said it did.

My own birth was a tale she told lightly. When I asked questions, she smiled and said I already knew what I needed to – I had seen Rika working, helping, and I knew what needed to happen. *It was like that*, Felicity said. *Like every other birth. Every mother is strong like that.*

But all her counted stories made me wonder how many births I might have. Do you get to decide? Can you make them happen?

4

M OST VILLAGES AND SMALL TOWNS GROW UP ALONG
one main road, which is like a spine or the trunk of a
tree, but the road through Aberlady had a sudden dog-leg bend
that turned sharply as if to say *that's enough of that, let's look at
the sea now*. The wind pushed at my back, rushing me out past
the edge of the village towards the house. The tide was coming
in and shining waves chased the light over mudflats. In the distance,
I could see the bridge now, the end of the shoreline and the
beginning of the burn, but there across the road was the house.

Houses play tricks on us, or maybe it's memory. I remembered
the house as enormous: wide rooms, oceans of carpet with rug
rafts in front of the fire, vast bookshelves reaching from floor to
ceiling, crammed full of books and boxes, and a step stool in the
corner. A giant's chair and footstool and windows full as the sea.

But whenever Felicity spoke about the house – with Bas or

Rika or with one of the girls — she called it a minuscule bungalow. I asked once what that meant, and she said 'A small house. Cramped and with no stairs.'

'Like a cabin, then?'

'No. Smaller.' But Bas laughed, so I didn't believe her.

Funny how the truth becomes real. From where I stood across the road, the house was both small and strange, sitting low under the tall trees and the whitewash looking too bright in the sunshine. I hadn't remembered the stepped roofline or the crown-shaped chimney pot, but the cheerful red-tiled roof was familiar. As I approached, crows flew up from the trees beside the road, calling out loudly to each other. They circled in the sky before settling again to their treetops, their nests loose jumbles of sticks in the high forks.

A small lane led from the road down to the house. The front door was hidden behind a half-wall, a sort of L-shaped windbreak. *L for Livia. L for love.*

Then I heard a sound in the doorway.

A shifting sound behind the half-wall followed by the stillness of someone waiting. I paused. It seemed a quiet village. But the house had been empty for a couple of weeks now. Someone could have found a way in and set up camp. I held my breath. Then I heard the sound of feathers.

Only a bird, then. Well, that was a relief. I waited a moment, and then another, for it to emerge, but when it didn't, I cleared my throat to startle it. Nothing.

'Hello?' A human voice would scare it away, I thought. Still nothing. But then another shift, so I took a step and peered around the half-wall.

A goose filled the space. It was startlingly tall and its long dark neck snaked from side to side, its white chin-strap bright in the shadow beside the door. When it looked over its broad brown back towards me, I balked and stepped back. Weird to see a Canada Goose here, I thought, but maybe it was thinking similar thoughts about me. I raised my arms in a sort of loose-winged flap and made a few hopeful noises, but the goose stayed put. It looked as if it was waiting, but obviously not for me.

'Go!' I said, firmly.

And nothing. The bird would not budge. It turned towards the door and looked in through the window, making throat-clearing sounds. The key felt heavy in my pocket, but I walked back down the path, sat on the low stone wall at the end of the garden and dug an apple out of my pack. Banished.

The wind blew through the tall grasses on the verge. Grey clouds gathered out at sea. By the road, tulips nodded heavy purple heads, and I wondered if they'd been Gran's idea. Did she fling out a few bulbs, let them fall where they might and bury themselves to wait for spring? I could imagine that. I could almost see her, standing here at the very edge of her garden with a fistful of bulbs, watching the cars pass by, waiting for the right moment. She'd glance back at the house to see if he was watching and maybe he was or maybe he wasn't, and she wouldn't mind one way or the other, and then, with the road clear each way, she would reach back and let the bulbs fly.

When I turned back to the house, the goose wasn't there. The key turned smoothly in the lock and I stepped inside, closing the door behind me. The house was quiet. Empty. Smelling citrusy. *L for lemon.*

I set my bag down in the hallway next to the teak trolley where the telephone sat watching, squat beside a bowl of keys and Gran's brown wallet. Right out in the open, the first place to look. Logical, I thought, and the leather felt soft in my hands, but there were only cards inside. No folded letter, no secret photograph. I picked up the phone and there was no dial tone. The lawyer's letter had said nothing had been disconnected and everything should be fine. Well, there's something to add to the to-do list. And I would need to find another way of calling Mateo, too, and maybe Felicity. I thought I should let her know where I was.

The living room was a shrunken version of what I remembered. Shabbier, too, but only from the passage of time. Everything looked faded – the ashes in the fireplace, the rag rug Felicity had made at the camp sun-bleached like the photographs on the mantel, familiar and distant. There was a well-dressed Victorian couple framed in silver, he in tweeds and thick sideburns, she with lace cuffs, and her hands folded on her skirt. Then my mother as a grinning toddler running across grass, caught almost in flight. My grandparents in a wooden frame, new parents, my mother a bundled infant, my young grandmother with her head bent, adoring. My grandfather wore a zippered cardigan under his jacket and met the camera's gaze, shy, defiant, present and looking at me as if I shouldn't be unsupervised in his house.

Their wedding photo was framed in silver. My grandmother was all high cheekbones and a shine in her eye, and my grandfather watched her, laughing. They held their hands up between them, fingers intertwined, as if they wanted the photographer to capture the new gold band on her finger. Linked. She wore an elegant fox fur around her shoulders and it must have matched her hair, though in the black-and-white photograph, both the fox and the hair looked silver. I'd grown up with the photo. Felicity kept a copy on the table in our cabin and I liked to look at it when I was small. That Klimt look on Gran's face and Granddad's laugh.

'Was it like that with you and my dad?' I asked once. 'When he was around?'

'Oh, Pidge, you're getting too old for that story. You know you don't have a dad. Only a father. And no, he wasn't like that.' She pushed her fingers up through the paleness of her hair, then smiled at me. 'If he was, he'd be around now, and I'd have to share you. And then what would we do? I couldn't ever share you.'

When I was almost twelve and we were up late together after a long night-birth, I asked why her dad hadn't been there when she was born.

'It was the war, sweetie. He was away. You can't always be where you want to be. Not when there's a war.'

'But Gran had help, right? There were midwives there?'

'A doctor. And her mum. She could have had a nurse, too, but there were enough people out that night already. That's what she said. But I think it was more about privacy, really. Your gran is a very private person.'

She made it sound like she would describe herself otherwise. Or maybe it was just a slip.

In the kitchen, the fridge hummed gently and the clock kept ticking, its electric cord twisting down to the outlet near the cooker. Pinned to the wall by the door, there was a postcard from the gallery. Felicity must have sent that over – a photo of the giant spider sculpture that sat between the gallery and the street. On the back, a note in her handwriting:

Dear Mum,

Hello from Pidge's shop – all lovely books, silk scarves & calendars. She's happy, I think, selling gifts – says it reminds her people are thinking of others & that's beautiful. She has a generous heart, doesn't she?

Thought you'd like the spider. 30 feet tall & her belly full of marble eggs. An elegance of legs and space.
All love,
Felicity

I opened the back door for fresh air and so that I could see tulips growing at the edge of a cobbled yard. There were several outbuildings – sheds and things – and beyond that, grass with a stone bench and a path that led down to a small orchard. I remembered these trees – just a half-dozen apple trees, too small to climb and wind-twisted even there behind the house. I could smell the sea, too. Salt. Coins. Rust.

Then a sound. I startled, half expecting to see – who? Gran? Granddad? Not Mateo. Or Felicity, suddenly arrived with suitcase in hand to surprise me, *hello* and *my love*. But no, none of that. Nothing as gentle. Instead, the goose paced across the cobblestones, honking and squonking, sticking its neck out and making a God-awful, ear-quaking racket.

5

MY FIRST THOUGHT WAS TO SLAM THE DOOR TO KEEP it out of the house. And the others, too, assuming there were others. Geese aren't solitary birds, are they? They come in flocks. Or is it skeins? Which sounded like something in flight and the one I could see certainly wasn't. It stalked around the shed, upturning stacks of flower pots, buckets and bins. Everything crashed to the ground, bouncing on the hard stones or shattering to pieces. I checked the lock on the kitchen door. It felt strange to be alone.

I slipped my shoes off and pulled myself up onto the counter so I could watch out the window more easily. With its hard, black beak, the goose hammered on the shed door and then, as I watched, pushed the door open and marched inside. Then, a bedlam of brushes and boxes, more broken pots and an imperious honk. More clatter and a yellow tin clanged across the yard.

Fry's Cocoa.

I supposed it didn't really matter how much mess the goose made out there. Everything would need to be sorted through and disposed of one way or another. You couldn't sell a property full of stuff. Besides, there might be something interesting to take back to Ottawa. Maybe not dented old tins, but something. A lantern. An old tackle box. Something antique.

I looked around the kitchen to see what was there and, on top of the cupboard, I spotted Gran's blue glass cake-stand. Mateo might like that. In the cupboard, I found an olive-wood cruet set, three pottery jugs, and a gravy boat. The coffee mill, which would certainly be useful. Folded paper napkins wrapped in waxed paper, empty jam jars, scrubbed clean, and a tall berry-dark bottle marked 'sloe gin'. Behind another door, a stack of lovely teacups – some chipped, but enough to make up a set, certainly. Then, pushed to the back, a row of squat bottles with ground-glass stoppers. Inside, there were dried needles like rosemary, seeds like apple, and dusty flower petals, pink, red and yellow. Nothing familiar, not quite at least, and I wondered what Felicity might make of them. I probably couldn't get them through customs. Not without knowing what they were. Mateo tried to bring sausage home last summer – a long loop that he bought at a Spanish market. I told him that it was never going to work, that he was really just buying lunch for the airport staff, but he shrugged, looking smug. I was right, of course, though he put on a show for the officials.

'I promise I will not share it. No risk to the Canadian population, I assure you. It will pass no other lips than my own. Unless you would like to try? I might share with you.'

The customs officer shook his head and Mateo had to leave the sausage behind.

Maybe I should just sell the lot. There was never going to be space in a new condo for these old things. I could call an auction house and have them clear the place. Sell everything and head back home.

Another tin clattered across the yard. Oxo this time.

Home meant Ottawa. Mateo. Work. Home meant routine and habit, and that didn't have much space for china teacups. Home used to mean the camp, but I left because it was time for me to choose. A free woman chooses – that's what they had always taught me, and I got to the stage where staying didn't feel like a choice any more. It was just procrastination.

I'd been working in the village store, selling cigarettes, groceries and booze. The kind of job teenage girls pick up after high school when they're waiting for life to start, and it was like that for me, too, in a way. After I mailed my equivalence tests in the province and they sent me my diploma, I started at the shop as a way of making money before my next step, but then I stuck around. It was familiar and comfortable – like everything else. Most of the year, I knew everyone who came in, though it was different in the summer, with the cottage people and folk heading north to go hunting. But mainly, it was routine. Mothers came in mid-morning with small kids. Seniors needed help finding things every week. Just after the mass at one o'clock, a grey-haired man always bought a two-four of Molson and told me to smile. Always the same. Except one day, he asked me what I was waiting for. He said I looked tired, like maybe I was drowning. Who was he to comment? But later, I wondered if he recognized something. I couldn't say what I was waiting for. People came through Birthwood and told us how lucky we were to have this slice of creation for our own. Maybe I was waiting to feel that. Bas and Rika did, obviously. And Felicity, too. I thought it would come with time or age. Except now, apparently, I looked like I was drowning. Well, that wasn't true. I was just – what? Caught in an eddy, going round and round and watching the same piece of sky.

So, I made up my mind and chose to move to Ottawa.

I'd leave most of my things behind: my old photo albums and papers, the bookshelves Bas made me and my work clothes. I'd rent a furnished apartment at first, I decided, and find a new job. I could learn to live alone in the middle of a city. Eat meals on my own, visit museums and galleries, maybe even find work there, and when I actually managed to do all that, I told people that was why I had moved. For work and culture. For art.

But that wasn't true. I moved to Ottawa because it sat at the end of the river. The T-junction of the Gatineau and the Ottawa. *T is for time to go.*

When I was small, the river map on the wall showed the Gatineau curled like Felicity's hair. It laced among a hundred lakes and Bas told me the name was Algonquin – *Te-nagàdino-zìbi* – which meant *the river that stops your journey.* There were rocks to portage around and narrow places where even a canoe couldn't slip through. But there was also a story about a French explorer who drowned in the river, and he was called Gatineau, too. Nicolas Gatineau. There was a high school named after him and I found his name in a history book. Some stories come twinned and some things are true.

Gran's tea towels still hung on the hooks by the stove, and her spices sat on the thin shelf with the egg timer. But no coat by the door, no teacups to be rinsed. I noticed these things and waited for grief. I expected it and watched myself, waited. But it didn't come. Instead, I felt disconnected and cold. I didn't know how to do this.

Felicity should be here. Well, not sitting on the counter. She'd likely know what to do about the goose outside. And about the cupboards and the cake-stand and all the photographs and books. She'd negotiate presence and absence all right. She'd cry and swear and find a way to be practical, too. And, apart from everything else, she'd know the house inside out. She'd know where to begin.

When Mateo and I had moved into our apartment on Cartier Street, she'd been full of suggestions. Shelves and rugs and paint for the window frames. I had to explain to her that it was a rental and that we weren't planning to stay. Mateo had always wanted to buy something new, something shiny. He had his eye on one of the glass condo towers going up in the Market with their beautiful views of the river, all those sunsets and sunrises, and miles between us and the sidewalks below. I agreed to see a model penthouse one afternoon and, after my shift, I waited for him in front of the gallery. I watched the sun catching the spires of the basilica, and a family lingering underneath the spider, their toddler dancing between the legs. I thought about what it would be like to live so close to work and in such a small space, too. Mateo had said that it wouldn't feel small – not with those views. When he came through the door, he told me I looked lovely in the light, and we walked together through the Market, past all the tourists and the tempting patios.

'Later,' he said, squeezing my hand. 'After we've had a look. Maybe we'll have a decision to make?'

The condo was beautiful, it really was. I liked the view from the kitchen, right up to the Gatineau Hills. He liked the quiet. 'It feels like there is no one else up here at all. No one living on top of us. No dogs or footsteps or tricycles.' He laughed and put his arms around my waist and I pressed my mouth into his neck, his skin dry and warm. 'We could be happy here. Alone on the top.'

Out the window, I could see the goose grazing between the apple trees. I felt hungry. The fridge, unsurprisingly, was empty. The lawyer's letter had also mentioned that all the perishables had been cleared away. Not words to send to a bereaved family, I thought. There must be a better way of describing a scrubbed kitchen.

I dug my own meagre supplies out of my backpack. A roll of biscuits. Two apples. A bottle of wine. I'd need more or tomorrow I wouldn't be fit for purpose. There was a fish and chip shop in the village, so I found my coat and flicked all the lights on before closing the door behind me. It wasn't yet properly evening, but I didn't like the idea of walking into the house in the dark. Overhead, more geese crossed the sky, a dark V on the bright air, their rusty voices calling.

6

FELICITY: 1967

MATRON CLAIMED TO BE MOTHERLY, BUT SHE HADN'T a clue. My mum never put her foot down. She had no God-forbidding anything. She was much quieter than that.

Ahead of me, a gaggle of student nurses made their way down the corridor, looking pert and starched. From their chatter, I could tell they were due up in Maternity where they'd watch the ward nurses teach new mothers how to swaddle properly. Not Matron, though. No babies for her. I could imagine her eating them, with her cracked red lips, her pocked chin, and her eyes like lift buttons behind those thick plastic glasses. Standing behind the nursing desk, she watched every footfall on the ward, utterly unsparing. To get the attention of errant junior nurses, she snapped tongue depressors. She never drank tea. That afternoon, she'd spent her five o'clock sermon on me, filling my ears with her God-forbids. She said she was being maternal. I should be more respectful. I shouldn't look up when receiving instruction, shouldn't distract or interrupt, merely pay better attention and perform. My job was to trot along behind the doctors with my neat nurse's basket, carrying the requisite tongue depressors, thermometers, scissors, and gauze. I was to be careful. Take notes. Agree. My questions were not needed. The litany ended, Matron attempted a smile.

'I know I must sound like a proper old battleaxe,' she said. 'But do try to take it on board. Just a little nudge to the straight and narrow and you will be happily with us a long, long time.'

She patted my sentenced hand and released me down the corridor.

I walked slowly and thought about my mother. I pictured her out by the bay, tall in my father's old trousers with the hems tucked into black wellies and her hands reaching up, picking sea buckthorn. Too early yet this year, of course. The berries would still be plumping back home and my mother focussed on raspberries in the garden, but when I conjured her, I saw her by the sea. I saw how the wind caught wisps from her bound hair and how small clouds scudded across the sky above her like impossible stepping stones set against the blue. She always took her time picking berries, making the day last as long as it might, and when I was little, I would be there at her feet, digging out caves in the sand dunes, hoping to find rabbits or buried treasure. Now in that bleached corridor, I remembered the berries' sharp stickiness and their smell like sour wine. Mum mixed them with sugar and cooked them down to make a marmalade bright as oystercatchers' bills. I missed her marmalade and all her jams – raspberry and bramble, blackcurrant from the manse garden, jellies from rosehips, haws and sloes from every hedgerow along the coast. At home, Mum kept them on a high cupboard shelf, closed away to keep their colour, and later in my Edinburgh flat, I set them along the window sill so they could cast their stained-glass colours on the cold floor. Here, I bought grape jelly at Steinberg's and spread it on white bread.

Outside the hospital, the afternoon was hazy, and the road filled with fast cars and buses. When my hospital contract came for the agency, I thought the road name completely romantic. *Côte-des-Neiges.* The side of snows. It had been the name of a long-ago village, sitting halfway up the hillside, looking down on Montreal. It must have been where the winter snows piled thickest, I thought, finding it on a map. There was a cemetery, too, called Notre Dame des Neiges, which made my heart almost break with a cold kind of loneliness. Now, walking the road every day to the bus stop after my shift, it was the width that held my eye. So very Canadian. So much space for anyone that wanted it. If I could pick up Aberlady with my fingers, all her crow-stepped roofs and whitewashed houses, the little kirk and the ancient trees, if I could carry her here and lay her down in this wide-open road, how much room would she take up? How little. With my back to the hospital and the mountain behind, there was no horizon here and so much space.

But Aberlady was moon-far away, remote and removed. Or rather, I was. I was the one who had done the leaving, after all. Gave my notice in an insufficient letter to Dr Ballater, and shuffled off. Sold my car, bought a ticket and packed my trunk full of nursing textbooks and uniforms, too – though of course they were the wrong ones. Matron soon set me straight and ensured I had the correct hem-length.

A bus pulled up to the stop and I ran down towards it, waving to catch the driver's attention. He waited and laughed when I stepped up into the bus.

'Every day, I get a running nurse or two,' he said. 'All the pretty nurses. It's a good route.'

I forced a half-smile and found a seat towards the back. The windows were open and, as the bus pulled away from the kerb, the air felt surprisingly cool. It was often crowded in the late afternoon, but that day there weren't many folk on the bus. Summer holidays, perhaps. Everyone away at cottages, spending time by the lakes. Some of the nurses had been talking about cottage weekends, which sounded delightful. Canoes and campfires and hikes in the woods. Everything I might have imagined, but not yet found. Early days, I thought. There would be plenty of time.

When I'd told my parents about my Canadian job, Dad had asked if that meant I was turning down Dr Ballater.

'Of course, she is, Stanley, and it's no bad thing,' Mum said. 'He hasn't tried anything with you, has he? Has he been pestering you?'

'No, nothing like that. He's been a gentleman. He's just not . . . It's not . . . It's hard to explain.'

Dad cleared his throat. 'You want an adventure,' he said, softly.

'I don't know. Maybe. Yes.'

Mum didn't return to the question after that, nor did she try to talk me out of anything. Instead, she helped me make lists of things I would need, even things I would like: novels, toffees, nylons, a pair of white sunglasses. We went into Edinburgh to go shopping and she didn't ask me how I'd made my decision or what I was hoping to find. She bought me a book about North American wild flowers and, walking out of Woolworths, tucked her arm through mine and grinned. She even suggested we go to a café for a spot of lunch, somewhere young, she said, and modern. But I knew she'd also brought along sandwiches in her handbag and I said we should eat them in Princes Street Gardens. Walking past the gardener's cottage, she told me about the air raid shelters erected there early in the war.

'It's strange to think about all that now,' she said. 'How dangerous everything felt and how every effort was made to make safe places for everyone.' She squeezed my arm again, and we found a bench where we ate our lunch. I hoped that she wouldn't speak again about Dr Ballater or ask any more questions. I didn't want to defend him, but I couldn't explain, either. I'd been shocked by the whole episode. Knocked for six. I decided then I wouldn't tell anyone else about Dr Ballater. About George. I would give him that much. No more stories or questions or hypotheses. I would let him be. Like my mother, I'd keep mum.

She'd always been good at that. A cultivated quiet with no need to talk everything through. It really wasn't necessary, was it? It was enough to be still together. Without words. Without shouting or slammed doors. All that unnecessary bluster.

I'd been good at bluster when I was twelve. Slammed the door and stepped into the rain. I only had my cardi on and that didn't matter then. I didn't even care. I just needed out. I'd hop on a bus and go somewhere, right? Only it was Sunday and I had no money, so no. Hitchhike, then? But I never had and, likely as not, I'd know the driver – or worse, he'd know Mum. Then it would be over. I'd be right back at that kitchen table and she still wouldn't be saying anything. I could tell when something was up. I wasn't stupid. And the way they were keeping the radio off and not letting me see the newspaper. It had to be about the Bomb. I knew it was. Ever since I'd read that article about Nevada and Las Vegas and Miss Atomic Bomb. And the mushroom clouds like opening umbrellas and the costumes they made girls wear in the clubs and the Dawn Bomb parties and Atomic cocktails and I got so angry and I couldn't sleep. I tried to talk to my parents about it, but they wouldn't listen. They didn't want to hear. Maybe they were just as scared as me. Or more scared? They acted guilty, as if they were to blame. As if all this fear was something they made and silence was a way of keeping it down. That door-slammed afternoon, the radio had been on and Mum suddenly – fiercely – shut it off and looked at Dad with something like excitement, something like fear, and I asked if it was the Bomb or another war or what, but she wouldn't talk. She bloody wouldn't talk and I stormed out and slammed the door.

I crossed the road and then the bridge and headed out to the sands. The tide was far out so there would be a good walk, and I didn't care how far I went. Wondered if I could live out there, even just for the night. Would that be possible? Not in this rain. It was easing off, but even a drizzle would make for a miserable night. It might be different if it were dry. I could stretch out under the sky and sleep on the sand. I'd see the stars, and the moon, if I was lucky, and then the larks would wake me up. They were rising now before me as I walked. Flying straight up out of the wet grass. Strange joy, as Dad would say. He always said that whenever there were larks. That's when I heard him on the path behind me; his paced footsteps, his whistled tune.

'Mind if I chum you to the shore?'

I didn't say anything.

'It's fine,' he said. 'Silence is good. And this is a good place to be silent.'

But he kept whistling and quickened his pace to keep up with me. A hare leapt out and for a moment, it sat frozen on the path and I saw the yellow of its eye, the quick black circle taking in the world as it crouched with long ears, black-tipped, flattened, and then it erupted and ran. A lolloping stride escaping into the grass. In the quiet after it was gone, Dad picked up his tune, humming this time.

I didn't mind. Really, I didn't. It was fine that he was there. That he thought to follow me. It was fine.

Oh June, like the mountains I'm blue –
Like the pine, I am lonesome for you . . .

At least he wasn't asking questions. Or being silent. I kept walking out towards the sands and he kept on with his tune. It was an old Laurel and Hardy number. Probably predated them, too, but it was their song as far as Dad was concerned. Sometimes he swapped *Jane* for *June* if he was singing when Mum was around.

. . . in the Blue Ridge Mountains of Virginia

56

On the trail of the lonesome pine.

I hoped he just kept with the song and didn't start with the slapstick to get a laugh. I wasn't in a laughing mood. The wet sand was hard under my feet and the rain stopped as we walked towards the sea. Dad quickened his pace now and it felt like he was the one leading the way, which was just fine by me. I didn't mind.

'Thought we could go and take a look at the submarines. Think the rain has washed them away yet?'

They sat about a half-mile from the high tideline out by Jovey's Neuk. Two wrecked subs that had been there as long as I could remember. Forever or something like it – though probably only since the war. There were fair-sized holes in both of them and the subs themselves weren't that big. Mum warned me not to go out here – not all the way out on the sand at least. She'd rather I stayed closer in, maybe picked flowers round the Marl Loch. She'd rather I didn't wander. But it was okay with Dad. He trusted me.

We walked across the sand together, our shoes wet through though there was only an inch of sea water on the sand. It was rippled and dimpled with puddles and the bay kept draining away. Further out, we saw the marks that seals make when they pull themselves back to the water. We almost missed the wrecks and had to veer left and in towards the shore, too. Their ribs stood out like something hungry.

'Not big, were they?' Dad said. 'Hardly seems like there'd be space, but four men would crew each of these. Volunteers, I mean. You couldn't make a man climb in.'

57

'I'd hate it.' My voice sounded rough from yelling and I wished it didn't.

'They probably did as well. But they did what needed doing. That's what they would have told themselves. But it must have been hell. Cold and condensation. And all the way up to Norway. I couldn't have done it. Not my field, of course, but there's no way.'

I thought he was going to say *hell* again and I waited for it. Then he laughed, but not like it was funny. He laughed with a seal's cough, I thought, or a mouth full of sand.

'Did you know that the engine they used in these XT subs was the same engine they used for a London bus? Gardner Diesels. Bet you didn't know that.'

'No.'

'Well, now you do. Look at that. You just got cleverer. I know, not funny. But that's why I followed you out here. I used to come out here myself when a laugh wouldn't work. Sometimes you need the space, don't you?' He shoved his hands in his pockets and looked up at the sky. 'Listen, chum. It's not about me, is it? This door-slamming tick of yours. About me and your mum? Because if it is, I want you to know that people jump to conclusions and talk rot when they don't understand and maybe when they are scared, but we're solid. We always have been. And your mum just needs quiet sometimes. Like you need space. I know you get angry and have questions and all, but she's doing her bit and her best, too. She's holding us together, you know.'

After this, he was quiet, and I was, too. We mooched out to the second submarine, squelching our feet in the mucky sand. I kicked the side and there sounded a dull thud. Above us, a skein of geese cut across the sky, and Dad raised his arms as if he was holding his gun, but he'd left it at home and they were flying too high anyway. I wondered what he'd do if the powers that be managed to get the bay pronounced a nature reserve. Less goose on the table, I'm sure. I teased him about that on the walk back and he pulled a grimace, then picked up his tune again.

And I can hear the tinkling waterfall
Far among the hills
Bluebirds sing each so merrily
To his mate in rapture trills
They seem to say 'Your June is lonesome, too,
Longing fills her eyes
She is waiting for you patiently
Where the pine tree sighs.'

Before I left Scotland, Dad told me about the whales found a thousand miles from the sea. Not in Montreal itself, but even further inland near a place called Cornwall where the river was island-strewn and slow. I asked how they'd managed and he laughed.

'Fossils, my dear. Ten thousand years old. They were found by men digging clay for bricks half a mile from the railway station and two hundred feet above sea level. White whales, I think. Proves the story of the long-drained sea, but then so does the clay. It's quick clay, tricky stuff. Formed under the oceans and riddled with salt. With the tides gone, the clay dries out, the rains wash the salt away and it shifts. So cracks appear on buildings or suddenly, a whole hillside slips away. Sometimes, fossils emerge that way, too. Sometimes, they're dug up intact.'

I wasn't sure why he told me this. A token fact to ease my way into a new country. And a nod to what he knew, who he was. Clay and old stone, deep time and soil. It could have been that. But later, walking through Montreal looking up at the skyscrapers, a new understanding started to surface. Above me, the half-moons of hotel windows, the ribs of towers rising, and under my feet, things still hidden.

Was I the fossil-hunter then? Or the whale?

7

PIDGE: 2006

Mateo was still at work and I was making salad when she called. Slicing cucumbers and preserved lemons, pitting green olives. When I picked up the phone, I could smell their sharpness on my fingers.

Felicity's voice was so quiet I thought she was ill, but she said no, it was only sad news. She'd had a phone call that afternoon from Scotland. One of the elders from the kirk in Aberlady was working through Gran's address book, wanting to let her friends and relations know.

'Kind of him, wasn't it? Not to leave it up to a lawyer or someone, but to get in touch personally. He said the funeral was yesterday. Prearranged. It seems your grandmother sorted it all out ahead of time. She didn't want . . . a fuss.'

'Would you like me to come?' I asked.

'Here? No, no,' she said. 'No, I think not. I'll be fine. It's just

I haven't seen her in a while. I . . . I don't quite know what to do. Now. What to do now. That's it. I don't know what to do now.' She let go of her breath, and I could see her, standing in the farmhouse kitchen, her hair falling forward to curtain her face. She paused, and I could see her hold her hand up to her mouth, her long fingers, the blue of her veins. Outside the window behind her, another evening was beginning, a greying sky above the trees, the lake still and growing darker.

'I'll come,' I said. 'I can take some time off work. Someone can cover for me.'

'No.' She sighed again, and I waited. 'I just wanted you to know. There really is nothing to be done, but I thought you should know.' She told me Bas sent his love, and Rika, too. The snow was melting and mud beginning to show between the trees. They'd started tapping the maples. The beginning of another year. She said she would be fine.

'I know,' I said, softly.

'Yeah. I know, too.'

When Mateo came home, I cooked fish and he opened a bottle of wine. I opened the window, so the kitchen wouldn't get hazy, and to the east, I could see streaks of light. For a moment, I wasn't sure what they were. They looked like scratches or tears on the surface of the sky. I watched as they changed, brightened, grew longer and strange. Then I saw they were only vapour trails catching the last light of the setting sun. I thought about picking up the phone again and calling the camp to tell Felicity about them. She'd like that. On the other hand, she might think I was checking in, prompting or trying to get her to say something else. Better let her be. I'd tell her when we spoke next, I decided, and then it struck me she might be thinking similar thoughts, out beside the lake. That she couldn't pick up the phone to tell her mother about the bright things that caught her eye. Not this evening or in the morning or later. She had to let her be.

At the bungalow, I'd decided to sleep in the front bedroom because that wasn't where Felicity and I slept. We were always given the back bedroom – her room before she left, now stripped and painted white. Felicity said that she'd asked her parents to do it – to make it neutral – when she left. She'd wanted to close a door like that. To make a fresh start.

Even so, the double bed with its nubbly white coverlet was utterly Felicity to me. The pillows might have only just been shaken out, the sheet folded over. If I lay down, I would feel her hands soothing my spine, her hair warm beside me and, in the morning, tangling over me so I'd wake laughing. I would be a child again, too young for this empty house, and I knew I'd never sleep for her whispered stories, her gentle questions, and my own held answers.

In Gran's room, I told myself the clock would be soothing, the photographs interesting, and the knick-knacks would leave no space for ghosts. The wash of the sea would sound like wind in the trees at the camp or like trucks on the highway in Ottawa. But, inevitably, I slept fitfully. Maybe the smell of her soap never quite let me settle. Maybe I was just overtired. A little after dawn, there were birds in the garden and I started to compile an inventory in my head.

The books. The photographs. The rag rug. All the boxes on the shelves. The letters. The things in the shed. The kitchen things, too. The teacups. The small jars. I might have slept again, thinking through the shelves and counting, but the blue glass cake-stand on the top of the cupboard brought Felicity's voice close.

'It was just this colour, wasn't it, Mum? Do you remember that? The blue moon when I was wee?'

I was sitting with two cushions wedged beneath me as she took it from the shelf. The collar on my new dress was itchy and wrong, but I held Granny's coffee mill tight between my knees, turning the crank to grind the beans. Granny sat beside me, the pen in her hand paused over a sheet of white paper.

'Goodness, Felicity. I'm surprised you do. It was a very long time ago. Be careful with that, dear. It was a wedding present.'

'But the colour was just like this, wasn't it? Don't you think?'

'Hmm. I hadn't made that connection before. I always wished it were green, which was more fashionable back then. Auntie Jean wouldn't have known that. She must have purchased it in Jenners, I suppose. Imagined it sitting in pride of place in my matrimonial home. That was the sort of thing the Morningside aunts said.'

'I don't remember it at all,' Felicity said.

'Well, when you were small, I didn't have much cause to use it. Too hard to make cakes on the ration. And people didn't come around then. At least, they didn't come here.'

'Well, they will come tomorrow,' Felicity said.

'Yes. They will. They will come for your father.'

Felicity placed the cake-stand on the table, tracing her finger around the rim, and I waited for her to say the words to our bedtime poem. *The moon is round as round can be. Two eyes, a nose, a mouth has she.* But you need a face for the moon and a cake-stand has no face, no chin at all to tickle.

'How's that coffee coming along?'

'Almost done,' I said. 'I can still feel a few scratchy bits.'

'Well, I certainly don't want any scratchy bits in my cup. Be sure to grind them carefully.'

'Was the moon really blue, Granny?'

'That night it was. A long, long time ago now. And the next night, too, though not so clearly perhaps. It was a strange sight. Like a painting of the moon someone had slipped into the sky, trying to fool us all.'

'Did Granddad see it, too?'

'Yes, pet. Your granddad saw it. He thought it was very special. In fact, he took his chair, that chair you're sitting on right now, and placed it in front of the window in the sitting room so that he could watch the moon travel right across the sky. He sat and sat, just watching that beautiful blue moon.'

'All night? I like to stay up all night.'

'Well, maybe not all night. Until it was bedtime.'

'Felicity lets me stay up all night when it's a full moon and there's a baby coming hard.'

'Having a hard time coming, perhaps?'

'Yeah. That's coming hard. Sometimes they do. Babies.'

'Your mum helps a great deal when that happens, doesn't she?'

'I do, too. When I stay awake.'

Gran put down her pen and laid her hand flat on the paper. Her skin was tea-brown from afternoons outside, and her veins ran like rivers under thin skin. She wore a thick gold wedding band, and a finer pearl ring set with small diamonds. I thought her hands were beautiful.

'Was it blue like veins, Granny? Or blue like the sky?'

'A little like the sky. But more like bluebells. It was a thin, translucent blue, and still very shiny. Perhaps like the blue in the very centre of a candle flame.'

'Why was it blue? It isn't blue now.'

'No, it wasn't blue for long. Just a couple of nights. They thought it was probably caused by smoke from forest fires drifting over from Canada.'

'Just like us.' She smiled when I said that and then held out her hand to Felicity. I kept on with my grinding and she continued. 'Some people thought it was worse than that, not smoke at all but something to do with nuclear activity, all that meddling about with the atom. There's one for your protest friends, Felicity. Ban the bomb or the moon will turn blue. They'd run with that one.'

'I'm sure they would,' Felicity said. She laughed and shook her head, her hair falling over her shoulders, almost down to her waist. 'A great slogan. See? You still have a knack for poetry.'

'Haud yer wheesht,' Gran said, but she smiled and that was all right and then the sound of the coffee mill changed in my hands, and the crank turned smoothly.

'Can I open it now?' I asked. She nodded and told me to be gentle.

'I will. This is the best part.' I placed the mill on the table and pulled out the little drawer with its perfect gold knob. Inside, a small mountain of fragrant coffee grounds looked like rich, dark earth, and I imagined I could make out a tiny pathway snaking up the hillside, tiny people walking in line towards the peak. I winked and the hikers looked up into the kitchen sky, my one open eye a shining blue moon above them.

'Your dad didn't like any of those explanations,' Granny said in a voice suddenly tired. 'He called them all theories. He wanted to believe the magic. Said that he believed we're entitled to a blue moon every once in a while. I can hear him saying that, can't you? Just like that. As if saying made it so.'

I was pulling on my jeans when I heard a honk. Under siege again. I opened the curtains but couldn't see the goose. The day was clear and the sky a swept blue. The house here sat below the level of the road, and the lane to the door ran downhill, but by a trick of the lane's angle, I could see the sea from the front bedroom window. Out on the water, birds were bright flashes diving white among the waves – gulls of some sort; fish-eaters. Felicity would know. Or Gran. I could only guess. But the goose was unmistakable – a run-of-the-mill, plain-as-my-face Canada goose. There was nothing else it could be. Big and brash and, as if the thought conjured it, there it was again. Another honk blasted from somewhere behind the house. Well, it could have the shed, if that's what it wanted. I'd spend the morning inside. There were maybe two jobs in hand. Or three. Yes, three. The first was the inventory and that was the biggest. The second was to look for whatever it was that Gran had left me. The third was the difficult one: to decide what to do next.

I'd thought again about the auction house idea but selling everything would be absolute. There'd be no chance to search and sort if I handed the house over to the professionals. And if there was something to find, perhaps I'd better be the one doing the looking.

I took out my notebook and wrote: *To keep. To rehome. To let go.*

I'd start with the desk. That was sensible. If Gran had left me something, it would likely be there. I opened each drawer carefully but found only tidy stationery supplies. Then an address book and a neat diary, mainly empty. A set of utility bills held together with an elastic band. There was a new set of blank postcards and a book of stamps. Nothing old at all. Nothing resembling news.

I turned to the bookcase, scanning the shelves. Was there a notebook wedged in backwards? A small box hidden behind the novels, containing – what? Something.

Gran must have imagined me like this. Searching. Looking for family secrets, reading the old letters, the dusty diary, finding the crucial photograph.

Everything looked dusted.

The flow of books seemed natural. Dictionaries to bird books, walking guides, then maps. Pebble identification. Edible wild foods. Mrs Beaton. Then poetry below, with historical fiction, anthologies and folk tales. A collection you might find on the shelves of anyone of a certain vintage and a certain class. Still, something wasn't right. Working in the gallery shop, I'd learned to read a shelf. What was missing, what had been moved. I stood, looking, balancing from the balls of my feet to my heels and back, trying to work it out. George Mackay Brown. Byron. *The King's Treasuries of Literature. Legends of Vancouver*. All interspersed with knick-knacks. A bowl of marble eggs was displayed in a willow-pattern bowl next to the Scrabble dictionary. French poetry books stood upside down so that their titles aligned with their English fellows, and each of the shelves was pristine and polished. Everything looked ready to be seen.

I needed Mateo. He never spoke about his work, but I pictured him like this, poring over bits and pieces, looking for patterns in a collection. I needed a good eye. An organizer. A curator.

But maybe that was it. That was what seemed strange. Everything had been made ready. Everything was ready to be seen. Like the start of every day at the shop. Everything was dusted and arranged as if at any moment, the time might come to unlock the door and let the day begin.

Was that how I remembered my gran? Ordered, polished and ready? I wasn't sure. I remembered the soft woollen rug with its tangled fringe, the warm electric fire and the bowl of marble eggs. I remembered her soap. Imperial Leather, and it smelled like the forest and cinnamon and sandalwood. And like geraniums, too, but without the prickle in the nose. The bar sat beside the bathroom sink – a heavy block the colour of maple cream, I thought, or the Caramac bar she would set out on the tea tray for me beside Felicity's mug. I remembered Gran standing at the sink, scrubbing our grey underwear with her Persil powder, sighing that our homemade camp soap never got anything white. She pinned the laundry to the line in the garden and I remembered chasing

Felicity through the cities of sheets and shirts, the wind itself white and clean. Then I remembered Gran combing out my hair in the evening, and Felicity saying yes, it was all right, as Gran lifted me up on the table to cut my hair off at chin level so it swung. *Just like a wee land girl*, she said. *Muriel used to wear her hair like that. You need a Kirby-grip over your eyebrow and then you'll be jaunty.*

I remembered Gran working hard and liking beautiful things. I imagined her readying this room. Standing here by the shelf, straightening the books and the photo frames. Maybe she caught her own eye in the mirror, too, and looked and wondered when, and then set things in order for me. Muriel said she knew I was coming. So, she knew she was going. And she made things ready.

My grandmother was tall, as was my grandfather. The height of the mirror was telling. As was the height of the bookshelves and the shelves where the boxes sat. Some were labelled in my grandmother's precise script – what my mother would call 'educated handwriting': *Photographs. Felicity's letters. Recipes. Buttons.* Then there were the boxes marked with Granddad's scrawl: *Pebbles. Scribbles & Poems. Feathers. Maybe.*

I pulled out the desk chair and climbed up. Felicity would like the recipes. An easy *to keep*, I thought. The box held neat bundles of pale-blue index cards bound with sensible elastic bands and marked with white tags. *Soups. Vegetable Sides. Game. Puddings. Sweet Treats.*

My gran's coconut macaroons were the most exotic objects in

my childhood. And her golden cheesy fish, baked in a casserole and covered in breadcrumbs that crackled in the middle and bubbled at the sides. Chicken in mushroom sauce meant a whole chicken breast just for me, and a white napkin to spread across my lap. Water in a cut-glass tumbler. Margarine.

I leafed through the recipes, hungry for the familiar. But you can't flick through memories like that. They don't turn on like the lights. You need to kindle them and wait.

Sloe gin

1 lb sloes
8 oz white sugar
1 ¾ pint gin

Sterilize a good strong darning needle in a candle flame, then use it to prick the tough skins of the sloes all over.
Place sloes in large bottle and add sugar and gin.
Seal well and shake. Keep bottle in a cupboard and shake every second day for the first week. After that, shake once a week and gin will be ready to drink in two months. Lovely at Christmas.
Note – Muriel's mother says to try this with brandy and blackberries.

To dry rosehips

Wash your rosehips, top and tail then finely dice and dry them on newspaper in the sun.

Tip the dried rubble into a metal sieve and shake gently to remove the tickly hairs. They will easily fall away, leaving you with clean dried rosehips, ready to be used for tea, jam or jelly. Good for preventing colds and as a treatment for stiffness.

Coconut macaroons

Line a sandwich tin with sweet pastry.

Mix in a bowl:
  1 cup coconut
  ¾ cup sugar
  1 switched egg

Smooth into tin and bake at 400° for about 25 minutes.

Sweet pastry Felicity likes

2 lbs plain flour
1 ¼ lbs margarine and lard (mixed)
½ lb sugar
2 eggs
Pinch of salt

Makes a lot so a child can play with extra as pie is readying.

8

THE BOX LABELLED *FELICITY'S LETTERS* WAS A NEATLY
bound archive, the envelopes marked BY AIR MAIL/PAR
AVION. I remembered these. The paper thin as onion skin. The
blue-and-red marked edges and the acrid taste of the glue. I could
see Felicity bent over the table in the cabin, writing by candlelight.
She filled page after page and sometimes let me add pictures, too.
Her ballpoint felt important in my fingers and awkwardly precise,
my smiley birds looking far scratchier than they ever did drawn
in crayon on Bas's cut-open paper bags.

Felicity drew pictures, too – little sketches perched at the beginning of paragraphs or squeezed in along the margins. There were
babies' faces and Rika's hands. The table in the birthing house
with its neat rows of instruments set out ready. A chipmunk in
the woodpile, its eye reflecting the shape of the treetops against
the sky. The rough-roofed cabins. The road into town and the

patterns of leaves. And among all the details and the sketches, in letters that predated me, I found stories I'd never read before.

Montreal,
January 1969

Dear Mum and Dad,

I guess I should start by apologizing for my last letter. Way too abrupt and I'm sure you were shocked. I could have managed it with more grace. Still, I wanted you to know about the baby, and I didn't know how to say it gently. I shouldn't have written what I did about keeping it or not. Let's just pretend I never did, okay?

It's beginning to feel like a real baby now. When I wrote before, I just felt sick and tired, but now it's moving about a lot. There are most definitely feet and elbows in there. The textbooks say it's supposed to feel like butterfly wings, but that's not right at all. A bit like hiccups, maybe, but with a completely different kind of anticipation. Jenny and Margaret are being lovely with hot-water bottles and they rub my feet when I come in from a long shift at the hospital. They've even given me the sofa cushions for my bed. I'm still feeling sick sometimes, though I've got through last month's exhaustion which is truly wonderful. I kept falling asleep at the nurses' desk and getting scolded by the matron. She assumed I'd been out dancing like all the other girls and told me that it simply wasn't respectable to come to work so shattered. Not sure what she'll say when she notices the real cause for my doziness, but so far so good. I seem to be more or less the same shape at this point. Well, a little wider in the waist, but there's room in my uniform. Last month, I was only thirsty but you won't believe how hungry I've been today. I ate two sandwiches for lunch. Which felt like a luxury but didn't break the bank.

I'm writing this from the deli on the corner. It's not quite as cold here as at home, and the man behind the counter is kind. He keeps coming by to fill my mug with hot water. He'd pour coffee on the house, he says, but I say no, it's fine, I like the hot water just as it is. Besides, coffee would make the baby jump and keep me awake, and it's my day off so when I get home I'll just want to sleep as best I can. Of course, I don't explain all that to the deli man. He probably can't even tell about the baby. I'm pretty wrapped up. It's a good thing it's cold like this. At work, we've been given permission to wear an extra layer and that's probably bought me another month of work. That and my snazzy maternity girdle. The glories of synthetic yarn.

The money at the hospital is decent, so I won't be putting in for a clinic job anytime soon. Anyway, I still like the bustle of the hospital. It's right in the middle of everything here and as crazy as the city. So many people, so many stories. When I first arrived, I thought everyone might speak French and that I'd be forever struggling to take notes from French specialists. As well you know, my spelling is rather atrocious — and sadly so it proves in French, too. I fudged my way through the interview with feeble school French and it was such a fluke they picked me up because officially, all the hospitals here are either French or bilingual. I was sure it would be just a matter of time until someone called my bluff and likely as not, it would come out in the middle of an emergency triage, some poor child's life dangling and my incomprehension making a mess. But it seems not. Half the nurses at the General are as bad as me and the first question every single doctor asks is, <u>Do you speak English?</u>

I hope you aren't too scandalized by all this. It might not be quite how you imagined this chapter of my life working out, but it's your grandbaby, so I thought I should let you know how it is growing, and how I am, too.

I haven't come up with a better word than <u>it</u> so far. <u>He</u> or <u>she</u> seems presumptuous and I don't fancy cutesy pet names at this stage. What did you call me before I was born?

It's taken some thinking but I might have a solution for the birth. Not the General, at any rate. I couldn't face that. So, I've been asking around for other options. Margaret – she's one of the girls in the flat – is active with the women's movement on campus. She's still a student herself – politics and art history – isn't that a great combination? She told me about a place in the woods where girls can go to have their babies. Not a Catholic home for unwed mums or delinquent girls or anything. It's really wholesome. A few families have built cabins by a lake and they are farming there, or at least gardening, and they welcome anyone who needs a place, and they look after you when your baby comes. She says they are amazing. A couple of McGill girls went there last year. I think I'll look into it. My job won't last too long at the hospital once the matron finds out the real reason for my snoozes, and I don't want to skive on rent here with the others. *I'm not coming home. I don't say that to hurt you, just to be honest about how things are. I came over here and I got myself into this . . . I was going to write* <u>mess</u>, *but I can't. I've got to keep my words precise and language like that isn't loving and it isn't positive and I can't bring a baby into the world in that frame of mind.*

I'm going to end here because I need to head home and forage in the fridge for some dinner. It's my turn in the kitchen tonight and I promised them something better than tinned to-may-to soup. See, I can even talk Canadian now. I miss you both and I'll write more soon.

Lots of love,

Felicity

* * *

Montreal,

February 1969

Dear Mum and Dad,

The weather is still cold. I've been absolutely living in that mohair wrap you sent over for Christmas. Again – thank you. The colour is perfect. Like East Lothian daffodils against the old drab snow of Montreal. At Christmas, there was romance to all that white, but now it's stale, scrubby grey and it's hard to feel inspired. I haven't seen the ground outside my building since November. Some of the doctors come into work in parkas with fur around their hoods. Wolverine, apparently, because it won't freeze regardless of the temperatures. Others wear black fur hats, something between a tea cosy and a Russian officer's hat. They are the senior doctors and don't even speak to the junior nurses except about patients, and hardly then. The students who come around to our flat all wear camel duffel coats with floppy hoods and toggles and most wear black galoshes zipped over their shoes. They leave these in puddles by our door and they drape their coats over the radiator or on all the kitchen chairs. The students themselves pile into the living room with Jenny and Margaret, spreading out newspapers, smoking like forest fires and arguing about the salvation of Quebec. The air grows rank and it all sounds foreign and zealous and strange, but I'm happy here. I feel I'm settling into something entirely new.

The light here is amazing. Cold and white and blue. New snow brightens everything, and then there are layers of reflections – neon and shop windows and all the cars. The snow piles up in high banks along the streets and on the spiral staircases outside apartment buildings. From my window, the fire escape looks both laden and lightened with all the snow. The city trucks come by and scatter salt on the pavements to melt the ice, but they call them sidewalks here like the Americans, or <u>les trottoirs</u>. Mincing along, trying not to slip, I think of pigs' feet. I read in the paper that there's talk of heating them from underneath so that the snow will melt on contact. Isn't that crazy? Very space-aged, like so many things here. Since the Metro system was built, there have been extensive expansions underground, so it's like a brand-new city just under the surface.

Shops and restaurants, even a church and a discotheque. Imagine all that under Princes Street!

Despite the cold, there is so much life in this city, so much feels just about to happen. And I love the mix of people. The whole world is here, all bundled up in a thousand layers against the freeze. French and English, obviously, and a fair number of Scots among the mix. But black people, too, with fantastic French accents, and Hungarians and Jews and even Chinese. I hope to go down to Chinatown soon to try one of the restaurants Jenny keeps talking about. I'll let you know all about it when I do. I wonder if foetuses like ginger.

Did I write to you about Expo? I know I sent the book about it, but I can't remember what I told you. Probably not much. I know I didn't write much when I first arrived – I'm sorry for that. Everything was so new and I was so ready to be far from home, but I should have been better at writing. Anyway, Expo was amazing. Space-age for real, with real Apollo capsules and an American astronaut suit. I first went with Jenny a month or so after I moved into the flat. We took the Metro and stood all the way to Île Sainte-Hélène, which is an artificial island made of earth dug out from the Metro tunnels and deposited in the middle of the St Lawrence River. Then everything was built on top – all the buildings of the world. I loved the American Pavilion. A 200-foot geodesic dome covered with a shiny acrylic skin. Dad would love it: a great clear bubble filled with spacecraft and Raggedy Ann dolls, Andy Warhol prints and totem poles, cowboys and neon, and Elvis Presley's guitar. Pure poetry. The Americans hated it. Not enough about technologies and arms, not enough about trade. Instead, it was all American imagination and so beautiful in its glorious gaudy way. But more than the exhibits, it was the space itself that I loved. A shining bubble floating above the island, the light shimmering in triangles. It was honeycomb and patchwork quilt and crystals and constellations all at once. A mini-rail train ran right through the building, and giant escalators climbed to the very top. Everywhere you looked, there were people moving, bright colours, and a sense of beautiful space.

Everyone came to Expo. All the languages in the world on one little Canadian island. Like the war was finally, finally over, and everyone was together in a place that was new and glowing.

It was all supposed to close at the end of October and all the countries were to pay for the individual demolition of their pavilions. But the powers that be changed their mind and opened it up again this summer. Renamed it, too. Couldn't very well be Expo '67 in perpetuity. Now it's 'Man and His World', which ticks Jenny off no end. Margaret, too, but Jenny is louder. All this mind-expanding globality, she says, and they go for the archaic misogynistic tag. I can't say I'm bothered, but she is, so we hear about it continually. It's even worse in French, she says. 'La Terre des Hommes'. And just when do we get our world, she asks over porridge and tea, waving her spoon about histrionically. I shrug and she says I've been brainwashed by the patriarchy and need to wake up, but I say I'm tired out by ten-hour shifts and a growing lump of humanity in my belly and I don't feel excluded by an historically accepted inclusive noun. She'd prefer

'Humanity's World', which suffers poetically, but maybe equality has higher value than poetry.

Jenny is from London and used to teach primary school, though that's impossible to imagine now. She's far too loud and bright and flamboyant for any classroom. Maybe things were different in London. She wears ground-trailing skirts and her hair is short and dyed jet black to match her mascara. And she's an actress now, which she says isn't a world away from teaching. She's managed to get leading lady roles in a few Shakespeare plays – says it's the accent that kills at auditions. She thinks it's a riot I'm still in nursing. A last-generation job, she calls it, perfect for old-fashioned girls. I'm not quite sure she understands wanting a stable life. And it's not like she has pots of money to prop her up. Before she moved into the flat, she had a basement room with no furniture. Just a mattress on the floor and a radio to keep her company. She says it did wonders for her Canadian accent, all that talk radio. <u>The prime minister is said to be very upset about this room-er. Tomorrow, the high temperature will be twenny-three degrees.</u>

Heat is supposed to be included in our rent, but the flat is still cold. Jenny walks about draped in blankets. Margaret says that the weather will be warmer by March. I've already been through a full year, but Montreal weather is hard to anticipate. Margaret keeps saying things like <u>when the snow melts</u> . . . and <u>that was before the dog days.</u> They roll off her tongue quite naturally, but then, she's from here. I should be keeping a logbook, I think, marking down temperatures and the superstitions of the natives. But she's right to remind me. Seasons

82

change quickly here, and spring doesn't linger. Last year, it was such a shock. Ice and blizzards one week and then the crocuses were up and gone the next. Blink and you miss it and everyone's in bare legs. Margaret says I should really call the folk at the camp soon and see if they can help, if that's my plan. She said it so sweetly. You'd like her. I guess I want you to know that I'm being looked after. We're a family of sorts here at the flat, the girls like sisters and guardian angels – their friends and suitors, too.

I'm not going to write to you now about my baby's father. I don't mind that you asked and I will tell you at some stage, but for now he isn't important. And I'm fine with that. That sounds defiant, or defensive. It isn't meant to. I am well and as peaceful as I can be in this cold and troubled city. Jenny says get used to it – not just snow but bombs, too. Bienvenue au Québec, baby. But don't worry about me. I am well and safe and more or less happy.

Lots of love,
Felicity

* * *

Montreal,
March 1969

Dear Mum and Dad,

So much for nonchalance. Even if I didn't have to, I'd want to leave my job now. Not because I'm tired out – though I am –

and not at all because of the people, because they really are lovely. But the work is getting scary and so is this precarious city. You probably don't hear much on the BBC, so here's the scuttlebutt, as Dad would say.

Last night, there was hell of a march. The anglo press is reporting it as a peaceful protest, but at the hospital, we see another side to things. Of course, they are comparing it to last month's attack at the stock exchange. No bombs last night, so no structural damage, but there were ten thousand people out on the streets, at least. From what we saw, the police got rough, or possibly the protestors did first. I was in the flat and there was so much noise outside. Someone lit a bonfire in the middle of the street like we were in a war zone or revolutionary Paris, and there were firecrackers or worse, too. Some were even shouting 'À bas la Bastille!' but it wasn't the prisons they were protesting about or even the government. It was McGill. For heaven's sake, a university. But a symbol, too. Everything is becoming a symbol, or a slogan. 'McGill au Travailleurs!' they chanted. 'McGill Français!' They're demanding that the university become a unilingual French, pro-worker institution. So much for art history and politics if that happens, though I suspect nursing would still get funded. They'd need it.

At the hospital in the morning, we saw a lot of bruising, twisted ankles, and more than a few broken legs, too. One boy, who was carried in dangling between two cronies, came in with a fractured skull. They were all grinning, which was perhaps the most disturbing part. 'Had a good night, boys?' one of the doctors asked, but they only whispered to each other in French and kept on grinning.

One of the students who had been demonstrating came by the flat this evening, and got angry when I told him what I'd seen at work. He's half French and mostly fervently separatist, but he likes hanging out with us British girls. I made a pot of tea and he told me about his grandmother – mémé. She had a digestive problem and it turned out to be cancer in the end and he spent a lot of time in the hospital with her, translating. Officially, everyone is guaranteed medical care in their own language, but he said it's never really that way. His mémé needed a specialist, but the specialist didn't speak a word of French and neither did half the nurses. Not like you, he said. You try at least. 'Bonjour' alone works wonders. He told me his mémé went downhill pretty quickly after she was admitted. He couldn't be with her all the time and she spent her final weeks fumbling through the few English words she knew, trying to make herself understood by the busy anglo nurses. That's no way to go, is it?

I see the injustice, but it's all getting scary. There were four bombs on New Year's Eve then three mailboxes exploded in the next few days. And those are the ones that get reported because they've exploded. I wonder how many other bombs have been found and stopped in time. Two exploded at the end of November at Eaton's downtown. Even Jenny is getting apprehensive. She's talking about heading out of town for a bit. I might try to convince her to come out to the camp with me. I called them the other day and the woman on the phone was lovely. No trouble at all, she said; come as soon as you like. There is a space where I can stay, and she wanted to know if the father was

85

coming, too. A gracious way of asking. I told her that he wasn't and she really gently suggested that I talk to him. Tell him where I was going. Give him the option, she said, so he could know and choose for himself. I don't know. I'd rather do all this on my own. It isn't like he's going to turn around and ask me to marry him. He's not that type. But he knows about the baby, so maybe I should talk to him before I go.

I've been having weird dreams, which isn't surprising. I dreamed the baby was stuck in a postbox and I couldn't get it out. When I looked down through the slat, I could see it all curled up on top of the letters like it was floating, way down at the bottom of a well. Then I dreamed that the baby was a package and I was wrapping it up with paper and string and worrying about the postage. What does it cost to post a baby? The woman at the post office was being difficult, and then, when I finally had it all wrapped and stamped, I realized I didn't know how to address it. Isn't that odd?

I hope this letter gets through – well, gets out of Montreal, I mean. I keep thinking about all those letterboxes. Sorry this is all so disjointed and rambling. That's just how I'm feeling myself. I hope you are well. Thanks for the description of Aberlady Bay. It's nice to think about things continuing on just as they always have – the wild flowers, the rabbits and the deer.

Lots of love,
Felicity

* * *

Montreal,
April 1969

Dear Mum and Dad,

I will be moving soon. Yesterday, I went to the campus with Margaret to talk with some of her friends about the camp – they looked like a bunch of radicals with long hair and jeans, but they were kind. One of them had lived at the camp last summer and the other – Annie – was friends with the folk who started it up. She says she goes back and forth a lot to help them out. I asked if it was a cult or anything, but both girls said no. Annie said the folks who started it were Christians and there are some hippies now, too. Some folk are radical, but not everyone. It's a real mix and it's just a good place to be.

She showed me photos of the farmhouse where the midwife lives. Just a humble log house, really Canadian with a porch along the front, and a swing and gardens, too. They grow lots of food, and anyone who wants to can share in the meals. It's about three hours away from Montreal, which sounds good to me.

Margaret's going to be moving, too. Not far, but also to somewhere pretty different. She'll be out along the St Lawrence Seaway in one of the new villages, living in her grandmother's old house. When the province flooded the Long Sault Rapids ten years ago and the Seaway went through, whole villages were abandoned and people relocated, but some houses were moved instead. Margaret's grandmother's house was one of those – picked up and planted in a new village made from *old homes. The Hydro Company promised the process would be gentle and everything would be safe. Even said they could leave the kitchen cupboards as they were, with all the plates and bowls still inside. It was that easy. The Hartshorne House Mover would arrive on the Thursday. All the family needed to do was pack a change of clothes and wait a day or two for their house to be delivered to New Town 2 where it would be built on a new foundation supplied by the Hydro Company. Safe and sound. Her grandmother worried – she hadn't cradled the family china all the way from Ireland thirty years before to be smashed up by a machine now. But her grandfather took the company at their word. Even filled a teacup and left it on the kitchen table to see what would happen. That was Tuesday. But when the Hydro men came by on Wednesday and cut all the elms behind the house, he stood on the porch and cried. Margaret's grandmother knew then that everything was changing.*

Last winter, she passed away after eight years on her own. Margaret said that neither of them really felt settled after the move. They'd talked of moving to the city to be near their sons, but never got around to it. Margaret's glad because it's nice to have a family house to return to.

It would make me dizzy, I think. A house you know in a strange new place with different views out of the windows and a different piece of sky overhead. Margaret told me that when she was small, she used to help her grandmother dig potatoes in the garden behind the summer kitchen and they stored them for the winter in a dry root cellar with a red trapdoor. Now, the garden and the cellar are both under the river, but Margaret says she doesn't mind. She told me she likes walking along the new shore. Everything still there, she says, but also washed away. You can see where the old highway runs right into the water. And Dad, it's not far from your whales — only 10 miles or so. I suppose if there were more bones still buried, then the waters have covered them again. Margaret says where there used to be hills, now there are islands and if I go for a visit, she'll take me out in a canoe to see. But that will have to wait until after the baby.

When I get up to the camp, I'll send you the address. Well, the post-office box anyway. There's a village not too far away, with shops and things, which is good because the camp isn't quite self-sufficient yet. There's also a sympathetic doctor in the village, and he helps out when he's needed. So, see? I won't be out beyond the moon — I will be okay.

Any thoughts about a name? Any advice would be great.

Lots of love,

Felicity

* * *

From the camp,
September 1969

Dear Mum and Dad,

Thanks for the box of baby things — perfect timing. Little Pidge is growing so quickly and much faster than even Rika can knit!

I didn't know you'd kept my things. I'll need to find a camera so that you can see how sweet Pidge is in that little lacy bonnet. Did you make it? I'd love to know more about all the bits and pieces.

We're settling into routines now, Pidge and me. She's nursing really well, which is such a blessing. I can't quite believe I'm coping. She's still dainty, but strong, too, and with a gorgeous mop of dark hair, and her eyes are so big, taking everything in. Rika says she looks really bright – not that it matters, but it's nice to hear. It feels like there is so much to tell you because she's perfect and this is working, the two of us, and I'm feeling so much better now. My energy is coming back and she's making me cheerful again, too. Everyone is being so kind and helpful and lovely. But it is you I want to thank, the two of you, because it was thinking about your decision about me that drove me to make my decision about her. I wouldn't have known how to love her – not on my own, not like this – if it hadn't been for the two of you showing me how it's done. You love because your love is needed, right? And it doesn't matter how that happened or what anyone else might say. You just love and that puts more love in the world. Anyone who says otherwise can go jump.

But blether enough, the baby's crying.

All love,

Felicity

* * *

From Birthwood,
January 1973

Dear Mum and Dad,

Just a short note today. I sent off a package for you yesterday with the finally finished rag rug for you and a long newsy letter, but I had to write again today to tell you what Pidge has been up to. Reading! Would you believe it? So little but she's picking it up so fast, like a duck to water. Or maybe a fish.

Rika and I were busy at the table, working away on our latest leaflets for the girls on campus, and Pidge was tucked away under the table with a pillow and blanket. I thought that she'd fallen asleep, she was that quiet. But then out she sprang and right over to Bas to show him something. He was kneading bread at the counter and clapped his hands together to get all the flour off, which made Pidge laugh and sneeze, but all the while she was saying <u>hat, hat, hat!</u> Because, of course, she had sounded out the letters that sat under the drawing of a hat. Absolutely magic! So out came Bas's notebook and the two of them sat down on the floor to make a list of H words, then B words and words for animals and things. You should have seen the two of them sitting like that on the rug. <u>R – U – G.</u> He told her that her mother had made it before she was born and I looked up, but didn't say anything. Then he asked her to name the colours and they traced all the letters onto a blank page in his book. <u>B for blue. Y for yellow. G for Green.</u>

'And L for Livia,' she said, putting her finger on a green

L-shape hooked inside a heart in one corner of the rug. 'She put my letter here. One of them.'

'Well, look at that. So she did.'

'She must have known I was coming. Before I was born, she knew it would be me.'

'Maybe she did, youngling. Maybe she did.'

Just perfect. I can't quite believe how quickly she's growing or how clever she is. I am so very, very lucky.

Lots of love,

your Felicity

9

I SPENT ALL MORNING READING THE LETTERS AND DIDN'T get through them, just emerged a bit nostalgic, a bit homesick. Not exactly progress, I thought. I was supposed to be sorting Gran's things, not working myself into a mope. So I decided to take up Muriel's suggestion of lunch at the hotel and muster more vigour in the afternoon.

As soon as I was out the door of the house, I spotted the goose – or rather, it spotted me. This time, it was up on a tall stump halfway down the path. I'd have to pass right by it. It looked at me and let out an almighty squawk, beating its wings in the air. I froze. Do geese attack? Bas told stories about geese guarding farmhouses in the Netherlands. Said they were loud enough beasts to frighten any intruders, all hissing and strong wings. Geese protect their flock. But would a solitary bird be fierce like that, I wondered. I could stand here all day and not know. Then the

Edinburgh bus rumbled past empty-seated and the goose settled down and tucked its beak under its wing. I took my chance and scuttled past it to the road, looking backwards to see if I'd been followed.

There were plenty of cars in the hotel parking lot and full tables in the restaurant. Muriel smiled to see me and asked if it was all right if she sat me up at the bar for my meal.

'We've hordes of golfers in just at the moment. You'll want to sit away from them anyways, I should think. They're full of noise and bravado, by the sounds of it.'

She brought me a bowl of soup and a large supply of bread and butter. 'Do let me know if you would like anything else, dear. Anything at all.' I thanked her, and she smiled warmly. 'Lunch-wise or help with the house. I want you to know I'm willing. And if it's strong arms you need for lifting, I can probably find a name or two to suggest.'

'I do have a question about geese.'

'Geese?'

'Did my gran like them? I mean, did she keep one? At the house?'

'A goose? I shouldn't think so. Not that I know of, at least. She didn't really go in for farming. She helped me with our pig, but that was back during the war. A long time ago. No, she never did mention geese.'

A man came through from the kitchen with a tray of food and set it down on the bar while he checked the orders in a notebook.

'I was only wondering because there's one coming into the yard,' I said. 'I don't know what to do about it.'

'Not a goose, I shouldn't think,' Muriel said. 'It's a bit late in the spring for geese. They'll have gone now.'

The man looked up. 'No, I heard them still this morning. Won't be long, but they haven't flown yet.'

'These warm winters must be confusing them,' Muriel said. 'They should be heading up to Iceland by now. But just one, you said? Is it a swan, perhaps. They're both big birds.'

'No, it's absolutely a goose. Do you call them Canada geese here?'

'Ah, that's it then. I thought you meant one of the pink-footed chaps out on the sandbar. They're our winter companions, but they do fly off each spring. Just passing through.'

'Like the rest of us. Excuse me, ladies,' and the man picked up the tray and carried it through for the golfers.

'Well, there's your answer. A Canadian goose. They don't migrate, you see. No call of the north in the spring for them. That's not their way. They're resident all year round. And noisy pests, but at least perhaps familiar for you.'

I asked at the grocery shop, too, because of a sign in the window for duck eggs.

'Geese? Well, no, I'm afraid I can't help you there. These come from Fenton Barns, but they don't keep geese. But if you are looking for information about them, you might try the library in Gullane. And there's Goose Green, too, isn't there? Can't say I ever saw a goose there, but ask at the library and the girl might tell you something; some history or the like. I do have postcards, if you're interested. Seabirds and scenery. They sell well.'

The rack by the wall was well stocked and I chose a postcard of shorebirds for Felicity and and a skilful sketch of a local castle for Mateo. Turning the cards over, I spotted the artist's name: Izaak Nowak. Well, then. That was something off the to-do list. Gran's artist – found. I thought about buying the duck eggs, too, but worried I might not manage to eat them all on my own. They looked too big and meaty.

All along the coast road, the wind circled me. If it could just pick a direction, I could adjust, but it seemed to come from all around. I pulled my hair into a ponytail to keep it from my eyes and thought about Gran's curtains. I wished she were here to talk to.

On my return to the house, the goose was standing sentry on the stump again, so I thought I'd go see the bridge. I walked past on the other side of the road, through the parking lot – this one empty – and found an interesting cairn commemorating a local writer who had apparently enjoyed this stretch of the coast. A sign warned about the nesting season and the importance of keeping to the path, and described the local flora and fauna, resident and invasive. At the beginning of the bridge, I found another sign:

Aberlady Bay LNR
No dogs please
Please take your litter home

All those disappointed puppies dragged back home. I could hear Felicity laughing already. She liked wordplay like that. Maybe that's what I'd write on the postcard.

The tide was out so the bridge sat tall in the landscape. I looked down through the gaps between the planks at the muddy water below. As a kid, this made me feel dizzy, and I remember gripping Felicity's hand tightly. We'd count our steps, too, but I was already halfway across. Something for next time, then.

Nettles and thistles grew thick along the path, and further on, there was bright sea buckthorn and yellow prickly gorse. Why do so many thorny plants grow in sandy places? Protection against invasive species? Or tourists? Or was it like cacti in the desert, hoarding water any way they could? Strange to think that could be necessary in drizzly Scotland. Today was clear, at least, and away to the left across the water, Edinburgh sat etched on the horizon, the church spires rising like handwriting. I sidestepped the prickles and followed the path inland where a small lake was edged with nodding, yellow flowers. Islands of seafoam gave it a strange arctic air and a pair of Canada geese floated serenely with their clutch of yellow goslings. I'd never really seen geese up close before. They were sky-birds at the camp, passing over in the spring and again in the autumn, heading north and south with the seasons. We'd hear them before we saw them, a dark string against the sky. Felicity told me they flew day and night, never worrying about the dark. They took turns leading, but the ones who followed were the ones you could hear, clacking encouragement from behind. On this small lake, they looked sculptural, tall and peaceful, but then one of the adults noticed me and clacked in a territorial tone, and the chicks darted off to the shelter of the tall weeds. They didn't want spectators. I kept walking.

The path led into a hawthorn wood and, stepping in out of

the wind, my ears felt muffled, my eyes dim in the shade. No coin of daylight marked the end, only the path stretching on through the trees. It might stretch on forever. Or dimly tunnel right into the earth, down into sunless caverns under the sea. More Felicity-thoughts whispered at me as the branches creaked and swayed close above my head, as startling as voices. Quick strides, hands in pockets, resolute, and then I found a sudden corner, bent like a dog's leg, like the main street, and the path now was brighter and ran on before me, higher and thicker with green, and louder with birds overhead. Brambles grew here and something with white flowers. It was an easier path and, with sunlight ahead, I relaxed – or almost. The darker path was still there behind me, a scarf caught on a nail. And I wasn't sure this path had been here when Felicity and I came to visit or maybe we had just walked a different way.

Out in the wind again, the world was open. Spring-bright and alive with purple, yellow and white splashed through the grasses. All wild flowers Gran would know. Because a resident would know. And what was I? Migratory? By no means indigenous. I knew lady's slipper, evening primrose, white trillium, Indian paintbrush and pennyroyal with its lingering scent. All those grew in the forest at the camp. The flowers here were only colours to me.

The path cut inland over sandy ground marked with broken shells and pebbles. Far away to the left, sheep grazed, and dune hills formed strange shapes. Like the hawthorn path, I couldn't decide if they were familiar. The wind must change this landscape all the time. The ever-working wind making everything strange.

A large concrete block sat out among the sheep, and further

up the path, more blocks were positioned in lines and groups, manufactured grey against the daylight. They had been planted there during the war to repel German tanks. Now they looked like stepping stones in the long grass. A few wore graffiti, the paint old and worn by weather. I walked between them, away from the path and out to the shore.

Two lines of seaweed lay washed up on the shore: one wet and close to the water, marking the recent tide, and a dried remnant up against the dunes, recalling the last storm. Broken boards and smashed plastic crates were tangled with frayed rope lost from fishing boats and all kinds of seaweeds – bladderwrack, flat wrack, tangleweed and laver. How did I know these names but not the flowers? Everywhere, there were limpet shells, sea-worn branches and pebbles of glass. Mermaids' tears, Felicity taught me – or maybe Gran. Maybe both.

Scavenging gulls and crows combed the wet wrackline, turning over the tangled weed, searching for good things to eat. The curious goose would have a field day out here. Like me in the house, I thought. Turning everything over. Seeing what came to light.

The letters raised the question of Felicity's decision. Which must have meant keeping me. A small missed step under my heart, though of course, I'd always known. A free woman chooses. That was what Felicity taught me, and Rika, too. Me and every woman at the camp. Choice of vocabulary, provisions for care, position in labour. They wanted every woman to feel enabled to make their own informed choices. And when the choices were hard – when nothing was easy – Rika still helped. She spent nights listening to scared women talking, crying and questioning, listening to everything they had to say and still there listening even when they were quiet. When they knew their answer and if they needed her help, she took down the jars out of the dresser drawers: pennyroyal and yew – bitter, helpful herbs – and evening primrose for the pain. It would have been the same for Felicity, if that's what Felicity had wanted. If I had been unwanted. Invasive. But she never told me that story. And here I was.

She had told me about my father. That he was handsome and intelligent. That he was cultured and interested. That he hadn't known how to love me, but that she did and that mattered. She said that I didn't look like him. She said that he was gone. Maybe if I read through all the letters, I would learn more. Gran might have meant me to find that. Maybe she worried Felicity hadn't told me enough and that I might want to know.

When I was little, I wondered who I looked like because my dark hair wasn't like Felicity's or Gran's, and judging your own face is difficult. I studied photographs of Granddad and squinted into the mirror, wishing I could remember his face. I remembered his funeral, but that was all. I'd only been small, and Felicity had tried hard to explain about his special box. She said that he didn't need his body any more. That they had put it in the box instead – *a beautiful box, see?* – and everything was all right. But she wasn't. She held my hand too tightly, and looked up into the sky.

I'd seen a dead baby once. Blue and purple all over, like a bruise. It was born that way, with its cord in knots. I imagined Granddad like that, lying in his box with a cord like a necktie. People at the camp didn't wear neckties, so they looked dangerous to me. Perilous decorations.

The baby was buried in the forest in a box Bas made from cedar wood. It only took a morning to make, and in the afternoon, he dug the hole with the baby's father, a tall, dark man named Gordon. He and Betty had arrived at the camp in a station wagon at the beginning of the summer and slept in their car, on a mattress in the back.

'It's lovely,' Betty told Felicity. 'When it's hot, we can just leave the back up and then the breeze comes right in. And we can always see the stars, you know.'

'Don't the mosquitoes get to you?'

'Yeah, but I'd be awake anyway. This guy's a real kicker.' She rubbed her hand across her belly, her smile broad and open.

After the birth, she'd held her blue baby all morning long. Rika said that Felicity and I should go back to the cabin to sleep, but we couldn't leave. We sat together on the porch outside the birthing house singing a bit and Betty cried a little, rocking her baby in her arms. Felicity's voice was beautiful. Betty told her baby stories, held him close and kissed his still fingers, then after a long time, she took the white shawl from around her shoulders, wrapped it around her baby's body, and passed him over to Rika.

'Thank you,' Betty said. 'I mean that. Didn't think I could ever say it, you know. But I can.' Rika held him carefully and smiled, slow and sad.

I was almost back across over the bridge when he called out to me. 'Do you know you're being stalked?'

I looked up and saw a man on the Aberlady side, grinning.

'No, not by me,' he said. 'Turn around. There's your fellow.'

Forty paces behind me, the goose stepped out, flat-footed and tall as the handrails. I flapped my arms and it stopped its parade, watching. I clapped my hands. It took a few shuffling steps away. I clapped again and it crooked its muscled neck and barked, low and threatening.

'Go!' I called out and the goose stopped. It gave me a curious look, a sort of nod, then shook out its wings and flew, tracing a wide circle over the mudflats.

'Do you two know each other?' the man asked, leaning against the railings. He rolled his Rs, but didn't sound Scottish. I couldn't place the flatness of his accent. He looked old and white-headed, but stood straight and held a large white sketchpad. The pockets of his tweed jacket bristled with pencils.

'Quite possibly,' I said. 'There's been a goose mucking about in the yard of the house where I'm staying. It might be that one. Unless all the geese here are so affectionate.'

'They can be right pests at times. Curious, noisy things. We tend to let them be out here, though. Not like in cities where their eggs get oiled or pricked. To keep populations down, you understand. Not to be vindictive. Mostly out here there is enough space and they're let be.'

'I wish that one would let me be.'

'I wonder if it recognized a fellow Canadian and wants company. Did I get that right? I used to be better at identifying accents.' His pencil hovered over the paper, but he looked at me, quizzically, then smiled. 'But, I will let you off the hook. My accent, it is Polish.'

'Thanks. I don't know that I would have guessed.'

'It is an old accent and rusty. Scottish rain, I'm sure.'

A few ducks took off from the water and flew overhead, cackling and calling their way across the bay, and I followed their flight. There was no sign of the goose now.

'Are you here for the birds?' he asked. 'You do not strike me as a golfer.' He put his pencil in his pocket and turned the notebook towards me. 'What do you think?'

The lines of the bridge were good, and he'd sketched the swimming ducks, too. Beyond the water, the land was flat, the low hawthorn wood dark against the land. 'It's not right yet,' he said. 'I don't think it is, but I cannot see how it isn't.'

'Well, it looks balanced to me. And the shapes are good,' I said. 'Maybe the distancing? Is that what's causing you trouble?'

'Perhaps. Yes, perhaps.' The man took out a charcoal pencil and held it elegantly in his fingers. 'Do you draw, then?'

'No. I don't. But I look at a lot of paintings. I work at a gallery. In Canada.'

'You see? I knew.'

'And you are Izaak Nowak, aren't you? The bird sketches.'

A shy smile. 'Pleased to be identified. And by one far from home. You must have been buying postcards.'

'Yes, but I knew your name before that. My grandmother told me to keep an eye open for your calendar. She lives . . . used to live in Aberlady.'

A pause and the intermittent calling of birds on the water.

Then he smiled again. 'I know your grandmother, perhaps. Are you Jane's, then? I should have guessed. All the way from Canada.'

'Yes. And she mentioned your sketches in a letter. She said you were good at drawing light.'

'Is that what she said? An interesting summary. Ah well, Jane was never very good at telling the whole truth. She did not lie; she was not that kind of lady. But she didn't tell the truth.'

'Felicity told me she was private.'

'Yes. Perhaps that is the word.' He sorted through a handful of pencils for the right one. 'A private soul holds the story close. But I always preferred sharing. When your mother was born, I was the one to send word to your grandfather. Mind, I didn't tell her that it was me, so maybe we're alike, too. I only thought that, war or no, there is a time for family to be close if they can be. And Stanley was grateful for the chance to hold his brand-new daughter in his arms.' He selected a pencil, nodding to himself and started shading. 'But you weren't here for Jane's funeral, were you? Did word not reach you in time?'

'No. But I came as soon as I could.'

'It was a dreich day of it when Jane was buried. But there it is. She is at rest now. And here you are. You won't be here for long, will you? Settling affairs and then heading home, I imagine.'

'Something like that. I'll need to decide what to do about the house.'

'I think the market is good these days. Seem to be a lot of new people around the village anyway. But your mother doesn't want it?'

'I don't know. She offered to move back once already. After my granddad died.'

'Well, I might imagine Jane said no to that, didn't she?'

'Yeah. Felicity said that she was surprised. I used to wonder what it would have been like if I'd grown up here.'

'You wouldn't have your beautiful Canadian accent, you wouldn't.'

'Maybe the geese would leave me alone then.'

He laughed, closed his sketchbook and pulled a package of tobacco from his jacket pocket. 'Do you mind? I feel I should always ask these days. So many people . . .'

'No, no, it's fine.' I shook my head. 'Really.'

'Thank you. Old age proves dreadful enough even with small pleasures.' He put the package on his knee, slipped out a paper to roll a cigarette with thin fingers. 'Outside, I don't think it matters much. Still, I like to ask if I'm with someone.'

'Thanks for that.'

Izaak puffed on his cigarette, his eyes watery in the wind. 'There is, I think, some story about geese and God, isn't there? A saintly connection, perhaps? I cannot remember. Some story there, though. I think I remember your grandmother talking about God and geese. And there's a story, too, about your mother and the saints. I think I heard you were born in a convent?'

'No,' I said, smiling at the thought of Rika wimpled. 'It was just a community. A commune, really. Some of the people there were believers, but not everyone. It was an open kind of place.'

'And you? You are a believer?' he spoke kindly, but the words stung, and I felt far from home.

After a moment, I said I wasn't sure. 'It's hard to put into words.'

'Yes. I might know what you mean. It is private.'

* * *

105

Felicity was a believer. There were many things she believed in. Cleanliness. Cheerfulness. Women's strength. That protest was a virtue but so was building sanctuary. That tree roots stretched as wide as their branches and the same was true for ideas. I thought she'd learned all these things at the camp with Rika and Bas, but they were all in the bungalow, too. In Gran's dusting and patience. In the careful boxes and the saved letters. History came in porous layers, with folds, cracks and creases, and stories broke into each other. Felicity's into mine, mine into Gran's and everything was in the same place and nothing was believably linear.

Just like the Roman roads and plastic sandwiches all over again and now God and Mother Goose, too. All these layering stories washed in with the tide, and what was I to believe?

I said goodbye to Izaak and left him to his cigarette and the wind on the water.

Closer to the house, the trees' branches stirred above my head, and I noticed a scrap of a bag held out like a banner as if to signal to sailors still out at sea.

10

FELICITY: 1968

A GRIMET DAY IN MONTREAL, AND THE FACE OF THE mountain was patched with snow. The day before, the wind had been warm and I thought that spring was coming but in the night, the temperature dropped again, and I woke with cold feet. My shift at the hospital started dark and early and when the sky finally brightened, it was a hard day to read. It could go either way.

Matron was likewise grimet – one moment smiling encouragement and rough as thunder the next, bustling us through too many tasks in just a splinter of time. A far cry from Dr Ballater's quiet afternoon tea. But wasn't that the point? I'd wanted a change, and now I was here, feeling fickle as the weather.

Grimet was Dr Ballater's word. I imagined he thought it sounded rural, but where he dug it up from, I hadn't a clue. Some old book, maybe. I never heard it from anyone else in East Lothian.

Still, it was a good word. Mum might like it. I'd include it in my next letter, I thought, and she'd also like the mountain and the snow. This cusp-of-the-season feeling. The strange sky.

I kept my eye out the window as I made up the empty beds along the ward. It was the last job before the end of my shift so possibly Matron was being kind. She usually assigned me occupied bed-making which was tricky and required two nurses. Empty beds could be managed alone, and, without a partner, I could take a moment to watch the sky. It would be a cold walk after my shift – a full half-hour to the Oratory to meet Asher. I'd imagined a stroll through a new spring afternoon with my hat folded away, my coat open and a warm evening ahead. It had been like that the day before. We'd walked in the sunshine together, right through the downtown, looking for a restaurant. It felt like spring had begun and we'd laughed about how much the weather had changed in the past month. It had only been a month since he'd followed me off the bus and already we were constant.

I'd been looking down at a folded street map, wondering if I might find the way into Summit Park. There were supposed to be pheasants there, up near the old radio tower, and I thought I might find them if I went looking.

'Is it the Oratory you're after?'

I looked up and saw a young man walking quickly to catch up with me. He looked pale and northern, I thought, with his dark hair and his strong jaw. I could imagine him chopping wood a thousand years ago in some Viking settlement. Or not a settlement, but a monastery. Remote. Celtic. Scanning the horizon, thinking of God. Yes, there was definitely something monastic about him.

'You got off a stop too early, really,' he said. 'For the Oratory. It isn't far, just up there. I'm . . . I'm going there myself.' He pointed, and that's when I saw the dome on the hill.

'Yes? You are?' It was hard not to smile at his earnest expression.

'Yes,' he said. 'If you are.'

Now we met as often as we could, for meals or coffee, whatever my shifts would allow. I teased him that I'd soon lose my overseas novelty. He teased me that I'd get lost in the city without him.

We'd wandered through the skyscraper valleys, certain no one else in the crowds was half as lucky, half as alive. We walked miles and we never found the restaurant, settling instead for a counter with smoked meat sandwiches and French fries.

'Next time, I'll take you for pizza,' he said. 'Have you been to Pizzeria Napoletana?'

'Is it new?'

'Hardly,' he laughed. 'Been the cornerstone of Little Italy since the end of the war. My uncle used to take me there when I was a kid. Slumming it, my folks said, but it is a venerable Montreal establishment.'

'Just like you.'

He laughed again and held my hand, so I kissed him and taxis drove past, red rear lights blurring as they turned fast corners and disappeared. Above us, the lights were on in every window and Asher stopped in front of a plush skyscraper hotel. It towered above us, all elegant, arched windows and modern concrete, like a space-age campanile.

'How about this one? You tried this?' he asked.

'A little rich for my blood, I think.'

'This old cheese-grater? It's already been open over a year. I hear the Expo guests wore the place right out. The chandeliers are half dulled with all their gawping. But I wonder if you'd like a night in it.'

'I'm not that luxe a girl.'

'Aren't you? But think of it – the finest views of Dorchester Square in the city and Mount Royal in the distance. And room service. Plush hotel towels. A gorgeous big double bed. I wonder if there's a swimming pool?'

'Do you mean it? It must cost the earth.'

'It's not the Ritz. I could probably manage.'

'I don't know.'

'I could wait.'

Asher was at the bottom of the Oratory steps when I arrived. Still waiting, I thought, but I didn't say it. He smiled and then I thought he looked handsome.

'There you are! Are you up for a climb? I wondered if you would be, after your shift. Are you tired out?'

'I'll be fine,' I said. 'The view will do me good.'

Snow clung to the corners of the steps, hiding in the shadows and shining white. At first, my knees felt cold and stiff, but they soon loosened, and we climbed quickly, side by side, step after step after step. Asher said some people climbed on their knees, every step prayerful. There was even a set of wooden steps kept for that purpose and roped off with a sign – *réservé aux pèlerins qui montent à genoux* – but I kept my Presbyterian feet on the stone steps and held Asher's hand.

We didn't go inside the church, not that day. We were pilgrims for the view. The city stretched out before us, the straight streets and the first lights coming on, then beyond, the old city and a river sunset. The Oratory lawns were white with snow, which stood out now, whiter from above. Asher turned to me, his eyes shining.

'Come, let's go,' he said. 'Snow-viewing till we're buried.'

When I smiled, he told me it was just a poem. A haiku by Basho. He'd spent the morning in the library and now his head was full of Japanese verse. He said he was struggling with *kireji* and that there was no real equivalent in English.

'They're cutting words – or letters, maybe – that slice a haiku in two. I think it's about breath as much as about revelation.'

'Come, let's go,' I said, and he laughed.

'I suppose he meant buried in snow, but I like the fatality of it. Very Montreal, don't you think?' He took out his cigarettes and offered me one.

'My mum read poetry at university. I wonder if she read any haikus.'

'You don't strike me as a poet's daughter.' We breathed smoke in the cold air.

'No? Well, she's more reader than writer. She has reams of it in her head.'

'And your dad? Let me guess . . . bagpipes craftsman?'

I swatted him, and he put his arms right around me, pulling me close and warm. He smelled of fabric softener, tobacco and skin.

'Okay, so not that,' he said. 'Shepherd? Politician?'

'Geologist,' I said. 'Well, sort of. Yes.' I knew this sounded wobbly. 'Yes, a geology professor. But he might not be my father.'

'I'm not sure I follow.'

So I ended up telling Asher about the war and all the men away from the village. About the date of my birth and how I couldn't sort it out with counting. Then about the looks I sometimes saw in the street when I was small and the scraps of rumour I finally heard at the high school. Sometimes I thought my parents were hiding the truth from me and sometimes I was angry but I wasn't really sure about any of this and I told him that, too, and how both Jane and Stanley were so loving and such rocks for me and he chuckled a little, thinking I was making a geology joke. I told him my half-story badly because I'd never told it before. I wasn't sure if you needed to understand a story to tell it. Asher listened and said it didn't matter. Of course it didn't, I thought. Of course.

After that, it wasn't hard for him to climb into my bed. And, with him, Basho seeped into everything. Montreal's warming spring. My memories of Edinburgh's cherry blossom. Everything.

> *In my new robe*
> *This morning –*
> *Someone else*

11

PIDGE: 2006

AT THE HOUSE, THE DOORSTEP WAS COVERED IN BIRD shit. Guano. Ordure. Droppings. But that made it sound solid and this wasn't. It was slimy, liquid muck. As green and rank as goose shit comes.

But the good news was the stump was empty and the goose nowhere to be seen. There'd be a hose in the garden. Or a bucket, at least. Maybe all this muck was a parting gift. I could clean it up. No problem. But first, a cup of coffee.

I'd been glad to find whole beans in the village shop. One bag amongst a whole row of jars of instant coffee. That felt lucky and then it occurred to me that there might be beans only because Gran usually bought them. The shop might stop carrying them now that she was gone. That was all I was thinking about – the beans, the shop and Gran – as I came into the kitchen and saw the back door was wide open. The paintwork around the handle was scuffed and scraped, and the back doorstep as mucky as the front. And then there it was. Standing in front of the sink, right in the middle of the black-and-white kitchen floor tiles – a fat, white goose egg. Perfect.

I was really going to need to do something about the goose.

The next morning, I checked all the locks. I must have left the back door open a little, I thought. I would have to be careful. I put the cold egg in the living room in the willow-pattern bowl with the marble ones. It seemed to balance all right on top but it looked immense. Then I spent the morning being serious: linens and lamps to donate, books and clothes and shoes.

In the afternoon, I drove Gran's car down to the next village. The locals on the hill called it Gillan, and perhaps they were right, but Gran always said Gullane. There were more shops there – a bakery, a butcher, an antique shop on the corner and a library where I hoped to find a computer.

I didn't know if Mateo would be worried that we hadn't spoken since I'd arrived. He never sent me notes or called to check in when he went away for work, though I suspected that he would like me to make the effort. And as for Felicity – who was probably waiting to hear from me – well, I really should make up my mind what to let her know.

The librarian wore her hair in short, dyed Nordic spikes and looked glad for the interruption when I approached the desk. Maybe it was just the surprise of a new face. By the window, a long wooden table was spread with newspapers, and a few old men sat there, turning pages, wearing tweed. I explained about wanting to use the computer to check email and I held Gran's library card, playing with it between my fingers as I spoke.

'None of that should be a problem,' she said in a soft German accent, her gaze direct and kind. 'I knew Jane well. She was in every week without fail. Not the kind of lady to use the computer system, still her account number will be registered all the same. I will find you a password.'

Over by the window, one of the old men let out a cough and another muttered under his breath, looked over at me and muttered again. The clock on the wall ticked loudly.

The cougher raised his voice. 'You her family, then? Come to dig her out of the dunes?'

'No,' I said. 'I'm her granddaughter.'

Another mutter but between the coughing and the accent, I couldn't understand the words.

The librarian copied a series of numbers onto a bit of paper and passed it across to me.

'I was also wondering if I could borrow books?'

'Sure. Not a problem. Those shelves by the wall are fiction, and biography is at the end. Non-fiction is over there,' and she waved towards where the old men sat.

'Do you have anything about birds?'

'Birds? Absolutely. You like bird-watching?'

Bird-watching or being watched by birds? I thought. 'Um, more care and maintenance, I think.'

'Did Jane keep birds, then? I did not know.'

There was more coughing from the table, and muttering. 'Daft old bird herself,' one said and the man next to him jabbed out his elbow and the muttering stopped.

'Well, no,' I said. 'She didn't. But I found one. Or rather it found me. It . . . she . . . well, a goose has been hanging about in the yard at the house.'

'She?'

'I found an egg. On the kitchen floor. I don't know how she got in the house. Is there a bird rescue centre or something like that nearby? Somewhere that could help?'

'I do not know. There is a bird-watching club that meets once a month, though not bird keepers, you understand. But they might know someone. A farmer with a flock, perhaps.'

'She isn't domestic. At least I don't think so. People don't keep Canada geese, do they?'

'Shoot them, more like it,' said the cougher. 'Best to wring its neck and pop it in the oven. Nice thing, roast goose. Haven't had one in years.'

'There's a lot hasn't happened to you in years,' said another man, adjusting his flat cap and turning the pages of a newspaper. The librarian pushed her keyboard over to me.

'You use this to search. There will be lots of information, I'm sure. Many birds come through here every year. Seabirds and water fowl, all sorts of things. You will find information about invasive geese, too, I am sure of it.'

I took my notebook out of my back pocket and turned to the computer screen. It soon became clear she was right: half the world seemed to be rescuing wild birds. My goose didn't seem to need rescuing; I did. Most of the stories involved something small – crows, magpies or garden birds like thrushes or wrens. Some were babies and others stuck somewhere – a chimney, a drainpipe, the mouth of a dog. Boxes and pet carriers were mentioned, the right way to catch an injured bird in a towel. And so many grocery lists and recipes too – egg yolks cooked and cooled and mashed with Coca-Cola. Dog food. Cat food. Baby food. Insects. Chicken. Wheatgerm. None of this helped, though I did find out that unlike ducks, geese are vegetarians. Comforting, that.

Under 'East Lothian bird rescue', I found numbers for national helplines but nobody local. Nobody who might come with a large net and a van.

I jotted down a few notes and then opened my email. Mateo wanted to confirm Gran's address so that he could send me a package about the condo. Things might be moving quickly there. He'd tried to call, but the number didn't connect. It would be good to talk. I wrote him a short note, mentioning Edinburgh and the drive, and the tulips in Aberlady, but I didn't mention the goose.

I sent word to Gran's lawyer, in case he had anything else to pass my way, and I emailed the telephone company. And to Felicity, what could I write? A telephone call would be better. Give her the chance to swear at me a bit for saying nothing and then climb back down. But I needed to get in touch and until I got the phone working, an email would fill the gap.

Hi Felicity,
Just checking in. I hope that you're doing okay. I'm away
for the week, all of a sudden. Thinking of you.
  Lots of love to everyone at the camp,
  P.

Incomplete and dishonest. Again.

As I left the library, the wind blew my hair from behind my ears as it rushed along the library wall, whispering into the small leaves on the privet hedge. A flutter of small brown birds scattered out onto the ground where they turned to pecking and bobbing for crumbs.

A mother came through the doors after me, her hands full of books and a toddler trailing behind. He tried to crouch down to watch the birds, but she grabbed his hand and pulled him away. The sparrows took flight as the mother hurried off down the path with her son. I watched as the wind ruffled his hair and caught the ends of her scarf so that it blew out behind her like a flag.

All through the winter, Mateo had complained about the noise from the people upstairs. There was always the sound of tricycles in the hallway. Or shouts from the bathroom or the bedrooms, the loud bang of dropped books.

'We should just go out,' he'd say in the evening. 'Find a quiet place for a glass of wine.'

'I'm sure they'll settle soon. It's only half past seven.'

'Every blessed evening. We should move.'

'Yes.'

'You say yes, so we should do something about it. I'll arrange another viewing. For this week.'

'Felicity is coming to town on Thursday.'

'Friday, then.'

'Yes.'

'All right – yes. Then yes.'

12

In the house, it was in the kitchen. She. That goose. No egg this time, just the goose standing there, calm as could be. Ridiculous. A goose in a kitchen is ridiculous. She stood there on leathery feet, looking huge beside the counters, shitting on my gran's floor, scaring me half to death, all on my own. I bellowed and clapped my hands and she looked right at me with dark, beany eyes as if to ask what the fuss might be. Then she opened her beak and hissed. The pale pink of her fleshy tongue flashed out at me and I could see small, strange teeth along her black bill; more dinosaur than bird. She hissed louder. I picked up the broom and swung it out, hoping to sweep her towards the open door. She beat her wings and jumped up into the air, hissing and raising a wind in the small room. I stumbled backwards into the hall. She kept coming at me, so I jabbed out with the broom and I hissed a bit, too, fiercely, or as fierce as I could manage, and she hesitated. I got my hand on the doorknob, but was scared to slam it in case I caught her neck. I hissed louder and let out a strangled shout. She backed off, just enough, and I got the door closed and that was that. No – she'd opened up the back door before, hadn't she? So I needed to lock this one. Of course, there wasn't a key – I'd have to wedge it shut with something. I pulled the desk chair from the living room and rammed it under the door handle, hoping that would do the trick.

Then I went into the bedroom and did the same thing.

I could still hear noises from the kitchen, but the hissing had stopped. She honked triumphantly. Well, let her think she'd won. It wouldn't last long. I'd figure something out. I would. In the morning. I'd have to.

The light was beginning to fade. I settled on the bed, with a blanket over my knees and read through Mateo's guidebook. Maybe I'd take a trip to down the coast. There was a seabird centre in North Berwick. I wasn't sure if Canada geese counted as seabirds, but maybe the people at the centre could help anyway. It was either that or bundle the bird into the car somehow and deposit it with Muriel at the hotel. Actually, the hotel was a rather tempting idea that evening. I could head over there, have a meal, and ask for a bed afterwards. Except that would make me look ridiculous, too, wouldn't it? I couldn't really explain why I wasn't going back to the bungalow. They'd think I was scared of the dark. Or ghosts. So I stayed put and wished I'd eaten more for lunch.

Out in the bay, waves crashed on the sandbar. A storm was coming. Wind in the trees and rain starting on the roof tiles. It would blow right into the kitchen through that open back door.

It might flood. Well, then the goose might float away. I wasn't going through there again. The trees along the road groaned with the strengthening wind and every window rattled. The blanket was scratchy but warm and I wished Mateo were here. I looked at every page he'd bookmarked, read every detail.

Later, I fell into the pattern of sleep and listening. The rise and lull of wind continued through every dream, and I followed it deep into the night, settling, unsettling and settling again with the waves until a sound came from the kitchen. A screech like something skinned.

Wide awake suddenly, I couldn't move.

Another shriek and the loud sound of wind now, but the shriek was animal. She was caught, trapped somewhere and bleeding. Torn and bleeding. She was hurt and panicked, and my ears were raw with her cry.

I felt for the light switch and closed my eyes against the glare. Another cry but this time softer. I stood up, wrapped a blanket around me, and moved the chair away from the door.

Light channelled into the darkness and, down the hallway, I could see that the chair I'd wedged by the kitchen door had fallen. I pushed it away, listened and opened the door slowly. The wind hit me first, my face wet with its cold touch. Then I saw the goose moving in the shadows. Her head twisted back and forth, her eyes blinked blindly as she croaked out harsh sobs.

'Hush, hush, beastie. Gentle now, hush,' and she came towards me, bleating. I crouched and let the blanket fall from my shoulders, unsure what I was doing, but there she was, coming towards me, bending her neck and pushing into me as if she wanted to hide. I reached down and pulled the blanket up to cover her wings and she let me. 'Hush,' I said again. 'Hush and hush.'

I held her. I whispered. I waited. She was a scared young thing in my arms and I held her until she was calm. She folded in on herself and settled on the floor, the half-tangled blanket still around her. I stood, still hushing gently and turned on the light by the cooker. She stayed still, almost trusting. I closed the door to the yard but left the hallway door open and she was still. Settled.

I went back to bed and kept listening.

In the morning, I found the house quiet, the floor cool under my feet, the trees outside the window still. The goose was in the living room, nesting in an armchair, her beak under her wing, her eyelids closed and lightly feathered. I hadn't known that Canada geese had white eyelids. Two small white circles like the moon. How strange, this intimate knowledge. This glimpse.

The kitchen was carnage. Water on the floor and feathers and the mess of more shit everywhere. She'd pulled the clock down from the wall and now it dangled, exhausted, from the plug. The blue glass cake-stand was in shards on the floor. Another egg, this time smashed. The white was an oozed slick on the tiles and the yolk the size of my fist. Felicity had taught me to salt a smashed egg. A handful of salt will absorb the wet mess, making it easier to scoop up. And a slice of bread for the broken glass to keep the splinters away from your skin. Neither trick would work with puddles or grime, but I found a stack of old newspaper beside the fireplace. Then, after the debris was dealt with, I would mop the floor.

* * *

I was just putting the kettle on for coffee when the letterbox rattled and something heavy fell to the floor. The address was written in Mateo's handwriting – jarringly out of time. It had only been the day before that I'd emailed him the address and here was an envelope already. A thick magazine slid out, with a note clipped to the cover. He'd been in touch with Felicity for the address. He was sorry. He hadn't realized that I hadn't told her and that she didn't know about my trip. Conversations between Felicity and Mateo were generally awkward. Neither of them quite understood how I felt about the other. Or why, perhaps. Perhaps the heart beats in secret.

The magazine was propaganda about the condo Mateo fancied. *Live above the ordinary* with a photo of a tower in the city sky. All those glass walls. When we first looked around our current apartment, he'd been so pleased with the glass shower surround and the clean white subway tiles on the walls. That was before he'd heard the kids upstairs. But I'd been grumpy and tired later when I described the bathroom to Felicity and she'd got the wrong end of the stick. She thought I was unhappy, so she came to visit. Trying to cheer me up, she brought along brushes and red paint and covered all that glass with trailing vines, leafy patterns and the shapes of birds in flight. Mateo did not understand.

'Happiness *is* bird-shaped, isn't it?' she said, grinning, brushing her hair back with her wrist, her fingers still holding a paint-dipped brush. 'Did I get that quite right? A feathered thing? My mother would know. She has all the poems at her fingertips. A crack mind, my mum.' She sat back on her heels and admired her work.

It took Mateo two weeks to get rid of the colour, scratching at the glass with a razor blade, clearing his throat and saying little.

I flipped through the magazine pages, past the sauna, the concierge and the penthouse terrace. The pages had a plastic smell, a slickness fitting for a glass house.

The goose walked into the kitchen. I kept turning pages. I wondered if she noticed that I'd cleaned. Then I wondered if she was hungry because she would be, wouldn't she? After all that had happened. I stood up, slowly to keep her calm, opened the back door, then returned to my magazine. The garden was hers if she wanted it.

The wind through the door smelled of churned sea and earth. She looked at me. Expectantly, I thought.

'You okay? You hungry or anything? You can go outside, if you like. The door's open.'

She honked quietly, her eyes still fixed on my face.

'You thirsty? There'll be a puddle in the garden. You want to go out?'

This was silly. Geese don't understand words. But you can't look into a face like that and not respond. It seemed rude. So I talked. She blinked. I talked some more. She pecked at the magazine and I put it down on the table.

Through the window, I could see the tips of branches and pale-green leaves pointed to the sky. The goose angled her head up, listening. Maybe she could hear the other geese calling. Sometimes I could hear them when the windows were open, but her ears might be more attuned. It was strange to think her family might be close by and here she was, alone with me. I wished I could let them know she was all right.

When I headed to the bathroom, the goose followed me. She watched as I filled the sink with water and, as I splashed my face, she jumped up to the edge of the bath, so I turned on the bath tap and put in the plug. She clacked amicably as the water ran. When I turned it off, she hopped down into the water, shaking out her feathers, stretching out her neck, bending and drinking and looking pleased with herself.

The water in the sink went cold, so I drained it and started again. Hot water, a clean flannel and Gran's soap. The goose splashed in the bath. I splashed, too. We got on fine.

After that, she followed me everywhere. I walked to the end of the garden and the goose walked along behind me. I crossed the road to look at the bay and she came too. When I walked out over the bridge to the saltings, she flew low over the water to join me on the other side. She kept close as I crossed through the dune country, and when we reached the concrete blocks, she flew up to perch and take in the view. I scrambled up after her. It was higher than it looked and I noticed words carved into the block's surface. Not graffiti – concrete's too hard for that. This must have been written before the concrete was dry.

WEDENSDAY 21st AUGUST 1940

A simple mistake set now in stone, back when my grandmother was young. *En* for endure. Stone without end.

Standing, we could see the wide world of the Forth, the water both silver and blue, broken by the wind. The goose opened her wings and beat them against the air, calling out with her broken voice. I thought she'd fly. That she was going to leave me. I waited and watched, and something like loneliness barked in my heart, a faraway cry. She paused, then met my eye.

'Oh, honk yourself,' I said. 'Go if you need to. You are a wild thing. I'm all right here.'

But she didn't go. She winged the air again, calling louder than before, and I saw how beautiful she was. Her feathers spread wide, each wing a perfect pattern of shaded shingles. Looking at her, angels made sense. Wings were naturally heavenly. I stretched out my arms to feel the push of the wind and she cackled. I was sure she was laughing, her shiny eye full of light, and I laughed, too.

May grew fat and the last tulips dropped their broad petals to the grass. I made lists, sorted through all the boxes and moved umpteen things from place to place. I threw away old utility bills and kept my mother's letters. I found nothing new. Only the usual bits and pieces, expected detritus and all the ingredients of a long life lived.

Meanwhile, the goose made herself at home in the living-room chair. She pulled suckers from the apple trees in the orchard, and layered them around the cushioned back, lining them with her own feathers to make a soft and rounded place to be. Things around the house disappeared, reappearing later in the growing nest. Bits of newspaper. Pencils and pens. A luggage tag. One of my socks. One morning, I watched her tear a large piece of the condominium magazine. She crumpled the glossy paper, creasing it with care. I let her. I wasn't particularly interested in reading about concierge service anyway. I read the library book instead and learned about goose habits. Seems young ones get confused and wander. Build solo nests in strange places. Get into mischief. I took notes and observed her caching habits as hairpins went missing from Gran's dressing table and coins from the pockets of trousers I left on the chair. The problem of bird grime spread. I had to lay towels over the furniture, and newspapers under the desk where she liked to hide after lunch. I learned to keep a paper towel in my back pocket and swooped down without thinking to wipe the floorboards and the tiles in the hall. The Persian carpets proved harder to clean, dusty traces remaining despite all my work with the vacuum cleaner. They had to be dragged outside and draped over chairs in the garden. I worked them over with a dry brush to remove the residue, then rolled them up and put them away under the bed.

She dropped feathers and I saved them in a jam jar.

Sometimes she laid more eggs and sometimes she didn't.

Whenever I left the house, the goose came too. She kept her eye on me. She didn't like it when I climbed into Gran's car to go down the road to Gullane. When I returned with groceries and more books, she was back on the stump, barking at me, but when I opened the bungalow door, she flew down from her perch and walked regally up the path, nodding graciously to me and stepping inside.

When the phone was connected again, I called Felicity but Bas said she wasn't there. He might have meant she didn't want to talk. I didn't know if he would tell me.

I told him about the goose and he laughed. 'It's good to live with animals,' he said. 'Isn't that why we kept you around?'

'Hey you, be kind. Don't want to make me cry, do you? I'm far from home and all alone right now. Well, almost.'

'You're a tough nut. You're fine, aren't you?'

'Yeah, I guess. Still haven't decided what to do with the house, but I'll need to head home soon. Has Felicity mentioned anything?'

'No. No, she hasn't. Have you asked her? She might like to be asked.'

'Tell her to call me, will you? I don't mind what time of day it is.'

He said he would and we hung up. I tried Mateo, too, but there was no answer.

One warm evening, the goose followed me down to the fish and chip shop and then we sat together on a bench overlooking the bay, sharing squashed chips. Seemed she liked them better like that, and I ended up eating just the fish. It was almost June. I would be heading home to Ottawa soon. A year since last summer already.

Last summer, it had been Spain. Mateo had had a conference to attend and I tagged along.

'To see my haunts?' Mateo asked. 'My childhood seasides?'

'Yes. If you like. You never talk about them.'

'Perhaps there is not much to say.'

I told him I also wanted to see Picasso's Margot. At the shop, we sold a book with her face on the cover, her lips as red as the roses in her hair and her eyes painted thick with colour, her haunting, confronting look. He'd given her a background painted with pointed light, gold and green like the Klimt, but miles different, too. Klimt's model stood untouched in a surreal setting, but Margot leaned solidly on a dark tabletop. Both would never blink.

One month before we flew, I knew I was pregnant. It was just like Felicity described it. An ache and a lift. A weird certainty. I'd never believed these symptoms – thought they were mumbo-jumbo and too early to be real. But it turned out she was right. Eight days in, I knew.

I didn't say anything, didn't do anything. Told myself my period was often erratic. I was coming down with something. The weather. The mussels I'd eaten. The flu. At the end of the month, I bought a test at the drugstore. But I didn't want to test at home, not even alone. I went to a coffee shop and stood in line for a coffee – just a small espresso. Sipped it slowly, watching the buses drive past.

Afterwards, I didn't call Felicity; I couldn't, and anyway, it was Mateo who mentioned abortion first and asked me if that was what I wanted. We hadn't planned this. We weren't going to. I said yes.

Is it love to want what your lover wants? That's love, right? I can't remember. The women at the clinic were professional and I felt foggy all through June, like the drugs weren't wearing off. I felt thin. I woke late at night and too early in the morning, feeling bruised, remembering things I wanted to pack for Europe or the smell of summer flowers at the camp, the names of children.

In Barcelona, I found Margot in a Catalan palace. According to the plaque on the wall, she was a woman of many names. *The Wait, Pierreuse, Red Woman, The Made-Up Woman.* She sat in Gallery 7, crowded with visitors, her scarlet dress striking against the flush of her skin. All around, her artist's early work stared out through clear, unfamiliar faces, suspended in the time before everything broke apart into his familiar shards.

While Mateo met with colleagues, I sat in a sun-bleached square, drank coffee and read the guidebook. I planned our hike at Montserrat. There had been a medieval monastery; Napoleon demolished it, but it was rebuilt, and now there was a wonderful museum there, with more Picassos, El Grecos and Dalís. More faces to face. We would take a narrow-gauge railway up the hillside – the *cremallera* – and, at the top, choose one of the hiking trails that led back down to the houses below. Local children once saw visions of angels there, and now pilgrims visit, but the way was clearly marked for hikers, too. I folded a napkin and slipped it into the guidebook at the photo of these serrated hills, then spent the rest of the afternoon exploring small city streets thinking of mountains and Margot.

In the evening, a restaurant in another square, a table with a white cloth, chairs and the tourist sounds of violin. I was tired from walking, the skin on my heel rubbed raw under my sandal strap. I drank a cold glass of water and noticed the buildings. Old windows, old shutters and chimneys, the plane trees with solid trunks the height of church towers and an impermeable hide, their leaves impossible hands. Mateo bought a costly bottle of wine and the air was heavy with roses.

'We never would have had all this, of course,' he said, with a soft smile. 'We might have been at home right now in the humidity with morning sickness. And loud bars on Elgin Street. Not a pretty thought, is it?'

I smiled. In the night, I was awake again as Mateo slept, his beautiful face turned towards me, and I remembered the roses and their cultivated perfume. At the camp, evening primroses bloom at night. I remembered that, too. And that night is when wild orchids are most fragrant. That pennyroyal is fragrant all the time, and it smells like peppermint tea laced with turpentine.

And a year passed and now I sat here.

The next morning, the post brought another heavy envelope, filled with folded information about the condo. Mateo wanted to go ahead and buy. He wrote that he'd spoken with the agent and with the bank. He needed my signature. He also wrote about the weather. Told me it was hot in Ottawa. 28 degrees yesterday. He'd had his dinner on a patio in the Market. The fish was good, I would have liked it – just the right amount of lemon. I should sign the documents and return them via courier to ensure both our names were on the agreement. He wanted me to read everything first. If I had any questions, I should call him – even at work. He wanted this to move quickly.

PART TWO

1

JANE: 1940

WE DECIDED TO MARRY IN THE VILLAGE KIRK. STORIES end with marriage, but ours doesn't. It starts here instead. The young minister was surprised when we asked him.

'Won't you be married from home, then?'

'No,' Stanley said, though the question was clearly for me. 'We want to be married in the church we'll attend together. You'll know my mother, I think. Mrs Hambleton down near the bend in the road.'

'Yes, I've had the pleasure of a cup of tea. A kind woman, your mother. It's good that you and your wife will be living nearby. I hear that you have been called up?'

'Yes.'

'But that isn't why we're getting married,' I said, quickly.

'No, no, I didn't think so.' He looked at us with kindly eyes, and pencilled our names in his diary. 'April is a lovely month for weddings, I've always thought. You will need witnesses, too. Will that be arranged, or shall I convince my wife and a friend?'

'My mother will be with us, and Jane's parents as well,' said Stanley.

I smoothed my gloves between my hands, chocolate brown with two buttons.

'That's lovely, then. I will see you in time.' He stood and shook Stanley's hand, and I stuck mine out as well. 'Lovely to meet both of you. I'm sure you will enjoy the village, Jane. And Connie will be glad to have another young wife nearby. She's a grand one at putting together ladies' gatherings. You will have plenty of company here.'

'Thank you,' I said, and hoped my voice sounded warm.

At the house, Stanley's mother had prepared egg sandwiches, which Stanley carried out to the garden. We sat on kitchen chairs set on the grass with small plates balanced on our laps. I found that the top of my sandwich was spread with butter, which made my fingers and my mouth greasy, but there were no napkins to be seen so I pressed my lips together and hoped they weren't shiny. Stanley caught my eye and smiled.

'I should bring a table out,' he said. 'That would be nice, wouldn't it, Mother? A little table for our plates.'

'Oh, I don't know. We're fine like this, I should think. You might scratch the doorframe.'

'I think I could manage. Just the small table from the sitting room. I'll set the aspidistra on the floor by the fire, and have the table out here in no time. Careful as can be.'

'If you must, I suppose. But we really are fine like this, aren't we, Jane?' She sat with her feet firmly together in her husband's old Oxfords. She had told me they were too good for the cupboard. Quality calfskin with ventilated inner soles. The brown leather looked waxy, and she wore them with the laces tucked away inside. I wondered if she would wear them to the wedding. Not that it mattered. Of course it didn't.

I offered to brush her clothes for her, if she liked, when the time came. I could pop down to the house whenever it was convenient. 'I have a good new clothes brush. It works a charm and I'd like to help, if I could.'

'Oh dear, you must think I'm looking shabby. It is hard, you know. On my own and with my eyes. You will forgive me, hen, won't you?'

I reached out to take her hand, but she kept holding her plate, so I laid my fingers on her skirt instead. 'That wasn't what I meant, Mum. I only meant to offer a kindness.'

'Of course. Of course.'

'I'll be here, Jane,' Stanley said. 'I can help her get ready.'

'Yes,' she said. 'He can help me.'

'You will have enough to do. Your hair and your parents and everything.'

'I hope they come. My mother only said that she would try. I'm not sure what that might mean. We shall see, I suppose.'

'All will be well,' he said, smiling again.

'I suppose it will. And what will be, will be.'

I decided I would wear my mother's fox fur on my wedding day. Warm for April, perhaps, but it would look smart. I'd had an old jacket and skirt adjusted instead of a dress because they would be serviceable afterwards for Sundays. The Edinburgh dressmaker had been surprised at my choice, but did not push after I dropped a few references to my husband's training duties. When I stopped by my parents' flat to pick up the fur, Mum's lips were thin, and she looked tired. 'I might have brought all that down to you on the bus,' she said. 'How is that little house? Is it damp? You'll need paper to wrap up the fur, if there is a chance of damp.'

'It's lovely, Mum. Small, but you'll like it. I have been papering the drawers in the kitchen and the wardrobe is already seen to.'

She crossed her arms and held her elbows. 'Are you lonely? I'm not sure it's proper, living out there on your own for no particular reason.'

'There is a reason. We promised to occupy the house immediately. That was the condition of renting it. Only Stanley's mother shouldn't be alone, so he'll be with her for a few more weeks and I'll be in the rented house. She needs him.'

'And she won't need him after the wedding? Or will you still be living alone then?'

'Oh, Mother. Don't be awkward. I've told you: we'll be in the rented house until he goes and then I'll see if she'd like me closer or if she can manage on her own. Everything has been arranged.'

'I've been worrying about your degree, too. You're not going to leave it, are you?'

'No, of course not. I couldn't. I just need to see how Mrs Hambleton settles after Stanley goes. If she needs me, I'll stay and read out there. If not, I can come back to the city. I can find digs somewhere else if you're worried about the space.'

'No, no, don't be silly. There's always space here. This fuss must just be nerves. I've never had a married daughter before, you know.'

'I know. But, we'll be fine, won't we?'

The day before the wedding, Mother sent word that Father was not feeling well. Sadly, they would not be able to join us. Well, these things happen. Stanley suggested that maybe it was a long way out from Edinburgh, after all.

I got ready on my own at the rented house, looking in the rented mirror. Brushed and set my own hair, wiped my shoes clean. I'd forgotten about flowers, but that didn't matter. My coat was a smart one as well as serviceable, and I swung Mum's fox around my shoulders. There. All set and ready. The small green glass eyes glittered at me, bemusedly.

'Right then, chap. What do you say we swagger off to the church and find a husband to bring home? I think the two of us can land a looker, if anyone can.'

Stanley and his mother were to meet me there. I hoped that he would have mentioned about my parents to the Reverend Thomson so that we wouldn't have to go out into the street to find another witness. I was sure he would have. He was sensible. But when I got to the church, he stood alone by the door, looking worried.

'She isn't with you, then,' he said, in a resigned tone. The church door opened behind him, and the minister emerged. 'She's gone. She . . . she got ready early and she was sitting out in the garden when I had my bath. I assumed she'd come down here, but the minister hasn't seen her.'

He was walking towards us now, his dark robe catching in the wind. 'She's nowhere in the kirkyard. My wife is out looking along the paths,' he said.

'Shall I go and look at the rented house?' I asked. 'Maybe she's in the garden? She might have come for the clothes brush?'

'No, you stay here,' Stanley said. 'I'll look. And then I'll check again back home. Perhaps she's gone home again and is waiting at the house.' I held out my hand and he took it, giving my fingers a quick squeeze.

'She'll turn up, love. She can't be far.'

'You look lovely.' He met my eye, and I watched as he turned and walked away.

The minister cleared his throat. 'Is there anywhere she likes to walk? Somewhere she may have gone, perhaps to calm her nerves before the ceremony? She may have fallen somewhere and be in need of help.'

'She doesn't go walking,' I said. 'She's very much a stay-at-home lady.'

'I suspected so, but she will be somewhere. You and I can wait here until my wife returns, and then we'll have a think about the next best place to look.'

But thinking and looking did very little, as Stanley's mother did not appear. The minister knocked on doors and found others to help in the search. They wouldn't let me look; I could only sit and wait. The minister's wife, Connie, installed me in her sitting room. She couldn't have been much older than me, with black curly hair and skin as pale as milk. She asked me about the rented house and about wedding gifts. Then she made tea and stirred two spoonfuls of sugar into my cup without asking. Morale-boosting, I thought. She'll do this regularly. Maybe ministers get extra sugar rations.

I looked at the photographs on the piano, each one placed on a lace doily.

Much later, Stanley came into the room and he, too, was handed a cup of sweet tea. The minister gathered a few more men, and Stanley told them everything he could think of that might be useful.

'She was wearing her good clothes,' he said. 'A bead necklace, too, and . . . and her hat. A grey hat. With a green band. She'd washed her face this morning, there were towels on the rail and she looked all clean and ready.'

'We'll find her, lad. We'll keep looking and we will.'

The sky was high and cloudless, and the sun lingered into a long, warm evening, the kind of evening for garden parties and cool wine, music on the lawn. My skirt was creased with sitting. I took the fox off and placed him on the tea table, my shoulders light and damp under my blouse.

It was almost dusk when they found her in the woods east of the village. Someone had seen her on the road nearby in the afternoon, but the searchers hadn't looked over the wall or into the woods until the light was beginning to fade. Among the trees, old stones sat moss-covered, marking the foundations of a medieval priory. There was a strange pond in those eerie woods, bright with green algae, and the searchers worried about its depth, but the algae on the surface was undisturbed. They found Stanley's mother sitting on the ground with her back to a skeleton tree and a skein of yarn on her lap. She held a single knitting needle between her fingers and wound the yarn around it again and again, mindlessly. That was how it was described to me and, yes, that was the right word. Her mind had slipped away, and it did not return. Later, in the manse sitting room, I saw her soiled dress, her hands still clutching the muddy yarn, her tired smile, but it was her vague gaze that would haunt me. Connie wrapped her in a bright shawl and more tea was made, poured out into good cups, drunk quietly while the mantel clock ticked on. Before the searchers could leave, Stanley asked the minister to marry us.

'Another day, surely. That would be best. You will all want to get home and rest.'

'If we wait another day, Jane will return home alone. I do not want that for her. Today has been enough.'

'She could stay here,' Connie suggested. 'I have sheets on the spare-room bed. It would be no trouble at all.'

'Thank you,' I said. Stanley gripped my hand, and I looked up into his face, worn and weary. 'Thank you, but no. I think Stanley is right. We should be married now. Here, perhaps. We don't need to go into the church.'

'Very well, then,' the minister answered, blinking. 'Let me get my book. And wash my hands. I will only be a moment. If this is what you wish.'

Stanley nodded and squeezed my hand again. Some of the searchers agreed to stay to serve as witnesses, and Connie went out to the garden to fetch some flowers. She came back with cuttings from the horse chestnut tree.

'So you'll have something to hold. The daffodils looked past it, but aren't these lovely and green with the candles just starting. Let me settle that fur for you. He is a lovely one, isn't he? Just perfect with your complexion. Wonderful. Don't you look the bride now? Would you like to step into the hallway so that you can enter?'

'I shouldn't think that's necessary,' I said. 'Seems a bit silly to leave only to return again. Let's just stay together.'

Stanley's sister arrived from Stirling a week after the wedding. We had sent her word about her mother's health, but she arrived on the arranged day all the same. Her name was Violet and she did not want my help. Such a delicate name, I thought, as I watched her rough hands sort through her mother's clothing.

'She will be safe with me,' she said. She folded skirts and placed them in the suitcase. 'We won't be staying long in this house – I've arranged for a cottage further north. I don't expect to be in touch, but I will send a note at New Year's to let you know how we are.'

'Thank you.'

'I'll write from the south,' Stanley said. 'As I can.'

'Naturally,' said Violet. 'As you can.'

There were planes over Glasgow a few days later – in broad daylight, too – though little damage, which was a relief.

'They must have passed right over the village. Can't think why we didn't see them,' Stanley said, winking at me.

We read about them in the newspaper as we drank tea in our garden. The Germans were getting bold, which was why Churchill needed more pilots. Stanley was scheduled to leave at the end of May. Until then, we spent every moment together, talking, touching, lying in bed laughing, and working in the garden in the bright spring sun.

'It will be just like school, won't it? All this training to go through,' he said, standing with his hands on his hips, looking down at the soil. I was on my knees beside the onions, weeding out the thistles. 'It will be exercise and games and all boys together.'

'Sounds dreadful,' I said, brushing my forehead with my arm.

'Yes, but that's war. We don't get to choose. I'll be fine.'

'I know.' I pulled off my gloves and sat back on my heels. 'What can you take with you? How many books can you fit in a duffel bag? Do you have a packing list? And where do you get a uniform?'

'Your mother might recommend Jenners, but I suspect the army will provide. That will be interesting. I've never been anywhere where they give you clothing before. All dressed alike – I'll lose myself in the crowd.'

'Like a school of fish.'

'A shoal of herring.'

'How will I choose when you all march home?'

'Just pick the handsome one. That will be me.'

'Always.'

'And forever, my love. And forever.'

That evening, we walked out to the ancient priory. A giant tree lay shattered among the ruins, its complicated roots heaved into the air, still clutching handfuls of earth and the broken shells of oysters. Stanley said that medieval builders mixed shells with mortar to give it strength. Beneath our feet, more ancient stones lay broken. Most of the building had long since fallen away, but one low arch remained, sheltering a large stone coffin. The coffin was cracked and broken, a dark emptiness exposed inside, and the carved knight on top was time-worn, his features erased, the stone surface coined with lichen. I traced the shape of his face with my fingers.

Then Stanley took my hand and kissed my mouth.

Beyond everything else, the vows we made in the manse, the ring, even my pleasure in the dark, beyond it all, that was the moment our marriage started. His lips were dry, his mouth open as if in speech. Or as if he would drink from me and be filled. And we would fill each other. Everything begins from there.

2

I MIGHT START WITH MARRIAGE, BUT STANLEY WOULD begin with stone. Ancient Archaean gneiss, limestone muds and Hutton's unconformity. Places where the rock was laid bare and the age of the earth could be seen. Then he would list the eras. Ordovician, Silurian, Devonian. Storms that lasted for millennia. Landmasses emerging, shaped by mud and sand, pulling and gathering oceans. Layers in rock grew like tree rings. Wide alluvial plains stretched. All these first facts Stanley taught me in the cool evening air, his mouth on my neck, whispering, the hollow of my throat filled with the names of ancient lands. Laurentia who would be Scotland. Avalonia, her southern suitor. They pulled apart four hundred million years ago, then crashed together again, a compelling marriage. Folding, faulting, uplifting, eroding. Inland sand dunes, the building of hills.

Perhaps foundations are important, too.

When we first met, I was standing on a ladder, counting boxes of powdered milk. There had been a recipe in the newspaper for rice pudding that used powdered milk and the Marchmont mothers were all coming by to pick up a box. I'd spent the morning repeatedly shuffling stock to the front of the shelf to make it look full. When Stanley came into the shop, I was up the ladder again and I'd taken him for an undergraduate, standing there with a book under his arm. Thin, clever, looking like someone who thought too much. He smiled as he called up to me, a great wide grin that made me worry my hem was caught up in my knickers.

'I'm looking for chocolate,' he said. 'An Aero, if you have them.'

'Flakes are better. You'll find them over there,' I said. 'By the counter.'

He gave Mrs Kerr the money and put the chocolate in his jacket pocket. On his way out, he stopped again by my ladder. 'I'll have to remember,' he said. 'This is a good place to buy chocolate. The shop with Fry's on the window.' Then he smiled at me and I smiled, too, but Mrs Kerr laughed when the door closed behind him.

'He'll remember all right, I believe. But he'll also find that every third shop around here says Fry's on the window. And it was a Rowntree's bar he was looking for. Young men!'

The second time I saw him, I was crossing Bristo Square. The evening air was cool and I hurried home, heading south to the Meadows. Funny how quickly you can recognize someone. The shape of his shoulders, the length of his stride. A wind blew up suddenly towards me across the square, tossing his hat into the air, taking it up and out of reach, then dropping it down at my feet and playing instead with the folds of my skirt like a cat. I picked up the hat and held it in my hands as he walked towards me, grinning.

'It's the chocolate girl again. What a lucky wind to blow us together like this.'

'Is it?'

'Absolutely. Now I don't need to pop back to the shop for another bar of chocolate. I can save my pennies and ask you directly if you'd like to come out to the films.'

'That's a funny way to put it.'

'Maybe . . . maybe I'm a funny fellow. Do you like Laurel and Hardy?' He stuttered a little, the words coming out nervous and uneven which made me smile.

'Well, I don't know,' I said. 'It's a bit sudden. I'm not sure I even know your name yet.'

'It's Stanley.'

'Like Laurel.'

'I hardy know him. I'd . . . I'd like to know you, though.' He grinned awkwardly, standing as tall as me, and his teeth were squint but the lines around his mouth handsome.

'You're a funny man, then.'

He laughed and took his hat from my hands. 'Only when I'm nervous. Ach, I'm sorry. I'm not used to this.'

'Me neither. Funny men don't usually make passes.'

He told me he was a geology lecturer at the university, and I told him I read Literature.

'Well, that's a relief. I was worried you were in medicine and would think I was entirely too frivolous to pass the time of day with.'

'Poetry is serious.'

'No, no, of course. I don't mean to offend. Not a jot. I've just had a recent run-in with a chap from medicine and came out rather wanting. Geology is a wee bit hard to defend in terms of its contribution to the common good. I worried that my feeble reputation might have gone before me and scuppered my chances with you.'

'And Laurel and Hardy wouldn't? I wonder if serious men have good taste in films.'

'Likely no. But I like a good laugh. It's good for your heart. Like poetry, I'm sure. Highly salutary.'

So I went along to the film. All up lifts, down ladders, dropping boxes, lighting pipes. It was ridiculous, all this falling about and confusion, all this absolute inanity and the fat and the thin of it. And I laughed. Stanley clapped his hands and doubled over laughing.

Afterwards, he walked me home slowly past the big houses in Morningside and tried to explain why geology.

'Because,' he said, 'a perfect day is spent somewhere outside picking up pebbles. How can you do better than that? Spend the whole day wandering, just letting your eye rove around. You never know what you might find. It's terrific! You should come sometime. If you like.'

'Perhaps. I don't know much about stones.'

'Well, Edinburgh is a . . . a nice teacher.' He always seemed to speak with a twinkle in his eye.

'I'm not sure what you're suggesting.'

'Only a terrible old pun, I'm afraid. A failing of mine to mention it, not yours to miss. Geologists. Really – you should keep away. But *nice* sounds like gneiss. It's . . . it's a metamorphic rock. A lovely layered thing.'

'Changed from one thing into another,' I said.

'That's it. Like me – from interesting to rather pathetic in an instant.'

I laughed and he shrugged a little, and smiled, too.

'But I meant it,' he said. 'Edinburgh is rich in good rocks. Volcanic substructures and plenty of interesting layers.' He told me about the black basalt under the castle, the layers of cooled lava and ash on Arthur's Seat, and the thin stony soil near the Crags where the gorse grows thick. A well-built city, he said. Slow and evolving. Geology takes time. Stone builds slowly.

So does poetry, I told him. It, too, needs to be sequential. You can't take it all in at a glance.

'I suppose you can't. I like that. Poetry like lines of sediment.'

'Do you read poetry?' I asked.

'Some. The Greeks at school. And Lawrence. I like him.'

'I like him, too.'

'See? We'll get on swimmingly then. You and me.'

Mrs Kerr was impressed when she heard he was teaching at the university. 'A university man. Well done, Jane. And out at the new King's Buildings, too. Very smart. It must be that red hair that gets you a dashing modern man.'

* * *

A grey day and we climbed the city's hills to see the shape of the land. Stanley told me how the Forth was a fjord, a sea estuary scraped out when the glaciers retreated ten thousand years ago. The Romans called it *Bodotria* and to the Norse, it was the *Myrkvifiord*. He talked of slow erosion and volcanic geology. Time, deep and slow, and all the interruptions. He said the Salisbury Crags were formed from steep dolerite and columnar basalt and they used to be sharper until the Victorians quarried them and sold the stone to London to pave the streets. A sudden change in the city's shape.

Stanley spent his days lecturing and his evenings at the art college, watching Alexander Carrick carve Scottish stone. For the past decade, the artist had planted memorials for the Great War up and down the country. He had no classical education, no credentials as a gentleman modeller, just a deep knowledge of Scottish stone. To the students in his evening classes, Carrick preached on his preference for freestone from the Cheviot Hills – fine-grained, soft enough to chisel cleanly, but as durable as standing stones. It would take the weather, he said.

Stanley sat on the hard art school benches, listening to the song of Carrick's stories. The sculptor had been a soldier in the Great War, and served and sketched in Belgium, just north of Ypres. He told of a day when a shell exploded prematurely in his own battery. He'd been untouched by the shrapnel, but something broke, the chisel slipped and he could not continue. The higher-ups refused to stick him in the military hospital to recover his wits, what with epidemics sweeping through and so many of the bleeding needing beds. Instead, they left him in the house of an old Belgian woman and she just let him sleep for days on end, time fallen away and the guns always booming in the distance like breakers on the shore. Stanley was touched by the story and tried to tell me why. But all these conversations were eras ago. And then there was love.

At first, a swooping, flying fear inside. Needing to know what he was thinking, where he was in the city and when he'd come to see me again.

What was love? New, of course. Yet hadn't love come before? Who can ever say it hasn't? So yes, I suppose, when I was younger. Love or something like it. How's that for an answer? There was a boy in my class, Donald, whose fingernails were always nice and his knees were bony and strong and he was the fastest runner by far. One day after school, he held my hand, which was embarrassing and nice and I thought I liked him. Then another day, I knew all at once that I needed him. Couldn't breathe without him. My heart, oh what does a heart do? Thump? Ache? Gallop? Words were rubbish and hearts were just a handful of muscle, clenched, unclenching, but I needed him. For four years, I was certain. It wasn't unrequited. We held hands, on and off, throughout high school, and even risked kisses, but we were always good. Almost good. I was lucky. A lot of girls didn't get to stay around for high school, or at least not all of it. Some girls made mistakes. A lot of families needed their girls to work. My friend Jeanie had to leave. We'd been close. Jeanie and Jane – and she looked like me, too. Some people even asked if we were sisters. Idiots. She left at fourteen. Hoped to find work in a shop or at least something clean. She said to me, on the last day she was in school, that I was lucky. To get to study, I knew that's what she meant, but also to stay with the boys. She looked at Donald as she said it, all swoony. That's when it stopped for me. Like an unwound watch. Flat stopped, out of love. Donald was just another long-faced boy in the hallway. I didn't need him any more. Relief. A little grief. A small pause and oh, Donald, I hope Jean did chase you and catch you up. Everyone needs something like love.

Because after needing comes want. And want is stronger. I can be stronger wanting. Want is hunger and hunger must be fed. Hunger is the openness that makes you strong. That's what I have learned since things started with Stanley. How hunger works and how strength lies across the fault.

Carrick didn't come to Aberlady. Stanley said the village decided to save money and use the old memorial – the one they had paid for after the Boer War. Sensible, he said. There was still space, and women came regularly to leave flowers. And, of course, there were two blank sides yet.

Stanley left for war on a Tuesday at the end of May. The paper said there would be rain soon. He would take the train from Haddington, heading south.

He held both my hands and looked into my face.

'Don't make this harder than it is,' I said. I didn't need last words at the doorstep, or worse, by the kirk where everyone gathered to say goodbye.

In the evening, when the lights went out in the village and all the way down the coast and the sky turned charcoal black, I disappeared, too. The door closed on its own, the rented house beyond it changed. The walls were rough, the floor unsettled as I walked invisible, without pattern or pride, indistinguishable from everything else. The windows were blind and there was nowhere to look, no stars to see.

After love, I am not ready for loneliness.

3

LYING IN BED ALONE, I LISTEN FOR THE SOUND OF THE waves. I wait for the roar in every silence, holding my breath, willing my heart to hush, but I am never sure. Maybe the house is too far from the water. A hundred years ago, ships sailed right up to the village, and rested at low tide on the soft clay bottom by the burn, safely unloading their cargo of cotton, coal and timber for Haddington. Practical wealth for town living. Even Aberlady had its weavers then, and five alehouses – a surplus, the minister believed. It is quieter now. The bay has silted up, and the shore lies out across a meadow, far beyond the kirk.

I'd read the local history in one of Mrs Hambleton's books. Before he left, Stanley had moved a box over to the rental house, full of village memoir and history. Celts and Saxon stories. Coastal plant life, wild flowers and pebble identification.

'In case you get tired of your school books,' he said.

'Good students push through.'

'Well, you might consider these the invigorating cups of tea that I won't be able to bring you over the next spell. How's that, then?'

Stanley has been away two months already, and this doesn't feel like home. I stay up late reading and listening for the sea. The sea is familiar, though the village isn't. My mother used to bring us here, just a little further along the coast, for two weeks each July. We'd come by bus, all together, bouncing about like peas in the pan, she said. We took the same cottage each year. My father stayed in town, away from the sand and the cottages, but we came every summer, even the grey ones. This is the weather I know and the summer seas. *Mackerel sky, mackerel sky. Never long wet and never long dry.* And always the cottage and a cup of tea to warm you up again. Dust the sand from your hair, stomp your feet outside the door, properly now, then come in and warm up by the stove.

In August, we'd go home again to Edinburgh and the full flat, the air always starched with the waft of boiling tatties, and us folded back into school clothes. My mother rolled her sleeves down, straightened her skirt and joined the ladies from the kirk for tea and missionary projects, respectable and proper, her hair pinned in place.

When I met Stanley's mother last year, I wondered if I should mention our summers in the cottages. I didn't know what the local people thought about us, traipsing out from the city to walk barefoot on the sand. Stanley said she might be interested, but I stayed mum. We ate a quiet luncheon in the kitchen, spring sunlight flooding in across the floor, and the glass water jug casting a bright reflection on the cream tablecloth. While his mother turned to refill the teapot, Stanley set his hand on my knee, warm, so warm, the kettle whistling, his mother in profile smiling by the stove, the plate of bread and butter white white white. After lunch, she wouldn't hear of help to clear the things away, no she wouldn't and the day was so fresh we'd best make use of it, so out we went into the wind and down to the sea.

'Watch for Jova, will you?' she said. 'Might catch a glimpse on a bright day like today.'

'We'll keep our eyes open, Mum. Shall I give him your love?'

'Wheesht, you,' she said, kissing his cheek. She reached out and squeezed my hand. 'Just enjoy the light. It's a good day for a walk. Clear the cobwebs away.'

Along the road, the trees were tall, their wind-bent branches sketched against the startling sky. When Stanley and I crossed the bridge, the water was high. Troll-drowning weather, he called it, and said there were times when the bridge itself was covered, only the handrails sticking up. More than once, he'd splashed across it with the waves coming in.

Stanley led me down the path, past the Marl Loch and out across the plain where the grey-green grass and the buckthorns grew. The larks flew up before us, singing high above our heads in the bright air.

'Why do they do that?' Stanley said. 'You only ever hear them singing in flight, don't you? Do you think the ground muffles their song?'

'Trying to distract us, I think. Lead us away from their precious nests.'

'Maybe. But they fly straight up, don't they? Never even a pace away from where they begin. Not very clever. Maybe they're used to fooling the angels.'

'So that's your mother's Jova then?' I asked. 'An angel?' I held out my hands to Stanley, the larks only pinpricks now above us.

He laughed. 'No. He's just a story she grew up with. And her mother before her, too. Must be a scrap of truth somewhere like as not, but it's hard to tell. Story goes that there was a hermit named Jehovah Grey who lived out here along the shore. Or he might have been Joseph or Jock. Or Jova or Jovey, as the storyteller likes. They say he kept an eagle in a cage. I can't think why. You don't see many eagles out here. Maybe it was blown off course or injured. Or maybe he was lonely.'

'You wouldn't put an eagle in a cage for company.'

'Company is hardly what you're after if you choose to live out here. No one ever walks out here. Most just call it the Point and keep to the streets in the village. Those over in Gullane don't even know it's here. But some in Aberlady still call it Jovey's Neuk.'

That afternoon, we found the outline of his cottage, when the slanting afternoon sun cast long shadows across the grass. We could just make out the limits of its two small rooms. One for him and one for his cow, Stanley said.

'See? It's the mushrooms. Continually prolific wherever there's been dung.'

'You're telling tales.'

'No, it's true. You think mushrooms would grow out here in the sand and wind elsewise? I tell you: cow.'

I found a flight feather from a goose – charcoal grey and tapered – and I handed it to Stanley.

'Remarkable,' he said, and winked. 'The Celts were fond of geese. Did you know that? Carved them all over the place, they did. Excellent artistry.'

'You have anything else to teach me, then?'

He laughed and took a notebook out of his pocket to slip the feather in.

Down at beach level, Stanley showed me Jovey's well. More proof to the story, he said. It was a piped stream with an iron spout that poured out in a small pool on the shingle. He cupped his hands, the water clear, offered. I shrugged, and he said it was sweet.

'The only fresh water you'll find along this stretch of coast. It's been a relief on a hot afternoon a hundred times. I wouldn't fool you, you know.' The corners of his eyes creased softly as he spoke, and I smiled. 'It's cold as January, mind, but deliciously fresh.'

I bent my head, my chin touching his palms as I drank. 'It's lovely.'

'Yes.' With a wet finger, he traced my jawline, the indent under my ear.

After we married, we crossed the bridge every day and walked the shore together. It was our own world, a little lonely and weatherworn, neglected now, perhaps. When Stanley's parents had been courting, things were different. Lively, even. There were tennis courts out there and open golf courses. The young people used to come here from Aberlady and Gullane; further afield, too. In the winter, they curled on a flooded pond beside the Marl Loch. Hard to believe now. There was nothing here but rabbits, wild flowers, long grass and the ruins of the clubhouse scoured by the sandy wind. A rickle of stones, Stanley said, and I told him this was better than all the jolly tennis courts in Scotland.

We spent our days among the grasses and the flowers and he picked armfuls of meadowsweet. Loved by Queen Elizabeth, it was, and lovely still, all tall, dark stems and dainty cloudy clusters. She had it strewn on her floors and all who loved her called it Queen-of-the-Meadow. In Stanley's hands, the flowers smelled of honey. I picked blueweed, its thick stalks rough, but its colour so like the sky, each flower an open throat. He told me blueweed is also viper's bugloss. From the Greek for ox tongue, the leaves rough as flesh.

We invented new names for the flowers around us. Gingerleaf. Dawnwort. Crimson Karst Creeper. Stanley told me about karst landscapes, how limestone dissolved into underground channels, sinkholes and caves. 'We'll visit Canada,' he said, 'and see the limestone by the Great Lakes. There are caves there with stalactites that grow four inches every thousand years.'

I said that sounded like poetry – a millennium to span a child's hand.

'Or two thumbs touching,' he said. Those were days for nonsense and poems, stories and stones and touching. Sitting on the shingle with the dunes behind us, I laughed as he wove stories of smugglers hiding in the old ironstone mines nearby. All their hidden loot long gone, still sought, and today just a song to sing in the wind. *Tea, brandy, gin and aniseed. French salt. Currants and figs, sugar candy, coffee, chocolate, Dutch cotton, Indian hand-kerchiefs, gunpowder, snuff.*

Another afternoon and we walked under grey skies with the city smudged from the horizon, only the sea before us. I wondered if the storm would blow inland, but Stanley thought it would stay out at sea.

'It's further away than it feels,' he said. I shivered, and he wrapped an arm around me. Rollers broke at the mouth of the bay, showing white over the distant sandbar. There were white gannets, too, out at sea, white against the waves, their long beaks like spears, their heads yellowed like the grass. They don't often come up as far as Aberlady, but there were hundreds of them that day, circling high, then with a plummeting crash, diving into the sea, hunting fish.

Then he told me the story of Sandy Gibb, who rambled this coast a century before. Maybe more. So many stories carry no dates. 'Poor man believed he was made of glass. Rather precarious in the wind, don't you think? But they say he loved to walk the shoreline. The trouble was, he would get stuck. Suddenly stopped stock-still by the fear of shattering. He would wait until someone came along, then call out, always the same thing: "I'll thank you for a shunt, sir." The locals understood and they'd give him a gentle push to start up again. Then, he'd go on his way.'

And what else did I tell him on those windy afternoons? That I loved him. That all this would remain – the sand, the shore –

and he would return. That there would be time for stories, for children. I never said enough, I'm sure of that.

The bridge feels longer when I cross it alone. Stanley and I counted the steps – when? Two hundred days ago. Two hundred paces. It is only one yard wide, so we never managed to walk side by side, though we did try.

The dog-leg in the middle of the bridge makes me smile. Crooked as the Aberlady high street, which feels as if the builders failed to agree, but Stanley said that the bend on the bridge was meant to counter the action of the waves.

I take the path to the left so that I might walk close to the sea. There are ducks on the Marl Loch, and a light breeze stirs the surface until it shines like fish scales. I've brought one of Mrs Hambleton's books with me and there is an old map printed there. The footbridge is marked and the Marl Loch, which looks longer on paper. There are rabbit warrens, and old fences marked too, old quarries and standing stones. Celtic, perhaps. Stanley hadn't mentioned those; I could try to find them and send sketches in my next letter. The books said stone pillars like these represented a link between heaven and earth. I wonder what Jehovah Grey would make of that. On the map, the Point is labelled Jophie's Neuk, so there's another telling of that story, too.

Down at the beach, the tide has pulled away, the saltings stretching wide before me and the sands are silver with light. Some beaches are good for seashells. If the currents are kind and strong in the right places, they are carried up unbroken to the sand. Here, you only find small shells and fragments. Broken mussels, razor clams and periwinkles. On a very lucky day, you might find cowries, white as teeth, small as children's fingernails.

I scan the beach for driftwood and sea coal, which would make a nice change from having to buy. The papers said that they are drafting Welsh boys to the coalfields now that the French and Belgian mines are gone. I wonder if they might do that over in Fife, too. A funny way to spend the war, though underground might be as good as up in an aeroplane, or better. Safer. And you could go home for tea. I wish Stanley could.

Out on the Forth, a few large ships sit heavy in the water. Regular visitors now, patrolling the coast to keep the bridge and Grangemouth safe. Even the ocean is crowded and almost as bad as Haddington's streets or North Berwick. Nothing solitary left. Everything is being done to keep us safe.

A crowd of rooks flies out over the waves, their wings shadowed and level against the level sea. More stand together on the sand, pacing and picking through the seaweed that lies stretched and drying in the sun. They look solemn in black robes, but their over-long beaks give them a funny dignity, not quite grim as they turn the seaweed over, looking for the soft bodies of stranded fish.

Beyond the wrack, a white stone sits on the sand, as round as a fist, and I think it might look rather nice on the window sill. Pleasing. As I step closer, I see that it isn't a stone at all, but a teacup. A perfect, unchipped teacup sitting impossible among the broken seashells, a blue Cunard stamp on the side. A crowned lion holding the globe. How strange to think of passenger ships in these military days. How long was the teacup out at sea? Or has it been buried here in the sand and only just surfaced? The glaze is not sanded or grit-roughened, but smooth to the touch, and it fits neatly into my cardigan pocket. I'll take it home and wash it out, rinsing away the sand and the salt, and set it on the shelf, one cup mismatched, saucerless.

Further around the shore, the ground is muddy, and my shoes grow heavy before I make it as far as Jovey's Neuk. I wonder about walking barefoot, but instead, I turn inland to walk through the dune hills.

Then I spot the soldiers. Their lorries are parked on the flat land between the hawthorn trees and a tall machine crawls across the grass on caterpillar treads. The soldiers stand with shovels and binoculars. Two of them notice me and the taller one waves to get my attention, his pale hair like the grass. I wave back, keep walking, and they must pick up their pace because they are beside me faster than I anticipate, stopping in front of me so I stop, too.

'You can't go on. You'll have to go back, miss,' the taller one says. He speaks with an accent and I wonder where he was born.

'I hadn't realized the coast was closed.'

'You could put it that way.'

The other man speaks with a deeper, local voice, an older, slower manner that isn't used to contradiction.

'We will be mining this coastline. It won't be safe for civilians to walk here henceforth. Defences, you understand.'

'Oh,' I say. 'That is unfortunate. It's a pleasant walk.' Ahead, the shoreline looks churned up, muddy and dangerous.

'Don't you worry. There aren't any mines in yet.'

'You will need to stop here, however,' the fair-haired soldier says.

'Stop?' I say. 'I'm not sure I understand what you mean.'

'Turn around or head inland.'

'Ah, yes. I see.'

'Public safety. Not a place now for civilians. Would you like to be shown the way?'

'No, no. I am perfectly all right on my own.' I stride out with straight shoulders and don't give them time to disagree. One of them coughs and I imagine a comment, and I don't turn to grace either of them with a look. Courtesy, even here.

That night, there is an air raid. The warden comes along the street with his whistle, a siren cutting the sky. Through the wall, I hear Miss Baxter's chair scrape and the cupboard door bangs closed. I collect my gas mask from the hallway, a folded cardigan, my framed wedding photo. Then every door on the street opens and out we all go, methodical rabbits emerging in the dark, hunch-shouldered whatever the weather and scuttling to the shelter in the yard at the end of the row. It is set back from the houses, a simple corrugated steel hut, dug away into the ground in among the gardens, covered with a thick layer of soil and turf.

Miss Baxter has trouble closing her front door, so I pause and help her along, the two of us the last through the door of the shelter. If the houses had all been occupied or the men home, there never would have been space for us all in the shelter, but as it is, we fill the benches, sitting squeezed together and listening to the planes and the siren. Beside me, Miss Baxter holds a hand-kerchief between her fingers, and she speaks into my ear, her breath warm and worried in the dark. 'Maybe I should go away.

165

My sister might have space. She lives out past Dumfries. It's the other sea there, you know. Not that it will be any the safer there, mind. Though perhaps I can help. Her grandchildren are there from Glasgow, and rations might stretch further when we group together.' She pats my hand, kindly enough, the handkerchief damp against my skin. She says she would return, in the spring, or after Hogmanay, depending on the weather and the war.

She said all this, just the same way, last week during the last raid. We sit in the shelter and wait for the all-clear. I close my eyes, imagining onions and potatoes growing in the gardens behind the row. Maybe it is the cool, dank air, or the smell of the earth. They fill my mind, their hidden skins and whiskery roots loosely gripping the soil, their flesh white and waxy under the earth, vulnerable.

When the world ends, I do not want to be huddled in a garden shelter, waiting to breathe brick-dust, or the slosh of spilled life around me. I want to be out in the wind. Where the birds catch and hold the air currents above the water. I want that space between the mud and the sky as my own. It is only hope that keeps them apart, isn't it? Only blind, ignorant hope. But most days, it works.

4

Dear Stanley,

We must be on the same wavelength, don't you think? Me about to send you poems and you already writing that you've got your mitts on some Lawrence. It would be interesting to hear just how an American edition ended up at Padgate. The tides wash in all sorts, even down south in military old England.

I thought poetry might be a good distraction for you, and Lawrence isn't rocks, he's earthy, so it seemed the logical choice. (Yes, I also remember you mentioned him, so there.) And yes, of course, my dear I hear why that passage spoke to you. <u>Direct</u>

167

utterance from the instant and the soul and the mind and the *body singing at once* – *that's you through and through. That's how we all should be and so few, so very few of us are; still, you are, my dear, sweet husband. I wonder how long that word will sound strange.* Husband. *Such an old-fashioned word, all cultivating and tilling the soil, but fitting and perhaps that's because you look after me well. And I, you, I hope, even at a distance. My love is strong and will enfold you. Oh goodness, why do all these words look so trite when I write them down? I am not becoming a sap in your absence. Nor a frustrated poet. I promise you that. Maybe it is just that I do so little talking alone in the house that I'm forgetting how to put words in a natural order.*

But now that you have a copy of the poems, I can save a few more pennies and keep my edition here at home. Look at that, a thrifty-housewife thought. There will be salvation after all.

Since your last letter, I've been rereading Lawrence myself and finding it such fitting stuff for this windswept place. The wild common is here, isn't it? The rabbits like handfuls of brown earth, and all the gorse, too. I love how Lawrence compares them to flame. Of course they are. How could they be anything but flame, now that he's given us the image. And then in the ending with all that is right, all that is good, all that is God takes substance. *It is such a happy accident that* God *and* good *sound so much the same in English, a fact that must have led a great many into prayer. Everyone rejoices in the good, and it could be there is gospel in that.*

With no book to include and no more poetic or theological thoughts, I can only send these poor words and all my love and more. Think of me tonight and always and know you are loved.

Your

Jane

Sometimes, I finish a letter and I can't hear myself in it at all. As though someone else has written it and it couldn't possibly be fair to Stanley to post it. How can we be connecting if I can't set my own words on the paper, just silly well-behaved, expected ones? Looking back over it, I might sound sweeter than I am, more literate – or trying to be. It isn't me.

I would like to speak with him about the other poems, the ones that haunt me. The young wife and the grey-haired mother and damn it, Lawrence found words for all that and if Stanley were here, we could talk about it all and find a way through. It is only ever the talking that helps. Nothing else is spontaneous enough. No, that's false. Touch helps when the talking is there, too. If it wasn't, touch could never be enough. What would it be? Indulgent? Mute. Perhaps whatever it is that the minister calls sin. I wonder if he and Connie can talk things through properly. The doilies make me doubt it, but I shouldn't judge. My mum has given me doilies, too. Ancient family things the aunts passed her way, packed between sheets of tissue paper like old leaves, their colour bleached away, their skeletons preserved as lace.

Doilies be damned. Stanley should have stayed at home.

We didn't ever try to concoct a reason or an excuse to keep him here, even a little bit longer. Surely, his mother might have been that reason, but he spoke of duty. Duty be damned, too. There's murder in it all, and I can't see anything properly. The haar has been rolling in from the sea these days, death-white and wet. It hides the laneway behind the house, the trees by the kirk and all along the road and all the fields will be filled with white and the streets feel cluttered with fear. East Lothian seems to be filling up with fog and foreign men. So many troops here these days and always more Allied aeroplanes overhead. Hurricanes and Spitfires, dreadful names all. Even the Mosquitoes are unpleasant. And every day, more news on the wireless to listen to all alone.

That's not quite true, is it? It's hard to be alone with Miss Baxter through the wall. I listen to her cough. My mother worried about the *other noises* coming through the paper-thin walls but it's not the involuntaries that concern me. It is the deliberate, subtle, mid-afternoon throat clearing. The thought. The pause. The second cough. Enough to get me on my feet whatever the weather and beat it outdoors. Which is better than staying at home and worrying.

I put on my cardigan, and tie a scarf neatly around my hair. I should do the neighbourly thing and go round to see Miss Baxter, but then I remember Connie mentioned afternoon tea in the manse. 'Just a wee gathering for the ladies. Better than knitting at home, perhaps.' She said to bring along whatever I was working on, then sensed the thin pause before I nodded, and kindly mentioned that there would be needles and service woollies patterns there, too, with suitable victory wool. 'It will be mainly mothers and widows, I'm afraid. Don't worry, though. They'll like you. They keep a friendly eye open for young wives.'

That was the hat to wear, of course. Young wife. How strange. From grand passion, all hands and mouths in secret, however much we tried to be good, and all that longing for even our fingers to touch, but didn't I long for more? And didn't we teach each other? Everything. And now, to be a wife. Sitting in a well-behaved circle of mothers and widows. Knitting damned socks.

I don't know if Stanley would laugh or weep to see me.

At the manse, I can't fathom why they painted the parlour green. The ladies' faces catch the colour like a smell. It is all rather grim, but I smile and make an effort. Connie looks so young and well tucked in, her yellow housedress crisp, the skirt sensibly calf length and her shoes polished. Square toes for youthful swagger, as the papers say. 'If you like, you can sit beside me and I'll get you started.' Tact, thy name is manse-wife. I smile again thankfully.

When I step into the parlour, they are sitting in a circle, which makes it sound communal, so perhaps it is better to say they sit around the room. On chairs, some soft, some not, and on the two chesterfields with their pale scatter cushions, their backs smartly buttoned. Mrs Scott is talking about her sons now, her brave and bonny boys, and she reassures us that Douglas would look after wee Johnnie, that it's right for them to be together. The grey sock she is knitting hangs stiffly from her needles, with threatening, even stitches. Connie starts me off with a ribbed scarf pattern that I can just about manage. Plain three, purl one, over and over and over again.

'It thickens it a bit to add the purls in. And after a few rows, the pattern will emerge nicely and keep you on track.' She is working on a child's vest, and I ask her if she is expecting, but she blushes and explains about the orphan packages the Red Cross requested.

'Did you see the photograph in the paper of Her Majesty knitting?' Mrs Gilmour asks. 'Sitting outside, too, in the sunshine with Elizabeth and Margaret Rose, all knitting for the troops. So good to see. It warmed my heart.'

There is a knock on the door so Connie sets her knitting down and excuses herself. 'It will be Muriel, I should think,' she says. 'She mentioned she might drop in.'

'Aye, Muriel,' Mrs Scott echoes. Her hands are red and dried like pigeon's feet, I think, which isn't kind but true. Would details like that work in letters to Stanley? Or would he wish me to be more graceful, more charming? How did he want to remember me now when he was so far away?

A girl as tall as me strides into the room, wearing a grey tweed skirt and a white shirt with dusty sleeves, looking too warm for the weather. The ladies smile and nod, mostly. She isn't a pretty girl, but not quite plain either. Her hair is cropped blunt-straight at her jaw, her oval face long and lean. Her grey eyes sit spaced a little wider than most, which gives her a feline look. Not a house cat, soft and aloof. No, Muriel is alive in the ordered room. She sits down beside me on the chesterfield and I feel too far from Edinburgh, stiffly brushed up and lonely with these village ladies who all know each other. The ladies don't seem to mind that Muriel looks out of place. Instead, they treat her like a returning hero, or at least a favourite pet.

'Now, Muriel my dear,' Mrs Scott says, with bright charm. 'How is your garden faring? You've had plenty of sunshine lately.'

'It's looking grand. Potatoes galore and you can't go wrong with potatoes.'

'Your mother must be pleased. Have you heard from your father recently?'

'No, Mrs Scott. I believe he is busy with the work.'

'All of the cities must be so busy, really, these days. And frightening, too. It's not just London, is it? Everywhere is suffering. Still, my sister says that as much as possible, life is continuing on as usual. Everyone is being so brave.'

'Margaret, you say that as if bravery were a virtue when it is merely moral duty.' This woman is stern-mouthed, her glasses thick and very clean indeed. Her grey hair is wiry, scraped back and rolled, and she wears a small tortoise-shell pin on her collar with a silver St Andrew holding his cross in his hands. A sweetheart brooch, Connie tells me later, from her father's days as a Cameron Highlander in the Great War.

Mrs Scott smiles. 'Duty, yes, of course, Miss Clarke. However, duty is not always easy, is it? Courage is still worth mentioning, perhaps. Wouldn't you agree?'

She turns to ask Connie about the biscuits on the plate – how *did* you manage with the sweetness? – and Connie tells her that she used honey and a little cinnamon, too, but that the trouble was with the margarine because the recipe called for 2½ ounces, which seems like a lot of the ration to begin with, and the biscuits really needed another half-ounce to hold together, which was difficult and she is so glad that Mrs Scott likes them. Would she like another?

I worry my needles between my fingers, the wool impatient, and Muriel leans over towards me. 'You feel as odd-pea-ish sitting here as I do?' she asks, grinning. 'What I wouldn't give to step outside for a long cigarette's while right about now.'

'I have some in my purse. We could go and puff away in the loo.'

'I think I'll like you.'

She says she's known Stanley from primary school and asks how he is. I tell her he has been made an officer because of his university degree and that he's been put to work training pilots.

'I thought he read geology.'

'Well, in its wisdom, the military marked his enlistment papers *scientist*, so logically, he's equipped to teach rudimentary physics.'

'Gosh. I guess gravity is gravity, rocks or otherwise.'

'It's better than bombing runs,' I say. 'He teaches them the basics – flight, weight, thrust and drag as well as how to read all the dials in a cockpit. He says he'll be on leave in October.'

'That's not long, is it?'

Miss Clarke clears her throat and Connie stands to pour more tea.

'We'll chat properly later. Because this is the moment for no' but

174

serious needlework.' Muriel buckles down with her socks and I return to my scarf. I feel hopeless when it comes to woollen things. My father once suggested it lowered my value on the bride market, as if such a thing were funny. Stanley didn't make the slightest enquiry into my knitting at any stage in our courtship. Cake was always more my pride, and I eye the tea things on the table now.

Muriel catches my glance and grins again, launching into a story about her grandfather's funeral, a grand affair by the sounds of it, with family from here to Glasgow and a table simply laden with the work of so many kitchens. Muriel soon organized her cousins, the boys at least, to set up camp under the table with pilfered plates of macaroons.

'Oh, your grandmother's macaroons were a treat,' says Mrs Scott. 'Soft and light like, well, like a tropical dream. Perhaps her far-flung brother inspired those divinities – oh pardon me, Mrs Thomson. Didn't he work abroad? Bahamas, wasn't it?'

'Yes, it was. Came home brown as a coconut himself for the funeral, and you should have heard how Granny cried when he handed her a bottle of rum. Too late, of course, for that kind of thing.'

'Oh dear, Miss Grant,' says Miss Clarke.

'I only meant that my granddad liked the rum and he couldn't drink it, could he? Because it was his funeral,' Muriel continues, her eyes wide and innocent.

'I know what you meant.'

'Yes, dear,' Mrs Scott says. 'I will need to ask your mother for that macaroon recipe. So very light. Though I wonder what I could possibly use these days. What might make a mock coconut? Well, it would be good simply to have the recipe. Once this war is over, I will make them for the village fete. When everyone marches home.'

5

RAIN FALLS FOR SEVERAL DAYS AFTER I MEET MURIEL. I stay at home and my knitting progresses slowly. Most of the time I spend filling pages with notes, sometimes about the poems I read, taking tender steps back towards my degree work, more often just thoughts for Stanley. I decide I won't describe Mrs Scott's hands and that I will mention the food and my tangled knitting. I wonder about the clothes he is wearing. Are his stitches even? Does he notice?

At the end of the following week, the weather breaks and I knock on Muriel's door. Her mother tells me that she is working in the garden. Along the walk, pots of geraniums, marigolds and seashells are set out in patterns. Laundry flaps on the line beside the house, white tea towels, pillowcases and aprons.

Muriel is standing on a stepladder in blue dungarees, picking runner beans. She drops them down into a square wicker basket on the ground.

'Goodness, I'm glad to see you. Everyone's been in a bit of a mood around here because of the soggy weather, and I'm all out of fags and compassion. Climb on up and sit down. There's space for two. I'd offer you a chair, but it's easier to keep out of the pig's way up here.'

A ruddy sow roots around under the trees at the end of the garden, ignoring both Muriel and the chickens pecking their way across the grass towards me.

'Here,' I say, tossing Muriel my cigarette packet and climbing up to join her. 'That will help dry you out.'

'Absobloodylutely. It's been awfully dreich, hasn't it? And all those aeroplanes and the awful kerfuffle of the ack-ack guns. Glad to have them there, though. Not a word against the defence. I just can't think for lack of sleep.'

'I wanted to pop by to say thank you for the other day at the manse. For your kindness. Connie was lovely to invite me, but it isn't really my thing.'

'Nor mine. However, my beloved mum sends me along to keep up appearances. And supply the brave soldiers with pair after pair of lumpy socks.'

'We all contribute,' I say. 'Those beans look super.'

'It's a good crop. Beans are easy. The more you pick, the more they grow. They need plenty of water, but that isn't a worry, is it? You can take some home if you like. We've got miles of them.'

'Thank you. That will be a bit of a treat.'

'I'm more of a choc ice girl.'

'You'll be lucky, these days.'

'I was the other evening, sort of. Izaak took me out in

Haddington. Bought me a shilling ticket at the pictures and then an ice, too. Not real, but it fitted the bill.'

'I don't think I could. The chocolate is like burnt Bakelite these days.'

'Better than mock coconut, I should think. Macaroons. Imagine. Well, I will certainly eat my fill when that fete comes around.'

'Do you think she believes it?'

'I think she has to. Two boys gone and her husband has stopped talking altogether. She says he's rather poorly, but my mum says only as poorly as any cushion might feel as all he does is sit up in a chair all day and watch the sky. He takes his meals as right as rain, and sometimes walks down to the end of the garden, but he won't say a word or lift a finger about the house. And Mum says there are sheets on the laundry line every blessed day. Mrs Scott has her work cut out for her. So she keeps cheerful as she can and ever optimistic. Always that rosy glow. I'll speak no ill of her at all. Did you know that she tucks little notes into each pair of socks she finishes? *Good luck, boys! Love, Mother.* That sort of thing. Sentimental and an absolute brick.'

'She seems fond of you.'

'Well, yes. She's auditioning for the role of mother-in-law for all she's worth. I've had a bit of trouble with her boys, and now she's quite certain we'll be family soon.'

'That sounds like a story.'

'No, nothing like that, you goose. Nothing serious. They've just taken turns walking me home and asking if I need any help digging the garden. Sweet boys, but not for me. Honestly, I don't know if I'll ever be bothered. It seems too brave a thing, loving another person.' She takes a long drag from her cigarette and kicks her feet against the legs of the ladder. Under the trees, the pig makes a satisfied gruntle, and Muriel grins. 'Who knows, I might get swept away. Some gangly lad will come along with a heart full of love for a skinny malinky longlegs like me and he'll fly me to the moon in his beautiful balloon. Is that how it was for you?'

'Yes,' I laugh. 'Yes, it was. Not in the specifics, but yes. Completely swept away. He came into the shop where I worked, looking for chocolate. Always keeps some in his jacket pocket. He has a very sweet tooth.'

'Look at you. You've gone all pink. You really do have it bad, don't you?'

'Yes. That's why I married him.'

'Heavens. And now you're living alone out here. Are you pregnant?'

'No,' I say, trying to sound just as blunt as she does. I smooth my dress, then take another puff on my cigarette. 'That's what everyone's thinking, with me all of a sudden out here on my own. But that's not why I married him. And not for the officer's income, either, which doesn't make much of a difference anyway. Not with rations. No, it was just love. Is that mad?'

'Sure, it's mad. Lovely, too. And lonely?'

'A bit. Not a lot of distractions out here other than knitting. But I couldn't stay at home in Edinburgh, going dancing while Stanley was away to war. For a while, I thought I might go to London. Train up as a nurse and do my bit. Only now Stanley says that Scotland shouldn't be drained of all its young people or how will it stand?'

'He wouldn't *let* you?'

'No, no, it wasn't like that at all. We talked about, well, everything. About how London might be valorous, glamorous even, but work has to continue everywhere for Britain to be properly defended. Like you and your garden. Life just has to continue, doesn't it?'

'So, what's your work?'

'Haven't a clue, to be honest. It was just the idea that convinced me.'

Muriel's mother came down from the house with a tray of glasses.

'Gin already, Mum?' Muriel calls out. 'Just the ticket.'

'I'm afraid not, girls. Hitlerism seems to be putting a stop to all good things. Except possibly the sunshine. Isn't it glorious? And don't those beans look good? They'll be just the thing tonight with a bit of ham.'

'As they were just the thing last night with an egg.'

'Wheesht, my dear. When we have beans aplenty, we eat plenty of beans. Now, Muriel, will you get down and shift that basket over here, so I have somewhere to set this tray. Glad to see you settled comfortably, Jane. Muriel says that you are the one who married Bunty Hambleton's son. Such a shame she's moved herself out of the village. A gentle soul, Bunty.'

'Yes,' I say. 'I like her. She's gone north with her daughter Violet.'

'Well, perhaps that's for the best. These aeroplanes are terrible overhead, aren't they? Is it hard on your own? You have a good shelter for the raids? You can come and camp here anytime you want company. Plenty of room in our Anderson shelter, you know.'

'I am managing quite well. It's all rather novel, being on my own. There was an awful pile of us at home.'

'Lucky lot. I wanted a houseful. That's what my sister got. However, for us, only Muriel came along, didn't you, my love?'

'Only Muriel. Aren't I enough? Dad says I'm better than a barn-load of boys.'

'And perhaps more trouble, too,' she says, laughing. 'But I wouldn't trade you for all the world, my dear, and you know that. Right in your bones. And where did you get that smoke, young lady? I thought we were clean out. Sweet talking the poor Polish boys again?'

'No, this one's from Jane.'

'I've plenty in the pack, if you'd like one.'

'Well, kind of you to offer. And maybe I will say yes. Keeps the spirits up, doesn't it? Thanks, that's lovely.'

The pig snuffles loudly and I startle, dropping my cigarette. 'Oh dear, don't let Rosie bother you,' says Muriel's mother. 'She's just on her feet because she senses someone new in the environs.'

'Just caught me a little unawares.'

'I imagine there aren't many pigs in Edinburgh's back gardens.'

'Not pigs, no. Some families keep chickens, but not pigs. Especially now that everyone is growing vegetables. There wouldn't be the space.'

'We've space above and beyond around here, and she seems to be easy enough to feed. We're still getting used to each other. I had a bit of a pause yesterday when I was preparing lunch, though. We've been giving her all the peelings, but while I was washing some of Muriel's gorgeous tatties, the voice of Churchill himself seemed to whisper in my ear, "Sacrifice and glory". All those good nutrients gone to a scraping waste. It's a shame, though. She likes potato skins, does our sausage. Well, we can always let her out into the wood on the other side of the wall and see what she might rummage around for there. Acorns and the like.'

'You won't be collecting those for us then, Mum? Or pine needles? Pebbles for a nice soup?'

'Oh you. I'm not quite at that level yet. We'll see how it goes, won't we? Really, I'd like to get another pig. They're such social animals and I've read that they put on more weight when they have company.'

'We'd be popular with two pigs. Bound to be with more bacon and sausages on the table.'

'You'll spread the word with all your gentlemen friends, won't you?'

'I'd be happy to contribute my scraps,' I say. 'If that would help. And bacon at breakfast would be a welcome change from powdered egg.'

'It can't be easy on your own, my dear.'

'Well, nothing seems to stretch, but I'm making do.'

'You'll still be at the playing-house stage, won't you? Just moved away from home and starting out as you are. And your husband – is he stationed nearby?'

'Not yet. He's still down at Padgate. But we are hopeful.'

'I'm sure it will work out. With all the new airfields around here, something is bound to open up. He's such a charmer, too. No need to blush, now. You've found yourself a good man. Gentle, too, like his mother. In days like this, that will be particularly important. Far more miles in gentleness than all the fancy manners and scent of the Polish boys Muriel has her eye on.'

'I haven't got my eye on anyone, Mum. Izaak just asks me to the films. And buys me ices, too.'

'And plies you with strange foreign cigarettes. Have to use your own teeth as filters with some of them, though it's good of you to share whenever you do get some. But this Dunhill is lovely. A classy girl, this Jane. Well, I'll just leave the two of you to your blether and get on with the day, shall I? Jane, would you like to be staying for some lunch?'

Muriel's house sits out beyond the village, away from the other houses and close by the sea. It is nothing like my parents' flat, which is always crowded with kids and middle-class civilizing efforts. Like the thin window in the room at the front, which enables you to glance out to the street for the children as you play the piano in the afternoon. There are high ceilings and decorative moulding in the front room, and you'd never know the boys slept there unless you stayed too late after tea and saw them yawning in the hallway. Muriel has a bedroom to herself at the back of the house, with space for a bookcase and a chair. Wealth untold. Mr and Mrs Grant sleep in the larger bedroom at the front of the house, and there's also a living room and a dining room and space in the kitchen for a fair-sized table, too. Everywhere, there are shelves and the pantry itself is large enough for a bed, with space for a dresser with a marble shelf.

Mr Grant works down in London these days and stays there much of most months. When he's away, it's the coast that he misses, Muriel tells me. The streets of London have nothing to compare with the light on the water. That's why they bought the house in the first place, so that they might have a spot on the water and a place to watch the sky. Muriel shows me his photograph on the living-room wall. He looks like her, I think, has her gangliness and her interested eyes, but he has a seriousness, too. He looks like a man who might need to walk beside the sea once in a while.

After the war, I will bring Stanley here to meet him, I think. And Mrs Grant and Muriel, too. We will sit together in these rooms, talk about pigs and poetry and listen for the comfortable sound of the sea.

6

THE END OF AUGUST AND IT CAN'T BE HIM, BUT I'M already running. No one knocks at my door in the evening, and if it is another air raid, I'd have heard the whistles. No feet in the street either, no scratch of a chair, just that gentle tapping on my door and my feet already running down the hallway. I've been sitting in the kitchen with another weak cup of tea and a book, not even thinking about him but I know. I just know.

The key is stiff in the lock. My fingers won't work properly. I need two hands to turn it like a child and it just can't be him but finally, finally the door opens and Stanley is home.

'Did you send word?' I ask, my arms already around him, already pulling him into the house. 'I didn't know. I thought leave was still weeks away. I . . .'

'Hush, lovely, and let me in.' He speaks softly, and he is already beside me, closing the door.

'You are here.'

'Yes,' he answers, laughing quietly. 'I am, aren't I?'

'Oh, but you're cold. It must be windy outside. And the last bus was ages ago. How did you . . .'

There is a strange look on his face, a faltering, I think, but it could be just the light in the hallway because he shrugs and smiles, slipping his arms out of his coat and hanging it on the doorknob.

'I had to walk. All the way from Haddington after the train. Thought about going across the fields, but I was worried I'd lose my way, so I followed the rail tracks out to Longniddry then the road after that.'

'Goodness, it must have taken ages.'

'A couple of hours. Nothing at all. It's beautiful tonight. Clear and quiet. There was such a cloud of bats on the wing at the Cottyburn Siding. I could have caught you one in my hat. You could have cooked it for tea. Are rations bad now? Are you starving? You don't feel quite like you're starving.'

'You were lucky it was quiet. We've had such a lot of noise here, all the planes overhead.'

'Should hear it down south, love. Piccadilly Circus every night. But look, I brought tea and fags. A fresh packet of each, too. We could have a veritable picnic, couldn't we? Tuck in bed and be cosy together?'

I suggest a bath first to warm him up but how can we wait? The water would need to boil and the bath brought through to the fire with the curtains and the blackout blinds all closed securely and then the lamps lit. We manage the blinds and no further. The sheets are cold against bare skin, and him warm, him so close, hard, strong, tender. I keep opening my eyes, not wanting to miss a single look and if they were closed it could all be imaginary no matter how good and real. So I open my eyes and everything is open.

It is later I notice that he hasn't got his duffel bag with him, that he didn't have anything at all in his hands as he came through the door.

In the dark, he speaks, lying on his back beside me.

'It's only for a day or two. Well, a few days now that I'm here. Don't get used to it. I can't stay.'

'Of course not. But you're here now.'

'Am I? It's hard to believe. I could be anywhere.' He rolls towards me and runs his hand down my side. We might have fallen asleep, easily. It's even likely, but we don't. We just lie there together in the dark. I want to feel easy. I want to feel that the world is whole again. It is so dark that I can't see the ceiling or the paleness of the sheets. I can't see anything at all. For a long time, we are simply together.

Later, we get up, slip on clothing, sit in the kitchen where my cup of tea is still on the table. I take the cheese from the shelf and unwrap the creased greaseproof paper. It is getting almost too hard to slice. The Ministry of Food pamphlet suggested letting it harden as it would stretch further grated. Unpleasantness stretches, perhaps. I slice the bread and grate a little cheese onto each slice, folding them in half, but the hard bread crumbles and I have to pass it to Stanley on a plate.

'No matter, my love,' he whispers.

'We don't have to be silent. We won't wake anyone. Miss Baxter's gone away for a few nights. There is no one to hear.'

'The whole country is emptying, isn't it? That's what I was thinking as I walked along the tracks tonight. There's nothing and no one left.'

'You won't feel that way in the morning. You'll see. East Lothian is heaving with military. Haddington is quite inflated, and even in Gullane, there are uniforms everywhere. Not as quiet in the country as we expected.'

'But you're safe? Yes? You feel safe? You're not scared?'

'No, I'm fine . . .' and I stop because his leg is shaking, jumping up and down like a piston under the table. 'Stanley, what is it?'

'I'm . . . I'm not on leave. I just left.'

'Left?'

'Yes. I walked. I didn't seek permission or tell anyone at all. I just walked away.'

'But that's desertion.'

'Is it? Is it? I don't know. Fuck, my love, I don't know anything any more.'

I lace my fingers around the Cunard teacup, bone-cold and silent. He holds his head in his hands for balance. I could touch him, but I don't. Then he stands, an awful lurch to his feet, and I stand, too, but he grips my stiff shoulders and shoves me back into my chair. My breath stops. He moves through to the hallway and the door to the street closes. Again, he is gone.

The dark is final. Moonless and it owns the earth. It fills the kitchen, my lungs, my heart. I sit at the table, certain the invasion will come soon. It has to. There will be landings here, up and down the coast, despite all the defences. The south will fall. London. All the fields. Dunkirk will be remembered as the first stage rather than the glorious withdrawal, the heroic stand. All the heartening stories are just whistling in the dark. The private yachts and the fishermen. The two sisters who pulled fifty men from the beach and brought them home safe to Blighty. I thought they were heroines, shining saints of the sea. God was with them and with us, shaping the nation's beautiful story. But they will fall, too, the saints and the sisters, the mothers at home, Mrs Scott, Muriel, and all these other women we watch. And who watches us and from what distance?

Because if he returns to the army, they will kill him. Isn't that what they do to deserters? It was in the last war, and isn't that the irony of courage? If it flags and you turn away, blind or suddenly seeing, they will gun you down. Methodical murder and none of this for heaven's sake.

Day comes, grey and with a gentle rain. I stand and will myself thoughtless. Drink water and do not bite the glass to taste the shards, the blood alone warm in my mouth. I will not. I cannot move past this moment, though the hours pass and it becomes a vigil. I will sit; I will not retreat. No stumble, no vicious light. Perhaps I only wait for the returning dark.

Footsteps outside, perhaps midday, and Muriel's whistle with a Hollywood song and dance up the walk, all lipstick and Izaak's blond hair in the dark of the double bill. I can't speak, can't tell her anything or ask her what to do. Her gentle knock on the door, once and then again. She calls my name and, a hundred feet below the tide, I can't answer. Only lie anchored while somewhere above, the gulls and gannets shriek and dive for pale fish.

When it is dark again, he opens the door and shuffles into the hallway. I meet him there, but he doesn't stop, doesn't meet my eye and we don't touch. Back in the kitchen, I sit, still empty.

'Where did you go?'

He sits opposite me and places his hands on the table. 'Out to Jovey's Neuk. I like it there. No one saw me.'

'It isn't safe. The army are building concrete blocks along the shore to keep the Germans from landing their tanks.'

'I saw them. Ugly things.'

'They say that they will be mining the sands, too.'

'I thought the ironstone was gone. More or less.'

'No, love. I think they meant explosives.'

'Oh.' He stretches out his hand towards me and I take it between my palms. He feels cold again, damp, and he looks emptied. 'It rained in the afternoon. For a long time, I sat in the dunes. I shouldn't have come here. It isn't fair on you.'

'What does that have to do with anything? You came home. I . . . I want to ask why.'

'I knew you would. I'm not sure.'

'I wondered where you'd gone.'

'What did you think?'

'I . . . I didn't know. Maybe walking. I wasn't always sure you'd been here at all. Maybe I'd made it up. A fever dream or something. Or I thought I might be . . .'

'You don't need to say it. I've wondered, too. Sane people don't walk away.'

'I don't know. Perhaps they do.'

Later he tells me that, after the rain, he went down into the ironstone mine. 'There were these wide white breakers out to sea and the wind grew cold. I wanted a sheltered place. Knew there was an entrance somewhere in the bluff behind Jova's cottage. Took me a while to find it, actually. The grass has grown up and there's been a rock-fall since I was a teenager. It was a bit of a tight squeeze, but I did manage to get in. Used to be easier. I've made a right mess of my knees. Once you crawl through the entrance, it widens out and there's room enough to stand. It starts with a broad chamber that you can circle pretty well if you keep your hand on the wall, and then there are all these alleyways and arteries that lead away into the hill. I remember it gets pretty windy down there sometimes, so there must be ventilation. There used to be bats, too, that made an awful flappy noise in the dark up above our heads. Me and Andrew from over by Drem. We'd gather driftwood from the beach and get a fire going in the mine despite the drafts. Maybe they helped. Made us smell like kippers, too, but nae bother there. And we'd go exploring, looking for smugglers' loot. We never expected gold or silver. Nothing extravagant. But opals, possibly. They're found sometimes where there's ironstone. Opals would be grand, and we had candles and shining sand from the beach to dribble out in long lines down the tunnels, so there was always a pale gleaming trail to lead back to safety.'

'Stanley, you can't hide underground for the rest of the war.'
'No? Perhaps not. Perhaps.'

He sleeps, his wet clothes bunched on a chair. I check the blinds, the curtains, the key in the lock, pad back to bed and light the lamp. Stanley does not move. He lies naked on the sheets, stretched out like a drowned bird on the strand. He is thin with ribs and ligaments, the meticulous structure of bones, hollow weight and length. In sleep, I cannot see his wide-horizon gaze, his inconceivable ability to fly.

Sometime in the night, I wonder if I might cut my life in two. Walk away. Or more sensibly take a bus. Leave, anyway. Maybe to London. I could find work, a room. I could just cut and run. Leave no explanation, just a tidied house behind. But that is the trouble, of course. That was what Stanley had done and now what? I can't leave him. I can't send him back. I lie beside him as he sleeps; the darkness of the room curls over us both, his breath soft and even.

If I could cut my life in two like an apple, you might see the seeds. You might see where all this is going. But nothing can be quarried to its core and keep its weight. Light will change everything, and these days need to be lived in darkness. Maybe I should hide away, too. Would Stanley's mine be big enough for two? That might be the answer when the time comes. But it isn't here yet.

The wind whistles down the chimney and he stretches in his sleep, rolling onto his back, then back towards me again. I turn out the light, the skies still silent above us. I can't see him, but I don't need to. He is here and that is enough. For now, night is a cover.

I sleep and wake, aware of him as of a twin. The other half of the apple. Sliced across, you find a star. Straight down, a heart. My mother showed me that when she first taught me to use a knife. She let me decide.

'Stanley?'

He wakes slowly, his hands holding the sheets.

'Stanley? You need to go.'

'I can't. A little longer.'

'It will be dawn soon. People will be waking.' I touch his face, his tired skin.

'All right, okay . . . might be awake now. I was dreaming I was awake, but I woke up . . .'

'And,' I say, picking up the threads of his silly quotation, 'found myself asleep.'

'Now that's Hardy funny, my girl.' He reaches over for me, but I sit up straight because there are things he needs to know.

'I've put a few things together for you. To take to the mine.' An apple. A few slices of crumbling bread. Cigarettes. A jar of water. 'There will be more later. I'll manage. But you need to stay hidden. You will. You know the lie of the land.'

'How are we going to tell the children about all this, Jane?'

'Don't. We'll say goodbye later. If we need to.'

7

FOR A FEW DAYS, HE COMES AND GOES LIKE THE TIDE, and landscapes change each time. He is bright or quiet. He can meet my eye. I trace the lines around his mouth and his gentle hands quiver. I don't know if this is love or tenderness. He tells me about the rooks coming down from the sky, walking the old wall-lines at Jovey's cottage, their pale-beaked faces bright-eyed and curious.

'I gave them some of my bread. Just a little, to be friendly. At first, they scattered, but slowly, they started pecking up the crumbs, hopping back and forth and always sure to keep a sharp eye on me. Then later, one flew back with a blue mussel shell in his beak and dropped it in the grass, quite close to me. Like a gift. Made me feel like Elijah in the wilderness, it did.'

* * *

Every night, we find each other. Everything is familiar: the rain outside, salt on the lips, the tongue, hands holding on, the quilt on our bed.

'If I could find a boat, I'd go down to the islands,' he says. 'Just down the coast towards North Berwick. Used to be hermits out there on the Bass and Fidra, too, I think. I'd fit in.'

'You stay put where it's safe. I can't even think about you on the sea.'

'Can't fathom it, can you?' he says, and I can smile. 'But I wonder if I could get a boat. Think I could sneak by without being spotted? I think I could make it. The rooks could bring me one: a very large mussel shell. What do you think?'

He tumbles me on my back and traces my face with a finger, telling me that the Bass was named from the Gaelic root for forehead.

'And Fidra?'

'Norse for feather.'

'It all comes together.'

'Yes.'

In the morning, the sky is clear again and I hang up laundry in the garden. Miss Baxter comes home and pops round to tell me about noises she heard in the night.

'Ghosts,' I tell her. 'Must be.'

'Oh,' she says. 'Perhaps.'

'I think so,' I say, trying to sound convincing. 'I'll listen tonight, too, and then we can confer in the morning.'

'Yes. Let's.' She draws her cardigan close with one hand and smiles quietly, holding out a glass jar towards me. 'I brought you jam from my sister. It's blackcurrant. Only made with honey, I'm afraid, so it is a bit syrupy, but the flavour is good.'

'Thank you,' I say. 'That's lovely.' I take the jar and hope there's nothing in the hallway behind me that might betray Stanley. Just in case, I won't invite her in. I tell her it's good to see her, that I would like to hear her news, but perhaps later? This might make it sound like she's caught me at a busy moment. I stand with crossed arms at the door.

In the afternoon, I walk along the road to Gullane to buy bread, cheese, eggs if I can find them and a newspaper. News of more raids over London and reports of courage and cheerfulness, too. *Most children are sleeping through the night. It is still comparatively easy to secure accommodation in country hotels.* Everything will be all right. That is the message. *Repetition of the experience tends to diminish rather than increase its effect.* I will put the paper away before Stanley comes. Maybe use it to start a fire. The evenings are growing chilly.

It is odd that there is no mention in the paper of raids on Scotland, too. It isn't just London or even the south. With all the airfields up here and Grangemouth, too, there are plenty of targets. When I went into town to visit my family in the middle of the month, Mum mentioned bombs in Marchmont, her lips pursed as she told me, as if no one should think of such a thing. But they fell anyway, regardless of what the Edinburgh folk might have to say. Five in one evening along Argyll Crescent, all unexploded, mercifully. And no mention in the paper. It must be the policy these days, keeping hush about specifics, though I wonder how they decide. Which bombs count? Which ones are worth knowing about?

When Stanley comes late in the evening, I make a pot of tea in the dim kitchen, and stir a spoonful of Miss Baxter's jam into his mug for sweetness. Black bits float to the surface, giving it a scummy look. He lifts them off with the bowl of his spoon.

'It's not bad,' he says. 'Better than treacle.'

'Can't think where you'd find treacle these days. Do you need anything else?'

'You.'

'That's not what I meant.'

'Let me see your face.'

'You know what I look like.'

'We can turn on a light. The blinds are down.'

'Finish your tea first. You'll be cold after a day outside.' I don't want to be prim, it's the last thing I'm feeling, but the words come anyway.

'Here, take my hand,' he said. 'It's you who are cold. You're shivering.' He rubs the back of my hand, his fingers rough and gentle. 'You'll be needing gloves in this house. And it isn't even really autumn. The geese aren't back yet.'

'I'm fine. Really. I am.'

'So am I.'

He holds me. Everything else can wait.

Then he tells me why, the words finally drifting down to the floor.

He tells me about the last bad night, the constant flights and the roar, flames and blindness, the shattered planes landing. 'We were worse than bridge-builders up there, or skyscraper men a hundred storeys above. We've got nothing tying us to the ground but gravity and that isn't a friend. Back on the ground again and we can't stop shaking, none of us, but no one talks about that. No one. A little whisky passed around, and we hold the flask in two hands, but then the planes need to be hosed out because that's how you do it. There's nothing left to lift. Just a slurry of blood and bone grime.

'I spoke with the chaplain. Even managed to ask him about fear and he offered a prayer. Then he smiled and told me there was a job to be done and he knew I could do it. All the way back to the barracks, I kept saying that, repeating his words just under my breath like a spell. A job to be done, a job to be done. I didn't decide anything, didn't have to think at all, really, just kept pacing out those words. A job to be done. But I walked past the barracks, I did, and out to the road. Don't know how I got there, out past the gate and there must have been a sentry. I might have spoken to them, I don't know at all, but I know I was walking and kept walking till I found an army train heading north. Climbed on with a crowd of men, all tired out, all blind in the night and maybe I slept or maybe not, but soon enough I'd made it to Haddington, slipped away on the platform and walked home. No knowing how much shtook I'll be in now. I just needed to be home.'

His eyes wide as he speaks, his fingers splayed and I surface somehow, listening. No lovemaking then, but he holds me and I cry.

'I'm scared,' I say.

'Of me?'

'No. I don't think so.'

'No. We shouldn't be. I just blew here on the wind. It's just the after-echo of fear we're feeling. Someone else's fear.'

'You're too clever for this.'

'It's not cleverness. Just poetry.'

He leaves before dawn.

I take my suitcase from the top of the wardrobe and put a blanket inside. Socks. Another jumper. The wedding photo. From the kitchen, I take the jam, the Cunard teacup, a spoon. I know that none of this is a solution. He can't stay and more furnishings don't change that. But I don't know what else to do, and so I follow him out to the sea like a ghost.

The air is heavy with sea before dawn. Sea or soundless cloud. I'd imagined a different kind of light, grey but dawning, and I'd hurry along the road, racing the band of light to the east, and catching Stanley before the bridge. But it isn't like that. Instead, the haar is back and the world looks white and empty.

If I'm seen here along the high street, I can always say I'm heading into Edinburgh. Too early for the bus perhaps, but I could feign confusion. If I've already crossed the bridge when the soldiers spot me, the story stretches, and I'll need to think of something else.

My head aches now, as with fever, and time and distances shudder through me. Edinburgh again and six years old, down in the Meadows with Jeanie, swinging arms and walking through the mist. The pathways were straight and the planted trees looked like the shadows of men. Jeanie ran ahead and I lost my footing on the slick wet grass. My knee stained green. When I stood again, she was so far ahead, a smudge, another shadow or just a faint reflection in a misted window, my own form doubled, my own arms swinging still. I stood, time-blind, unsure if I could catch up or simply stand and my reflection vanish.

Somewhere ahead, Stanley is hurrying through this same mist. If he makes it to the mine before me, I will never find him. I will need to turn back. I could leave the suitcase, though the army might find it. What would they make of that?

My ears feel fog-filled as I cross the bridge and pass the Marl Loch. There are no birds. A single silence covers the bay and the flat dune land beyond but my heart beats like something wild, a fierceness that helps me keep going. When I find Stanley, I can rest. He'll show me the mine, and we'll both burrow in.

A voice behind me calls stop.

A man. Not Stanley. I freeze, hold my breath as if I could disappear by stillness.

'This way is closed.' His accent comes through the mist behind me, strange and familiar. 'Ah, it is you. But I have told you that this way is not for you. Are you . . . are you all right, miss?' I do not turn and he steps in front of me. I can see now that it is the blond soldier. 'You are far from home too early.'

'I'm fine,' I say, and I feel my lips thin. 'I was walking.'

'Yes. I was, too.'

'I hadn't realized that the coast was to be patrolled as well as mined.'

'No. It isn't. I was just walking. But it is not safe for you.'

'And for you?'

'I know where we put the mines. Here, let me take your case.'

'No, I want to keep it.'

'I did not mean to take it away. Only to carry it for you. You look worn out.'

'Do I?'

'Yes. And lost perhaps.' His voice is kind, safe even. By now, Stanley would be in the mine, so time doesn't matter, does it? I wouldn't find him now. The blond soldier holds out his hand and I let him take the case. He does not let his face express its weight, merely lifts it and continues to walk. 'I will show you the blocks, if you like. They are finished now. Perhaps you would like to see?'

We walk together, and the sun must be rising now because the air itself is luminous, as if overexposed, though the fog still hides the shape of the land. My fingers feel numb with cold. Away to the right, there are trees. I can hear birds beginning to argue, their voices ragged in the damp morning air. A hill rises under our feet and he touches my arm, motioning away from the track. Here, the ground is rough, the surface churned by the heavy treads of tyres, and the grasses are all scraped away. At measured intervals, concrete blocks sit heavy on the ruined earth, row after row like something emerging from the soil, pushing up into the fog.

'They look strong,' I say. 'And old.'

'We just finished them last week. But you are right. They look as if they have been here a long time. Like standing stones.'

'Do they teach you local history in the army, then?'

'No. I pick up things. I am curious.' I know he is looking at me, but I will not meet his gaze. Instead, I set my hand against the block, its surface ridged and rough.

'Is he your husband? The man you are looking for,' he asks. I want to hold stillness around me, to be stone deaf, but the soldier bends to meet my eye, smiles, and the stillness is gone.

'Yes,' I say. 'He . . . he shouldn't be here.'

'Yes. We can end up in strange places.' He tells me then how he left his country last year. The sudden attack, the city under siege. Bombers destroyed the waterworks and left no water to drink, let alone to put out fires. So many fires. It doesn't take long for a burned city to starve. Then horses were flayed in the street in front of the bank, its classical facade watching bone-white, respectable. Every day, he had to visit his father in hospital. Pneumonia and not unusual for an old man, but now? Such a peaceful sickness was strange as Grecian columns in the smoke. The hospital was modern, bright with windows, so much glass. And every night, more bombers. So the nurses moved the patients down to the basements. His father wouldn't go. He wanted to stay near the statue of the Virgin. She would protect him, wreathed in stars. She was his only health, he said, and the doctor telling the son this story cried. Later, an American journalist came, his Bell & Howell camera strung around his neck. He filmed the shattered windows, the Virgin's stars, and the quiet nurses carrying buckets. The son met him on the street and told him stories about the maternity ward in another hospital where the babies were tied to pillows because there were no unshattered cots. When the siege was over, the American would smuggle the footage home, the film wrapped around his chest like a bandage, newspaper around a glass, a hidden blade. The son would also slip away, taking a long escape from his homeland, a breath held until at last he pulled himself onto this grey and rainy island.

'And now, I seem to be a soldier,' he says. 'I do not know if my father would like that. He was a peaceful man.'

'So is my husband.'

'Yes,' he says, as if he already knew him. As if the fog hid nothing.

He tells me he can help Stanley and that I should trust him. I am not sure what trust means. Only that I am scared. And that doesn't seem to matter.

'It is getting cold,' he says. 'I can't imagine that he will want to stay here longer.'

'You won't send him back.'

'I said I could help. I will.'

'The suitcase . . .'

'Leave it with me. I will find him and he will have it.'

'Is this risky? For you, I mean.'

'I don't think so. You should go home now. When I can, I will send word. Do you know Muriel? With the garden?'

'And the pig. Yes, of course.'

'I wondered if you might. Perhaps I can send you word through her.'

The fog lifts and all that is common and kenspeckle returns. The day beyond our words.

8

I GO HOME IN THE GROWING MORNING LIGHT AND I wonder about going home to Edinburgh. Mum said that there would always be space for me if I needed it. But Stanley might still need me, too. I should be where I can be found.

Aberlady will be waking up and if I am not quick on my feet, Miss Baxter will be meeting me at the door. I could tell her that ghosts kidnapped me. Or scared me off? I should never have mentioned ghosts.

My mother believes in ghosts. More or less. She believes that the self continues after death, not in some vague paradise far removed, but here among us.

'If they choose. Some must choose other places. Hilltops, woodlands. Or far out to sea. Places where you cannot live with a body, but without perhaps you might.'

She told me this at night when I was small. I'd woken afraid, the new cot in the corner casting strange shadows on the wall and the baby fretting. Mum came through to settle us both, and all I could say was *ghosties*. 'Nothing to be afraid of, pet. They're just real, like you. Only they've finished with their bodies. Must be grand, don't you think? I wonder where we might go. Up on a mountain? I'd like to be up in the air like that. Near the eagles. I've never seen an eagle. I think I'd like to.'

'But what about heaven? Mummy?'

'Oh, it comes later, doesn't it? On the Last Day. That's when the graves will break open and the Judgement comes. Heaven will start after that. Isn't that what the minister says? I'll let him worry about the details. It's the bit that comes first I'll look forward to. Give this old body a rest and turn away for a while.'

She told me she'd seen a ghost once, not long after she was married. She meant to soothe me, I'm sure. She said she had been thirsty and my father sleeping soundly, so she left the lamp unlit and stepped carefully through to the kitchen where she found a woman standing by the window. It was a thin white woman standing so still with her open hand pressed flat against the glass, leaving no trace. My mother startled and stepped back, the floorboard sounding behind her as she found her balance. She thought she must have mistaken her own reflection. Just a trick of the light against the glass. She smiled at her folly and waved but the image remained fixed. Then she understood. 'Quietly, you know. Like she was something I already knew but just realized or remembered. Nothing to be frightened by. Not really.'

My mother left the kitchen without turning away, then went back down the hall and climbed into bed again, still thirsty.

Night after night, the thin woman came back. My mother lay in bed, listening to her sighs. Later, she was braver and would go and sit with her for a lonely hour in the night. 'Not reaching out or saying anything, you understand. Just sitting in the moonlight together. I always thought she looked as if she were gazing out to sea. Not that you could see it through that window. There are trees and flats and half of Marchmont in the way, and then the castle and the rest of the city, but beyond that, the sea. I knew it was there and I felt she did, too. Who knows what the dead can see. And I did wonder if she might prefer to be out there, really. Out by the sea with the white waves and the wind.'

Remembering it now, this story feels different. As a child, I was fascinated by the ghost's hand on the window, the thought of watching together in the moonlight. Now, I think of my mother climbing back into bed where it would be warm, where her husband was heavy, his breath steady and maybe he turned in his sleep or perhaps he woke, drawing her cold body close, the sheets warm and safe.

My parents moved from that flat two years later in the summer my sister was born. My mother made a point of leaving a gift for the ghost on the window sill. A small pebble, sea-smooth and grey. Just in case.

Back inside the rented house, I kick off my shoes, shrug off my coat, lie down and sleep without deciding, without dreams.

There are birds arguing with the sun before I open my eyes. They must be over the road in the kirkyard's yew trees. I roll over and the pillow is cold, the room too sudden. I wonder how long I've slept and then I wonder about Stanley, and then about the soldier who took the case. What an idiot I was. What would *he* do to help? Probably pilfer the socks and the jar of jam. Leave the case sprung open in the dunes. Stanley might even find it out there and figure out my idiocy. Not even worth coming home to. But that was it, wasn't it? He hadn't come home to me. He'd just come home. Frightened and running, back to the place he knew. Pulled to the old landscape and the stones. Like gravity.

Next door, a window crashes open and the birds take flight with loud, abrasive cries. I push back the blanket and step into the day, still wearing yesterday's clothes. In the kitchen, I drink a glass of water. There are mouse droppings on the floor and Stanley's chair is pushed in slant against the table. I wish he'd left me that mussel shell he told me about. The one the rook brought him. I'd carry it about in my pocket all day, hidden and blue like a bruise.

Towards the end of the month, Muriel comes round again. I hear her whistle outside, then her syncopated knock on the door.

'You okay, hinny?' she calls. 'Yoo-hoo!'

'I'm coming. Hold your horses.'

She stands on the doorstep, hands in pockets, not quite smiling. 'I was right. You do look bleak. Mum says to give you space, but there's space and then there's neglect. And I had the feeling something was wrong. Are you poorly?'

'No. Yes. Not right, anyway.' I step back and let her in; her heavy shoes weigh down the carpet as she walks through to the kitchen. 'You hungry?'

'That's not the point. Mum says to bring you round for tea, if that's what you fancy, but I wondered if the films might be a better solution. Get you out of a funk, perhaps?'

'I don't have money for the films.'

'Me neither. But Mum slipped me a little for the cause and I'm sure we can find someone to smile at for a couple of choc ices.'

'Getting a bit chilly for that now.'

'Smiling or choc ices? It's never too chilly in Haddington. We'll be fine.'

It would take too much energy to say no to Muriel, so I let her sweep me up and bustle me off. I'm slow to gather a cardigan, slow to finger the buttons through the right holes, not wanting to shake. Muriel takes a scarf from the dressing table and ties it over my hair, gently tucking in the stray ends. I try not to notice or I might just cry, but she's all businesslike and jolly and makes sure I have the house key in my pocket so I can come home again.

Outside, there are two bicycles propped against the wall. Hers is a rusty old man's bike her father cobbled together from bits. She's borrowed Connie's bike for me so I'll ride in comfort, all good leather handles and a wide basket buckled on the front.

Out past the dog-leg in the high street, we set our backs to the sea and cycle inland past the fields and down the long road Stanley walked to get home in the dark. Muriel keeps the pace up, throwing the odd glance over her shoulder to encourage me along the way and chattering about the films.

'There's no point holding out for hope and high drama, I'm afraid. Mostly Laurel and Hardy these days to keep the spirits up.'

'Well, here's another nice kettle of fish you've pickled me in.'

'You didn't strike me as a fan.'

'I pick up things,' I say. 'I'm curious.'

'I always like the bit when Laurel makes his fist into a pipe and lights it with his thumb. A bit of good magic, don't you think? We could all use a little of that.'

After that we cycle in silence, the cold air catching my breath and my eyes beginning to run. Ah well, let them. The sun is bright in the fields and it's a brisk wind, but I've a clean handkerchief to tidy with at the end of the road.

Coming onto the high street in Haddington, Muriel swings a leg over her bicycle frame to balance a moment on the pedal before she steps down onto the road. I brake and hop down, too, jolted and out of breath.

'You can't let me forget about brambles,' she said. 'Mum's been dropping heavy hints about some likely bushes down by the river. I must remember to go and take a look for her. And I'm to tell you that Rosie's due for slaughter next week so there'll be sausages for you, if you like.'

She props her bike against the stone wall by the church and rakes her fingers through her hair. 'Anyone you know?'

She's caught me scanning the street. Maybe I'm looking for Stanley. Maybe I'm just looking. There's such a number of people walking up and down and it feels like ages since I've been in a proper crowd. 'Not a soul. You?'

'We'll have better luck by the picture house, I should think. There's always someone there to chat with.'

* * *

The picture house isn't plush like the one in Morningside. No stained-glass peacock or Art Deco tower here. Inside, there are dozens of soldiers in the seats, mostly uniformed but you'd know anyway because anyone from a farm would be outside on a day like today. The weather is turning, but it hasn't turned yet. Some of the soldiers have girls with them, East Lothian sophisticates, but mostly it's just men. There are children, too, and five years ago, they would be clutching paper bags of sweeties, their mouths sugar-crammed and sticky, but not now. A few have carrot candy, instead, and they suck on it for a turn, then pass it down the line, all through the newsreel. Aeroplanes over London and footage of the streets. Churchill's Few are praised and he's playing Prince Hal for all he's worth these days, but it seems to work. The soldiers clap and cheer, and the air feels thick with courage and the floor under my shoes is sticky. I can't stop thinking about Stanley, that look in his eyes and then what he said about hosing out the plane. They don't show that on the newsreels, do they? I'm on my feet before I know it, pushing past Muriel and out to the door, but I make it, just make it out to the street before I'm sick over the railing. The laughter of children, then the street is quiet, but I'm shaking and the tears come, too. I'm glad Muriel had fixed my hair, that it is out of the way, that I didn't have any damned mascara to wear. I wipe my mouth on my sleeve and try to stop shaking. There's a hand on my back now, which must be Muriel, but when my breath returns and I can open my eyes, I see that it isn't. It's that blond soldier and he's passing me a handkerchief.

'Thank you.' I straighten and turn away from the railing, holding the folded cloth in my hands. 'I—'

'Yes,' he interrupts, then smiles. 'You are welcome. It is for your eyes. The handkerchief.'

'Of course. Thank you.' I dab them with the cool cloth, and Muriel is through the door now, her voice loud and warm. 'Goodness, Jane, that was dramatic. Must have been all the sun and cycling that did it. A first-class case of the collywobbles. How are you doing, duck?'

'Wobbled,' I say. 'Glad to have got outside in time.'

'It's so warm in there, isn't it? And the smell of all those men. That can't have helped. You look absolutely grey.'

'I'll be fine. Really. I just need some air. I'll come right in a minute.'

The soldier cleared his throat. 'Some water to drink, perhaps?'

Muriel turns to see him and then she grins. 'Izaak! Always the ideal gentleman. Jane, you picked the best rescuer of them all. Izaak is a real brick. The brickiest.' She puts an arm around me and gives me a squeeze.

'I think she might need a cup of tea.'

'Yes,' I say. 'I'd like that. And I think I should probably sit down.'

They walk me down to the Italian chippy and find me a seat. I pass Muriel my purse so that she can pay for tea for three. As she steps up to the counter, Izaak leans towards me across the table, his voice soft and subtle.

'We will talk later,' he says. 'About Stanley. Trust me.'

'Did you find him? Did you give him the suitcase?'

'Later. Not now.'

My face warms and I hear Muriel laughing at the counter, the woman there saying something and laughter again, but when she comes back to the table, she hands me a cup and looks at me oddly and I only look at the tea. It is weak, naturally, but lovely to know that my ration at home isn't reduced by this cup. I sip slowly, and when I look up, Izaak meets my eye, smiling. Then he smiles at Muriel.

'I wondered if you two ladies might know each other.'

'I hadn't realized you had met,' she says.

'Yes. We were out walking near the shore. I had to turn her away.'

'I was getting too close to the defence lines. Twice.'

'The area was closed to civilians.'

'But it is safe, isn't it? The shore, I mean. I . . . I wouldn't have been blown up.'

'Perhaps not. But you might have spooked the boys in the pillboxes. They are doing their best to keep a good eye on the coast. Best to stay away. As I said before, people shouldn't be out there, no matter how pleasant it seems.'

Muriel digs in her pockets for a pack of cigarettes. 'Jane, you are perfectly peaky. You should have said something. If you had, I never would have dragged you out here.'

'How are you feeling now?' Izaak asks.

'I'll be fine. It's nothing.'

Izaak excuses himself and steps outside, saying he's sure he will see us both later. Muriel grabs a menu and looks it up and down, chattering on about the lovely grub they do here, and I drink my tea.

'Look,' she says, suddenly. 'There's a dance coming up. Do you want to go? I need someone to go with.'

'Won't Izaak be going?'

'I wouldn't know. Haven't a clue. I wish you wouldn't tease.'

'I'm not. I . . . No, I don't think I could. Not without Stanley.'

'Oh, it'll be fine, really. He's sure to be off dancing, too. Everyone is these days. Really, it's a matter of morale. Civic duty to keep cheerful, don't you think? Anyway, I'm sure there will be masses of people. Air Force and Poles and everybody. Lots of farm workers, too. And land girls. I've got half a fancy to sign up for that game myself. Listen, if I do, you could take over my garden, couldn't you? That would be just the ticket. Rosie's time's up, but there might be another pig and Mum could help you out. Then I could go, and I wouldn't be leaving anyone in the lurch. And you'd have work. Cure the waiting blues in no time at all. That's all it is, isn't it? You missing him?'

'How did we get from let's-go-to-a-dance to look-after-my-pig-and-potatoes-won't-you? Muriel, you could talk anyone into anything.'

'Part of my charm. Anyway, the dance is Saturday night. You'll be feeling better by then, I should think. We could get the bus up and walk home again together, no bother. Take your mind from your troubles. Dance for victory and all that.'

'I can barely get my mind around my shoelaces.'

'I'll come round your house to help you. The dance won't start until ten, but it should keep going until two at least, if it's a good band. They even muster midnight sandwiches sometimes. The Polish families bring them along. Call them sausage, but it's only

214

spread and rabbit from the dunes. Tasty as anything, though, especially with all the dancing. How are you feeling now? Still peely-wally? I think the tea's brought back your colour. You ready for a choc ice?'

'Not on your nelly.'

I say I'll take a bus home and Muriel says she'll come too, but I remind her about the bicycles. I ask if she thinks Izaak might be able to ride Connie's bike home for me? That will give them a long time together to smooth things through. Muriel grins and squeezes my arm.

'Might be for the best, really,' she says. 'Wouldn't want you to have a wobble on the way back and end up in a ditch somewhere.'

She leaves me at the bus stop and says she'll come round to check on me in the morning. All the way back to Aberlady, I watch the ditches and the hedgerows and worry about Stanley's suitcase.

9

I T IS NOT UNTIL NOVEMBER THAT IZAAK PASSES ME WORD
of where Stanley is. I come back from the shops in Gullane
to find a yellow square of folded paper slipped through the door.
Birthwood Cottage, Biggar.

I don't know if he has been there long, or if he has only just
arrived. But it doesn't matter. He's away from the coast now and
out of the mine.

In the afternoon, I sit down and try to shape words on the
page. My fingers smell like soap powder and the pen feels oddly
weighted in my hands.

Dear Stanley,

*Right off the bat, I got the address from Izaak. I assume that's
your first question, seeing my awful scrawl and wondering how*

I found you. Doesn't that sound just like something they say in the films? Right off the bat, darling? I wish we could go to the films tonight, me and you. Sit in the dark, hidden away. And laugh. That would be nice.

Of course, I should tell you I am well and then spill all the local news, and I will, but I can't yet. It's you I want to focus on, not shift over to me. I want to know how you are and what it's like where you are and what is happening. Izaak told me so little. We managed to chat at a dance last week and he told me about your sympathetic chaplain, but I imagine he doesn't really know much anyway. The military is all rather need-to-know, isn't it? Did he do right by you? That's what worries me the most. Was I right to trust him? Because I did. He said this would be counted as a sort of leave for you. There must be some other category. Convalescence, perhaps. Izaak said it wouldn't be detainment, but he couldn't promise there wouldn't be a trial. Oh, they don't call it that, do they? All this military process and jargon and bloody— sorry, Stanley, but it is. It's a bloody, bloody war.

No. I can't do this. I should take a clean sheet and try starting this letter again. Write some cheerful words, all full of hope and charity, but I won't. This, too, is the lie of the land and we promised intimacy, didn't we? But you — I wanted to start this letter with you. Even if it can only be how I imagine you rather than how you really are. I know you're in a cottage near Biggar, so I'll imagine that and maybe sometime, you'll manage to write to me and correct all my shoddy, poetic assumptions. The hills are lovely there, I think. Steep and rounded. I don't think it's rocky land, is it? What will you find to look at? But maybe the hills will do. You can imagine the glaciers that shaped them and the long years of wind sandpapering their slopes. The cottage will be stone, too, won't it? A shepherd's cottage nestled in the crook of the hills. You can lay your palm against the quarried blocks and dream of past ages. I like the name. Birthwood conjures all sorts of dreams. Trees, naturally, and the possibility of something new. It's green, too, I'm sure, and green feels important these days. Even when everything is bleak and precarious, or loud with aeroplanes overhead, it feels important that there are still green things all about. Things with roots. Things that grow. It seems to me that the important things are not things that happen, but things that grow. Your walk home only happened. What grows from it will matter. Of course, it will.

And this is where you need to tease me out of my lecturing or remind me that this all sounds like nonsense to a geologist. But I'll one-up you, my fine fellow. You won't have guessed yet, but when you reread this letter, you'll surely tell me I am no good at keeping secrets because every line has already been telling you my news. What I mean to say, what I can't help but say, and by now you do know, is that I'm expecting. What a thing to tell a husband in a letter. But there it is. All being well, the baby will be born in the spring. Around the middle of May, I think. And all is well, so don't worry about me. I'm hungry, which my mother says is a sign of health. At first, I wasn't, and I could hardly manage a cup of tea, but I chalked it all up to worry about you. Took me far too long to understand the real cause, but when I did, I headed into the city and visited Dr Graham right away. He says I'm right as rain. Sound as a workhorse and would manage heartily, which hardly sounds ladylike, but I found cheering, and as he's known me since day one, I'll trust his words.

September and October have been busy. Muriel got me involved with the harvest. Nothing taxing because of my suspicions, though I hadn't told her anything. Mainly, I have been hauling up vegetables, sometimes in her garden, sometimes elsewhere. The onion sets you planted here came up beautifully. You can't find them in the shops now for love or money, so I'm not telling anyone about these beauties. I lifted them in September and they've been keeping well since then in the garden box you lined with those dried dune grasses. Do you remember the day we gathered them? All that sky above us. I would send you that day again, my love, if I could, and it might brighten these November rains. And I'll send Lawrence's stormy raindrops that cling like silver bees to the panes. And his child sitting under the piano, pressing the small, poised feet of his mother who smiles as she sings. That will be me. Imagine that, will you? East Lothian rain all down the window and me at the piano, singing, my feet tingling and longing to dance.

A pretty picture, I suppose. I want you to know that I am keeping up. I worry. I work. I find ways to be cheerful. Now that the harvest is done, I'm keeping busy with getting things ready for the baby. More knitting and I'm getting the hang of it. Baby things are so small they knit up quick as anything. As

219

fast as lickitie, quick as hickitie, as my granny used to say, but my mother never did.

I don't know anything about your grannies. What were they like? It occurs to me that this baby of ours is going to have twice the ancestors I do. Isn't that wonderful? Every generation doubled, all those stories we might share, if only we knew them.

I'm sending you a book from the minister. He said that you would be interested and I think I agree. It's all about local carvings, but older than Carrick's. Did you know about the fragment of the cross found here at the manse? Seventh-century sandstone and carved with Celtic birds, all intertwined. It was found built into the manse garden wall, but it's over at Carlowrie Castle now. Maybe we can see it after the war. Make it a long day on bikes and see if the people who live there will oblige. You could flash your university credentials and we could have a jolly day of it. But you'll see there is a clever reproduction in the book. Reverend Thomson said he thought they were wild geese, an ancient symbol of the Holy Ghost. Something else I didn't know, but you might.

I put in a few more feathers for you, too, in case you needed a bookmark.

Write to me, if you can. Tell me how you are. Tell me about the land, about your heart. Know that I love you and won't stop. Ever.

Your

Jane

* * *

It's a mess of a letter, but honest, I think. And it does raise the question: is spilling out on the page like this more honest than crafting something carefully? Is craft meant to conceal or clarify? I'm not sure I know any more. Where do the poets get with all their half-said thoughts, prettily arranged? Though, perhaps if they said what they really wanted, we'd all be fit to be tied. And if that's so, what sort of critic might I be? I can't even open my degree books these days. I just sit and read Lawrence and listen to the rain.

But I wish and even pray that this letter may speed its winged way to Stanley. Like hope itself, that thing with feathers, and thank you, Miss Dickinson, for that lovely image. Why didn't I give Stanley that one, too? I think about adding it in, but annotation would spoil the flow and if the letter is to be honest, then let it be unpolished, too.

As a scientist, Stanley will appreciate the letter's actuality. Not a news report, but a record of the weather. And somehow we'll weather this. It was a strange wind that blew Stanley north, away from the barracks and almost to the sea. But the land caught him, the mine snared him and hid him like a rabbit in its heart, keeping him safe. I hope he is safe now. I hope that Birthwood Cottage, whatever else it may be, is a haven. Such a fairy-tale name. Rather fits with Stanley's rooks who brought him presents. And the godly geese, too. All these feathered fables. Why do storks bring babies? Who first fancied that idea? Is it German? Germans are good at fairy tales. I wonder if that's why they're good at war. They dare imagine darkness. But then, so do we. Ghosties and ghoulies and long-legged beasties and things that go bump in the night. Wild god-geese on the sandbar and selkies and kelpies and all of the saints. There's a Scottish story, too, about a raven, although it might be a crow, who drops a gold ring into a goblet. I can't remember if it's for good or for evil. I'll need to brush up on my fairy tales before the baby comes. The baby with mussel-shell eyes.

I went to the manse last week to talk to Connie about knitting patterns. When I first asked, she seemed pleased and talked about the poor orphans, so I had to explain that these wee projects were for the local home front. Cheeky, but she grinned, and then turned grave. When she didn't ask, I knew she was counting.

I haven't told Muriel yet, but I will need to soon. That feels like a decision I have to make. She's asked me to spend Christmas at her house, too, and I think I will. Save Mum and Dad the worry of where to put me up at the flat.

I wonder about writing to the baby. Is it strange to write to an unborn child? Unlucky, maybe? But she's no less real than Stanley. No less alive. Not having heard from Stanley for months now, I imagine that he can't reply. That he is dumb, muted somehow, perhaps by the air in the mine, his voice gone underground, his thoughts in hiding, too. Like the child, he might hear me if I send out words his way, but perhaps like her, they will carry meaning only in tone, only in the shape of sounds, the mood of breath as the words pass through.

What water walls contain him now? Do the Scottish hills womb him round? Is the sky a mother's tautness above? And what might he kick out against?

This isn't helping. It was the child I was wondering about – or perhaps only my desire to connect. It is so easy to feel lonely these days. So here I go, I will give it a try and write her a letter. Her? That's based on nothing. Only feeling. Or just hope. Because I might understand her better. I try to stay unconvinced. But then the quiet voice returns, saying *she*. I imagine it is the baby's voice. She reaches out for me, sending certainties up through my jangling nerves, into the space that holds my heart. So I reach out for her.

Dear Baby, My lucky love. I want you to know that you are wanted. That is the place to begin. Everything else will grow from there. If you ask, I will be honest. You surprised me. I had my eyes on other things when you crept up on me.

Will I, really? Be honest like that? I'd like to. And over time, I will. I am sure of that. Because I think you should hear your story. I will shelter Stanley. I won't tell the world that it was really him, but I must tell you. How else will you be able to make decisions? Our decisions shaped you. You will need to know.

But not yet. Not when you're little. And soft. For now, I will simply tell you that you are born of love and longing. And I want you.

You are a half-made thing, but so am I. Half said, half thought, half aware, I'm sure, of all that's going on around us both. And maybe just as hidden as you. Hidden and conspicuous. And so is your father. He's hidden, too, hidden from me. But I trust that we'll emerge. We'll all emerge from this darkness, this mad noise and fear and be able to see each other. To look each other in the face and tell the truth, if only through silence.

10

THE KITCHEN IS DARK. I PUSH THE BLACKOUT CURTAIN aside to let moonlight into the kitchen and a shadow walks up the garden path, hops onto the wall, pauses and licks paws before easing through Miss Baxter's open window. I turn to the table and slice a thick wodge of dense brown bread, then a precious onion, too. There are still drippings in the pan from yesterday, so I scrape them out with the knife and slather them on the bread like glue for the onions. My stomach makes appalling noises. No end of indignities when blessed with child. But the sandwich tastes good and I eat it slowly, the onion sharp, sweet and crisp. We used to eat onion sandwiches with cheese, me and Stanley together out in the dunes before the war. We even believed the water was warm in those days, took off shoes and socks and waded up to our knees in the blue, blue water. Now the sea looks different with winter. A November sea is corpse-cold, hungry and grey as old pans.

There are never enough eggs in November. Not enough light so the chickens give up, and that means no cake. When my mother came to visit last week, she seemed surprised by this.

'But you've all the farms out here,' she said. 'And all the garden space, too. Surely there must be many families in the village with a decent supply of eggs. Haven't you been making friends?'

She wants me to come home and go back to being happy. I am not sure what she means. I told her about Muriel and her mother, about Rosie and the scraps and the sausages that followed, then about Connie and the minister.

'Well, I am glad,' she said. 'It is good to have friends on hand. You'll be needing them soon, won't you? Are you getting your energy back, my dear?'

'I'm managing.'

She smiled, because she understood. There were enough of us at home.

'Of course. You'll manage just fine. It does take time to learn, but I know that you will manage beautifully.'

Beautifully is hardly the word but she's right. I am trying. Halfway through already and trying. And hungry. I can't stop myself thinking about food. So much of my brain is occupied with food chatter. Egg and cake and onions. Mum brought me a gift from home: my granny's cookbook – *Everybody's Pudding Book*, by Mrs Georgiana Hill. The recipes are arranged seasonally, starting with January. Another eggless month.

'The shelves of all good housekeepers should still be stored with a fair share of preserves of different descriptions, which, with the numerous farinaceous substances such as sago, tapioca, rice and others that are always readily obtained, our resources of festivity will be found to be most ample.'

Ha. To give her credit, she does note that it is also not the best time of year for milk, cream, or butter and, with that in mind, she gives the recipe for simple currant fritters without eggs. Half a pint of mild Scotch ale, flour, and currants, fried in a pan of boiling lard, then sugared and served with lemon juice. A thoughtful touch.

But not on the ration. Today, I resorted to the newspaper's recipe suggestions which feature an 'elegant eggless ginger cake' recipe. I thought it would look nice on the blue cake-stand. Cheerful. But it was false and boring, even with the suggested mock cream on top, gritty goop that it was. Bland, false and boring and sweetened with flavoured gelatine. I wished Rosie was still in the land of the living because then I could donate the failed cake to her and that would mean more sausages for me.

I've been spending time copying out recipes onto careful cards, looking forward to the impossible tomorrow when they will mean something again.

Tonight, tea was only tea, but at least I slept afterwards.

I suppose that is one good thing about living alone. Stanley would be horrified to see what I'm eating. As would my mother, I was jolly well sure, if she looked past my brave face and tea-party sandwiches. But hell's bells, if I am to stiff it out here alone in the wind, I might as well eat what I like, that's for damned certain.

I need to sleep better. The aeroplanes are loud at night and it's making me rather Anglo-Saxon, I'm afraid. My language is usually cleaner than this. I wonder if the baby knows. Can she hear me? I mean, all the unspoken bits. Thought vibrations, maybe? The energy of vulgarity passing through the womb walls?

Yesterday, she moved. So early and I thought I must be imagining it. How can she be big enough yet to feel? I'm too skinny, that's what it is. Not enough meat on these wartime bones to give a bairn a cushion. But it was wonderful. Just a little flutter somewhere behind my navel. I was sitting by the window, trying to get into a rhythm with my knitting. I can manage, but the stitches all need to be so deliberate. I've none of Connie's momentum, her clickity-clackity stitch-after-stitch-after-stitch. I need to think it through. So I sat there thinking, working the grey wool in my fingers, not too loosely, not too tight, wondering if Stanley was warm enough at night in the cottage. What a mothering thought, that, and then there they were. Bubbles in a glass of champagne.

When the war is over and Stanley is safely home to stay, we'll drink champagne. Nothing but, and bucketfuls. It feels close to the end now, but the end of my tether or the end of the world, I can't know. When the world does end, I want to be out in the dunes. Drinking champagne, yes, and with Stanley, of course. I want those ugly concrete blocks all swept away, the wind empty and strong around us, and the grasses to grow wild again. We'll spread out a blanket on the sandy ground and there will be larks and rabbits and geese, too, out on the sandbar or flying over the waves in their family skeins and because it's the end, there will be no more shadows, no planes overhead, no warships on the Forth. All that will be swept away and we'll have time to be together just as we are, unafraid after all and love and love and love until the day is over. That's how the end will be.

I'm not sure the minister or Connie would approve. These aren't quite godly thoughts. I'm finding church hard now. The pews are uncomfortable and so is the lack of men. Old men come, but there are far too many women and and they stare at me. I'm sure they do. It's far too early for them to tell, but I feel their eyes anyway. They know. Maybe they can see it in the way I walk or in how tired I know I look. Or if they don't and I'm making it up, they'll figure it out soon enough, anyway. A baby bump out of season. What will they be imagining? How on earth can I keep Stanley safe? Only one way, really, and though hard, it's sure to work because Stanley grew up here and he's their golden boy. And me? The suspect floozy. I won't mind. I'll carry that. And everything else I must keep hidden.

Miss Baxter is awake through the wall. I heard her close her window after the cat, and then the springs on her chair eased down again. I still haven't gone round to see her, not properly. Only spoken with her during the raids, and when we've come up from the shops at the same time. She must be my mother's age, but thinner. I'll go round in the morning. I wonder if she'd like the eggless cake.

* * *

There was a suggestion in the newspaper about adding a grated carrot to a cake for moistness, and it's not a bad idea, really. I think I'll add it to the Christmas cake I've promised the Grants. I've been setting aside sugar for weeks now and Muriel says she will contribute an egg to the cause. She pops in to see me, gangly, awkward with her hair cropped shorter and uneven. She looks unhappy. She tells me her mother is planning a rabbit with bacon for Christmas Day.

'Your pig is keeping us all fed these days,' I say. 'Makes the best dripping I've ever had.'

'The butcher thought she was a bit too fat. He said we should have had her earlier. Mum said we're all needing all the fat we can get these days.'

'Me too,' I say, but she doesn't laugh. She fumbles a question about when Stanley's coming home on leave. I tell her I don't know. We find other things to talk about.

Muriel says that she's candied some rosehips and offers some for the Christmas cake. I tell her I've dried some apples by the fire and have some sultanas saved, so that should do for dried fruit. I draw the line at turnip. I'm no good at this wartime housewife game.

Muriel refills our teacups and the second cup is stronger. The kitchen feels warm with two of us sitting there. I push up my sleeves and ask about her garden, her parents and then, after a while, I ask about Izaak. She fixes her gaze on the stained doily. When she does speak, it is slowly.

'Well, I wouldn't know how he's doing, would I?' The spaces between the words are precise and sharp. 'Isn't it you who keeps track of Izaak these days? You have some nerve sitting there, asking after him.'

'What do you mean?'

'As if . . . as if you really believed I didn't know about the notes you two sent back and forth. As if I didn't suspect you'd been meeting. You could have told me. Should have.' Muriel's face is flushed and unhappy and I can't help but straighten in my chair, though she isn't being fair and she's raising her voice now. 'You're married! You have some nerve.'

'Muriel.'

'No. Don't. Please. I don't want to hear anything else. It's not worth fighting about.'

She doesn't stay. At the door, I try to hug her but she is nothing but shoulders and elbows and my breasts feel sore when I try to reach around her. She shrugs me off and pulls her collar up against the rain. On the walk outside, she pauses for a moment and looks at me with a crumpled, angry face and it looks like she's going to say something else, only she just jams her hat on over her ears and scuttles away down the deaf and empty street.

This won't get any easier when my bump starts to show.

Half an hour passes and I hear the door again. I want to ignore it, but can't. I'll need to tell her something. Maybe everything. Can't, I think. Can't, can't, can't as I walk down the hallway, then the key turns slowly in my hand, the rain on the street, the sound of a cat.

'Miss Baxter,' I say. 'Come in, please, come in.'

She stands on the threshold, her head tilted, her face soft. The cat in her arms dark, sleek and patient and the sleeves of her jumper catch the raindrops. 'I wondered if you might need company on such a wet day.'

'Yes,' I say. 'That would be lovely. I have been meaning to knock on your door. I just . . .'

'Well, now there is no need. Here I am.' She wipes her feet on the mat and follows me through to the kitchen. I test the kettle to see if it needs more water, but she stops me. 'No need for that, either,' she says. 'I'm sure you used plenty of tea when your friend was here.' She sits down in the seat where I had been sitting, sighing a little as she eases herself into the chair. Her hair twists into coils over her ears, the moisture creating a soft halo around her small head.

'Is it all right if I let Basil down? He likes to explore new places, but he won't cause mischief. He's very good.'

'Of course. Make yourself at home,' I say.

'I call him Basil, you see, because when he was small he liked to sleep in a plant pot, so the name suited. Silly really, but there you are. He's my company.'

I watch the cat walk the perimeter of the room on careful feet as if the tiles are untrustworthy, though I imagine it's just the same tiles on the other side of the wall. He sniffs the small mat by the back door, the bristles of the broom propped up in the corner.

'My sister thinks I'm daft to keep him. Recommends giving him sleep instead. Isn't that a grisly way to put it? Sleep. But so many have done precisely that. My sister read about it in the London paper, and told me it would be a kindness. I could never.

231

It's not right. Not out here in the country. He'd never go hungry here, which is what they fear in the cities, I suppose. You can't get rations for pets. Here, there's no need and he copes fine with whatever mice and birds he finds.'

The cat weaves himself around me, the soft pressure of touch on my legs and I have to turn away, blinking. Miss Baxter reaches out and lays a gentle hand on mine. 'There now, my dear. There now.' Her voice is so gentle.

It doesn't matter, does it? That I am not alone, that Muriel isn't fair, doesn't understand. It doesn't matter that Stanley is gone and I can't I can't I can't talk about it or tell anyone or he won't be safe and I don't know if he is safe at all these days or if I will ever find him again or

'There now. You make as much noise as you need to. What a lonely stretch of coast out here. We must all be mad to live like this.'

'I . . . I'm sorry. I shouldn't . . .'

'Shouldn't say shouldn't. Tears come. Let them.'

So I do. I let the room fill with tears, the table a raft that rises as a black line of weather covers half the sky and horror hovers like barrage balloons. Miss Baxter is a quiet hill and anchors the room as I rage.

'And I've . . . I've . . . promised to spend Christmas with them. I can't. I just can't. Not knowing what she thinks.'

'No? Mistakes shouldn't matter so much. Maybe I should come along, too. Do you think you might ask Muriel's mother if there would be room at the table for another poor lonely woman who can't travel this terrible Christmas? If you would like the company.'

'Would you? You'd come with me?'

'Of course. Would it help if I mentioned that your husband had been home? What was it, four months ago that he helped me with my blackout curtains? Five? Such a nice young man. Handsome, too. Shame it was such a quick visit before he was reposted. Is that the word? I could tell all sorts of people about that. Or would that be the wrong information to spread? Which might smooth the way for you, my dear? You think about it.' She sets a cup of water in front of me and I find I am thirsty.

'You are so kind.'

'It will be all right,' she says. 'Things settle. In a small place, they get stirred up easily enough, especially in difficult days. But they will settle. By the time your bonny baby is here, you'll have dozens of offers of kindness again. I am sure of it. But then you might choose to move, too. A change might be good for you. And the baby.'

'You mean somewhere away from the talk.'

'Perhaps. It might be good to have some space around you. That would be nice. Oh, God bless you, child. You will find it, if that's what you want. Or it will find you. Things turn up.'

'And Muriel?'

'She won't ossify. There is too much life in her for that. She'll soften again, I'm sure. You won't lose her.'

A few days later, the wind is high and Miss Baxter knocks on my door again, asking for help with a rattling window pane.

'It keeps me awake in the night and I worry it bothers the cat, too. Just a little noise most nights, but on days like this, it can be loud. A silly thing to bother you about with all the other noises in the night, but I thought perhaps you might have an answer?'

I find a scrap of cotton and tear off a small piece. Outside, the trees beside the kirkyard point their fingers to a pale sky, storm-broken and grey, and I think of Tennyson's yew, which changest not in any gale – that was it, wasn't it? And something about yews smoking with pollen when touched by wind. These rags of poems are the words in my head as I work the cloth between the frame and the glass with a blade and Miss Baxter sits on the edge of the bed, her cat curled beside her.

'My mother once told me that men like the wind,' she says. 'Men like the wind, but women don't. Do you think she's right? I love the wind myself.'

'Me too.'

'It's lively and so . . . so moving. It makes the world a lovely thing to watch.'

The snow comes in December. In the middle of the month, someone puts a shortened Christmas tree in the Anderson shelter and wreathes it with paper streamers. The week before Christmas, the tea and sugar ration is increased and I think about going home to Edinburgh after all, but there is a notice in the paper about a travel advisory – fuel conservation for the war effort. Well, Mum will understand that one, at least.

I am hungrier now, even with my maternity rations. I drink water to keep full and promise myself to forage the hedgerows come summer for more provisions. That and plant more onions, if I can find the sets.

There are no church bells this Christmas. Not here in East Lothian nor in Edinburgh, nor any city up and down the country. Since the summer, a ban has been instituted so that the bells might be reserved to signal a German invasion. And so it stands, even at Christmas. The silent bells hold both fear and joy, and I wonder how we'll hear them when they do ring out again.

Mr Grant comes home from London with plans to stay for the rest of the winter. Mrs Grant slipped on the ice and has done something nasty to her back, so he's concerned. I hear this from Miss Baxter who heard it at the kirk.

On Christmas Day, we go together to the Grants, Miss Baxter and I. The morning has been crackling cold and frost has iced every blade of grass, every yew needle and the stones of the kirk tower, too. Now the wind has sharpened and the walk to the house is cold. Beyond the trees, we hear the wild geese in farmed fields, gabbling among the precious winter wheat.

'Are you feeling ready?' Miss Baxter asks.

'For dinner? Or for conversation?' My coat feels tight and my fingers are cold in my pockets, but she smiles softly at me and takes my arm.

'Christmas itself, I suppose. That's all I meant, my dear. Christmas has a way of coming even when all else is strange and cold. But goodness, the wind is dancing today. Just look at the white out on the water.'

She offers to carry my bag full of packages and I let her and listen as she tells me about her breakfast of hot porridge and a celebratory fourth cup of tea.

* * *

Along with the rabbit, Muriel's mother prepares baked celery with a cheesy crust, a recipe her mother used during the Great War. 'Served elegantly as its own course, too. Just like the French. My mum liked fine manners.'

'There won't be much French about this feast,' Mr Grant says. 'The occupation's done us out of all possibility of good postprandial brandy. Think we can muster some whisky?' He winks at Muriel and she laughs.

She is warmer than I expected. Friendly enough, as if I were the neighbour's visiting relative to be cordially entertained. She says nothing about my condition and I wonder if she's noticed. But all her talk is about the land girls and the work ahead. Come February, she says, she will be down in Drem bunking at a farmhouse there with two other girls. She's looking forward to it. Her father says he'll miss her and she kisses the top of his head. His thin hair, her close, soft cheek. I can't picture the top of my father's head.

'I'm not gone forever, you know, old man,' Muriel says. 'Not even getting married. Just off to work.'

'I know, I know. But I worry. And now, with your mother's back, too.'

'Och, you. I'll be fit in no time. All this food is sure to strengthen my resolve.'

'Ah, but.' He stops and says no more, his hand reaching across the table to take hers.

'Will you be getting another pig?' I ask.

'Well, now, we haven't quite decided. We'll need to evaluate what to take on without Muriel.'

'Jane can lend a hand,' Muriel says. 'Easy as spit. Rosie practically raised herself with all the rummaging she managed under the orchard trees. All that is required is simple maintenance, really.'

'I'm happy to help. Of course I am.'

'That could be one answer, then,' says Mrs Grant. 'You're such a helpful lass. I'm sure we'll all manage together, won't we?' She smiles at me and fills our teacups, and we listen to the BBC broadcast from Coventry Cathedral. Amidst the ruins, the provost preaches restoration, pledging that after the war, he will work with those who have been enemies *to build a kinder, more Christ-child-like world.* I try to catch Muriel's eye. She holds her teacup carefully.

Towards the end of the meal, I begin to feel dizzy and have to excuse myself from the table. I step into the pantry and lay my hands flat against the cool marble shelf. Mrs Grant follows me and stands close.

'You all right, my dear? Too hot in the other room?'

'Yes. I'm . . . I'll be fine.'

'Would you like to lie down? Might be better for your head. You'll be finding it harder to lean over to stop the dizziness these days, I imagine. It was like that with Muriel. Such a head I had! My mother was always telling me to stand up straight to make it better and to give the baby space, but I only ever wanted to set my head down on any table I could find, close my eyes and wait for the months to pass. But they will, you know. They will.'

She lays a gentle hand between my shoulder blades and her voice is quiet and reassuring. 'Waiting is always difficult, my dear, but difficult days do pass.'

Later, she sends me home with a thick slab of cake and leftovers to feed an army. Miss Baxter is given a jar of marmalade and a bit of cheese for Basil and she thanks the Grants for their kindness. Mrs Grant stands at the door with her arms around Muriel and they both wear brave smiles as they say goodbye and Happy Christmas and joy of the season and goodwill to all and peace, peace, peace in the days ahead.

Hogmanay comes and goes and I ignore it. Most do. The minister opens the kirk for prayer on New Year's Day, and I watch cold figures pass my door on their way over the road, but I stay at home. I write to Stanley, as I do every week, and hear nothing.

I grow fat. The winter grows still colder. There's talk in the shops of farmers finding their sheep shorn and shivering and the foreign airmen are suspected of stealing the wool to stuff their palliasses. The butcher made a weak joke about Polish mattresses and local pale lasses and I pretended I hadn't heard. In the newspaper, there are reports of *considerable telephonic disruption* due to wet and freezing snow clinging to overhead telephone lines. They can't tell us where the bombs are falling, but they can conjure up all these careful images of weather. I imagine strange white snow birds like pale-feathered rooks, their frozen feet snapping the wires and all the broken words of our local conversations tumbling out like frozen eggs to shatter on the cold ground.

Miss Baxter and I share tea most evenings now. She leaves Basil at home or out in the garden. Sometimes she watches him through the window, though mostly we sit together at the table, warming our hands around our cups. There's been talk on the radio about parachutists on the south coast, and even sightings up here. You'd think that all the airfields would quell fears, but everyone is keeping alert and aware.

'Ah yes, it's parachutists this time, is it? There's always something to watch for.' Miss Baxter pulls at the cuffs of her cardigan, looking for a handkerchief. 'And parachutists are a frightening enough prospect, but what about the clouds behind them? Is anyone talking about that, I wonder? What about the fear and the doubt that are crowding in? And all the suspicion, hunger and hate? And loneliness, too, and greed and decay. What about everything else that comes with war? We're all too distracted looking out for parachutists to watch for any of that, aren't we? We don't notice the heavy dark clouds blowing in over Europe. And then it is too late.'

'Stanley would like that,' I say. 'I think he'd say you understand.'

'Maybe I do, a little. My brother was a conchie in the last war.'

A pause and she doesn't ask about Stanley.

After a little while, she tells me about the men her brother met at his meetings. All kinds, she said. Some clever and privileged, coming from the right schools. But there were others, too, who were just regular boys like Mack.

'Such courage, the lot of them. No one really recognized it. Because it takes courage to walk away. They had strong ideas about life and God and wouldn't let anyone bully them into killing. Well, in the end, Mack was lucky and he was assigned non-military work. Of National Importance, they called it. But we had some hard times because of him.'

I ask if the family understood his conviction.

'No, not at all. There was nothing irregular about us. Regular

Sunday school kids, and my father kept a bible on his bedside table all his life. But my brother picked up some new ideas. Met some older boys and said he'd learned to read the scriptures differently. Still, it wasn't anything shocking. Perhaps a little more serious, that's all. It was only when the war came that it made a difference. That war changed many things.'

She doesn't say more then, just watches the cat flicking his tail back and forth, and the sparrows flit from the wall to the paving stones, then back to the wall.

Late in January, I'm feeling heavy and catch a bus along to the shops in Gullane. The weather is bleak again. Bleak and dreich, flat-skied and grey. When I say as much to the butcher, he says not to worry a jot as the days of Bride would be coming soon. My cheeks warm and redden. I know he's only referring to the story of St Bride and the first days of February when the weather tends to warm, but it feels like a personal dig.

The butcher asks after Stanley and I say I haven't heard yet this week. As if he writes weekly. I wish he would.

'He went last in May, didn't he?' The butcher looks down as he asks the question, but I don't.

'Yes,' I say. 'He went south with the others at the end of the month.'

Thick fingers wrap up my sliver of beef, then add a slice of fat on top. 'That's for the wee one. You'll be wanting more meat, the both of you.'

'Thank you.'

'Nothing said, nothing minded.'

'Of course not.'

I'll mince the fat and mix it with tomato paste and breadcrumbs to fry up as faux sausages. Another idea from the newspaper, though the ladies around here all say fox.

11

Then spring comes but not warmth and I still wear socks to bed. Mornings come earlier, with daffodils and taller grass in the kirkyard, and everything is filled by the wind. The front room. The trees across the road. Miss Baxter's pillowcase on the laundry line. I, too, am restless. Muriel has been out at the Drem farmhouse for a month, or a little more. The geese left last week, wave after wave lifting from the sandbar, a pandemonium of honk-a-lonks and trumpets, Mrs Grant said, like half the world a-wing with the dawn. She had stopped by with a heap of old baby clothes she says she found put away in a drawer. I suspect she had been around the village and collected them from a few drawers at least – that, or Muriel had the most clothes of any baby in Britain. I'll wash them today with my extra-ration maternity soap and pin them up on my end of the line. Every day now, the light is stretching and the days last longer. It's easier to hope with this wind and strong light.

Mrs Grant tells me that last week Mrs Scott had a letter returned by the censors. The franking read: RETURNED BY CENSOR, and on the back of the envelope there was a stamped note which read *No permission to ask for parcels or rationed goods or rationed food from overseas.*

'She was terribly upset. It hadn't occurred to her that she was doing anything wrong. She just kept saying *why don't they tell us these things? How can we do the right thing if we just don't know?* The poor dear, I don't think she'd ever been scolded like that before in her life.'

Miss Baxter gets a letter from her sister, franked with red ink. RELEASED BY CENSOR. Inside, the letter is scored through with black and hard to read. Together, we glean that her sister hasn't been able to sleep, and that she is worried, but we don't know what about – something she has heard in the night.

'It must be terrible,' Miss Baxter says, 'for someone to take the time to cross all this through. Still, there has been no news of any raids in the north. I can't think Stirling would be much of a target. Maybe further west. Glasgow? They might have had a bad raid. Do you think she'd have heard that in Bridge of Allan? Maybe that's what she's trying to say.'

Still no word from Stanley. I've written to him again, and I said that I wouldn't write again now until after the baby is born. It can't be long now. The baby is heavy, sitting low and shifting awkwardly. When she pushes into me, I press back with my palm, prodding gently and breathing softly to give her space.

One morning, I decide to take a walk. Fresh air and a bit of a stretch. A bit of shopping and then on the way home, I'll stop at the Grants with bramble tea. It's been a good week for drying things in the sunshine and I've read in my granny's cookbook that bramble tea is a delicious change from the usual kind. She wrote this in the margin next to a recipe for orange pudding, which sounds so very nice. I slip a paper packet of dried bramble leaves into my net shopping bag and walk down to the bus. I mean to go along to Gullane where I'm registered at the shops. I have my ration book ready, and my money in my purse. I'll buy a little sugar, some butter, some cheese. The coins for the bus sit in my hand and I mean to cross the street, walk down past the Mercat Cross and wait, but a bus is coming along just now around the bend in the high street and towards me, so I hold out my hand, flag it down, and it stops. *A single to Edinburgh*, I say without thinking, dropping the coins in the slot. I slide myself into a seat, and the bus pulls away, on to Longniddry, Port Seton, Prestonpans. In Musselburgh, I wonder if I might admit my mistake and go home. I'm not expected in Edinburgh. Only the driver knows I paid all the way into the city.

When the bus turns into St Andrew Square, the city feels warm around me. People walk about in the sunshine, smiling as if summer may be around the corner after all. I cross Princes Street, and climb the Mound slowly, the hill a challenge, my pace slow past the bank and over the cobbled Royal Mile. Down in the Meadows, allotment gardens have been dug and potatoes and carrots grow in straight rows. I will need to plant some myself pretty soon, I think. Only six months or so until the baby weans and then the two of us will be needing our vegetables. Mum will give me advice, on both the planting and the weaning when the time comes.

She meets me at the door with her sleeves rolled up. 'Goodness, you shouldn't have come. Just look at you.' She doesn't need to say anything at all; I can see she's worried. I smile as strongly as I can and rub my belly.

'I'm fine, Mum. I needed a change of scene. The bus was running anyway. And I wanted to see you.'

'Oh my love, look at you. You're . . .'

'Full.'

'Yes. And lovely. Let's get you inside. You'll be needing to sit yourself down. Goodness, all this way like that. Come in now.'

The flat smells like vinegar and it's quieter than I expected. I'd hoped for a crowd. The boys and their jokes, all my little sisters smiling, sitting as close to me as they could, smartly plaited hair and falling-down socks. But the kitchen is empty. Newspapers are spread out on the table, and Mum's copper pans set out in a row.

'I might have brought mine along with me,' I say. 'They could do with a good polish.'

'Everything could, these days and I can't find lemons for love or money. This takes a little more muscle to get anywhere near a reasonable shine. Here, sit down and rest those ankles of yours.'

She pours me a glass of water and I take a sip.

'Your da is sleeping now. His nights have been busy with fire-watching. He's been taking his turn down at the high school.' She tells me how he sits up on the roof tiles with sand and a stirrup pump, watching for incendiary bombs. 'If they hit his roof, he has to be quick. Has to quench them before they take hold, you see. It's hard work but he's good at keeping wakeful.'

As she speaks, she looks out of the window, her eyes soft and worried, and I imagine him, too, sitting there perched with the city at his balanced feet, his eyes fixed north to the sea.

'He liked Roosevelt's speech last month. When he wakes up, he's sure to talk to you about it. Gave him a lot of hope, it did. Every help promised from the USA. Rather encouraging. Did you hear it?'

'No. I've been focusing on other things. Trying not to worry.'

'Yes, indeed. That's the best course of action. And how is Stanley?' She strains the words, which isn't fair, but I see she doesn't mean it to hurt. I tell her I haven't a clue. 'You haven't heard from him? I thought he was only stationed in England. You haven't . . . argued, have you?'

'No.' I swallow the story again. Not because it feels necessary this time. I've simply grown accustomed to hiding Stanley away.

'It must be hard,' she says, 'being so far apart. So many people are these days. I think of that every time I pass the postbox. All those things you can't say on paper. Yet people are always putting things in the post. It can't be easy. Maybe that's why we have children. Easier to talk to.'

'He'll write when he can,' I say. 'I have been writing to him. All about the baby and the village. About the birds, too. He is interested in the birds.'

'A good habit for a pilot.' The copper pot in her hands brightens, and throws the light onto the ceiling like a watch face. 'It's nice that you write. I had a letter from your father once. It wasn't long before we were married and he was away down south, I can't remember why. Something with his father, I think. That doesn't matter. He'd been away from the street for a week or so when the envelope came for me. What a thrill it was. A clean, white envelope with my name written on so neatly. It wasn't even my birthday and I didn't ever know his writing, I didn't, and still I knew it was from him in an instant. My father wanted me to open it up right away and read it out, but I didn't and my mother backed me up. She scurried me outside, down all the stairs and out under the blue sky and I leaned on the railings with that letter in my hand. You know, I can still feel the scratchy brown wool of the jumper I had on that morning. And I think of that sky every March, I do. A sky clear as clear as March should be.'

'Was it lovely?' I asked, but she didn't understand. 'The letter, I mean.'

'Not a bit, I'm afraid. Rather stilted and formal. He didn't really say very much at all. Sent me his father's regards and hoped I was keeping well. That sort of thing. Didn't matter. It was the letter itself. That clean envelope and my name written on carefully. I'll never forget that.'

'Here. I brought this for you. Dried bramble leaves. They make a nice tea when they've been dried. Stretches the ration.'

'Now, aren't you a good girl? Even if you've made up your mind to live so very far away.'

'Mum, I'm married now. It wasn't—'

'Yes, I know. Married and alone and pregnant and of course I worry about you. Let me. I'm your mother.'

It strikes me then that Miss Baxter is going to worry, too, when she finds I'm not at home. That's just what Aberlady needs – another lost Mrs Hambleton.

'Can I use some writing paper, Mum?'

'Yes, if you like.' I go over to the table by the window and look among the papers there. 'It should be in the drawer, I think. You'll find a pen, too, and some ink if it needs it. Can't remember the last time it was filled. Is everything all right? You look flustered.'

'No, I'm fine. I just remembered a message I need to send back to Aberlady. But a telegram would be faster, wouldn't it? Oh dear, I can't think this through.'

'It's not to Stanley, is it?'

'No, of course not. He's not at home. It's just the neighbour. I didn't tell her I was coming into the city and she'll be beside herself.'

'I only wondered. You're flushed, dear. Sit down. You should rest.'

'I'm fine. I am.' A telegram would be best, so Mum gets me organized and we walk down to the post office in Bruntsfield.

'We won't pop in on the Morningside aunts,' she says. 'It would be too sudden for them, and you will want to see about the telegram as soon as possible.'

Such a lot of trouble to cause, I think, but I just nod. I picture the telegram boy on his bicycle, the faces at the windows all along the street in Aberlady. Well, perhaps it serves them right for all their staring and muttering. Let them worry that he's coming to them. Let their hearts stop just a little. Miss Baxter's won't, so that's all right. She'll wonder and she might worry for me but only for a moment. When she sees him at her own door, she'll not panic. She won't mind that I've sent word like this. She'll be calm and curious, that's all. Not like the rest of us on the street. She won't feel the kick in her heart at all.

There are allotment gardens down on Bruntsfield Links, too, and Mum makes a comment about pushing golfers out of the way to plant potatoes in the holes. It's so strange to see the grass shrunk away, the black of the soil and green blades of vegetables. Strange, too, to see the railings cut away in front of the terraces, and the darkened windows in all the flats. But the jackdaws are the same. They haven't been scared off by all the changes. They swoop close over the new gardens, their overlapping calls *chew chew* and gentler than the ragged rooks by the sea. I watch as they wing circles around the church spire, then glide down with grace to hop on the grass, with grey hoods and silvered eyes.

Mum and I walk briskly together, matching strides. I feel as if I could walk forever, but when we stop at the post office and my mother goes in to see about the telegram, I lean against the wall and feel things change. A tightening. A swoop. Here and, in a moment, gone. The bricks are cool to the touch. I pay attention.

On the way back across the Links, I don't say anything. It isn't anything anyway, is it? Just another strange pregnant feeling. A pause. A shift. A change. It comes and goes. It isn't anything. I keep stride with my mother, and she glances at my face, holding my arm more tightly now.

'There,' she says. 'You have grown strong, haven't you? You'll be fine.'

At the flat, I don't want to sit down, I've stayed too long already.

I tell her I should be heading back to the buses, but she lays a hand on my arm and tells me to wait for the others.

'They will all want to see you, you know. They won't forgive me if I let you go. And your father, too. It has been a long while since you've seen him.'

So I stay and I don't sit down because the baby is low and it's better on my feet, rocking the weight, swaying a little, then walking up and down the worn carpet while my mother smiles. I follow her into the kitchen and she slices bread. There are children on the drying green outside. I can hear their voices, calling, singing, the sound of a ball thrown against a stone wall, rhythmic, and then my mother hands me a plate.

'Eat, my dear. You need your energy. Even a little will help you on your way.'

'I'll eat back home. Don't waste your ration on me.'

'But you'll be staying here tonight. You can't travel like that. You aren't comfortable. Would you like a chair now?'

'No, I'm fine on my feet.'

'It's starting, isn't it?'

'No, it's too early. I'm just feeling sore.'

'Let's walk a little more to loosen up, shall we?' We walk up and down the hallway again and she says that there won't be buses back to East Lothian in the evening now. It is too dangerous with the raids and besides, the telegram was sent, and no one would worry now. Best to settle in. Walk out the cramps. Eat if I could. The family will be home soon for their tea, and don't begin to worry there, the stew is already cooked. Mainly turnip and potato, and a handful of greens, too, because they're full of iron.

'I think I should lie down.'

'All the excitement of travel and I've walked you too far now, haven't I? And talked too much. You need to rest.' She takes me into the girls' bedroom and helps me out of my brassiere. 'You can sleep in your slip. I'll tell the others to be quiet when they come in.'

The sheets are cool and the pillow smells of home. I wish my sisters would come and wrap their little arms around me, nuzzle little faces into my hair and bring in the smell of the garden, too. Another swoop and a tightening getting tighter and it's starting to hurt. I pay attention. I breathe into the pillow, hold on, let go.

It's almost midnight when the sirens start, jolting me, and fear floods in with the wheeze of the sirens. Then pain pushes up against me, squeezing out my breath. My mother is there, her arms around me. She says the children are away, wrapped in blankets, hiding in the shelter in the garden. We shouldn't be scared by the loud noises. We shouldn't be scared, she says, and she rocks me, telling me the children are safe, and so are we. She gives me words of prayer and they are comfort. God is close. The planes will pass over and she will stay, she will, she says, and she repeats herself, she will stay. She says I am strong. Then she shows me how to breathe, how to find the space in between the pushes and she pulls me to standing, helps me lean against the chest of drawers, holding on, learning, letting the keen of the sirens be the blood within me. I let go of the fear. She rubs my back. I breathe.

The doctor will come soon to check on you she says.

Then a cool cloth to wipe my face, a warm blanket around my

shoulders. Waves, wind. Breath and time dark as the room, pushing against me, with me, blind.

You can push now. Words in the dark and still the planes and sirens and the sound of far-off guns down the coast. In between, I learn, I'm taught by breath and by spirit and I learn to approach, to squeeze past and through, pushing away from the voices and the cotton sheet gripped in my fist, but not beyond the sounds and now I'm carried among them up along the searchlight beams, out over the water and into the dark, the guns steady, steady below.

Then comes a small, high, furious wail above it all and I'm pulled back down to earth, afraid that the planes will hear the baby's voice and find us in the dark. I open my eyes to the grey-blue room, my mother's face close at the end of the night, pale and smiling. Then with absurd appropriateness, the all-clear cuts through, its continuing note like a psalmic amen and now I can feel something warm against my knees, soft and wriggling.

'It's a girl.'

When dawn comes, my mother rolls away the heavy blinds and the wind catches the white curtains, blowing them big-bellied into the room like sails and it makes me laugh because I see that Felicity's eyes are as blue as the sea. Deep, deep blue.

The zoo was hit that night and Milton Road down near Portobello Park. But not the railway and none of the churches. In the shelter in the garden, my brothers were sure that Arthur's Seat had crumbled. They heard the crack, they say. Rockslides and earthquakes and maybe a great big hole. As soon as the sky was light, they ran down to the Meadows, blinking, and saw that it was still there, its bulk still holding the city in place. When they tell me all this, their faces are flushed, relieved, and laughing with the thought of it then serious again when they remember to worry about the giraffes. I hold Felicity in my arms and when they bend down to look at her face, I see that they are gentle, too.

I stay at the house for a week. My sisters take turns holding the baby, sitting with their bottoms right against the back on the chesterfield, a cushion balanced on their laps for support. My mother washes me with warm water, brushes my hair and helps me to my feet. She makes me porridge without the sugar and the salt is good on my tongue. I feel like a sailor home from the sea, the floorboards uncertain, untrusted underfoot. I don't walk far.

When my milk comes in, I dream of butter, of tigers running circles around the garden trees, turning and churning. Isn't that how the poem goes? My sisters might know. Felicity must dream only of milk, her small mouth nursing even in sleep, her skin pale and creamy.

She is ten days old when we climb back on the bus to Aberlady. My mum comes, too, just to get us settled. She carries a bag filled with things she's collected: nappies, blankets, soft cloths for swaddling and for after the bath. On the bus, my breasts ache and the baby fusses, turning her mouth towards me, but that will have to wait until we get home. We see the shore at Seton Sands, the rocks and the grey gulls out on the water. I watch for gannets, or seals. It is warm on the bus, the window open and sky clear and blue with summer ahead and Felicity in my arms.

As the bus passes the house, I catch a glimpse of the open window and worry that I've left it open all this time. Basil might have got in. Slept on my pillow or worse, in the drawer I set on the top of the dresser, padded with a pillow and ready to serve as a crib. Then, climbing down from the bus, I worry about my door key and the food in the pantry. My ration book. Miss Baxter and the telegram. And I see him standing by the Mercat Cross, uniformed, hatless. Stanley.

'Oh, I so prayed, my dear.' My mother's voice is quiet. 'I so hoped for an answer and that he'd come . . . oh, here, let me take the baby – please don't run now – oh!'

PART THREE

1

FELICITY: 1969

WHEN I GOT OUT OF THE VAN AT THE CAMP, THE first thing I saw was a huge girl down on all fours, scrubbing the farmhouse floor. She didn't even have a mop, just a rough brush and a bucket of water. She was enormous. She had to squat to get up to her feet, heaving up her heavy belly. Grunting. Grinning. Like this was all great fun or something. I didn't know where to look or what to say. She stood there in front of me, rubbing her giant belly like it was going to grant her a wish. My own hands fluttered, too, trying to protect my little bump – my barely-there-at-all bump – trying to keep it safe so it didn't grow ghastly and huge like, like, like *that*. She must have been having twins. Triplets. She was as big as a landscape.

Annie had pulled the van right up to the farmhouse door, so I could go right in, which was kind. It had taken us four hours to drive to the camp, down the highway from the city and up into the hills. I'd been a bit nervous at first, partly because Annie had a canoe tied to the van's roof and I wasn't sure it looked all that safe. She laughed and said it was fine; she did this every weekend. During the week, it lived in the basement of her church, but she liked to have it up at the lake whenever she was there.

Once I relaxed, I could see it was a really pretty drive. Lots of trees and old farms. There was a covered bridge, all painted red and about a hundred years old. The land was rocky, and you could see that anyone trying to make a life here would have had their work cut out for them, but it was all beautiful enough in its way. I liked looking out of the window at the fields going past, putting distance between me and the city. But other than the view, a lot of the drive wasn't great. I had to ask Annie to stop the van three or four times. Anyway, she was cool with it, said there was no point in being embarrassed. It was just my body's way of saying that it was time to put down roots in one place. Bellies need balance. That's what Annie said.

It was just after noon when we left the city and, by the time we got to the camp, I was ravenous. I'd worked myself into a bit of a state about food, which was kind of dumb. I knew where we were going but I'd let myself imagine it as every perfect New World farmhouse with a warm and open kitchen and a table heavy with maple-glazed Sunday ham. There would be an older woman, a real Quebecois farmer's wife, apple-cheeked and ample-bosomed. She'd welcome me in with just enough pity and a good dose of humour, too, settle me at the table with a hot cup of tea and a thick slice of warm tea loaf dripping with butter. Then everyone else – whoever they were – would come in and join us for a hot meal, and I would feel at last I'd come home. That's what I wanted. And she'd deliver my baby, of course, along with two or three junior midwives. Maybe one of them would have long shining hair and an old guitar and she'd be singing just as my baby was born, so soft and tender, and I wouldn't feel sick any more.

'Come on inside and careful on the wet patch, okay?' the giantess said, holding out a hand and helping me over the threshold. 'Don't want you ass-over-tea-kettle first thing here. Look at you, just starting to show. And me about to burst. Scrubbing floors is supposed to help. Which would be great because this little bugger has kept me waiting for almost two weeks.'

'You're the only one who's been counting.' A soft voice behind me, a tall girl, thin as a stick, her fine brown hair tied in a pony-tail. 'Babies know their own time.'

A big man came through the door behind her and gave her shoulders a squeeze. She looked up at him, smiling, then turned back to the giantess. 'You know, it's going to be fine,' she said. 'That baby knows what she's doing. You just need to get yourself ready.'

'And the house, apparently,' said the giantess. The man went over to the stove and lifted a lid off a large pot. Steam came up and fogged his glasses, so he pushed them up on top of his head, then gave the pot a stir.

'Well, floors need cleaning,' the girl said. 'No one wants to have a baby in the dirt.'

'I'd have this baby anywhere. Anywhere, anytime, how about now? You hear me in there?' She tapped on her mighty belly. 'You really think this one's a girl, Rika?'

'Well, I don't know. That's what it feels like to me, but it's easier to tell when the labour pains start. I'll get a better sense of things then.'

'You just watch,' the man said. 'She'll be right. Usually is. Felicity? Bas.' He held out a hand to me, and his grip was warm and easy. 'Welcome to the camp. Good drive up?'

'A bit rough in places.'

'That's the way it is,' Rika said. 'Annie show you the outhouse yet? Or you can use the toilet upstairs, if you like. We just need to be careful not to overuse it. The septic system's not built for a crowd. Dinner's just about ready. Carole's gone missing again, but she'll surface when she's hungry. How about you?'

The room was wide and open, with a kitchen at the back and a long table positioned at the front of the room, surrounded by stools and benches. There was a dresser with open shelves, stacked with plates and mugs, and a sofa against the wall, too, with a red-and-yellow blanket spread along the back. Like something in an Aberlady front room, except then there'd also be velour cushions and a fringed lampshade. Instead, Rika had a rag rug on the wooden floor and, on the table, an embroidered cloth with windmills and tulips outlined in blue thread. There were candles, too, set in glass jars on the window sills and along the dresser shelves, unlit in the bright room.

Bas lifted the pot from the stove and brought it to the table, while Rika filled a kettle at the sink.

'Tea, Bethanne?' she asked.

The giantess sat down on a stool at the head of the table. 'Yeah. That would be good. You said it helps, right?'

'It can. It might. If the time's right.'

'If it's all a matter of timing, then the tea won't really do anything, will it?'

'It still tastes good,' said Bas. 'And honey makes you cheerful and sweet. Works a dream on Rika.'

'Oh, you. I'm always cheerful.' Rika set the kettle on the burner and brought a stack of brown bowls to the table. 'Are you hungry, Felicity? Sometimes girls can't stand the thought of food when they first arrive, but you look like you might be an eater. What do you say?'

'It smells wonderful.' I took a deep breath. 'I could smell it as we drove up to the house.'

'These pregnant noses, they are something else,' Annie said. 'But be warned. Bas's stews tend to be on the garlicky side. Good, but garlicky.'

'There's nothing wrong with garlic.' I said. 'Makes the blood strong, doesn't it?'

'And moose is full of iron and that's good, too,' Rika said, passing full bowls down the table. 'Bas, you say a blessing and then we can all tuck in.'

'Right. Let's see. What words for today?' He raised his hands and closed his eyes. Annie and Rika followed suit. Bethanne caught my eye and grinned, then bobbed her head down, too. 'How about this? *We are surrounded by God's benefits. The best use of these benefits is an unceasing expression of gratitude.*' Bas's voice was soft and strong, and Annie murmured in agreement. I wondered if we were all expected to contribute something, but no one else spoke and then, after a pause, Bas said amen and everyone picked up their spoons. Moose. Well, I was hungry enough not to let that worry me. It proved a little gamey but beefy, too. I'd need to remember to mention it in my next letter home. Mum would like to hear about moose meat for sure.

When the kettle on the stove started to whistle, Bas took a teapot down from the shelf and Rika stretched her hands across the table towards Bethanne.

'Want me to feel how the baby's doing?'

'Would you? Since it's dropped, I'm not sure about anything any more.'

Bethanne stood up and went over to the sofa. Rika followed her, rolling up her sleeves and rubbing her palms together to warm them as Bethanne lay down and opened the buttons on her dress. Her skin was taut, and even from the table, I could see the dark line that zippered from her belly button down towards her pubic area. The *linea nigra*. I'd read about it and seen textbook photos but it was still too early for me.

Rika moved her fingers over Bethanne's belly, humming softly, and Bethanne laughed.

After dinner, Annie walked me over to the bunkhouse. She seemed different from how she'd been in the spring. She smiled more, moved more slowly. In the city, she'd worked to convince me the camp was a good, safe place, and I'd wanted to be convinced. I'd been looking for an answer as much as she'd been trying to help. I wondered if, now that we were past all that, we might be friends.

'Do you always pray at mealtimes here?' I asked. 'Is that part of this?'

'Yeah, I guess we do. Just something simple, though. Nothing heavy. We take turns. Bas likes to use something he's read – I usually just say *thank you*. But if you don't want to, you don't need to.'

'I don't mind.'

The bunkhouse wasn't far. I'd expected a barn or something, because the small cabin surprised me. A simple step up to the door, no porch here, and thin curtains on screened windows. Inside, there were rag rugs and cushions on the floor of the central room, a small woodstove and three doors like in a fairy tale. Annie said these led to the bedrooms and I could take my pick.

'Best aim for a lower bunk. We keep the tops for storage or extra guests.' Mostly, the bunkhouse was for girls who showed up on their own. Some came as soon as they knew there was a baby on the way and spent their months working at the camp, helping out. Others only arrived at the end of their wait and headed home quickly afterwards. Annie said Rika advised mums to stay for at least six weeks after the birth in order to heal and to get good milk into the baby, but some of the girls couldn't handle that. Particularly if they were leaving their babies at the camp. And that's why some girls came. Rika could find a home for babies who needed one. She had her networks and she knew who to ask to find sympathetic families happy to make room for another kid. And letting the girls know that this was an option meant that fewer of them ended up at dodgy clinics.

I settled on the room to the right, which was the smallest and looked empty. Annie stayed for a while, chatting while I sorted through the few things I'd brought with me. Books and bedding.

A postcard to pin on the wall – the island of Manhattan, the river a crazy blue. A mug painted with mermaids. The yellow mohair wrap from Mum and Dad, which I laid out on the end of the bed.

Annie smiled and said it all looked snug.

'You going to be okay?' she asked.

'Yes. I'm just tired out. Is it okay if I just go to sleep? Or will I be expected back at the farmhouse?'

'I can tell them you're tired, if you like.'

'Thanks. I am.'

'Bethanne probably won't be along until later. She's been taking walks in the evenings. And Carole will be here when she's here. She's a bit harder to predict. But if I see her, I'll let her know that you're already in bed and sleeping. She'll be quiet. You rest up, okay? Things will feel less strange in the morning.'

The night before I left for the camp, I'd brushed my hair a hundred strokes. It was shoulder-length now, with a centre parting like everyone else, and kirby grips over my ears. The girls were out – Jenny to a play, Margaret to the library – and I had the radio on, but it was just pop songs. Boppity-bop love and hearts, but I couldn't handle talk. Jenny had left me a box of chocolates with a little note on top that said *Break a leg*. I sucked on a caramel one and kept brushing my hair.

I'd told the hospital I was leaving to spend time with family. Which was true, wasn't it? But I felt terribly Edinburgh, proper and false as I said it. The matron suspected I wasn't coming back; she made sure I left my nursing basket behind. But she didn't check my purse so she didn't find my nicked copy of the pink book – *a doctor discusses pregnancy* by William G. Birch, MD. They may not breathe a word about contraception but they hand these books out like candy. I liked the lower-case title – I think they were aiming for modern and chic. On the bus ride home, I flicked through the pages, the neat line drawings, the words of scientific assurance.

You who are expecting a baby in this modern era can make your nine-month wait one of the happiest adventures of your life. You are safe in the security that medical science has devoted countless years of research to help your doctor help you have a happy, healthy pregnancy and childbirth.

Behind me, the hospital and maybe my career. And before me? A weekend bag and a hairbrush, a few new clothes, and a stolen book.

Jenny's chocolates were a nice touch. A little bit of grace there. We'd argued a while back – about how I made decisions, about the baby – and she told me that she thought it would be best to end it. Said she knew someone who could help. As safe as could be. Margaret had backed me up, but it was obvious she, too, thought the baby was a problem to be solved. But it wasn't. It was just what was happening. Like Asher. Like leaving Scotland. Sure, it would change things for me, but change happens, right?

The hairbrush was a gift from Mum before I left home. A Mason Pearson Handy. She'd be glad to see me using it diligently. I hadn't yet had a response to my last letter, and in her previous one, she hadn't mentioned the camp or the baby at all. Only said that she was glad I was feeling more myself and that I should be careful of my health.

That first night in the bunkhouse, I woke in the night, feeling blind without streetlights and achingly aware of my mistake. I wasn't really pregnant at all. I couldn't be, and how was I going to tell the others here? As soon as Rika placed her hands on my belly, she'd know for sure, and then what would she say? They'd all think I was crazy. So, I'd leave, I thought. Get up now while everyone was sleeping and head back out to the highway. Hitchhike. But where? East again. South. Guided by the stars, right? Or I could walk down to the lake and not stop. Not dip a toe or test the temperature, but just calmly walk straight in. Step by step. Feeling light and empty and free. And then, just as I imagined my toes pushing away, the lake taking my weight, that's when I felt it. The sudden tumble inside. The shift and shuddery shove of shoulders and elbows and knees. And I knew there was no mistake at all.

2

Morning and a knock on the front door. 'You up yet?' Rika's voice, and a bed creaked in one of the other rooms. Light fell across the floor like a strip of white paint on the boards. Back in Aberlady, there was a photo of me with light like that, falling across my face. I stood next to Dad, a small child next to a thin, towering man, and sunlight like paint brushed right across my face.

'Is it breakfast?' A voice from another room.

'Lazybones,' Rika answered. 'Of course it's breakfast. It's almost nine.'

'How's Bethanne?'

'I'm just popping over to check. You up, Felicity? Did Carole tell you about Bethanne's baby? You can come see her with me before breakfast if you like. Or are mornings as hard for you as they are for Carole?'

'Oi!'

''Strue though, bird. You struggle.'

A groan, but nothing more and Rika laughed.

'I'll be up and dressed in a minute,' I said.

Rika was sitting on the steps when I came out of the cabin. The woods were full of the sound of birds and then a sudden loud noise overhead startled me, and something fell to the ground. Rika looked up, squinting. After a moment, she pointed up at one of the pine trees.

'See him? Just there, where that branch meets the trunk.' A small red squirrel sat high above the cabin roof, chattering away. 'A pine squirrel. Cousin to your Scottish red, I think.'

'And just as noisy,' I said, but Rika had turned away and headed down a fern-lined path. I followed, combing my fingers through the curled green fronds as I walked.

'Do you eat fiddleheads in Scotland?'

'No. I don't think so at least.'

'Might be my favourite springtime food. A bit like asparagus and really tasty with butter. These ones are getting a bit old and woody now. You stay around for next year and you'll see.'

I thought of telling her about Mum's foraging – her rosehip jam and sloe gin, but the path was narrow and Rika walked quickly. Maybe there would be time later.

Just as the birthing house came into view, she slowed and turned towards me. 'You're what now? Four months to go?'

'I think so. I haven't seen anyone yet.'

'No? Well, that's likely fine, if you feel well. But good that you're here now. Lots of time to settle in.'

The birthing house was an A-frame cabin facing the lake, with a porch like the farmhouse. A rocking chair sat beside what looked like an old milking stool with a horseshoe-shaped seat. When we came close, a chipmunk darted out from under the log steps, running away into the trees. Inside the house, someone was humming softly. Rika tapped on the screen door and the humming stopped.

'Come in,' Bethanne called. 'We're both awake.'

'Hey. Look at you. You're all glowy this morning. Can I open the curtains for you or are you happy with them closed?'

'Open them up if you like. Let's let that day in. Day One. Holy Moly. Hi, Felicity, good to see you here. Sorry you weren't with us for the fun last night.'

'I was sleeping. They didn't tell me.'

'I thought it best to let you be,' said Rika. 'Who knows how late we might have been and you were pretty tired out from the travel anyway.'

Bethanne was sitting propped up in bed, under a patchwork quilt. She wore a plaid shirt over her shoulders, all the buttons open and the baby she held looked chubby and red.

'It's okay. You can come closer and look if you like. I don't mind. Help you get used to the idea and see what they look like. Crazy little space aliens. You sleep well?' I nodded, and she smiled, shifting her gaze down to the baby, her mouth latched onto her mother's swollen breast, sucking away.

'You picked a name yet?' Rika asked.

'I think I'll call her Ember. It suits her, don't you think? Check out her hair. It's wild.' She gently took off the knitted hat to show a tangle of damp spikes. 'She looked such a little ghostling at first. All blue and streaked with white. Then Rika rubbed her all over, getting her started, you know, and she started breathing and she got redder and redder all over. Like a little fire. It was amazing to watch the life coming into her.'

'It's a great name,' I said, taking a cushion from the pile and easing myself onto the floor. I needed the toilet. Rika perched on the edge of the bed.

'She's a little doll, isn't she? And it looks like she's taking to the breast right well,' Rika said.

'Yeah, she's a dream.'

'You, too, my dear,' said Rika.

'It seems to work after all. You were right.'

'I said you'd remember.'

'And you were right about her being a girl. I didn't want to hope for a girl this time round, but you knew, didn't you? And here she is.'

'So, you have others then?' I asked.

'Nope,' Bethanne said, her eyes never leaving her baby's face. 'Not any more. Ember is my first to keep. I had a boy when I was fifteen, but they made me give him away.' Bethanne pushed her hair out of her face, and the baby squirmed and stopped nursing, so she blew softly on the baby's cheek until she opened her gawping little mouth and tried again. 'She's funny, isn't she? It's so different this time. And the weather is so much better, too. I can handle anything in these cool spring days. Last time, it was stinking-hot July. And out on the prairies. 'Man, that was something. My parents sent me to a home near Winnipeg. Nothing like here. Not open or kind. Didn't even let me name the baby there, but they taught me how to nurse. Every three hours, they pinched my arms hard to wake me up and hauled me into a chair with this cracked fake-leather covering that my dress stuck to. Completely ruined it and I had nothing else to wear that unbuttoned in the front. Just ruined. Guess I wouldn't have wanted to keep it anyway, but you never know. Probably not.'

Rika watched Bethanne, a soft smile balancing on her lips. 'You ready for me to take a look? I want to see how that cunt is doing this morning.'

I flinched.

'It's okay,' Rika said. 'Just a word. I can use a different one when it's your turn if that suits better.'

'I'm feeling okay,' Bethanne said. 'The cool cloth helps.'

'You remember the witch hazel like I said?'

'Of course. I'm good at instructions, aren't I?' Bethanne started to sit up, but Rika stopped her.

'Hey, watch those belly muscles. You might think you can do everything, but you're still soft. Just be careful with yourself and let me take her from your arms, okay? I'll get a blanket ready. You just lie back and relax. We've got all the time in the world.'

'Hey Felicity, you want to hold her?'

'The baby?'

'Yeah. It would be good for you. She's not made of glass. That's okay, right, Rika?'

'Absolutely. Babies are for sharing. Well, some of the time.'

'I do know about babies,' I said. 'I'm a nurse.'

'Great,' said Rika. 'Another set of hands. How's your birth experience?'

'I haven't really done birth. A little infant care during my degree, but not since then.'

'You should see some of the girls who come in here. Never seen a little one at all and just about to pop. It can be a steep learning curve. We try to pass the babies around so that everyone can get some cuddles in. It helps. We make each other comfortable and everyone feels better about life.' She took a small blanket from a basket on the floor and set it flat at the foot of the bed. Gently scooping Ember from Bethanne's arms, she laid her down on the blanket, wrapped, smoothed and tucked her neatly, and then passed her into my waiting arms.

'Hey, little Ember,' I said. She felt so light and warm cradled in my arms, my elbow against my own belly, my own baby pushing softly inside. 'Happy birthday, wee girl.'

Bas was holding the coffee pot when we came through the door.

'The bannock will be ready in no time,' he said. 'Bit more of a crowd for you this morning, Felicity.' He put the pot on the table and turned to Rika. 'Carole not with you?'

'No, but she's fine. Just a bit sleepy. I think she walked too far yesterday.' She put her arms around him and he kissed the top of her head gently. I found a seat at the table.

A woman in glasses and a green headscarf sat with a toddler who played with pebbles on his plate. At the end of the table, a blond man filled a coffee mug and passed it up to her and the woman smiled. Between them, the child sang out a counting song – *one, two, trois, quatre* – his face café au lait and hers cocoa. Down near the window, Annie sat reading a newspaper.

'Hey, everybody,' Rika said, loudly. 'This is Felicity, come from Scotland by way of Montreal. Felicity, you know Annie, then Eleta, Soleil and James. The localest locals, you might say.'

'As opposed to the passers-through?' I asked.

'You can stay as long as you like,' said Bas. 'That's the deal here.' He was bearded and wore a blue checked shirt and jeans with a notebook crammed into his back pocket. He had a nose like Rika's, but while she was slender, he was built like a bear. Under his dark eyebrows, his eyes twinkled.

'How's Bethanne? Awake yet?' Eleta asked. 'Soleil is counting out the moments until we can see her baby.'

'Well, isn't that wonderful? An after-breakfast visit is a great idea. She'd love a visit. And what about those chickens? Have they been fed yet today?' Rika said, sliding in beside them to play pebbles with Soleil and to hear about his plans for the day.

James turned to me, smiling. 'So, how did you find out about our little camp up here? You another of Annie's McGill girls?'

'No, a nurse. At the hospital. But it was Annie who told me about the camp. Seems like a good place to have a baby. I couldn't face being in the hospital – not alone.'

'Well, you won't be alone here,' Rika said. 'And, as Bas said, you really can stay as long as you like. We're trying to convince James and Eleta here to put down roots. So far, they've only agreed to build us a new cabin.'

'Digging's done now,' said James. 'And the roof won't be long. It'll be done before the blackflies, I should think.'

'It's nice up here,' I said.

'You wait for the blackflies.'

After breakfast, the room cleared out, leaving me and Rika together.

'How's it been so far?' she asked. 'You feeling confident?'

'More or less.' I didn't know how to do this. And I didn't know what she was going to ask next. It better not be about the father, I thought.

She looked at me and smiled. 'Hey, it's okay. We'll just need to get to know each other a bit. Everything else will follow. Then you can see if you've made a good decision in coming here.'

'Thanks. I'm just a bit nervous.'

'I know. It's new. But maybe I'll start by telling you a bit about my own hospital work. We have that in common, you know. I'm not just some girl in the woods catching babies.'

As she wiped the table, she told me about the American hospital where she'd worked as a nurse–midwife. A real eager beaver, she'd taken every opportunity to learn new practice and new technologies.

'Continuous electronic fetal monitoring, enemas and forceps, episiotomies and DeLee catheters. The whole kit and caboodle.'

I laughed at her weird Americanisms and we both relaxed a little.

'It was fine. I enjoyed it. We seemed to be helping a great number of people, and what with the social changes going on, more and more poor people were able to come through the hospital system and find the help they needed. That felt good.'

She went over to the dresser and opened a drawer, taking out a white cotton case. 'But then, well, a bunch of things happened. Things around me, but also my brother's wife died, and he needed me. I may have needed out, too, but he most certainly needed me. So, I left the hospital and followed him out here and here we are. Not quite fixing the world, but we're doing what we can.'

I wasn't sure if I should say *thanks*. Almost the right thing, but not quite.

'Have a seat, okay? We'll do this together.' She unclipped the case and took out a stethoscope. I sat down on the sofa and she smiled again. 'Have you been taking any notes?'

I pictured the pink book and its directory page inside the front cover. All those blanks to fill in. Meant to be handy.

Doctor's name: ....

Office phone: ....

Home phone: ....

Answering service: ....

Doctor's associate: ....

Phone: ....

Office nurse: ....

Phone: ....

Hospital: ....

Address: ....

Phone: ....

Pharmacy: ....

Address: ....

Phone: ....

Household help: ....

Phone: ....

Neighbour: ....

Taxi: ....

Husband's phone during day: ....

'No. Nothing at all.'

'That's fine. Absolutely. I just asked because I've had nurses show up before with full files. Weight, temperatures, blood pressure, all that. One even had lab results from a pregnancy test to show me. How she managed that on the sly, I can't quite fathom.'

'I haven't done a test,' I said. 'But it's been about five months. I can't say I have any doubts.'

'I'd say. You have the right look. I don't really like these tests anyway. Why kill a rabbit to see if you're carrying life? There must be some more ethical way to figure it out. Or just wait. It doesn't really take that long to know. You want to lie down now? We can see if the heartbeat's clear.'

She checked me over gently, and it felt good. We talked a bit about my medical history and family, and she checked my weight and my legs and feet for troubled veins. It turned out the dresser drawers were a regular surgery of supplies. She said we didn't need to do the pelvic examination if I didn't want it. She'd want to know that I trusted her first because otherwise it could be awkward and not very helpful. And she could see that I was pregnant, and strong, too. Outside, I could hear chickens clucking away, and it all felt the utter opposite of anything that happened at the General. I wondered what she'd think of Dr William G. Birch.

She'd folded the stethoscope and put the blood-pressure cuff away and was standing by the dresser sorting the drawers when the farmhouse door crashed open and a girl stomped in. She was small and looked tough, her hair cropped short like a boy's, her wrists sticking out of her cuffs. Under her donkey-coloured sweater, her belly was round – bigger than mine – but her movements were quick and sharp. Rika turned and smiled, and the girl came close and wrapped her arms around her, their faces forehead to forehead. I sat up, focused on buttoning my blouse, tucking it into my skirt.

'Felicity,' Rika said in a warm voice. 'This is Carole. She's also here on her own.'

When I looked up, Carole was standing with her hands on her hips.

'Hey,' she said. 'Another one of us dumb, duped girls, eh?'

'Hello.'

'We're going to be compulsory buddies, then, right? Single girls united. Rika says you're not even from here. How'd you end up with us, then?'

'Gentle, Carole.'

'No, it's fine. I emigrated. I'm from Britain.'

'Land of tea and crumpets.'

'Something like that.'

Rika spoke softly, with a little smile on her face. 'Speaking of which, you'll be needing breakfast. Why don't you sit down and I'll see what I can put together for you? Cheesy eggs sound good?'

'And buttered toast?' Carole asked. 'And salt, please.'

'No to the salt, but the rest is fine. Don't want you to get puffy. Not that it's likely with you, I suppose, my strong girl. That was quite the hike you went on yesterday. You might want to start taking it easy, okay?'

'I'm fine. Really. Just full of energy.'

'And of baby. I'd like to get a measurement on that belly of yours today. It looks like your rate of growth is up.'

'Supposed to be, right? I'm eating for two.'

'Absolutely. But it's best to keep our eyes open. Paying attention pays off.'

Rika broke two eggs into a bowl, whisked them with a fork, then crumbled in some cheese. I watched Carole as she opened and closed the dresser drawers and fiddled with the knobs.

'This place is filling up,' she said. 'You'd think we could all sort out what was causing it, eh?'

I smiled, but she didn't and then I wasn't sure what to do. Rika didn't say anything, just poured the eggs into a frying pan and started to stir. Carole kept moving.

'You settle down, bird. You need to sit and eat now.'

'Okay, okay. Just feeling up, you know?'

'Sit. And no talk about politics, either. Felicity doesn't need that.' Rika put a plate of food down on the table and Carole pulled out a chair. 'I'll pour you some water. And when you've finished that plate, there's a letter for you. Annie went into the village for the mail.'

'From Charlotte?'

'They're all from Charlotte. You two are spending a fortune in stamps.'

'She worries. And she wants to hear everything, too.'

'I suppose you two need to keep your stories straight. Is she still sending you a copy of everything she sends home?'

'Of course she is. If she didn't, I'd slip up for sure.'

'You could just tell them the truth.'

'Don't need to. It's fine, really. You're looking after me. I'll have the baby and Charlotte will bum around India for the year, writing home for the both of us. By the end of the summer, it'll be done. You found a home for the baby yet? Is that settled?'

'Not yet, but it will be. The answer will come. It does.'

I thought she was going to talk about God then, and I looked at my shoes. Patent leather toes didn't really suit the camp. I should have left them in my bag.

Carole scratched her plate with her knife.

'Hey now,' Rika said. 'You don't need to worry. There's still plenty of time.'

'Yeah,' Carole said, pushing the eggs around her plate. 'Plenty.'

I wished she'd finish soon and leave so that I could talk some more with Rika. But she didn't. She dawdled like a child over her food until Rika sat down beside her and stroked her back. In the end, I left, saying I wanted to do some reading that morning.

Back at the bunkhouse, I arranged a nest of cushions in the

front room so I could sit where the light patched the rug. I lowered myself and tried to settle comfortably. No new turns from the baby, just a little heartburn and increased girth. I picked up Dr Birch, the pink cover the colour of Pepto-Bismol. What to expect?

In our world, abounding in miracles, there is still none so old or awe-inspiring as the birth of a baby. How nice it would have been had nature included a tiny, transparent TV-like panel over a woman's abdomen so she could observe the miraculous changes that occur in her body during pregnancy.

3

At midday, Bas appeared at the window. He startled me, though he only tapped gently on the glass, and his smile was tender.

'Everyone's picnicking today,' he said. 'James and Eleta are up at the new cabin, and Rika's hunkered down with Bethanne and Carole at the birthing house. I thought you might be hungry, too, so I brought this along.'

He held up a reed basket, topped with a checked cloth. 'Just left-over bannock and a wodge of cheese, I'm afraid. And a little fruit. Enough to keep you going. We'll have a bigger, fattening meal at dinner.'

Stepping into the cabin, he looked immensely tall, and I tried to stand up, but he said not to bother and set the basket beside me on the floor. The bear calls on Little Red Riding Hood, I thought. Which wasn't quite right, was it? A bear would change that story. Not sly enough. Too comfortable.

At the thought of lunch, my stomach growled wolfishly.

'Right on time, then,' he said. 'Sounds like you're ready for it. I've also put a map in there. Just a little sketch I made, so you can go exploring if you like. Dinner's at half past six. If you need anything before then or want company, I'll be around the farmhouse.'

'Thanks.'

'No problem. Thanks for coming.'

I watched him walk down the path. Lumber? No, he wasn't clumsy. Just big. And I wasn't little. Just feeling out of place.

I wondered what Asher would say to see me here. And if he was back in Montreal yet, looking for me. He'd probably think the camp was dangerous – that I didn't know these people, didn't know their training or experience. I was taking too much at face value. But wasn't that the better way? No point in being scared of everything. And Montreal wouldn't feel any safer these days, not with the letter bombs and politics.

Asher had been a lesson in getting over fear. It was all *what the hell* and looking into his eyes. It's easy to fall in love like that. Or more or less in love. I took him at face value, and he, me. Risk only surfaced in the single moment before we touched, a moment of seeing and being seen. But then the harbour of arms, lips, joining – not falling, not reaching, but finding a way between us. The first time, I knew there was no going back, no need to go back to the flat coastline, the sand dunes and the grey. I could go on instead into a country still young with trees.

He borrowed a car and we drove up the mountain, Montreal

below us bright like broken glass, and even sex felt safe. Stupid, but it did. In the car, outside even. Whatever safe meant. Later, it felt like something I was remembering, even as he pushed into me, our mouths open together, his hands in my hair. He was the constant, there in the middle of my life, waiting for me, and I was always approaching or slipping away.

The map Bas gave me was simple, the farmhouse and the bunk-house marked, along with the birthing house and a few other cabins and outbuildings around the curve of the lake. Hills, criss-crossed with paths, extended to the north, and there were railway tracks at the far side of the property. Simple enough. I'd just remember where the lake was and loop back. I'd be fine. I'd take an apple in case I got thirsty and wear my new boots. They were black, thick-soled beasts, ugly as sin and just as strong. I'd bought them at the army surplus on St Laurent near Maisonneuve. *You'll keep your balance in those.* That's what the man said when I tried them on and I hoped he was right. I also bought a pair of trousers that would make my mum quiver to see. Not that she would. They were only for the duration. Vast, army-green things with useful pockets. But I wasn't big enough yet to wear them, and my smart blouse and skirt weren't the thing for hiking. I dug about in my bag and found the dress that Jenny had made me, a soft brown A-shaped thing with an elegant Peter Pan collar. Looked spunky with the boots, but maybe the thing for a solo hike.

An old-fashioned walk out of doors is healthful for everyone and the pregnant woman should make an extra effort to include a hike in the country or window-shopping jaunt in her daily routine.

I followed the path to the woodshed, where a thick stump sat out front, ringed with woodchips and broken bark. Annie's van was parked beside the shed. The canoe was gone, and a large puddle had collected in the space between the tyres. I hadn't heard rain in the night; I must have slept soundly. The path climbed the hill behind the shed. If I was reading the map right, I could follow it up to a lookout place and loop down again out to the spot where the railway tracks met the road, then back to the camp.

The ground was rocky, and a split-rail fence snaked through the trees. The fence looked old, but the trees were young. So the farm wasn't new, I guessed, and wondered about the folk who'd left.

Halfway up the hill, a house-sized boulder sat, covered in green and yellow lichen. It looked like something a Cyclops might throw. Dad had taught me about boulders like these: erratics, he called them. Carried by glaciers and interesting because they have a different lithology from the bedrock around. He taught me you can use them to discern the patterns of glacial flow. With the woods growing up all around, it looked abandoned and forgotten. I wanted to climb it and see what the woods looked like from up high. Maybe after the baby.

Further up, the path veered away from the fence, and the woods grew thicker and wilder. A flash of yellow caught my eye, a strip of cloth tied around a tree trunk. It felt good to know that I was going the right way. Unless the yellow was a warning to go the other way. A heavy bird flew between the trees and the air above my head was loud with its wings. From underneath, they were white with black fingers. I watched it land in a tree and saw the red feathers on its head, then heard the hungry thwack of its beak against the wood. Then the sound of crows higher over the trees and, for a moment, the woodpecker was silent before it started again to hammer, and I kept climbing.

At the top, there was a clearing with a circle of stones for a firepit, one larger stone set nearby as a seat. A lonely spot. It was different from the view of Montreal from the Oratory, but similar, too. The height. The way the water caught the light far below you. The feeling of space all around.

From the top of the hill, the lake looked perfectly round, but there was more of it than I could see. In Bas's sketch, he had left it open, like a waxing crescent moon. The village must be away to the left, hidden by the hills. Then I spotted Annie in her canoe, a red shape moving across the surface of the lake. Someone called from the shore and Annie raised her paddle in greeting. The crows took sudden flight from the tall pines and circled the bay together, their voices harsh and calling.

The path down from the lookout was steep and muddy and, standing at the top, I worried about going down, so I dug my boots in sideways and kept close to the trees. It wasn't easy to walk downhill pregnant; it made me feel more pregnant than I was. I had to take a break partway down for a pee. At least the A-frame dress made that easy enough. I was almost at the road when I heard the train stopping, screeching and heavy like something was wrong. I stopped to watch, not quite hidden by the trees, but not yet out in the open.

A door on the train opened, a green duffel bag landed with a thump beside the tracks and then another fell beside it. A man climbed down, a girl following him, so he turned, smiling, to hold out both hands to help her. She wore a pale wool sweater, cabled and heavy like jumpers from home, and a full skirt. She was bright as a falling leaf catching the air as she jumped down to the ground. So perfectly present and then she laughed when she landed, her long dark hair falling in her eyes, catching her arms around herself, still laughing as she backed away from the tracks towards the woods. The man waved an arm up at the train, and the door closed. Then the train pulled away, leaving the couple standing by the tracks.

He heaved one duffle bag onto his shoulder and tried to take hers as well, but she took it from his hands and slipped her arms through the straps, easing it up onto her back like a rucksack. As she straightened again, I noticed her belly. She must have seen me standing there among the trees because suddenly she froze and stopped smiling. I raised my hand to wave, but she turned away, grabbing his hand, and walking away down the tracks towards the road.

At the bunkhouse again, I changed back into my skirt and blouse, then took a cigarette outside. The wind in the trees sounded like traffic and like the sea. I closed my eyes, listening, and when I opened them, Carole was at the window. She was watching me and, with her short hair tucked behind her ears, she looked like a woodland creature, or a fairy.

'You shouldn't smoke those things, you know.'

'Yes?' I wondered if her ears were pointy.

'You're a nurse. You should know better. They don't really calm you down. That's a corporate lie. They're just poison. They'll fucking tar your baby.'

'Hmm.'

She was probably right. Right but malevolent. I thought that, if I could help it, I probably wouldn't invite her to the baptism.

4

From the camp,
May 1969

Dear Mum and Dad,

A long-awaited letter home.

I'm out in the woods now, as you'll see from the return address. It's not really the back of beyond – only two hours from Ottawa, which sounds far but isn't at all by Canadian standards. We're about that distance from Montreal as well, but the roads here on the Quebec side of the river are fairly poor with all the logging trucks. In the village down the road, there's a doctor (and a post office) and a hospital only a forty-minute drive away. And our water comes from a tap and I'm not sleeping in a tent. All of which is to say that you needn't worry.

The folk here are great and really helpful, too. The midwife is a dear and I get a good feeling from her. She works with a sensible combination of science and old wisdom. You'd like her, Mum. She knows her plants and she knows when she needs a textbook and a bottle of disinfectant. Her brother Bas does most of the cooking and everyone has their jobs, but I haven't found my place yet. I'm sure I'll be nursing later but so far, it's been peeling carrots and washing clothes for me. Which suits me fine.

I'm even getting used to the outhouse, too. Ha. It's not too bad really – the mosquitoes do tend to swarm and it can get a bit fruity but we layer in pine needles and then it's much fresher. Really.

Okay, enough with the reassurances. I'm sure you will think I'm trying to convince myself as much as you, but be reassured. I am all right.

It's a lovely location here. The lake isn't very big – you can even swim right across it – but I haven't even been brave enough yet for a swim. Just dipped my toes in. It's lovely to be by the water. Reminds me a bit of Aberlady Bay. And there are fresh-water mussels in the lake – is that strange? Bas calls them pocketbooks and says they're a nice addition to soup. More Quebec surprises. Fish, I expected, but nothing with shells.

The nights are still cool, and in the morning, there's mist on the lake. There are birds, too – herons along the shore and mergansers and northern divers. They call them loons here. When I mentioned them to one of the other girls, she thought I was being poetic. It's funny – speaking the same language and continually tripping up on all the little differences.

She's here on her own, too. Carole. I can't quite figure her out. Feisty, but that's just self-protection. She doesn't try very hard to make friends. The midwife says she's carrying twins and needs to be careful because twins can come early, but she's restless, so she tends to walk a lot. I don't think she should be alone, but she hasn't taken kindly to my suggestions of company.

There's a family here, too. Draft-dodgers from the States, with the most adorable toddler. And a new girl arrived a few days ago. Marie. She's very young, but Rika says that happens. Apparently, you can get married at fourteen. I shudder at the thought, but hey ho, that's Quebec. New place, new customs. Her husband is a friend of Bas, and they're talking of staying, once their kid is born. They've been drawing up plans for a cabin and looking at stove catalogues. Rika says she'll get us all organized to help sew curtains and bedding, and Marie is so excited she can barely keep her feet on the ground. We're all feeling a bit big-sisterly towards her, I think, and maybe a little green-eyed that she's got a solid man and a place to root in. Well, here's to happiness and hopes for the future.

I'm copying out a recipe that I think will make you both smile and suit you fine over a cup of tea. Bas says that a teacup should work fine for measuring. Enjoy!

Cranberry bannock

3 cups flour
1 teaspoon salt
1 tablespoon baking powder
1 ½ cups water
1 cup berries or diced apples

Mix the dry ingredients, then add the water and stir loosely before adding the berries. Tip into a skillet and, with wet fingers, pat out the batter to the edges. Takes about twenty minutes to cook in a hot oven. Slather with butter as you like and think of me.

Lots of love,
Felicity

5

'YOU HAD ANY ROUND LIGAMENT PAIN YET? SMACKED crotch, it feels like. A real bitch.' Carole had a way of dropping words like plates, and Rika always smiled. Not like it was a joke. More like Carole was sweet.

We were together in the farmhouse and I couldn't relax. It might have been the rain or maybe it was Carole. She and I sat on floor cushions, doing tailor-sit stretches Rika had showed us that morning. She said they'd be helpful.

Carole's voice broke into a groan. 'Ma-aan, this sucks. You just wait, Felicity. It'll be your turn next.' She rubbed her hand against her pubic bone, and made a horrible noise.

'No one said it was going to be easy,' Rika chuckled. 'But you can be strong.'

She'd say these things and they made sense. She could bring peace into a conversation just like that and I thought she was remarkable, but then Carole would say something else ugly and Rika reached out for her, massaging a leg, a shoulder, the stretch of her belly. I looked away.

The wind threw more rain against the farmhouse and the chimney whistled. No one had gone outside since breakfast, and Bas had kept the teapot filled. Eleta spread newsprint and crayons on the table and Soleil and James drew trees, castles and dragons. On the sofa, Bethanne balanced Ember on her knees, their faces close and absolutely eye to eye, Ember making soft, open-mouthed mewing sounds.

'She's perfectly lovely,' I said. Bethanne looked up and smiled, then patted the sofa beside her. I stopped stretching and, as I eased myself to my feet, Carole threw her foot out and kicked me hard on the pubic bone.

'Sorry,' she said, smiling. 'Foot cramp. You got to work them out, you know, or it's more pain and agony for the preggo girl.' I swallowed and gave her my stoniest glare, then shifted out of her way.

Rika hadn't seen. She couldn't have or she'd have said something. Surely. Bas took a cookbook down from the shelf.

'How do donuts sound?' he asked. 'Do you think dragons like donuts?'

Soleil nodded, laughing.

'Yes, I think so too,' Bas said. 'And it's that sort of day, isn't it? Hans here used to be a fan of donuts, if I remember correctly.'

'And what is this? Bas, maker of donuts? What about Bas and the revolution? Bas waving the workers' flag. Now Bas and the apple peeler? The rocking chair? Is that it? I didn't expect to find you in a nursery.'

'Revolutions need nurseries, too,' Annie said. Hans shrugged and laughed.

'That is certainly true,' Hans said, catching up Marie's hand and holding it to his lips. 'Nurseries and donuts. And love, too.'

'We all find our work,' Eleta said.

Hans smiled. 'Thank you, my friend. I am particularly glad of your work. You and Rika are so good. We didn't know where to go, in the end.'

'I'm just glad I have a site cleared already.' Bas said. 'That will save you a lot of work with the brush when the rain stops. But we would have found space for you anyway.'

'You building a town, then? Carving out a new country for a new generation here in the trees?'

'Not quite. Some folk just drop by for a visit. But it's home for us. The only place we're going from here is deeper.'

Rika looked up and caught Bas's eyes. 'I like that. That's good.'

Bas scooped flour into a bowl and measured salt and baking powder. Then he grated in some nutmeg and the room smelled warm.

'Do you have a workshop here?' Hans asked. 'If we can stay, I'd like to do some work. Make a cradle. Maybe some bookshelves. And what about a sign for you? You could stick it out by the tracks. We weren't too sure we were in the right place when the train stopped.'

Bas rubbed his forehead with the back of his hand. 'Not sure what you'd put on it. The train men just know us as the freaks on the farm by the lake.'

'When I asked for the stop, I left out *freaks.*'

'And they stopped anyways? Fancy that.'

'But I could make one that said "The Camp". That would be fine, right?'

'Might look a bit odd written out.'

'Or vague,' Rika said. 'What about using the lake's name?'

'That might confuse folk looking for the village,' Bas said. 'A new name might be good. What do you think, Carole? You must be thinking about names these days.'

'I'm not. It's not like I'm keeping them. They can be A and B until they're adopted. I can do that, right?'

Rika just smiled and said she could do what she liked. Bas cracked eggs against the side of the bowl and stirred them into his batter.

'The farm must have had a name before you arrived?' Hans pressed.

'Just the family name,' Bas said. 'MacDonald's Point. But they've been gone a long time. Maybe it's time for something new.'

There's a moment in a conversation like this, when you hit on a suggestion and you know that it's right – absolutely perfect, in fact, like it always was the answer and you've remembered it somehow – but instead of speaking up so everyone can hear, you hold it for yourself, just for a moment so that before it's real and everyone knows it, it can be yours. I watched Carole, flat on the floor and looking up at the roof beams, blinking, her lashes spiked, her nose peppered with freckles. Just a kid. Scared and scratching out.

'What about Birthwood?' I said, my voice lidded.

Rika turned towards me and smiled.

'Yes,' she said. 'That's . . . apt.'

Carole rolled over and looked right at me, but she wasn't fierce now. She smiled, and Bas smiled, too, putting his wooden spoon down on the table. The knock and settle of wood against wood.

'Yes,' he echoed. 'It's just right. Couldn't pick a better name. It's a new beginning.'

Of course, Dr Ballater should know. I'd have liked to let him know that I remembered the name of his childhood home and was putting it to good use. That I remembered our chats and his stories. That it hadn't all been forgotten or wasted. I could write this down and send it to him. One airmail envelope and then he'd know. I could even tell him about the new kind of community we were trying out, a simple place where the war really was over and anyone might put down roots. I could tell him Birthwood was a new beginning. But it wouldn't work. I didn't want to hurt him. And I'd have to mention why I was there and then tell the story of Asher. Then while I was at it, I'd write to Asher, too, and tell him. I'd have to. Once you start these things, they grow.

6

I FOUND IT ALL EXTRAORDINARY. THESE PEOPLE LIVING together but separate, too, building their homes and measuring time in seasons, not shifts. I'd fallen into a new world. Mornings baking and afternoons in the garden. All day, the sound of hammering was loud between the trees and, at the dinner table, we talked about fireplaces, shingles, freedom and peace. I had time to read and wander and nap. I stopped thinking about bombs and learned to dodge Carole's moods and swerved away when I needed to. The days were warm and the forest path inviting. On Sunday mornings, we all sat together on a flat rock by the lake. No one preached, though sometimes Bas told a story. It was enough.

Morning and Rika asked for my help.

'I need to redo the birthing packs,' she said. 'The ones I have will be expiring soon so they need to be done.'

'Are you expecting someone?' I asked.

'Not really. But I wasn't expecting Hans and Marie either. It happens. Sometimes, people just show up ready to have a baby. And babies don't wait for equipment to be ready.'

She hung up her tea towel and we headed over to the birthing house together. Bethanne and Ember had moved into the farmhouse, leaving the birthing house empty again. I liked the idea of it sitting empty, waiting. Belonging to everyone.

She opened the curtains and all the windows and turned on the radio. A CBC voice talked about an upcoming interview with John Lennon and Yoko Ono from their hotel-room bed in Montreal. All HAIR PEACE BED PEACE, whatever that meant. I wondered if there would be singing or only politics.

'Here's the list of equipment,' Rika said. 'Just take a good poke around the room and I think you'll find where everything is kept. You can set things out on the table and then we'll make up the sterile packs together.'

'How on earth do you sterilize things out here? Just soak everything in Zephiran?'

'Not everything, though some bits need it. For most instruments and all the towels and cloths, heat is sufficient. I wrap things in heavy paper, truss the package up with string and bake it in a hot oven for two hours. That does the trick nicely. You just need to remember to put a pan of water in the bottom of the oven so the pack doesn't scorch. And, of course, wash up thoroughly before you touch anything.'

'You should have seen how they taught us to scrub at the

hospital. A full two minutes and up to the elbow with Matron standing over your shoulder watching.'

'I think I can trust you to be sensible and clean. These packs will last for a week and then we redo them, so you'll need to mark the date on them clearly. It can be easy to lose track out here.'

The birthing house would be Carole's next. I heard her up at night in the bunkhouse. Feet on floorboards. Opening and closing the windows. I lay in bed listening and watching the moon through the thin curtain. What Asher would call a woven moon. Asher, who liked Basho. At Expo, he'd bought a pocket paperback in the Japanese pavilion, and read poems to me beside a fountain. People walked past, girls in their miniskirts, pigeons pecked around our feet, and I saw them all, but I heard Asher.

> *Mountain path –*
> *Sun rising*
> *Through plum scent*

'Perfect.'

'Yes?'

'Yes! There's nothing clever there. Or obscure. Just a moment snatched from time.'

I dipped my hand in the fountain, nodding because he didn't expect a reply.

'He places it all so well. An exact moment. Those plum trees long gone to dust, but we have them, don't we?'

I lifted my hand, listening, happy, watching the drops collect on my fingers, fall.

'He catches them, gives them to us, and we participate in their reality, proving we are . . . alive. Whammo. Alive.'

Stethoscope, haemostats, scissors on the table.

Sponge clamps, speculum, foetoscope, scales.

Rika showed me how to fold the towels and gowns, the gauze pads and cover sheets to be sterilized in the oven along with the instruments. It felt good to be working again with white things, metal things, clean and hygienic, and odd suddenly to be wearing army boots. Since I'd left Montreal, I hadn't felt like a nurse. Almost since I left Scotland, because in Montreal, we didn't wear capes, and no one recognized me on the street. Even on my way to the hospital, I might have easily turned down another street and been someone else altogether. Maybe I did, and who was I here anyway, in army boots and my growing hair, this tumbling belly full of what? Who knew? Who.

'That's okay,' Rika said, reaching for the roll of gauze that tumbled unravelling across the floor. 'I'll get it for you.'

Then she asked me about Asher. Or rather, about 'the baby's father'. If I wanted to call him, to let him know where I was. I didn't. Because I didn't know where he was. Not really.

He left the city before I did, before we were over. He had to; his brother was ill in New York. His brother was dying. He would come back, of course he would. He might be a while. His brother would die.

He sent me those words on postcards. The Statue of Liberty. Central Park. Cherry blossom. In longer letters, he told me about his parents, their history, their hunger. He told me about watching them holding his brother's hands, about their hungry eyes, their clutching hands. His mother was German and couldn't understand what the nurses said. His father, full of fear, refused to speak German to her in the hospital, just in case someone heard. Neither one had spoken Yiddish since they were children, but now over the starched sheets and gripping fingers, she whispered *bubeleh bubeleh bubeleh*. Darling, Asher wrote. That's what it meant, and they were all scared.

I left Montreal before he knew. No. Before he found out. Before he came back and before I might tell him. Because I didn't want him to know. I didn't want to share. Maybe I didn't want to need him. I didn't want his trailing families, or worn-out history like stones in rivers, stones in pockets. I didn't want old countries and languages, old wars heavy in my veins, my baby weighed down already. We needed to be quick and light, to skim across the shining surface. We needed to get away.

And what's a father anyway? Only the beginning. And after that? A fairy tale. A useful story. Is that right? If he's gone? And if he's there?

Because Stanley fits in here somewhere, doesn't he? I couldn't really ask Rika about that. Or explain how, despite the high-school rumours, I still believed that Stanley was everything. Wasn't he? Everything. As good as could be. As good a chance of happiness as any mother could find. That's how I understood it. And my mother said nothing more. In the evenings, they would sit together on the bench behind the house. She leaned on him, her head on his shoulder, his hair caught by the wind and I remember standing behind them in the doorway, my hand on the wooden frame, aware of the grain beneath my touch and the continuing sound of the sea. I stood and watched, but they didn't move. They never did. I thought I understood.

But we can never see things as they were, can we? In the days that came before us. We can look as long as we like, but we'll only see things as we are. A daughter, looking. And now, a lonely almost-mother, looking back.

'You and Carole are in the same boat,' Rika said. She handed me the gauze, the look in her eye necessary, nursed.

'Because we're housing bastards?'

'Not quite how I meant it. Because you're on the brink. Is that fair? So much is changing for both of you, and whatever decisions you make, the changes are real.'

'I'm keeping my baby.'

'Are you? That's big. Exciting. We can talk about this. But I wasn't asking yet. I only wanted to say something about Carole and about you.'

She leaned against the tabletop and folded her arms over her flat middle. I could see her taking a moment before she spoke. Leaves brushed the roof of the birthing house, a soothing sound. Something to listen for when it was my turn. 'You're sensible,' Rika said. 'And she's scared. Of course, you probably are, too. That's natural. But I'm not sure that Carole's going to be able to help you out. I've seen you watching her and trying to tag along on walks. It's okay. She hasn't talked with me about it. But I want to warn you that it might not help. She's too much on edge. See if Marie wants company. She's not going to be able to do a whole lot to help Hans build the cabin. It might be nice if the two of you could spend some time together.'

Driving a wedge – was that it? Or was she keeping Carole to herself? It wasn't as though Carole was the best of company anyway. I'd only wanted someone to walk with. A dog would have worked just as well. Better. He'd be faithful and confident. Make me feel a little safer among the trees.

But I was managing on my solo walks just fine now. I'd found a path that led around the shoreline and spotted some good mushrooms I might pick for Bas: fairy rings and mica caps. A foraging walk is always a gift and besides, it was a gentler hike than up the hill. Carole made it clear the lookout was hers. Told me that she'd been the one to heave all the stones into the firepit, that the seat was perfectly placed so she could look down at the lake and that she wasn't going to share. I didn't know what to say. Absolutely couldn't imagine shifting stones like that whilst pregnant. Of course, she had pains. She might have ruptured something. Or possibly that was the point.

I didn't tell Rika any of this. Didn't think it would make her my friend.

7

I DECIDED NOT TO MIND WHEN CAROLE WENT OUT walking alone the next day. I would focus my energy elsewhere. I wouldn't even think about it. Marie wanted help starting a rag rug and Rika said we could use the farmhouse floor. She helped us push the furniture against the wall and set up the frame Hans had made. Then she found a basket of fabric scraps somewhere upstairs and Marie and I tipped them out on the floor. Gold and red like a Rothko and a hundred forest greens.

'Perfect,' Marie said. 'It's Christmas morning.'

'I didn't know what I was saving those for,' said Rika. 'But if you can use them, they're yours.'

Marie had an old potato sack she'd cut open and in the centre, she'd traced her own handprint and Hans's, too, in thick black marker, the palms spiralled with lines and stars and all around, she drew trees, hearts and flowers, swirls and circles within circles.

'I think it will make a nice pattern, *non*?' Marie said. 'Very lively.'

I helped her hold the sacking taut as she tacked it down to the frame, and then she showed me how to cut the scraps into strips to hook along the line she'd sketched.

'My grandmother makes these rugs. My mother when she has time. She made one for each of us, with the letter of our name hooked in the middle. We set them all out beside our bed – four girls all in one bed, so four little rugs lined up all pretty. We took turns getting out of bed in the morning, each hopping right onto our letter and no one else's. Very important.'

She chose a felted blue sweater and, with swift scissors, sliced it through top to bottom, the fabric falling away in long strips.

'These will be nice along here, I think,' she said, pointing to a line along the edge. 'Just like a lake.'

Eleta opened the door and Soleil came in like a cannonball, throwing himself towards Marie.

'Hey, you hooligan,' Eleta called, pulling him back. 'Cool it. Give Marie some space.' Soleil looked glumly up at his mum and Marie laughed.

'It's fine. The boy needs a hug. Anyone can see that.'

'He's been talking about you all morning. You have a fan.'

James came through the door behind her and Rika put the kettle on the stove.

'None for me, thanks,' James said. 'I thought I'd head over to the new cabin to give Hans and Bas a little help.'

'They're peeling the logs again today,' Marie said. 'The foundation still needs time to cure.'

'Won't take long, I shouldn't think. You'll be out of your tent and arranging furniture in no time.' He was dressed for work, wearing dirty jeans and a clean, white undershirt. The hollow of his belly button was marked by a small slack circle. My own belly button stuck out under my shirt like a cork.

'What else can I do to help?' I asked Marie. 'More strips?'

'Sure, that would be nice. Not too wide.' She laughed as Soleil scrambled onto her knee to get a closer look.

'Careful, *p'tit chou*, I have a baby in here.' But it didn't look like Soleil believed her. He pulled more scraps from the basket, searching. 'Not in there, silly. In here.' She leaned back and rubbed her belly, grinning. 'It is a funny idea, *non*?'

'Marie, if you want that monkey to leave you be, you just need to say.'

'No, he's wonderful,' Marie said. 'He makes me feel at home.'

'You used to little ones?' Eleta said.

'Yes, I guess. My family . . . lots of little ones.'

'Careful, Soleil. You be gentle with Marie.'

'He's fine. If he gets tangled in my hair, I'll gobble him up.'

'I'm not a donut!' he cackled, tossing back his tangled head, and Eleta laughed, too.

'It's wonderful to have someone new to amuse him,' she said. 'So much of the time, we're mucking about with the cabin and he plays on his own. This place needs more children, I think.'

'I think we're working on that one,' Rika said, smiling at me.

'And me. And then I will have another and another and we will all stay,' Marie said.

'It would be nice if Carole stayed, too,' Rika said. 'I'd like to get to know her twins.'

I shifted on the floor, my hip joints uncomfortable and maybe my heart a little as well. I watched Rika set the teapot on the table and take the mugs from the shelf. She sighed, smiled, pausing with her fingers hooked through the mug handles. 'But that's not her plan. And I'll find a family for her babies.'

'The offer stands,' Eleta said, softly.

'Oh, my dear.' She set the mugs down and stepped through our piles of scraps to wrap herself around Eleta. Rika was all elbows and knees, and her hair was a curtain around them both. 'I thought you and James still needed to discuss it.'

'We have. And we're ready. And if another baby comes our way, well, aren't we just in the perfect place to deal with that?'

'You are a blessing.'

'And you sound like Annie.'

'We'll need to talk it all through with Carole. And give her lots of time to make up her mind. She doesn't take well to anything like instruction. Even keeping her from rambling about has been almost impossible.'

'She up the hill again this morning?'

'Likely. I wish she wouldn't.'

'It's lovely up there,' I said. 'Such a great view and the firepit and everything.'

Rika looked at me strangely. 'She's one for secrets,' she said. 'Can't get a straight story out of her. But this restlessness is to be expected. We just need to keep our eyes open to be there when she needs us.'

'But not telling her family? Not even her mother?' Eleta shook her head. 'I cannot understand. My mother needs to know. How can she pray for me if she doesn't?'

'Does it help?' I asked. Marie glanced at me, her eyes darting to hide their surprise.

'Yes. Of course,' Eleta said. 'For me, it does. My mother's prayers are power in me. It is like . . .' She needed to look for the words, then she smiled. 'It is like God put a homesickness inside me. It calls out at night and knowing my mother is praying is like another voice calling back.'

'Yes,' said Marie. 'I think it can be like that.'

Over lunch, there was talk of the summer. Annie said students on campus were asking if they could come and pitch tents somewhere on the property. They wanted to be part of the community – help with the gardens, or with building cabins, too. Bas thought it was a fine idea, but Rika wasn't convinced. She was all for hospitality – that had always been part of the vision – but she wasn't sure of the wisdom of letting tourists in.

'It might be exciting,' Bas said. 'A new development, right? Change can be beautiful. We have to keep our eyes open.'

'Which reminds me,' Hans said. 'I'd like to head into Ottawa to buy a television.'

'What do we need a television for?' Rika asked. 'You running out of things to look at?'

'The moon landing, my girl,' said Hans. 'Not till next month, but I thought if we got one sooner, we'd have time to sort out the signals well in advance. Besides, it might be hard to find a set closer to the time. Everyone's going to want one.'

'It is amazing to think about,' said Eleta. 'Man on the moon. I'd like Soleil to see that.'

James wondered if they'd be able to pick up the signal, but Hans was fairly confident that it would work. Especially given the lead time. There'd be time to practise.

'No sweat,' Carole said. 'The radio signal comes through clear enough.'

Hans wasn't sure it worked like that, but said it was worth a shot.

'Can I come too?' I asked. 'I'd like to see Ottawa.' It sounded almost as far away as Aberlady or New York. Or the moon. My dad once told me that the distance to the moon was the same as the length of all the coastlines in the world. I wondered how the astronauts got their heads around distance. I bet their wives were buying television sets. I wondered if my parents would.

'Me too,' Marie said. 'I've never been to Ottawa.'

'You don't want to be trailing around the city. In your condition, I mean.' Hans wrapped his arm around Marie and kissed the top of her head.

'These girls aren't sick,' Rika said. 'Just growing people. A bit of new scenery isn't a problem. Mind, it's getting a bit close for you, Carole, but Felicity and Marie would be fine. Do the two of you good to see something new. Big city and all that. Take a walk along the canal. Or see the gallery, if you like.'

'That would be nice. I've never been to a gallery before, either.'

'Is that so?' said Hans. 'Goodness, I had no idea.'

Bas offered seconds on soup. 'Soup days in June. You never know around here, do you? But the rain doesn't seem to be hurting the berries. I've never seen so many. Maybe we should start selling them. A stall at the road-end – what do you think?'

'Let's tackle the television and the moon first, shall we?' Rika said. 'Middle of July, Hans? It'll be a waxing crescent then. Felicity's baby might be here.'

'Too bad it won't be full,' said Carole. 'That would be something, wouldn't it? A man walking about on a big-ass full moon.'

'We won't see anything from here, you know,' Hans said, reaching for the bread. 'Just on the television.'

'Don't worry, Carole, it'll be a broadcast to remember. Which is probably half the goal anyway,' Bas said, wryly. 'The Russians can't compete with that.'

8

From Birthwood,
(That's what we're calling the camp now.
Fitting, don't you think?)
June 1969

Dear Mum and Dad,

Thanks for your letter – it was so good to read. You said you had no news, but the birds on the bay were enough. I could see them there, bobbing about like fragments of cloud, just as you said, and then the sound of the geese on the sandbar at night. That's home.

It's been clear weather here recently. We had a good view of the full moon last night and I sat outside for a long time with the girls. You would have liked it. It was warm enough for bare legs, even at ten o'clock at night, and the lake was so flat

311

the moon was reflected perfectly. James and Eleta took a canoe out, and they offered to paddle me around, but I didn't feel I could even climb in. I'm really heavy now, and my joints get achy in the evening. I made a point of going out early today, though. A canoe is a beautiful thing. You are so close to the water, and the boat is thin beneath you, so you feel the lake through the hull just under your knees. Thin like an eggshell, like Dad's stories about witches in eggshells. Do you remember? You taught me not to break them after I'd scooped everything out, all the soft-set white and runny honeyness of the yolk. You said if I left them whole, then witches could use them to sail out to sea and stir up storms. I wondered how they could possibly steer an eggshell boat because wouldn't it just go round in circles? I'm always spinning in circles now, and especially in a Canadian canoe. Annie has been showing me the trick of steering. You need to look straight ahead and find a point on the far shore. Then, without shifting your gaze, you pull your paddle straight back through the water, twisting a little each time to compensate, not letting the point shift left or right. I'm getting the knack. Tiny adjustments will do. Isn't that the way?

I've seen the loons up close a few times now. They'll suddenly surface right in front of the canoe, and they surprise me every time. Their bodies are large and black – silhouettes at noon – and their necks are strung with pearly bands, their eyes strange and red. Beautiful. The pair on our lake have a nest somewhere at the far side. I haven't found it yet, but I'd like to. Not that they will be returning to it often now, since their chick has hatched. It might have been abandoned altogether. I am curious to see it anyway. Annie says that they are almost not nests at all, just a jumble of sticks as close to the water as possible, but you can sometimes find feathers there, and I'd like that. If I do, I'll send one over for Dad.

This loon chick is still covered in charcoal fuzz and I got quite a good view the other morning. I came up right behind them and when they heard my paddle, the baby hopped up onto the mother's back and nestled down into her feathers. She swam away quickly, heading out to the middle of the lake. I say she, but it's impossible to tell. The two adults look so much alike, and they both take responsibility for the chick, tag-teaming on fishing and diving demonstrations. Annie says they mate for life. I wonder if that's true.

I should tell you that I haven't been honest. To you, I mean. I wrote that I had told the baby's father, but that wasn't true. I didn't. And I won't. We're not in touch. I don't know why I told you that; maybe I thought that's what you'd want to hear and probably I was a bit ashamed, but anyway, that's how it is. I am on my own with this kid and I'm going to be okay. It's not like there's gossip these days. The world's wider now and anyway, no one minds here. I've decided to stay here for the autumn, at least, so I will have community in the early days with the baby and that will help. They need me here, too, actually. Rika says that my nursing will really come in handy, as will the fact that I worked in Montreal. It seems the local doctor is concerned Rika doesn't have qualified help. He got wind of Carole's twins and has been awkward about that. She thinks that having a trained nurse on site will help get him on side if she needs to call him in an emergency.

How was birth for you? I've never asked. What did it feel like? How did you manage? Maybe you could write and tell me a little. I know the story about visiting your parents in Edinburgh, how the family doctor stopped by and insisted you stay in town. I've often imagined you on the bus on the way to Edinburgh, not knowing just how soon you'd be meeting me. I would love to hear how it all felt, if you remember, and don't mind sharing. I'm shaped like you, so I suspect we might have similar experiences. I should ask Rika if it works like that. Is that foolish? I don't know. I can't think clearly right now and I'm trying hard not to worry, just to be interested in everything I can learn. Rika's been teaching me good stretches and squats for birthing and I'm trying to rest, but still feeling restless. I keep thinking about Montreal and all the people in the hospital. There have been more bombs this summer. I can't think why everyone doesn't just leave, but people don't. They think that nothing all that terrible will happen to them and chances are it won't. But I think about them anyway.

Maybe you know something of what I'm feeling, Mum. You were on your own, too. Maybe I should have come home. Well, too late for that now, and I'm just getting sentimental, close to baby time, I guess. I send you both my love, of course. Of course and of course.

Lots of love,
Felicity

9

To keep Rika happy, we promised we'd be back from the city before sunset.

'I'm not jumpy,' she insisted. 'Babies just tend to come at night, and I'd rather have the van on hand. So the sooner you lot can be back on site, the happier I'll feel.'

'Nothing is going to happen,' Carole said.

'Course not. Those babies of yours are going to be eons late. Three months at least. But I want to be cautious.'

'And you don't want to miss us too much,' Bas teased. 'I get it. The woods get scary without your brother around.'

'Is it the dark?' Hans asked, grinning.

'Oh, you two. I'm going to bed. I'll see you all tomorrow when you get back.'

On the way back to the bunkhouse, Carole was growly.

'Do you want anything from Ottawa?' I asked. 'I can pick something up for you, if you like.'

Carole snorted out a chuckle and said no.

'I don't mind. And you don't need to worry about money, if that's a trouble. What would you like?'

'Nothing. Really. Just leave me alone.'

She bolted down the path and slammed the bunkhouse door behind her. My mum would say she was asking to be followed but actually, I didn't have much choice. Couldn't exactly sleep in the woods. Curl up under a tree and use leaves as blankets, the moon above white as a pebble, as breadcrumbs.

Carole had the light off before I was through the door and she didn't answer when I said goodnight. Well, goodnight, anyway, I thought. May you dream of stepmothers.

The sun was not yet properly over the hills and there was nobody on the road, but still Annie stopped at the traffic light. Looked both ways. Turned right onto the highway. Kept going. Highway was a misnomer. Highways ran flat and straight across America, and were spotted with diners. There were motorbikes, mountains on the horizon. This was just an empty road with scrubby woods on either side. Away to the left, I could see mist shawling along the river below.

Halfway to Ottawa, we stopped to stretch our legs in a gravel car park. Railroad tracks ran between us and the water, and two boys, baseball-capped, burnt-eared and blue-jeaned, were testing their balance. They startled when the van door slammed and ran away down the tracks towards the centre of town. Hans and Marie crossed the road holding hands and came back with a punnet of strawberries and a newspaper.

'How can you let the world in on a day like this?' Bas asked. 'And you should stop buying berries. We've got more than enough at the camp.'

'But they taste like summer,' Marie said. 'And I was hungry again. This is the perfect place to live. I can see why you chose it.'

'Luck of the draw, really,' Bas said, adjusting his glasses on his nose. 'A lady at our church said she had land that needed people on it. I needed a new place to be, and Rika, well, she wanted to keep an eye on me, so she came too. Everything else followed after.'

'Hans told me about Sally,' Marie said. 'I am sorry.'

There was a pause before he answered, the sound of the river running through. 'She would have liked it here, I think. The river is lovely. Look at that — how the water moves, but the light stands still. Maybe that's just the last of the mist I'm seeing. I could stay here all day watching that. Looks like light walking about on the surface, doesn't it?'

Back in the van, we opened the windows wide and the warm wind blew in, ruffling hair and clothes. For a while, I pretended to sleep, letting my body slouch and feeling all the vibrations of the road. Annie sat between Marie and me, turning pages in a book, while Bas drove. He spoke with Hans, half-sentences blowing between the seats, some English, some Dutch, but too few words to follow. When I opened my eyes again, we were crossing the bridge. I could see the Parliament Buildings, blazing in the sunlight, their roofs coppery green, like the dome of the bank in Edinburgh. Green like lichen, green like pennies. When I was small, my dad taught me to wash pennies in vinegar and set them on the window sill. If you could wait and keep your fingers away, the pennies would turn green. Fairy money, he said. Perhaps if you left them under the orchard trees, you might find fairy gold left in exchange. But I hid mine instead, wrapped in a rumpled handkerchief at the back of my sock drawer, the perfect green saved.

Annie parked behind the old teachers' college on Lisgar Street. More green roofs and a sign high up on the wall read: DANGER. BEWARE OF FALLING ICE. Dandelions grew on the thin strip of grass beside the kerb. We walked along Elgin Street past a church, a movie theatre, a grocery shop, old women in day dresses pulling flowered shopping trollies, with dogs on coloured leads. Annie bought a bag of cherries and shared them around and I remembered I'd finished my airmail paper and popped back into the store. When I came out there was a discussion about the best place to find the television set.

'Bank Street? Or the Hudson Bay Company over on Rideau? Where's the best price going to be?' Bas asked. The image of him trading in beaver pelts amused me, but I didn't say anything. Maybe they'd make the same jokes about Woolworths and fleeces.

Annie leaned over and gently touched my arm. 'You girls going to be okay? I don't mind sticking with you, if you'd prefer.'

'No, we'll be fine. Happy as clams at high tide.'

'Price doesn't matter,' Hans said to Bas, rolling up his sleeves. 'I've got the funds. But you'll look after Marie, Felicity? She isn't used to big cities, you know.'

'Hey, that's not fair. Big cities don't scare me.'

'Yeah.'

'And Montreal turned out completely fine, if you ask me.'

Hans put his bare arm around Marie's slight shoulders and gave her a squeeze. 'Better than fine. Couldn't have been better. I just want Felicity to know to keep an eye on you, that's all.'

'I will,' I said. 'And she can keep an eye on me. Bellies stick together, right?'

'The gallery's up the street, about ten minutes,' said Annie. 'If you get up to the British High Commission, you've gone too far. But the canal's close by, too, if you just want a shady place to sit. It's going to be a hot one.' Annie checked her watch. 'Back here about noon. Does that suit?'

'Don't worry about us. We'll be absolutely fine.'

The gallery was a block building built like a ship – all concrete, brown siding and windows. Inside, we were given a map and invited to explore.

'The Rembrandt exhibit won't open till next month, but there's plenty to see in the Canadian Collection. And Contemporary American and British Prints, if you like. It's all on the map.'

The floating stone staircase made us both a little dizzy and we held hands to keep steady as we climbed. The rooms upstairs had low, tiled ceilings and fluorescent strips that washed the paintings in modern light.

Let's see. Canada. The frozen north, indeed. Just the sort of thing I'd imagined in the North British lobby. We wandered past snowy forests, lonely teepeed prairies and strange saints with cringing faces. A continent of longing, strange and wonderful, and after a while, Marie let go of my hand and wandered off to look at more trees. I walked slowly and was caught by gold. Gold and a vast pregnant belly. Obviously one of Klimt's and she was naked, the walls around her stark and white. Gold the tuft of hair at her sex; red-gold the hair on her head, wild and flecked with forget-me-nots. Her nipples stood red and her pale fingers, clasped together, were thin and protecting. Behind her, there was a blue panel marked with Japanese block prints, reminding me of Basho and then of Asher.

But her face. Her face. Her blue eyes were calm, her brows slightly raised. Her mouth, those thin lips, might be my mother's, her pointed nose. Her hair. My mother not my mother. I stood and stared at her wondrous naked face.

No one was naked when I was growing up. Maybe because there were no other children in my house. I couldn't compare with anyone, and my parents' naked bodies were unimaginable. My father rolled up his sleeves to wash the dishes and my mother held up her skirt to paddle in the sea. Nothing like naked.

Even children's skin was only exposed for needles, vaccines, stitches, examined for rashes, flushed with fevers, but never flaunted, never really seen.

I remembered Bethanne nursing, holding out her nipple like a cigarette and teasing her baby's opening mouth.

I stood a long time with Klimt's portrait before I noticed the skulls behind her, or the black ribbon entangled around her legs, the clawed hand emerging from the shadow. She stood before a complicated darkness, encroaching but held back by her naked-ness. The painting was called *Hope*. No, better than that – it was called *Hope I*. Like more hope might follow. Hope and again there might be hope. Despite all those skulls, there were things yet to be born.

'She looks like you,' Marie said, startling me, and I laughed.

'No, I don't think so. Her hair is so red. She's lovely, isn't she?'

'Do you think she's scared?'

'Could be. But strong, too.'

'Yes,' Marie said, holding her own belly. 'Yes, I think so too.'

'Come on, you, let's find some fresh air.'

But stepping outside, the sun was hot and the air heavy and humid. My skin felt sticky as we crossed the street and found steps leading down to a shaded pathway beside the canal. That was better. It was like a sunken green tunnel here, and cool in the shade. A pebbled concrete wall held back the slope of the hill and Marie climbed up to walk along it, holding out her arms for balance like a child. I was happy to sit down on a bench, my hips sore and my legs heavy.

A tour boat came through the shadow under the bridge, women sitting on plastic benches with sunglasses and headscarves, husbands with cameras. One woman waved at us, her hand bright white in the daylight. Marie pirouetted and waved back, then retraced her steps to sit cross-legged beside me.

'Do you have ideas for names yet?' she asked.

'No, not really. It still feels early.'

'Time isn't long, though.' She smiled and gathered her hair, twisting it into a rope and holding it up off her neck.

'But what about you?' I said. 'Any names? No – first, boy or girl? What do you think?'

'I'm not sure. I don't know what knowing would feel like. But I hope a little for a boy. Like Hans.' She let her hair fall down over her shoulders. 'But if it were a girl, I could call her Felicity. It's a beautiful name.'

'You're sweet, Marie.'

'Either way, I will choose the name. Hans said I could. So, I will have to think hard about it. But Felicity?' she said, hesitating. 'Can I tell you something? Would you promise not to tell?'

'If I can, yes.'

'It's just I don't want Hans to know because it feels like a lie now. My name, it isn't Marie. I made that up.' She picked at a mosquito bite on her leg, the crust of skin flaking off under her nails, a little blood showing. 'It's Eugenie. But I don't feel like a Eugenie. And my family called me Lunette. Which just sounds silly. I don't like that, either.'

'It's pretty,' I said. 'A little moon?'

'Yes. Silly. But I . . . I don't know. When he asked, I didn't know what to say. I was so scared. We'd just met. So, I said a little prayer – silently, of course, to the Virgin – and then when I opened my mouth, I just said *Marie*. Without thinking about it at all. But don't tell him. Please. It doesn't matter.'

'Of course it doesn't matter. Marie is a lovely name. And he loves you as Marie, so Marie you are.'

She threw her arms around me and laughed, surprising the ducks on the canal, who quacked loudly and splashed away.

'Yes,' she said, grinning. 'Yes!'

* * *

We hadn't meant to stay away so long. Traffic was bad over the bridge, and we sat for ages in the still hot air. Mosquitoes took advantage of our open windows, Annie climbing over the seats to squash them. Marie and I sat together in the back, our babies both kicking, so we rolled up our T-shirts, placed our palms on each other's bellies and laughed at how strong they were getting. Finally, the car ahead of us moved, and we headed up the highway. Bas drove quickly, and that must have been why we blew a tyre before we got much further. We were lucky, though, because it was just on the edge of a small town with a garage that could fix us up. An old school bus was parked at the edge of the lot, *Casse Croute* painted on its side in ice-cream colours. Hans bought us paper bags of chips laden with cheese and gravy, and we sat at a picnic table, eating with plastic forks. There were other people at the tables, too, children and thin men in baseball caps, women with thick jellied arms, bare and sun-browned. They wore their hair curled and tied with bright scarves, tight, bright sandals on their feet and thin gold chains around their necks, hung with charms or tiny crucifixes. Bas used the payphone but there was no answer at the farmhouse.

'They'll all be swimming on a hot afternoon like this,' he said.

I asked if I could use the toilet at the garage and was led past rubbish bins, pin-up-girl posters and a disassembled motorbike on the grease-stained concrete floor. The toilet was screened from the rest of the garage by a dirty gingham curtain thumb-tacked to the wall, but once I drew that closed, everything looked surprisingly clean. The walls were white, the soap uncracked and the floor scrubbed. On the wall above the sink, where I'd have expected a mirror, the sacred heart of Jesus hung, framed in gold.

The farmhouse was dark when we drove in.

'The bugs will be bad,' Bas said. 'Everyone's hidden away.'

Climbing down from the van, my back felt a wreck. 'Isn't it weird how you feel more pregnant at the end of the day? This baby gets so heavy.'

'Well, time to sleep then,' Bas said. 'Should have had you home hours ago. Rika's going to give me a talking-to, I imagine.'

'Toilet first,' Marie called out, scuttling towards the farmhouse. 'Better here than the outhouse with the bugs.'

'I'll find you some citronella candles for the bunkhouse,' Annie said, heading inside.

James came down the path, the tip of his cigarette like a lightning bug. 'I heard the van. Everything okay on the road? Rika's been worrying.'

'We blew a tyre,' Bas said. 'We called, but there was no answer.'

'You missed the trouble here.'

'Carole? Is it time?'

'She's gone. Seems she called her parents and told them everything. They came to pick her up this afternoon. Rika's inside.'

* * *

She sat at the table with a glass of water.

'The little bird flew,' she said, but she didn't cry. She sat at the table and her wrists looked like things made of wax as she held that glass of water, and looked dead ahead, her brittle voice straight as a road.

We sat down to listen. Bas put his hands on the table, his ring sounding against the wood, and Rika's face was set.

'It will mean surgery,' she said. 'I told her that, but it was too late. She'd already called home. But no hospital these days lets twins come naturally. If she's really lucky, she might get to deliver the first one, but the second will be C-section for sure. And full electronic monitoring throughout. And an IV. No space to move or figure out what she needs or anything. Imagine Carole all tied up like that. It'll break her.'

Bas reached for his sister's hand. 'They'll be doing it to keep her safe. You know that. They will be trying their best.'

'I know, but . . . I know.' She stroked his fingers as she spoke, and her voice was level and paced. 'She must have used the telephone when I was swimming. I went down to the lake after breakfast and when I came back, she had this look on her face. Stung, I thought. I wondered if she was starting. So I gave her some space and some tea. After a while, she came to find me in the garden and she told me what she'd done. She spat the words out at me, like I was the one who was running away. I tried to talk her through it. She was hurting and not listening. When her mother arrived in her city car, she leaned on the horn to get our attention. James and Eleta came running to see what was happening and it was a mess then, it really was. She assumed he was the father and said some ugly words. And . . . and Carole climbed into the car and they drove away.'

Her eyes stared from a face flattened by the day, and she looked out towards the lake, but it was too dark to see. Annie found candles, set them on the table and lit them with a long fireplace match, the flames reflecting and doubling on the window panes, and Rika stayed quiet. Marie tucked herself in under Hans's arm and asked what would happen to Carole's babies.

'I imagine they'll be adopted in the city,' Bas said. 'Split up probably. They might end up anywhere.'

'In a sad way, that might be for the best,' Hans suggested. 'Carole could never have managed them, even if she had changed her mind.'

I asked how Eleta was taking the news.

James shrugged. 'Philosophically. Faithfully. Says it wasn't meant to be.'

Bas nodded and looked away.

'I'm sorry,' I said.

10

Soon after that, the students started arriving, setting up tents in the field beyond the farmhouse. The summer days stayed hot and Annie stayed at Birthwood. She said there was nothing happening in the city these days and the woods were a better place to be. Hans finished the cabin and helped Rika and Bas build a stall for the end of the road where Annie might sit to sell our extra fruit. It was a simple box with a counter and space for a couple of chairs. I liked the idea of sitting out there, surrounded by fruit baskets and all the fragrant pies and tarts Bas baked from the berries too soft to sell, but I couldn't hack it. The road was dusty and the men who stopped stank, their snap shirts wet at the armpits, their hands dirty. Annie was good at grinning and teasing them in lazy French. I stuttered, shrank back and rearranged the pies.

As July wore on, Marie and I spent our time sitting in front of the birthing house. Hans moved the rug frame outside so we could work together in the shade where it was cooler and the orange wood-lilies grew tall as children. Annie had said she was more than happy to manage at the road stall by herself, which made Marie laugh.

'How can you be *more* than happy? Doesn't happiness fill you up?'

She did look full of happiness, sitting on her stool in a brown sundress with her skin browned to match. She kicked off her sandals and planted bare feet on the soft pine needles, the basket of cloth strips beside her. Blue and green and gold.

'Doesn't the light dance on the lake like diamonds?' she asked. But that was easy and not even apt. No, the sunshine on the lake came in broad sheets of light in those afternoons, layered and shimmering like feathers or fish scales. At home, July brought days when the sea was flat slate grey under a warm dull sky. But when the light did come through, even just a crack, it could catch on the surface and run right to the east with a bright skelf of silver. Diamonds were too easy and out of reach. But Marie wasn't used to living by the water. She told me the house where she'd been born was surrounded by trees, and she drew more blue wool through the sacking of her rug, widening the river again.

The shocking colour is necessary, she said. The clash of violent pink against soft blues and greens. It sets the whole piece. Rug makers call it poison but it brings sharp life into being. It makes the image sing.

Sometimes Rika sat with us, knitting baby shoes. 'Just in case,' she said. 'They always come in handy.'

I might have expected a sadness about her, or a briskness to keep sadness at bay. But Rika wasn't like that. After Carole left, she grew softer, slower, more willing to linger. She took time to admire the colours of Marie's rug and asked me questions about Scotland. Sometimes, she told us local stories, too. Stories about the woods, the villages both French and English, and the things she'd learned about the land. About healing plants, logging camps and old farms, travellers along the rivers, Algonquin traders and Nicolas Gatineau. Stories you'd tell children, and she soothed us with them, drawing us close. She spoke as if she'd been there a long time, though the camp was still new. Five years before, it had been empty, and they'd lived different lives. Now this was permanent. A place with roots and with a tomorrow. That's why they spread the word about Rika's midwifery skills. All part of the plan to be self-sufficient.

'Forty years from now, fifty, these cabins are still going to be homes. That's our hope. Maybe our homes or maybe someone else's. It will keep going. There's virtue in persistence and from that, freedom. Which is what we're looking for. Long term, ongoing goodness and freedom. And babies and berries and tomatoes.'

When it grew too hot, Rika went inside to lie down, and Marie and I sat on the flat rock to cool our toes in the lake.

'I think I could tell you anything,' she said. 'I don't think you'd be shocked.'

'Really? I might be.'

'No. You're easy.' She wiggled her feet, sending ripples across

329

the surface. 'I could tell you about . . . about stealing the host when the priest wasn't looking. I hid it in a handkerchief and ate it in bed at night when my sisters were sleeping. If my tummy gurgled, I knew it meant I was full of Jesus, pregnant like Mary with the Christ hidden inside where no one could see. Mine alone. Blasphemy. You shouldn't laugh – I was very wicked. Still am.'

'I don't think so, Marie. You're a lamb.' The rock was warm on my bare legs, the water cool, and I watched the sunlight move across the surface of the lake.

'I ran away, too. Lots of times. I hid in trees, once in a ditch. I watched my mother cry.' Little minnows came curious to nibble at our toes. 'She loved me anyway. She worried. I got fed up and ran further. I left school without telling anyone and got on a bus to Montreal. That's where I met Hans. At the bus station.' She splashed her toes, and the minnows scattered. 'He looked at me and I knew I loved him. Right like that.'

'That sounds easy.'

'Yes.' One minnow emerged from the shadow and tentatively made his way back towards our toes. 'Scary, too. He was older. And Soeur Perpétue had warned us about men like that. I'd just come off the bus.'

She kicked her feet a little more, the splash coining out across the lake. Then she told me about the town up north, the school, the hallways and the classrooms and Soeur Perpétue teaching her music.

'It wasn't a bad place,' she said. 'I didn't like the singing, and I didn't want to stay, but it wasn't bad. Soeur Perpétue said I could teach the little ones and be safe inside the walls. Said it would be the best life for me. That was after my sister's broken arm and everything. And when my sister left home, Soeur Perpétue made me promise I'd never hitchhike. She told me the bus was just as bad – bad men would find you at the station – but she didn't make me promise about that. I was so scared getting off that bus – and so hungry for a sandwich. I thought if I could just find a church or somewhere someone could help me . . . But Hans found me. I was scared of him at first, but it turned out I didn't need to be. He isn't like that. With him, I'm safe.'

Later, I realized I didn't ask if she went home again. I didn't ask about her mother. I was distracted by the water and the heat, the way I could see the ripples on the surface and the minnows underneath. A large fish darted out past the shadowed rock and chased the minnows away. In the bright emptiness, it paused, and I glanced up to see if Marie noticed, but she was looking out across the lake. When I looked back, the fish was gone. I wondered if it was camouflaged against the rock, or if it swam away. Or it hadn't been there at all. Like Asher, I thought, and that was ridiculous. But as the days slipped past, Asher felt further and further away, the little swimmer tumbling inside me far more real than he. When I slept, I dreamed of swimmers and rivers, and Nicolas Gatineau who might have wandered this way, might have stayed and drowned or never been at all. That story surfaced in my dreams and felt as strong as a current, tumbling over all I'd rather have kept submerged. Because there wasn't an off-switch for love. Even in absence, it kept flowing. I pictured my heart as a river in the night, the shores unseen. *Beautiful Asher, wherever you are now, I hope you aren't lonely for me. Go look for love again,*

look for living love, and when you find it, hold on and don't let go.
I wanted to say I was sorry, that I missed him, but morning
rippled in and I woke with my hands around my belly, worrying
about names. The baby would have my last name, of course. I
couldn't take Asher's. But what else? What name could I wrap
around this little life? What story was strong enough, bright
enough? What was best?

By the middle of the month, I wasn't sleeping any more. Not
at night, anyway. I could manage a nap mid-morning or late in
the afternoon, but at night I felt restless. I went out walking
through the dark woods, finding my way by looking up at the
spaces between the branches where the sky was brighter than the
path beneath my feet. I watched the moon grow fat each night.
One night, I lay down under the birch trees by the shore, the
cool lake air helping to relax my muscles and the sandy ground
holding my weight. Over the lake, the sky was bright with stars.
I could breathe it in, I thought. Inhale deeply and fill myself with
tiny lights, the path of planes and planets and the deep colour in
between. Half an hour, I told myself, just half an hour and then
I would go back to the bunkhouse and to bed. I didn't sleep there
on the ground but time passed strangely, and then came quiet
laughter in the woods behind me, and I heard Marie's voice.

'There's someone there already,' she whispered.

'It'll be folk from the tents,' Hans said. 'It is a good night for
a swim.'

I heard splashes behind me, and turning, saw women in the
lake, swimming far out from shore, their heads sleek in the bright
water.

I rolled over and called out to Marie. She skipped down the sand, light, slight, despite her swelling belly.

'Isn't it beautiful? I'm going in.' She pulled her T-shirt over her head, and pushed her long skirt down to her ankles, leaving it like a puddle on the grass.

'You are a birch tree, my love,' Hans called.

Marie laughed. 'Birches don't have belly drums. And I'm browner than that, too. Come on, Felicity. You'll come in with me?'

Hans was climbing out of his clothes, too, his body thick and shadowed with hair. I wasn't prepared for that, for the feeling in my own body, looking. I felt like a statue, solid, weighted, smooth, and shifting now. My fingers brushed at the buttons on my dress.

Marie swung her arms, readying herself for the water. 'Felicity, you'll come with us, won't you? Rika says she won't let us back in the water for at least six weeks after the babies come and for me, the lake will be practically frozen by then so I need to swim now. Every day. And night if they're nights like tonight.'

Hans's voice was deep and warm. 'These are nights to remember when February comes. Wherever we all are then, we'll have this.'

'But we'll be here, won't we?' Marie said. 'Even in the snow and ice.'

'Yes, of course we will. But we can still swim for February.'

I stood, looked down, unbuttoned my dress. I slipped it off and set it on the sand, folding my underpants, my unclipped brassiere carefully on top. The air was fingers on my back and soft around my ribcage where the cotton cut tight. I turned to face the others, but no one was waiting or watching at all. They had walked down to the water, and stood facing the lake, almost hesitating, but maybe that was still me. They looked like a couple at a train station, looking up to check the schedule. They held hands.

I ran in.

The sand felt sharp under my feet, then the water cold and the women in the lake hooted as I splashed out towards them. I dived under, a shallow dive but not shallow enough because my belly scraped the sandy bottom, then the water was cool all around me like fresh sheets or the palms of Asher's hands. With my eyes closed, I rolled over under the deepening water, then over again to feel the rush of this water against my skin. Alive.

I'll need to remember this, I thought. It's a story for the baby – this water and the sky tonight. I'll tell how we all swam together, Marie and Hans and the strangers laughing in the shadows, and how I floated on my back and we were an island floating, the two of us together, an island under the stars.

When I came out of the lake, Rika was sitting on the sand with a cigarette between her fingers.

'Hey,' she said. 'Gorgeous night, isn't it?'

'You couldn't sleep either?'

'No. Wide awake, it seems. It doesn't feel like a night for sleeping. But how're you feeling?'

'Marvellous. I was a bit off earlier, but the water helped.'

'Here, you should wrap up.' She took her flannel shirt off and slipped it over my shoulders. 'Don't want you to get chilly. I once swam in Lake Superior. Not late at night like this, though. It was early morning and so cold that you could see your breath, but I just had to go in. It felt like the whole world spread out in front of my eyes, just for me. Silver and blue. Like I was God and everything in creation was dancing in light. So beautiful. I didn't want to talk to anyone after that, not for days.' She rubbed my shoulders, then gathered my hair between her fingers and squeezed the water out onto the sand.

'Come on,' she said. 'I'll walk you back to the bunkhouse. You should try to get some sleep. Prop that beautiful belly of yours up with pillows and settle down to rest for a while. Dawn will be coming soon, but you rest as long as you can. I'll save you some breakfast if need be.'

11

FRIDAY AND THE FARMHOUSE KITCHEN WAS STICKY WITH jam-making. Rika's hair sprung into curls over her ears, and she wore her sleeves rolled high as if about to catch a baby. In her hands, she held the forceps, shiny, sterile pinchers, but they were for the jars boiling in the kettle. I melted wax in a small copper pan, ready to make the seals, and Bas stirred the cauldron of jam. It was syrupy and thick, a deep, bright red. Bethanne had gathered a crew from the tents and they'd spent the day before down by the railway tracks picking wild raspberries, which were far sweeter than the ones in the garden. I'd wanted to go, too. I used to help my mother pick berries – raspberries, brambles, sea buckthorn along the coast and rosehips from the hedgerows, filling pots and baskets and then the biscuit tins we'd packed with sandwiches and emptied at lunchtime, all possible space used to save every scrap of sun-fed sweetness we could find. Once I found a toad under the berry canes, sitting flat-bellied in the shade. I crouched to watch his mysterious breathing in and out, the flicker of his ancient eye. His skin was dry and ridged, sedimentary and strange. After that, I always looked, but I didn't find him again, that stone-coloured toad sitting hidden and heavy as a heart.

Are there toads like that here in Quebec? So many things can't be marked on a map or true stories found in a book.

Jam bubbled and more berries sat in bowls on the table, swimming in cool water so that the bugs might rise and be removed. White bags of white sugar sat waiting, too, printed with their Montreal address and *Granulated Sugar – Special Fine*.

We'd get two batches at least from all these berries today, and no point in heating up the kitchen two days running, Bas said. Not with weather like this. I sat down behind the table sorting lids, matching rings and disks and discarding wonky ones. A low tightness was starting to stretch under my belly and every so often, I shifted on my stool to change the pressure.

'You okay there?' Rika asked, her face glowing with the steam. 'Need some fresh air?'

'Yeah,' I said. 'Sitting feels awkward right now.'

'I'll just get these jars onto the tray and then I'll be out to join you. I could use a breather, too.'

Coming out to the porch a few minutes later, she asked if I wanted to walk, but I didn't. I just wanted to stand with my back against the solid farmhouse wall, looking at the lake. The loons were out on the bay, diving and surfacing, travelling underwater further than I imagined, surfacing together, catching me unawares.

'You might be starting,' she said. 'You crampy?'

'A bit.'

'You want to lie down? See if you can nap at all, and when you wake, we might see if anything's going on.'

She held out her hand to me and I took it like a child, or a lover, trusting. The wind blew through the pine needles overhead and she walked me down the path to the bunkhouse.

'There, it's cool in here, isn't it? And quiet. You can rest here. And if there are any cramps, don't hold onto them, okay? Just let them be. Don't try to make anything happen – that won't get you anywhere.' She helped me into bed, eased my boots off my feet and smoothed the hair from my hot forehead. 'Sleep, love. Don't worry. You're fine.'

The afternoon slipped away and maybe sleep came, but I didn't notice. Everything came and went in waves. Cramps and thoughts, doubts, too, and imagining those loons out on the lake, swimming and diving, dark and graceful, sometimes seen, sometimes hidden. That's what that afternoon felt like. To keep steady, I thought about the shoreline constant every year and then every year the loons returning to dive again, fishing, nesting, hatching, coming up for air. Evening came around and I found I was ready. All of a sudden full of energy, almost crazy with it, knowing that this was really happening at last. I got out of bed and took a work shirt from a nail on the wall, then walked myself down to the birthing house, stopping on the path only twice to lay a palm against a tree and breathe. Rika was there already, waiting for me.

'Ah good, we were right, weren't we? Let's get you something to eat, if you can manage it. Fuel for the work ahead.' She gave me a glass of water to sip as slowly as I could, and a bowl of berries. They were sweet and wet on my tongue, the night warm around me.

I'd thought it would be textbook: waters breaking, contractions building through to transition, breathing and finding an opening calm – like Rika said, a way forward – and then the desire to push which I would manage and work with carefully, but it wasn't like that at all. That was only a view from outside. A Dr Birch view and translation at best. Inside, everything was different and I only knew words when I came up for air.

Pain travelled through me, pushed me to the edge. Pain made me scrabble up and out of my body. When it grew stronger, I could not ride through it with breathing. My waters hadn't broken yet and how long would I have to ride this pain? I stretched my neck and craned to pull away and Rika's gentle voice called me back.

'That won't work, honey. Chin down is better. Put the force where it needs to be. Open. That's the way. Open your eyes and look at me, okay? In my eyes, there. Yeah, there. It's time for that now. Open and push.'

I heard her words or her voice between the words. Another translation and I found her eyes, the sweetness there. Strength. Time stretched out and everything was moved towards the feeling that was and wasn't pain. I learned to crest each wave, to push, to hold and let go.

Then, before dawn, he was born. Squeezed past my bones and out into the wooden room, into Rika's hands. There was no cry, no sharpness in the moment, as she lifted him to my belly, placing my hand on his small back, his soft, wet hair. 'That didn't take long,' she said. 'Just a little guy, look at that. I thought for sure you'd have a girl.'

He felt so small outside me, and when I bent up to see him, his eyes were already open, his small mouth, too, and he made a gentle coo hello.

'Hi, little one. You're here. You're . . . you're Stanley, I think. Does he look like a Stanley?'

'Sure,' Rika said. 'It's a good name.'

She wrapped a blanket around my shoulders and Eleta was there, though I hadn't seen her come in. She held out her hands for Stanley.

'I'll look him over for you,' she said. 'Toes to count and all that. Don't worry, I'll keep him warm.' She cradled his head in her palm, her eyes soft and loving as she looked into his little face. Rika pressed her hand high on my belly and I felt small rushing cramps. For a moment, I pictured another baby – a twin like Carole's – another small, perfect face, but as I shifted, I knew these contractions were the afterbirth coming away. A few small pushes and Rika caught it in a bowl and set it aside. She'd want to examine it and make sure it was healthy, and I might have asked if I could help, too, but I didn't. Instead, I lay back against the pillow, and felt like I was floating under an open sky, suddenly surfaced to find the shoreline changed.

'He's small,' Eleta said. 'But perfect.'

'Have you done his numbers?' I asked. Eleta and Rika both laughed.

'And colour and tone. His temperature's a little down, but it should go up once he's tucked in beside you. And I've dressed him in the kimono you chose, but I left the front open for skin-to-skin.' She passed him into my arms and as soon as he was close, he opened his mouth wide to nurse, which made us all laugh again.

'As I said: he's perfect.'

He knew just what he wanted, this small burrowing being at my breast. And I expected that, but I hadn't expected that I would know. Not how to nurse – that would take time – but that I wanted to. It was a desire that surprised me, and I didn't understand. No one talked about that want. That warmth and softness and close breath and its urgency, its complete necessity. That love that was new that was old.

'There,' said Rika. 'Now, you're both happy.'

I wished my mother could be there. I wanted her to see my Stanley. I wanted to tell her what it was like. And I wanted Marie, too. I'd reassure her. I'd let her hold him and I'd show her the tiny whorl of his ears and the light hairs across his forehead.

Rika sat beside me on the edge of the bed. I asked her about Marie.

'She'll be along in a little while. Everyone will, in turn. But maybe you'd like to rest first. That was a lot of work. You rest now, okay? Eleta will stay with you, and I'll be back in a little while to bring you something to eat. Sleep if you can. You'll want to be awake for the broadcast later. The next show on the agenda.'

Usually Rika encouraged new mums to stay around the birthing house for a few days, but this was different. There wouldn't be another first moon landing. It was afternoon when we walked slowly down the path together, one step at a time, and Eleta carried Stanley. When I got to the farmhouse, there was a white sheet hanging from the porch, catching the wind like a flag. WELCOME STANLEY, it read. OUR NEWEST ASTRONAUT HAS LANDED!

A crowd of folk came outside to see us, and Soleil danced about with a tambourine whilst James and Eleta led 'Happy Birthday'.

I never cry, but I did. So goofy and wonderful and everyone was there. So many people. Of course, they came for the broadcast, but we were family all together and that made it special. Some people from the tents brought cases of beer, and Bas made vast trays of sandwiches. Once inside, Rika helped me settle with Stanley on the sofa and she sat close by to help.

'Pride of place for you, my dear. You two comfy now?'

Hans built a tower of wooden crates and he set the television on top, the picture grainy but clear enough.

'Well, will you look at that?' Rika said. 'It works.'

'You sound surprised,' Hans said.

'Well, I expected we'd be needing the radio, that's all.'

'A little bit of faith, please.'

Bas said that they had been fiddling with it for a few days and had missed the launch itself, but managed to catch the footage later.

'Every time we've turned it on, someone's been talking about man's journey to the moon.'

I thought Jenny would raise an eyebrow at that, or more likely a fist. I'd received a letter from her at the beginning of June, postmarked Vancouver. Said she was working with an avant-garde group – she described it as 'very confrontational' – and was living halfway up a mountain, surrounded by raccoons and hippies. She sounded happy. She'd be watching the broadcast, too, of course. Half the world would be. I'd have to remember to send her a card about Stanley.

'Cronkite is in fine form,' Bas said. 'He's confessed to sweaty hands but he's managing to keep the show on the road. I half expect him to cross himself.'

'Him and all of NASA,' said Rika.

'Do you think astronauts are prayerful types?' Annie asked.

'Anyone who launches folk into space hoping that they will collide safely with an orbiting rock better be. Fourteen minutes to go. Clever how they make the numbers flick down like that, isn't it?'

'Big bucks for animators,' said Hans. 'Not bad modelling, is it? You could almost believe the real thing looked like that.'

Marie said she thought it looked like a lightning bug.

'Why's it Apollo, anyway?' Rika asked. 'Isn't he a sun god? What about Artemis? That would have been more appropriate, I think. Protector of the moon. And childbirth, too, I think – wasn't she?'

'Your kind of woman,' Bas said. 'Or maybe we should call you Artemis.'

'Hush it. I want to hear what they're saying.'

Beeping and faraway voices making official sounds and comments. Cronkite cut through with a laugh. *They say it's better than the simulator. That's consoling.*

Altitude now 2100 feet, still looking very good.

Four and a half minutes left in this era.

I nuzzled my nose into the warmth of Stanley's scalp as the lightning-bug ship shuddered on the screen, the numbers closing in. It looked like something from a kids' programme, something half made. There should be music in the background, someone ready to dance. My parents would be watching this, too. Or listening to it. Maybe they would go along to the hotel or down to Drem to be with Muriel and Andrew. I wondered if there was a television at the manse.

Correction on that velocity. Now reading 760 feet per second.

That's pretty slow for space flying.

It is. It's as slow as man's ever flown in space.

It sure is.

5200 feet. Less than a mile from the moon's surface.

We're go.

2000 feet. Into the egg.

'What did he just say?' Marie asked.

'Shhh!' Everyone focused on the numbers counting down, but Stanley startled at the sound, his small eyes opening, blinking, alert.

'It's okay, little buddy,' I whispered to him. 'We'll be quiet together, okay?' I traced the softness of his cheek with my finger, and his mouth opened. I tried again to nurse, but he turned away sleepily.

On the floor, Soleil sucked on the corner of a pillow, his mother resting her hand gently on his head. The screen flickered, the voices continued, and everyone held their breath, listening to the numbers until the words appeared on the screen:

LUNAR MODULE HAS LANDED ON MOON.

Hans was the first to cheer, then the room erupted but Bas clapped his hands, and everyone stilled to hear Cronkite say, 'Man on the moon'.

'We copy you down, Eagle,' a Houston voice declared.

And a voice from the moon answered, 'Houston? Tranquility Base here. The Eagle has landed.'

I held Stanley in my arms as everyone hollered and shook hands, hugging, some crying, all eyes shining, the same thing over and over in this new world, and my baby's eyes were galaxy deep and my heart filled with plain, old-fashioned wonder, the noise of people believing, unbelieving, and I held Stanley.

After that, some drifted back to the tents and some decided to stay up for Armstrong's walk. I went outside, and, over the lake, the moon looked sturdy and reassuring. Stars were reflected on the dark water and down by the village someone set off fireworks, a few bright ladders climbing up to heaven, echoing off the quiet hills. In my arms, Stanley slept, and I didn't want to wake him, even if everything was beautiful.

Each night, I took Stanley outside and showed him the moon. I liked to watch the darks of his eyes open in the half-light, the pale of his face soft like a moth's wing. He was so small in my arms, such a tiny weight, but my arms ached from holding him, and my breasts from nursing. I was tired and didn't sleep, but I was happy. Stilled with happiness with this sleeping baby in my arms. Rika taught me how to alternate sides for nursing, and

Marie made me a bracelet of braided cloth that I could switch between my wrists when I was too tired to remember which breast he'd emptied last. I felt full, heavy with milk, dulled and happy. Rika weighed him and told me it was natural he'd lose weight in his first fortnight. She held him and measured him, took notes and I thanked her. She wanted me to sleep and I tried and when he woke, Stanley watched us with wide, grey eyes.

In the mornings, I sat by the lake holding Stanley and watching geese fill the sky. A hundred vee-ed together over our heads, even a thousand or more, and I heard in their voices the end of summer arriving and winter drawing close. My childhood had echoed with wintering sandbar geese, their voices loud behind every silence and stillness only coming with their departure in the spring.

But these northern hills knew a quieter cold. This wild-goose song was just passing through. A pilgrim refrain caught on the wind, a stranger's song gone back into the world.

An August afternoon and Rika told me she wanted to take Stanley into town. She stood with her back to me, changing his nappy. Her hair hung down her back and her feet were bare.

'The doctor should have a look at him. He might have suggestions for getting his weight up a little more.'

'You worried?'

'A little. You know that. He's kinda small still, and sleepy. And he's not soaking his nappies as much as I would like. Best to consult, I think.'

Hans said he'd drive if we liked, and Marie wanted to come, too. She sat beside me in the backseat, the morning already sticky and humid and we sat on pillowcases so our legs wouldn't stick to the vinyl seats. I lay Stanley on my lap, his clothes undone so he'd be cool, and I think he liked the bumps along the way because he smiled up at me, a sweet, milk-soft, reassuring smile like everything was fine and perfect and lovely. The radio played the *White Album*, the organ's drone matching the hot and hazy day, and Marie pointed out a field of dandelions out of the window, a pick-up truck parked in the long grass, a horse lying down.

Marie wanted to buy some things in town, so she said that she and Hans would meet us later, when we were done at the surgery. They crossed the road together and Marie turned and waved, a split grin on her face like it was a holiday at the seaside. But the fan in the surgery ticked as it turned, and the nurse was only a kid in a tight white skirt and glasses, a tiny crucifix at her neck. I wondered if she liked the Beatles, her job, the doctor behind his closed door. When it was Stanley's turn, she looked surprised that Rika was coming in too, but the doctor smiled, and she withdrew.

'My friend,' he said, and Rika smiled. 'How are the woodland babies? You are looking well, yourself. Not overworked on your own?'

'Not on my own. There are lots of folk to help out. This is Felicity – she's a nurse herself. And this is Stanley. We're finding he's a sleepy baby and thought it wise to get another set of eyes on him to be on the safe side.'

He nodded, and I lay Stanley down on the bed.

'A foundling? He has the look of an orphanage baby.'

'No,' Rika said. 'And not a difficult birth. But we've noticed low pulse amplitude and low pressure at times.'

'Perhaps *mauvaise alimentation*? You have checked his mouth? No obvious cleft?'

'No, all seems to be well. He simply isn't fattening.' She asked what he would suggest.

'Supplemental formula is the best approach. And a little water in the afternoon so that the heat does not trouble him.' He took his glasses off and polished them on a handkerchief. Without them, the skin around his eyes looked bruised and weakened. 'Keep him close and come back when you need to. It should be possible to turn poor feeding around.'

Outside the surgery, I asked Rika if she thought that was really the answer – that I was doing it wrong. She smiled and said she didn't think so.

'But we'll keep a closer eye. And ear with the stethoscope, too, and weigh his diapers, I think. It's good to know the facts.'

There was a gate at the end of the path to the church and Hans stood there, shielding his eyes from the sun. He told us that Marie had gone inside to pray.

'She likes to, whenever we come into town. Usually it's open. Sometimes, there are ladies around doing flowers or ironing cloths, but she has it to herself today.'

'Do you think anyone would mind if I slipped inside to nurse Stanley?'

'Make yourself at home.'

Rika stayed outside with Hans, saying she'd warn me if a priest appeared. I found Marie sitting near the front with her hands folded over her belly, her face tilted towards the ceiling, but her eyes were closed. I sat down softly a few rows back and settled to nurse. Stanley seemed to know what he was doing. I relaxed and felt the milk let down, his mouth soon showing wet and milky against my skin. Maybe he didn't nurse long enough. That might be the problem. He'd soon turn his face away and I'd encourage him with the other side. But there was always milk. He must be getting what he needed. Perhaps he'd perk up when the cooler weather came. Right now, I thought he looked content. A quiet soul, small as a loaf of bread, his hair the colour of wheat.

Marie stood up and came towards me.

'I was praying about names, you know.'

'And did you hear any answers?'

'No, not yet. But it will come. I'm not worried.'

I thought she might ask me then about Stanley's name, and I would have told her, but she didn't. She just stood there smiling and looking around at the church. The arc of the ceiling, the peeling white paint. I'd expected more ornamentation – gilt, candles, saints, that kind of thing – but this church was simple. Not modern like the Oratory, but small, old-fashioned and simple. On a small table near the door, someone had placed a vase of wild flowers. They looked fresh, as though they'd been set there that morning, and the cornflowers a Marian blue. In the kirk at home, the stained-glass-window Mary wore blue, too. She knelt on the ground with her cloak pooling around her, her son lying in its folds and when I was small, I used to think she was the lady of Aberlady and that she was buried in our kirk. She was only mentioned at Christmas, but from the Sunday school bench,

I could see a marble carving on an ancient lady in a pleated bonnet, her eyes closed, her veined hands pale and folded peacefully on her breast. She had a mother's strong face and all the grace of one favoured by God. It must be her, I thought, though I didn't ask, and no one thought to tell me who she really was.

Marie circled the church, examining everything, and I looked down at Stanley. He'd fallen asleep again with his small mouth open. I could feel his gentle breath against my bare skin, and see his fair hair sweaty on his little forehead, shining.

'Here,' Marie said, holding out two closed hands towards me. 'I have gifts for each of you.'

She opened her left hand and offered me a cornflower blossom, which I took and set against Stanley's thin blanket.

'And for the little one, something that lasts longer.' Her left hand was empty, but wet and she laid it against the soft paleness of his hair. 'Holy water. A blessing for your baby. May he be righteous and devout.' She laughed as she spoke, then made the sign of the cross with her thumb on his forehead. 'He is a little lamb, isn't he?'

Stanley lived that half-summer, and half September, too. The morning I woke and found him cold, I didn't cry, just closed my eyes and wished only that I could contain him again. I wanted to hide him, to take him inside the still-soft folds of my belly and give him whatever strength he hadn't found the first time. Instead, I had to give him to the earth. Bas dug a small grave under the white pines. I told him that I didn't want a coffin.

'That's okay, right? I don't have to. He'll be safe enough.'

'Yes, of course. Just like the ancients. Held in the arms of the planet.'

Rika said these things happen. Sometimes souls slip away and we can't see why. Liver difficulties, perhaps, or a defect in his heart. It was hard to know for sure. Sometimes, there isn't a reason.

We buried Stanley in the evening, wrapped in his blanket, his head and his feet bare. Marie helped me arrange cornflowers around him, their blue encircling him, while high above us, geese filled the sky, calling, wild and free.

12

SEPTEMBER PASSED AND THE WOODS BEGAN TO EMPTY. The folk in the tenting field had packed up, and Annie was back in the city. Bethanne and Ember moved west to live with her sister. I moved into the farmhouse, and Marie made me a rag rug for my floor. Rika sat with me but never suggested anything other than rest or a cup of tea. And the days kept passing.

Across the lake, the leaves turned red and gold, and Marie told me that every morning, she found the beginnings of ice. First on puddles along the path from their cabin to the farmhouse and then in a gentle ring around the lake itself. Bas said he thought that there might be an early snow. I was glad to be sleeping in the farmhouse now. I woke up early most days, still uncomfortable with milk. Rika said it took time to dry up completely and I should be patient. Walking helped a bit, but better was coming back to the house afterwards, seeing the smoke rising from the chimney and knowing that Bas would have the coffee ready.

I thought it was a blessing when Marie's labour came on quickly. All afternoon, we'd been slicing the first of our apples in the farmhouse kitchen and threading them on strings to dry. Marie kept popping the rings in her mouth.

'They're so sweet,' she said, crunching. 'Tempting.'

She thought the first cramps were just too much fruit, and headed up the stairs to the bathroom, hollering that she'd be down in a minute. Rika sent me down to the birthing house to fetch a kit.

'Just in case,' she said, checking her watch. 'Take my cardigan if you like. It will be getting chilly out there now.'

The loons were on the lake, silent and lovely. Evening shadowed the hills, but the lake held its own light, the silhouetted birds tattooed on the surface. They'd be heading south soon, following the geese. Yesterday Rika had told me again that I could stay as long as I liked, that she could use my help, but I wasn't sure. Maybe I'd work again in Montreal, or head west. Nothing quite fitted, but I would need to decide.

When I came back to the farmhouse, Rika was rubbing Marie's back.

'Where's Hans?' she asked. 'Can you find him? And do you know if we have any booze? Ask Bas about the wine coolers, maybe? We might want to slow this down a bit. Feels a little too fast for my liking.'

Marie knelt beside a chair, her elbows on the seat and her hair hanging down so I couldn't see her face.

'Is she all right?'

'Right as rain and working. This feels like it will be a fast one and that can be hard the first time through. We've had the waters while you were away and they're clear, but I want to slow it all down if I can.'

Marie moaned, a low drawn-out sound nothing like her voice.

'There, that's right,' said Rika. 'Make it a song. Can you look up now? Find my eyes? I want to see how you're doing.' Then softly, to me, she said, 'I need Hans. And Bas. I need help.'

'I'll find them. They'll be out at the new cabin.'

'We need phones out here. We need something.'

'I'll be fast. I'll run.'

Rika wrapped her arms around the girl and tried to pull her to her feet. 'Let's get you lying down, love. I'll prop you up with pillows, and you'll just relax and try to breathe real slow. Slow as you can, okay? And Felicity? You go fast.'

'I will,' I said, but I paused for a moment at the door. '*Lunette? Il n'y a rien à craindre. Le bébé arrive.*'

She looked up, her face pale and her eyes not seeing, but she tried to smile. '*Oui. J'espère.*'

I left the farmhouse again, and the evening was darker now. I couldn't see the roots or the stones along the path so I picked up my feet as I ran. Out at the new site, the men were sitting down by the lake, the half-built house a shadow behind them, the smoke from their cigarettes drifting out over the water.

'Bas.' My voice sounded rough.

'Hey, Felicity.'

'Rika needs you.'

'Is it time?' Hans asked. 'Marie's started?' He smiled as he spoke, and I wished he wouldn't.

'Yeah, but it's going too fast. Rika said she needs help.'

Then they were on their feet and running, and I ran, too, but couldn't keep up. My body felt loose and aching, my breasts heavy and useless. I crossed my arms in front of them and kept running. By the time I reached the farmhouse, they were both inside, Hans kneeling beside Marie, stroking her hair and Bas speaking quietly with Rika.

'No, I don't think so,' she said. 'It's going fast. She'd only deliver on the way. But I think I want the doctor in the village to know. Just in case we need him.'

After the men were there, we managed to slow things a little. Marie could focus between contractions, smiling and holding Hans's gaze. He told her she was strong and beautiful. That in itself helped. Rika kept her voice warm and measured, and she told a story about another birth, a mother whose older children were there with her and played cat's cradle at the end of the bed. Marie laughed and told us that maybe it would be like that later when more of her babies had been born.

'One at a time, don't you think?' Hans said.

'Or two,' said Marie. 'We could have twins next, *peut-être*?'

Then another contraction rushed through her and her hands gripped Hans's arms, her voice rising.

'That's right,' Rika said. 'Keep your mouth open. Open's what we want. It's getting strong.'

Night passed, Marie's energy building. Rika helped her walk across the floor, tried to get her up the stairs, but she said no.

She wanted to stay in the open. The bedrooms upstairs were too small, she said. She wanted us all to be close. I gathered more pillows and spread sheets on the sofa so she could lie down with Hans, riding through the rushes of each contraction and trying to stay loose. When the pushing started, she wanted to stand again though the energy made her legs shake. Hans held her in his arms as she bore down.

When Stanley was born, the pushing had seemed to pass quickly. I'd been surprised by how much I had wanted to push and how good and active it felt. But Marie's pushing was hard. She kept her eyes closed and arched her neck. Rika tried to talk her through, to focus her attention on her child's crowning head, but Marie struggled to hear.

Finally, the head was born. I could see the dark hair, the white cream thick at the base of the neck, and the curl of each ear. The baby's eyes were still closed and for a moment, everything felt still, not quite started. Close and not yet, not yet. Between my own breaths, I felt Stanley close enough to touch.

Rika's voice was slow and soft. 'A couple more like that,' she said, 'and the baby will be in your arms. These are the easier ones now. Almost there.'

Marie flushed bright and strong, pushing again and the baby was born in a rush of blood. Marie's face softened, her hands still holding Hans's, and the baby already crying out. As Rika gently lifted her, we could see her tiny face all red and wrinkled, her arms and legs unfolding and reaching and strong.

'There we are, lovely one,' Rika said softly. 'Looking perfect, *maman*. The cord is a little short, so I'm going to put her here on your thigh, okay? She'll feel slippy, but I'm keeping her safe. That's a good strong voice right away, isn't it?'

'She'll sing,' Marie said. 'Like my sister.'

'She's lovely. All her fingers and toes accounted for. Good colour, too. Good and pink. A blanket, please, Bas.'

'She's okay?' Marie asked.

'Yes. She's perfect. We'll get that cord tied and cut in a minute or two and then I'll pass her up to you, okay? Felicity, you can see about the haemostat and the scissors, too.'

I fell into the rhythm of the work. Checking the instruments, the clean cloths, my wristwatch and the notebook Rika had set on the table. It was good to have work to do, to know that Marie was through, so good to hear her baby's voice. When the cord was cut, Rika helped her bring the baby to her breast and try to nurse. After a few minutes, she passed the baby to me so that Marie could deliver the placenta. 'Check her temperature, tone and reflexes, okay? Keep her warm.'

The baby's hair was dark, her eyes wide and interested. As I took her in my arms, she reached out with long fingers, and I wrapped her in a blanket and held her close, her little weight warm against me. Hans stood beside me and set a gentle finger on the baby's scalp.

'She is perfect,' he said.

'You sound surprised.'

'Guess I worried. But look at her. She's . . .'

'Yes. Unspeakably perfect.'

'Yeah.'

I wanted to know her name, but asking Hans didn't feel right.

Marie would tell us what she'd chosen. Naming Stanley had been easy. When he lay on my belly all naked and new, he'd looked like he was asking for a name. And then when he cooed his first hello, I knew I could give it to him, that he was Stanley, so I just told everyone. It felt like I'd always known. This little girl looked like she needed a name, too.

I set her on the table so I could get a proper look at her. Her breathing was good and so were her pulse, colour and temperature. I jotted notes on Rika's paper, wiped a little blood and vernix from her head and shoulders, and trimmed the ends of the string that Rika had tied around the stump of her cord. Then I dressed her. A clean nappy, a kimono and a knitted cap and boots that Rika had made, all soft wool and clean, new cloth. Hans stood beside me with his arms crossed, watching everything with wet eyes.

Behind me, I felt things shift. Marie was lying down flat now and Rika massaged her belly with firm hands.

'The placenta's not come,' she said. 'And she's passed a fair amount of blood instead.'

'What do you need me to do?' I asked.

'Methergine, I think, and then we'll get her feet up. There now, Marie love, we're going to manage this just fine. You'll be worn out from that quick baby.'

'How is she?' Marie's face was pale.

'Beautiful,' I said, handing the baby to Hans. 'How's her blood pressure?'

'One methergine shot now please. We'll see about the pressure after that.'

'I can't hold her,' Hans said, handing the baby to Bas. 'You take her.'

After that, it was only Marie, and Rika's hands working and my own with the syringe and cotton wool. The needle deep in her muscle. The pressure of fingers on flesh. Marie started to shake, and I'd read that mothers sometimes do because of the tension that builds up with birth, and sometimes the shakes come on strong. You need to keep them warm and encouraged and, with time, they will settle.

But Marie didn't. Hans sat by her head, his arms around her and his face close to hers as Rika and I worked.

'She's torn,' Rika told me quietly. 'I can't see where. Pretty high up, which is unusual in labour.'

'I'll call the doctor.'

'No, I need you here. Bas, go and call now. Please.'

He kept the baby in his arms while he made the phone call and I took over massaging Marie's belly, willing the muscles to contract. Rika tried everything. Another injection. Compression of the uterus and she removed the placenta manually, but the bleeding didn't stop.

'*Lunette*,' I said. '*J'essaie*. You are strong. And we are helping.'

'*Ça suffit. J'ai besoin . . . besoin de ma fille.*'

'She only wants her baby. Nothing else right now. Can you bring her close?'

'Yes,' Rika said. 'That's good.' She made space on the pillow for the baby so Marie didn't need to move at all to see her little face. I took off the baby's cap, and Marie stroked her dark hair. They both looked so new, so fragile lying there with their faces framed on the white pillowcase, two children tucked up in bed, ready for sleep.

By the time the doctor arrived, Marie's face was white and she wasn't responding any more. He asked me to take the baby away and he gave Marie another injection. Rika stayed close, whispering in her ear, but Marie's eyes were closed and I wondered if she could hear at all.

When it was over, Rika left the farmhouse, closing the door gently behind her. Hans stayed beside Marie's body and for a time, I sat with him, still holding the baby in my arms. She was so quiet, her little breath a steady rhythm in the quiet room. After a while, Bas touched my arm, holding out his hands for the child.

'Let me,' he said. 'I'll look after her. Poor little doddle. You go outside with Rika. She'll need a friendly face right about now.'

Rika stood by the water. As I approached, she turned towards me, but I couldn't see her expression. It takes a while for eyes to adjust to the darkness.

'We did our best for her. You know that, don't you?'

'Yes. I think so.' My voice sounded strange and small, but Rika reached out and took my hand, so I knew she'd heard me. She was strong, this skinny midwife. Strong as all the matrons in Montreal and in Edinburgh, too. Stronger than starch and aprons or hard reserve. But that wasn't fair. They were strong, too. Just different. All these strong women, coping day and night, holding on and teaching younger women to do the same. We stood there for a long time, waiting for the loons to surface.

* * *

That night, the baby slept in my room upstairs in the farmhouse. I put her in the basket where Stanley had slept, all swaddled safely with clean white sheets. When she woke in the night with a small mewling cry, I took her to my breast without thinking and nursed.

Outside, I heard Hans's voice.

'I shouldn't have brought her here.'

Bas answered, but so quietly I couldn't understand his words. Then Hans again, hard and rising.

'But she should have been at a hospital. I should never have thought . . .'

The door closed, and I thought they had come into the farmhouse, but then Rika spoke.

'She's young – this shouldn't have happened. I'm sorry. I must have missed something.'

'It was her that did it,' Hans said. 'When she first knew. She did it to herself. She said there was a lot of blood then but it didn't work.'

'What are you saying?'

'She tried to end it. But she didn't do it right and the baby grew strong anyway.'

'She didn't tell me,' Rika said.

'She didn't want anyone to know. It was in Montreal in my

apartment. I'd gone out somewhere, to the library, I don't know. When I came back, she was in the bathtub. I thought it was her wrists, but she'd . . . she'd tried with a knitting needle. And it didn't work. She bled for days, but she said it was the wrong blood. When she got better, we thought that meant the baby was meant to be.'

The baby in my arms fussed and wouldn't nurse. She couldn't be getting much milk, I thought, so I stood up and danced her round the room, singing softly and trying to ignore the voices outside. If everyone could just hush and be quiet, maybe she would sleep, maybe we could all fall asleep and be still.

'You should have told me.' Rika's voice rose higher. 'I never would have been so relaxed if I'd known there was a risk. I didn't even know I was taking a risk. You knew.'

'What do I know about pregnant girls? And she didn't want anyone to know. But she came round after that. She absolutely did. She really wanted the baby. And I thought she'd healed. Didn't you take a look? Isn't that your thing?'

'I only look in labour. There's no point in looking earlier unless you're trying to interfere. I don't do that.'

'Maybe you should have. She needed interference.'

'Sounds like she already got that from you.'

'Rika,' Bas said.

'God, I don't need this.'

In the morning, Eleta knocked on my door with a mug of coffee. The baby was sleeping again in the basket, her face small and peaceful. Eleta looked tearful and strong.

'Hans has gone,' she said, handing me the coffee.

'Gone?'

'I don't know. Maybe. We can't find him. He'll probably come back. How's the baby doing?'

'Sleeping well, I think. She's a little dear. Should I bring her down now? Is Rika up?'

'She'll come find you when she's ready. You drink up now. You'll need the warmth. It's cold today. Really fall now, all of a sudden.' Eleta sat down on the edge of the bed. 'And you? How are you doing this morning?'

'That's not an easy question.'

'I thought I should ask. We're all a little shaky today.'

At the breakfast table, Bas told us that Hans had taken the canoe out last night after everything. He didn't go anywhere, just paddled out to the middle of the lake and drifted. Bas sat down on the beach and watched. The moon set and the air was cold, his breath a cloud before him, the water flat and still.

'Sat out there all night, just sitting with his paddle balanced across the gunwales. When the sun rose, he picked it up and pulled his way back to shore. Then he sat on the sand with me for a bit. Didn't have much to say, but that's natural.'

'Is he coming for breakfast?' Rika asked. 'I want to apologize.'

'No, he's gone away. Just for a while. I drove him into town so he could catch a bus. He said he wanted to head east to tell Marie's parents and then he'd come back for the baby.'

'But he can't,' I said.

'No?' Bas asked, looking at me cradling the baby. 'Of course he can. She's his daughter.'

'No, I mean he can't tell her parents. He doesn't know them. He doesn't even know her real name. It isn't Marie. She made that up.'

'Why?' Rika asked. 'How do you even know that?'

'She told me.'

'And she didn't tell him?'

'No. Everything was to be new with Hans.'

We talked about what to do for a while. Whether Bas should try to follow Hans. Whether we could find Marie's family – or rather Lunette's. Eugenie's. It was hard to speak of her by her real name. It would have been hard enough face to face, but now it was next to impossible.

I told Rika about nursing the baby and asked if it had been a bad idea. Because I didn't really have much milk left and I worried that she'd go hungry trying. Rika smiled softly and said no, not at all.

'The baby needs closeness now. In a few days, milk will be necessary. But who knows, maybe we can turn your supply back on.' She opened the dresser drawers and found jars of fenugreek and blessed thistle for tea. She stirred in honey to soften the bitterness and encouraged me to try it. It tasted of burnt nuts and brittle things. Pine cones. Cracked bark. Shadows. The heat of it needled through me, better than coffee, strange and unfamiliar.

We'd mother her together, we decided. Rika, Eleta and me. A way of holding on. Perhaps we needed that closeness now. While Hans was gone, Marie's daughter was always in our arms. We never put her down.

* * *

Rika wanted to bury Marie in the woods but Bas thought the cemetery in the village was better. I thought so, too. She'd like to be near the church, and when I said that, I expected Rika to offer a rebuttal, but she only shrugged.

'As you like,' she said.

We didn't wait for Hans. We didn't know how long to wait. And we couldn't contact her family. We didn't know her family name; we couldn't find a telephone number. Besides, it was Hans's news to share – if he could find the family.

The priest said there was a space available in the corner, underneath a birch tree. Some of the nearby graves were decorated with plastic flowers and others with small photographs of the dead. On the day of her funeral, we brought the last of the daisies from the garden at Birthwood and tied them together with red and gold leaves to make a bright bundle. James helped Soleil set them on top of the casket, which made it look like a decorated table. Marie would have liked that. She would have laughed. We walked silently through the cemetery, the men carrying her casket on their shoulders, the hems of their jeans growing damp from the grass. I carried the baby wrapped in one of Marie's shawls and someone must have telephoned Annie because she met us there, too. Probably Bas. He would have thought to. At the graveside, the men lowered the casket so gently into the ground, like they were tucking her in to sleep. I was glad of the priest's prayer book, his knowledge of what needed to be said. He prayed in French, which also felt right, and no one sang because we couldn't. Not under that sky.

November came and brought the cold. We didn't name the baby – called her Marie's daughter when we needed to – and sometimes we talked about that in the evenings, but we couldn't quite bring ourselves to do it. We were waiting, I think, for Hans. I didn't think he'd come back. Bas did, but we didn't argue. We kept the farmhouse warm, kept Marie's daughter fed, watched television and worried about the world. Down in the States, there were marches and strikes. Momentum was building against the war, and Eleta and James talked about heading south, taking part. James said it was his fight after all, and maybe he'd better take a role in it.

'Won't you be arrested at the border?' Bas asked.

'There's ways of getting across. I know folk who can help. We'd be okay.'

'But not till spring, right?' Rika asked.

'Our truck can manage the snow. It's not made of sugar.'

Snow came the next day and covered the ground till everything looked black and white. I sat by the window and watched it fall into the lake. It wasn't frozen yet, and the dark water was an open mouth, the snow vanishing. In the evening, Marie's daughter was fussy and crying and wouldn't settle to either breast or bottle. Rika thought the evening air might help and sent the two of us out for a walk. I cradled the baby under my coat, and all the way down to the road, I shushed and swayed, cold feet on the cold ground. The puddles crackled with ice, the water underneath splashing up onto my boots and thoughts surfaced of Marie's gift of holy water and Stanley's sweet, wheaty hair. Tiredness, of course.

We were all exhausted. None of us were sleeping well. My mouth was raw with bitter tea but my breasts had filled again just as Rika had hoped and the baby seemed to be getting enough milk. Whenever she was hungry, her cry was strong and insistent, which was reassuring, though it kept us all from sleep. She settled now in the cave of my clothing, and I kissed the top of her little dark head, then turned back towards the farmhouse.

I knew when I saw there were too many lights on, and the unfamiliar car parked out front confirmed it. I thought of turning around because I wasn't ready. Eleta and James might let me stay at their cabin with Marie's daughter until the morning. But Rika would worry and come looking. I didn't want to do that to her, so I opened the door.

Hans stood in the kitchen with Bas and Rika. He looked as if he hadn't slept since he'd left Birthwood, his eyes scanning the room the way a thief might. Bas put the whisky bottle on the table and we sat down, ready to listen if that's what he wanted. Only I kept my coat on and hoped that baby would keep sleeping. Rika said nothing.

Hans told us he'd left without really knowing what he'd do. He knew he should visit her family, but the news felt impossible to carry. And he didn't know if she'd told them about him; she'd never called them when he was around. By the time he got to Montreal, he was certain he should turn around and head back to the camp. Maybe if he had the baby with him, it would be easier to meet her family. But what did he know about looking after a newborn? She was better where she was.

He saw the moon rising over the cross-topped mountain,

mocking him. A hotel was impossible – the white sheets, the soft pillow. He felt a fever coming on and set off down the street to outpace it. Streets and corners, cutting through alleyways, under-passes, city parks. A stone man looked down from a colonial plinth. Traffic lights, car horns, shouts and lights, sirens coming closer so he turned away again and headed for darker places. In time, he found himself surrounded by trees, the hill dark around him. Then a clearing and he lay down, the dirt against his back. He closed his eyes to close the world.

In the morning, an old man's face looked at him. Old and rough, bristled like an animal. The man stood against a tree, with bags at his feet and an old man's hat on his head. Hans said hello, but the man shook his head and walked away.

It took him an hour to find the bus station and when he got there, he was tired and hungry. He bought a sandwich and tried to eat it. Girls stood around – there were always girls – and he looked away from their dark hair, their open eyes. He used the public toilets and washed his face. He didn't look in the mirror.

Bas poured more whisky and I sat quite still.

'She'd always said she was from a place called Sainte Anne. North, I thought, but I didn't know. Anyway, I couldn't find it on the map. Sainte-Anne-des-Plaines, Sainte-Anne-des-Monts, Sainte-Anne-du-Lac, Sainte-Anne-de-Bellevue, Sainte-Anne-des-Beaupré. And more, too, but no Sainte Anne. I wondered if I had the saint wrong. Sainte Angèle, Sainte Agathe, possibly. I couldn't think. I didn't know.'

'But you must have known something. You could have asked . . .'

'I had nothing, okay? Nothing. Only bad news to confess and

no one to tell. What was I going to do? Show up in some random town with fucking dreadful news and find some priest to confess to? What would that even do?'

'But you looked. You must have. You've been gone a long time.' Bas's voice was level, convinced.

'No. I told you, I couldn't. I wanted to, but there was nothing I could do.'

'Where did you go?'

'You know what I'm like.'

'Yes. That's why I'm asking. And because you've come back to your daughter.'

Hans didn't say anything for a while, just sat and looked down at his glass.

'I wonder if she's better where she is. How . . . how is she?'

'Beautiful,' Rika said. 'Thriving. And sleeping, I think?'

She turned towards me.

'Yes. Quite settled.'

'Can I see her?' Hans asked.

'Yes,' I said. 'If you like.' I unbuttoned my coat and eased her into the open. The baby opened her eyes in the light, and I worried she'd cry, but she didn't. She looked peaceful and sweet, her little hands curled up by her face, her eyes slate-grey and lovely.

'You want to hold her?' I asked. He took a deep breath and I lowered her into his arms, showing him how to cradle her head. He brought his head close and whispered into her ear. He smiled. Rika turned to me and spoke softly.

'Felicity, why don't you take her up to bed now? You two must be tired out. We'll be up for a while yet, I imagine. We've got more whisky to drink. But don't worry, I'll fill Hans in on how we've all been managing.'

* * *

The stairs creaked beneath my feet, but the baby didn't wake. In the bedroom, I set her down softly in the basket beside the bed and she didn't stir. I lay down and watched her, listening to her breathing, to the hush of voices downstairs, and soon, surprisingly, slept.

Hans was gone by morning. The rest were half breakfasted by the time I came downstairs with the baby. James and Eleta sat at the table, talking about passports.

'I'm not sure we could add her to ours. Not without a birth certificate and we haven't seen about that.'

'We could, though,' Eleta said. 'It would just take time.'

'It would have to be a proper adoption. Because if we do get stopped, that would be one more crime on our list. Would you be ready for that?'

My belly clenched. The baby fretted in my arms. Rika offered to take her, but I shook my head and I wondered how long this conversation was going to take and how soon I'd have to let her go. She'd have formula, so that was all right. She was even good with a bottle. And I'd find work. I'd buy new clothes. I'd travel. I sat down, adding these things up, and Rika put down her coffee mug and reached for my hand.

They'd been up late, and Hans and Bas had still been at the

table when Rika went to bed. Bas said Hans had told him he'd spent the month living rough in Montreal. He hadn't been able to face his apartment. He couldn't bear being inside. 'It's the walls,' he'd said. 'I couldn't stop watching them. Felt like I was in a box. And Marie was still in the bathtub – she'll be there forever, you know. Lying there with her eyes closed. I couldn't face that. I was half crazy all month, and I thought that if I stayed out under the sky, I could keep her somehow. That some living part of her hadn't quite blown away in the wind yet, and she might find me if I stayed up on the mountain. Might settle in the folds of my clothes like snow. Travel with me. Stupid, but that's what I held on to and I slept on the ground. But then it got too cold for that and I ended up in doorways and there were girls and I couldn't, couldn't not . . . everything was neon and concrete and wrong and I . . . I couldn't hold on to her any more.'

In the end, he'd sold what he could to buy the beat-up car he'd driven up to the camp. He said he couldn't face the cabin, but he'd sleep in the car. Bas had given him an extra blanket and a hot-water bottle. They'd talk in the morning, he'd said. They'd figure it all out then. But instead, he left.

'I don't know where he'll go next,' Bas said. 'He didn't say anything. And I didn't push because I was sure there'd be time.'

'He might come back?' Eleta asked.

'I don't think so. He only came back to see that the baby was safe. And real, maybe. He's not thinking straight. It's best she's with us.'

'I want her,' I said. 'I'm staying here.'

'Oh, Felicity, you don't have to,' Rika said. 'We all loved Marie.'

'Yes, I know that. But I have milk and I can stay. And it's not complicated like it would be for Eleta and James. Then if Hans comes back for her, he won't find her if she's not here. I want to stay, too.'

Eleta smiled and said she thought that was beautiful.

'Because you need each other, don't you?' she said.

'Yes,' I said. 'I think we do.'

Rika gave me Hans's mother's address and his sister's, too, in the Netherlands. She said it was sensible to have them to hand, in case I ever needed them for medical history or family accounts. In time, postcards started arriving from Hans, always from different places, and they said little. No news of Marie's family or the place she came from. Sainte Anne remained just another saint on the map, and there were far too many to count.

I put the cards away in an envelope with the addresses. Keeping a record seemed a good idea. I might give it to her, I thought, when she was old enough. Then she could decide what to do with the story. It would be hers to choose.

And, of course, I named her.

It took me a little while to find the right name. I leafed through the books on the shelf. I didn't know what I was looking for. And just like that, I found it. *Columba Livia* – the rock dove. It sounds beautiful when you say it aloud and, though it's just the common pigeon, it gave me back the clatter of wings over Princes Street and the way the light broke through just in time. All those wings and gold, too. That's what birth should be like. It isn't, though.

It's hard work and scary. It hurts, and it makes you fragile and you have to do it. You have to move through it. Messy and powerful and real and that's good. And it happens to everyone. That's what brings us all here.

Pigeons are common, too, and at home everywhere. In every city, they find a place to roost and be settled. Then they wheel up over the rooftops together like a great flag flying, like one bright, lifting decision. As if to say *Look, life is like this.* Magic.

So that's what I gave Marie's daughter. That choice. That moment. Flight.

CLOSE

PIDGE

I OPENED THE SLOE GIN AND CANCELLED MY TICKET home. You can't leave a house with a goose in it. You certainly can't sell it. I told Mateo I wasn't finished and then procrastinated on signing the condo paperwork. The gin was delicious.

As the days grew warmer and longer, I found I could read in the orchard late into the evening, if I had a sweater around my shoulders. I worked through all Felicity's letters but felt no further ahead. The goose built a second nest under the apple trees and kept the grass trimmed.

In Gran's living room, I looked at maps, tracing the coastline with my finger – Gullane, Dirleton, then inland to Drem, East Fortune and Athelstaneford. In her letter, Gran had suggested that I explore. North Berwick along the coast, the islands and Tantallon. It would be a long day for the goose alone at the bungalow, and I didn't fancy the greeting I'd get when I returned. So I'd need to take her in the car and just how was I going to make that work? I covered the backseat with towels and layered them with large handfuls of grass so that she'd have something to graze on. Then I opened all the doors wide, stepped back and hoped. And in she hopped, surprise surprise, and she settled right down in the backseat.

The drive was worrying, but she kept quiet with her wings folded. I was lucky. Well, some people drive with dogs, don't they? I was just pulling into the car park at Tantallon Castle, out past North Berwick, when I realized the goose had fallen asleep. When I turned the engine off, I could hear her gentle snores.

I opened the windows wide and shut the door as softly as I could. The car park was almost empty. Luckily. She wouldn't be disturbed.

I bought a ticket in the small visitors' centre and crossed a wooden footbridge towards a ruined gatehouse. The grass was closely trimmed and neat, carefully kept, and there was Izaak, standing with an easel and facing the sea. The gravel on the path crunched under my feet and he turned, then smiled.

'You again, I see. And on your own this time? That goose has flown?'

'No . . . she's . . .'

'Ah, then. Still under siege. And so, you have come looking for doo'cots. Me too. Come and see.' He fluttered his hands, beckoning, and I stepped close. In the background of his sketch, the Bass Rock sat like an iceberg in the water of the Forth. In the morning light, it looked stark and stately, and the doo'cot stood on the grass like a landlocked reflection. Its roof was stepped and, in the sky above, a faint moon was clear and almost full, a thumb-print on the blue.

Izaak held a charcoal pencil elegantly in his fingers. 'How is it?'

'Perfect. The balance is just right.'

'Yes, I thought it was. I hoped so. Thank you.' He pulled another pencil from his pocket and added a few smudging lines to the surface of the moon. 'It is difficult to show just what the eye sees, I find. Especially when the face is so familiar. We should all be able to draw her in our sleep for all that we see her, but we can't. She can be difficult.'

A couple walked past us, their dog on a lead, pulling them across the grass towards the doo'cot. It was greyer than the ruddi-ness of the castle, and blind with no windows.

'Perhaps you look for ideas of a goose house?' he asks, grinning. The wind unsettled the pages on his sketchbook and his eyes looked bright and wet.

'No, she's fine on the chair in the living room. Well, almost fine. She's laying eggs all over the place. And I'm not sure what she's going to do when I leave.'

'Tricky. You cannot leave her inside the house and you cannot take her with you. You have a wild-goose problem.'

'I just need to find a bird rescue centre or something.'

'When do you go?'

'I don't know. I need to sort that out, too. And decide about the house. And . . .'

Izaak put away his charcoal pencil in his pocket and pulled out a large white handkerchief. 'I ask too many questions – I apologize,' he said, wiping his eyes. 'You were right to worry about me – an old man who cannot mind his own business. I do not have your grandmother's grace, I'm afraid. But I've remembered her story about godly geese. I found an old notebook of mine from the war and I'd jotted her story there, next to a sketch of a skein of geese out over your bay. She said the Celts saw geese as a symbol of the Holy Spirit. Fitting, I thought, because what is God if not free and maybe unpredictable, too? Wild and calling somewhere high above our heads, making us look up.'

'That is a good image,' I said.

'Yes, I thought so too. Compelling.' He fussed with his jacket buttons. 'I wonder if it's true. Hard to know what anyone really thought when you stretch back so far, isn't it?'

Yes, I thought. In many ways, but he was following his own train of thought and didn't wait for an answer.

'But they might have needed it – whoever came up with the story. A necessary fiction. Things were difficult during the war. They might have needed that kind of divine wildness.' He shook out his handkerchief, then folded it carefully and inserted it back in his pocket. 'You know, I think your grandmother would like that idea. And she would like your goose, too, I imagine.'

'But what do you think she would do about it?' I asked, seeing the eggs on the kitchen floor. The nest in the armchair. The mess of gooseness all over the carpets. Izaak shrugged, smiling.

'Likely make omelettes. Pragmatic, don't you think?'

I left Izaak on the lawn with his sketching and headed towards the castle ruins, the clouds shifting overhead. As the sun hit my face, I turned towards it and I noticed the doo'cot's roof also faced south, angled to catch the sunshine and shelter from the northern winds. Clever, that. A well-thought-through design. Stepping inside, I found the space above me higher than I expected. And still. So quiet the blood thrummed in my ears, and the space, too, was divided rhythmically. I could see why Izaak liked these places. There was space here for a thousand roosting birds, and for each one, a perch, a nest, a space to be inside this honeycombed bell, this house full of letterboxes.

Of course, letters are written to be delivered. Delivered and read. Like all the letters in Gran's boxes. Read and saved to be read again. There may have been others; there probably were. Misplaced, discarded. Slipped into books or piles of newspapers and forgotten. Burnt even. But the letters in Gran's house were the letters she'd saved and left for me. Maybe she even thought they were necessary. Hard to tell without asking. A box of letters can hold such a lot. Or such a little.

The letters I left at Birthwood were still unread. I'd chosen that. Felicity had said that I didn't need to open them until I wanted to. That when I did, I could read about my father's family history. She'd never made me feel anxious about what I might find. It was just a box of additional information, should I want it at some stage. But I've always thought I knew enough. Enough came through. Not the details like dates, place names and the names of wild flowers, but stories enough. Pulse through an eggshell. Wind in a sail. The love that sustains.

* * *

Back at the car, the goose was awake and preening her feathers. I unlocked the door and she looked at me, blinking.

'Hey, you. Snooze well?'

A quiet, rusty squonk.

'You want out? A bit of fresh air? The grass here looks nice for grazing.' I opened the door wide, but she stayed put, so I reached in and ruffled her feathers. That's what she liked – not a stroke like a cat, but a bit of a muss, my fingers digging into the warmth between her feathers. She stretched up towards me, leaning in, then when I stopped, she shook out her head, amicably, and honked. 'Well then, goose, time to be heading off, I guess. Home? Yeah, home.'

Driving back towards Aberlady, I noticed all the old stone walls. Must have been thoughts of castle ruins in my mind or the way the stones fitted together. Or maybe just the beauty of the overhanging chestnut trees with their broad-fingered leaves and the last of their candles fading as summer crept in. In places, the wall was difficult to see at all amidst all the green, and I wondered how long it would stand. I thought of the useless fences in the woods at home, the way the forest claimed the land. How long before this coastline would grow wild again, if given the chance? Before the stone walls disappeared into the trees, the trimmed castle grounds grew tangled with dune grass and the concrete blocks by the coast started to crumble? Or for the road itself to crack and grow green with long grasses, the creek to flood and the sea shift inland, drowning the fields and the walls, changing everything.

A strange thought. Or maybe a lonely, or just a tired one. I parked the car and when I opened the door, the goose pushed past me, rushing to get out.

'Hey, easy there. Lots of space out here.'

She flapped her wings and, in a slim moment, was up on her stump again, standing sentinel and looking out over the bay.

'See? You're back, aren't you, goose?' She'd need a name, I thought. I couldn't just keep calling her 'goose'. It didn't seem friendly. I'd think of something.

She turned towards me and stretched her wings. The wind ruffled her feathers and I felt it catch my own hair, too. Then she called – a long sustained cry, tossing her head back and calling again and again in broken song. A flutter in my heart at the sound. She shook out her wings, caught the air and took flight. With slow, easy wing beats, she flew over the water, over the bridge towards the dunes and then back to the shore, turning, circling, still calling. I watched her, a sketch on the sky, her wings wonderful. Then, she headed out towards the mouth of the bay. Out past the sand spit, out to open water where the surface caught the light. I didn't need to wonder then. I knew she was flying away.

Inside, the house felt empty. Fragile and porous.

The kitchen clock ticked. A seashell rested on the mantelpiece among the photographs. A feather lay fallen on the floor. Then the wind blew in through the open window as it did every evening. It blew right through me, unsettled the petals in the garden, every leaf trembling, and knocked the apples from the tree, the eggs from every basket, and unfettered my heart like a field gone wild. All things become themselves in time. Every necessary thing.

When I came down to earth, I stood by the mirror and watched the reflections and the changing light. Then I sat at the desk, picked up Gran's pen and started to write a letter home.

JANE: 2006

T HE CURTAINS ARE BALLOONING INTO THE ROOM AND I put my pen down, only half hearing the rack of the sea. It's always there, and sometimes I listen.

The letter is ready for the envelope now. I wonder what Pidge will make of it. If she comes here, she's bound to learn more of the story, and that's just fine. I can't hide that. But I have tidied what I can and burnt the rest. Those letters had nothing about her father that she needs to see. Just gossip more or less. It is an odd feeling, being finished. Nothing else to do except the walk. The dunes will be enough. I can't very well sit out here forever, forgotten by God. That's what it feels like. I've been overlooked. Omitted and forgotten and growing simply ancient, waiting. I'm still not very good at waiting. I live best in seasons.

Over the years, I've spent a lot of time thinking about the end.

Maybe that's just natural or maybe it's something my generation does because of the war. But Felicity does it, too. She used to sit at the kitchen table on her visits home and tell me about protests and preparations. Like us, they really did believe that everything would crumble. It hasn't yet, but I'm not sure that's comfort. It still might.

There's the sea sound again, washing away sand and shells and pebbles. I wish it could take thoughts, too, and leave me with peace for these last few hours. Or simply take me with it.

Felicity called last week, and it was good to speak with her. She told me that she'd been to Ottawa to visit Pidge. The two of them had walked through the gallery together, looking at snowy forests and lakes, the Tom Thomsons and the Varley I like, too, with its wind-shaped pine. I could imagine them there, sitting side by side, with all that colour around them.

Felicity said that Pidge seemed down, but she hadn't wanted to talk. She doesn't have Felicity's ease with storytelling. Perhaps she takes after me. I find words get difficult when they matter most. One of the reasons I let the poetry lapse. That, and learning to mother was complicated enough.

My mother once told me that fairy stories and lullabies both keep nightmares at bay. Felicity loved fairy stories, and Stanley could weave a tale out of anything. A teacup on the shelf. The feather he used as a bookmark. A footprint in the sand. I opted for lullabies. I see that now. Lullabies and the moment just after. That peace and the quiet moment as sleep comes on. This moment now.

Still, I should have told her more, perhaps. When she was little,

I felt I had to keep mum, of course. I couldn't let people talk. Stanley stayed home after Felicity was born and managed to spend the rest of the war stationed nearby, but I was never certain that he was safe. Superiors made promises, but what can you trust? So I kept quiet. It wasn't until '53 that deserters were pardoned. Churchill made a show of it with a speech in Parliament, another layer to the coronation celebrations. We read about it in the newspaper and naturally it was all over the radio so it might have been easy to tell her then – but was twelve old enough? Perhaps not. Later, I thought she knew. When that letter came over from Quebec marked 'From Birthwood', I was certain she was letting me know. All the rest had been marked 'From the camp' – so why 'Birthwood'? Why Birthwood? When did she learn our truth? And why did she choose that moment – that letter – to gently let us know? I almost wrote to ask. Stanley suggested it might be best not to. She would bring it up if she had more questions. And she never did.

It will be dark soon. I can hear the geese settling out on the sandbar. When he came home, Stanley told me how he missed the geese whilst he was out at Birthwood. Every night, he'd listen for them and only hear the wind in the trees or sighing over the crest of the hills. The chaplain told him there was comfort in the quiet sound, that it was ancient and soothing, but he missed the hurly-burly of geese by the shore. All hugger-mugger with their half-mad crowding, but he was sure there was order there, too. Had to be. There were too many of them for it to be meaningless. There must be moments of chaos and fear, but it wouldn't last because, with each sunset, they settled. Whatever the weather, they found their place. And when they flew, they flew together.

When we moved out to this bungalow after the war, he was glad to be closer to the geese. They are louder here than in the village. Miss Baxter was right – a move had been what we needed. Funny how things work out. I couldn't understand why Muriel's parents wanted to leave after the war. They would have had to meet all new people and start over again. Maybe that's what they wanted. I only wanted a chance to dig in. Curtains in the windows, rows of preserves in the pantry and potatoes growing in the garden. Chickens and beehives and Stanley.

Here at the end – because that is what it is and I can be naught but honest tonight – I find myself wanting Miss Baxter. She was a good neighbour to me. Helped me more than she could know. She'll be long gone now. Twenty years or more, I should think. I never heard, but then I never really kept in touch. It can be hard to keep a connection close when there is to be no return. For a few years, I sent a Christmas card with a newsy note and a photo of Felicity, but somewhere along the way, I let that lapse. I'd like to sit with her again now. She'd like to hear about Pidge, too, I think, and we'd drink bramble leaf tea in the evening and talk about age and the land and she'd talk again about God. I could tell her about being forgotten. I'm sure she'd have something to say about being remembered. Wish I knew what it was. She made God feel close, just as near as a neighbour through the wall. As if we all might live side by side companionably, hearing the coming and going next door, unseen but known. As if any evening, I might just clear my throat and be heard. Or hear. It would be simple enough. A word, a cough, even. A cry from either side would carry through.

I felt that closeness when Felicity was born. I remember the feeling. That God was near and present in my distress. Isn't that how my mother would have described it? Yes, present. The skies that night were loud with bombers and the sirens cut through. I can still hear that wail in my heart, but I wasn't afraid. God was close. My hands, my fingers held onto the chest of drawers as I rocked back and forth, my mother's hands on the width of my back, pushing, and I was safe and held apart from the fear in the powerful work of beginning.

I remember and it was strong. For years, I held to that beginning memory with no words but the holding. I held it so long that it frayed in my pocket and now when I remember, I am not sure any more. Perhaps I am only remembering the last time I remembered. A step away. And another. A way of borrowing time.

Well, I've been living on borrowed time for long enough. Back when I had that spell – the one I didn't tell Felicity about – that's when I should have gone, by rights. But the doctors were clever and sorted me out. Gave me prescriptions for my heart and for my blood. Tablets and timetables to remember. Later, Felicity thought I sounded cold on the telephone and she asked what the matter was. She wanted to know if she'd said something. I should have said goodbye then and just let things be. Accept the end. But the doctors don't let you do that. It isn't an option. You have to keep going, for good or for ill.

But no. I won't. Not any more. I will let time be finished

because it is time, regardless of what they would prescribe or what God remembers and who God forgets. I might be accused of bringing it on, but it isn't quite like that. I've been responsible. Eaten all my meals and put myself to bed on time. I've done nothing dangerous. I've left the yew on the shelf. But it's only the medication keeping me going and that's false. An artificial prolongation of life. So, I'll stop. Let nature take its course. That's not playing God, is it? God knows. Maybe it's just emptying the teacup back into the sea.

I'm glad to be able to end it here. There isn't anywhere but this dune country, not really. This is where I'll always be, out here in the wind and with Stanley. Tonight, the Forth will be calm and bright as silver, the Lomond Hills looking close as close can be under the moon, but Stanley closer because I'll be seeing him soon, won't I? I'll cross the bridge and walk along the shore, then find a place in the dunes where I can sit and wait, my hands in my pockets, my will held firm like Jova Grey and Sandy Gibb, too, long before I arrived. I wish they could come and keep me company tonight. I'd like to tell Sandy not to worry – that, in the end, we're all glass, really. Just changed sand, and sand itself only old ground stone. We'll wait for the night together, for the falling darkness and the sound of geese calling out on the sandbar. It might be hard, I know that. The medication keeps my heart in check and without it, there is bound to be ache and pain. But I'll leave it in my pocket and let the saints around me hold me up.

Then when the sun rises and the gorse is aflame with the coming day, Stanley will be there to meet me on the other side of the shadows. His wide smile, his funny face with those lines beside his mouth and the wind and his hair, his hair and skin and here we are again, already. The sun is already on the water, rising and Stanley is there, holding out his hand. The war is over, all flags flying and we've made it through.

Acknowledgements

Thanks to Joan Barfoot for encouragement, reassurance and wisdom, Sarah Agnew for reading, Sharon Davidson for early inspiration.

Thanks to the Humber School for Writers for community and to First Thursday at Chapter Arts Centre, Cardiff for the space to share early pages.

Thanks to my publishing team: Cathryn, Holly, Ann, and Suzie.

Books are born from many books, but these four volumes were my close companions through this writing journey. Ina May Gaskin's *Spiritual Midwifery*, Nigel Tranter's *Footbridge to Enchantment*, William G. Birch's *A Doctor Discusses Pregnancy* and Basho's haiku as translated by Lucien Stryk. I'd love to gather their writers for a meal. Maybe one day. Who knows?

And thanks to Mike for waiting up with whisky.